Praise for the Cupcake Lovers series

"Rich with emotional complexity and a cast of wonderfully rich characters, *Fool for Love* is an absolute treat."
—Kristan Higgins, *New York Times* bestselling author

Praise for Beth Ciotta's previous novels

"Enchanting contemporary romance . . . fun and sexy . . . Ciotta's fans will undoubtedly be looking forward to the next." —*Publishers Weekly* on *Charmed*

"An amazing charmer." —Heather Graham on *All About Evie*

"Wonderful characters and a delightful adventure."
—*RT Book Reviews* on *Into the Wild*

"A wonderful, savvy, sexy and suspenseful romp. Ciotta has woven a terrific tale with characters to die for. This book will definitely leave you 'charmed.'" —Jan Coffey on *Charmed*

"Four Stars! Gives readers a full quotient of fun and sexy excitement." —*Affaire de Coeur* on *Charmed*

"Fast-paced, sizzlingly sexy fun!" —Karyn Monk on *Jinxed*

"The hijinks of Ciotta's charmingly imperfect heroine make *Jinxed* a hip, witty, fun read!" —Nan Ryan

St. Martin's Paperbacks titles
by Beth Ciotta

Fool for Love

The Trouble with Love

the trouble with love

BETH CIOTTA

St. Martin's Paperbacks

This is a work of fiction. All of the characters, organizations, and events portrayed in this novel are either products of the author's imagination or are used fictitiously.

THE TROUBLE WITH LOVE

Copyright © 2013 by Beth Ciotta.
Excerpt from *Anything But Love* copyright © 2013 by Beth Ciotta.

All rights reserved.

For information address St. Martin's Press, 175 Fifth Avenue, New York, NY 10010.

ISBN: 978-1-250-00133-7

Printed in the United States of America

St. Martin's Paperbacks edition / April 2013

St. Martin's Paperbacks are published by St. Martin's Press, 175 Fifth Avenue, New York, NY 10010.

10 9 8 7 6 5 4 3 2 1

To my family. In blood, in name, in heart.
You enrich my life and inspire my art.

ACKNOWLEDGMENTS

Although I spend much of my time locked away in my writing room with my laptop and imagination, I am not alone in my literary journey.

My undying gratitude to my agent, my friend, Amy Moore-Benson, who keeps me sane.

A heartfelt thank you to my editor, Monique Patterson, who "gets me." Your support and enthusiasm are priceless! Plus, how can I not be inspired by your avid love of cupcakes?

Thank you to Holly Blanck for her amazing energy and to my copy editor, Barbara Wild, for her continued caring expertise.

I've been blessed to meet a few of the warm and enthusiastic people who help to bring my stories to life via St. Martin's Paperbacks, but there are so many more and I am grateful to each and every soul connected to the Cupcake Lovers series. A special shout-out to the art and marketing department, publicity and sales, and the entire editorial staff—Thank you!

My deepest appreciation to my critique partners Barb Justen Hisle (aka Elle J Rossi) and Cynthia Valero for being with me every day—in spirit and guidance.

A special thank you to my cyber-friend, Melissa Lapierre, a native of the Green Mountain State and a fellow lover of moose!

I'm blessed with an amazing support system of family

and friends. You know who you are and I thank my lucky stars you're in my universe!

To my friends (patrons and co-workers) at the Brigantine Library and my support system throughout the Atlantic County Library System . . . To my friends—readers, booksellers, and librarians—on-line and in life . . . Thank you for your fantastic support and enthusiasm.

To my husband Steve—my hero, my friend—I love you.

AUTHOR'S NOTE

Though inspired by a northern region of Vermont, please note that Sugar Creek and the surrounding locations mentioned in this book are fictional. Escape and enjoy!

CHAPTER ONE

Seize the moment. Remember all those women on the Titanic who waved off the dessert cart.

—Erma Bombeck

"Delicious."

"To die for."

"Had me at the crystallized ginger."

Rocky Monroe glanced around her grandma's dining-room table, smiling as everyone sampled her cupcakes with a blissful moan, pumping a mental fist as every member of Cupcake Lovers—at least the ones in attendance—concurred. Her proposed contribution for the club's Creepy Cupcake booth at the upcoming Spookytown Spectacular was a hit. She'd always had faith in her cooking skills, but when it came to baking there was nothing like a thumbs-up from the four senior members, Judy Betts, Helen Cole, Ethel Larsen, and Rocky's grandma, Daisy Monroe, who'd been baking for charitable causes since before the Vietnam War.

"Brilliance, sweet pea."

"Thanks, Gram." Rocky's generous, purple-haired grandma had hosted tonight's meeting even though it was Rocky's turn. Rocky's home, which was also a bed-and-breakfast, was undergoing extensive renovations. So instead, they'd gathered at Gram's humongous three-story colonial, a home brimming with folksy knickknacks, antique furnishings, and generations of Monroe family love. Personal nirvana for Rocky.

"I'm digging the gingerbread and pumpkin combination."

This from Rocky's cousin Sam McCloud, the only male member of the local baking society. He caught a lot of flack for that, especially from their male relatives, of whom there were many, including Rocky's two older brothers, Luke and Dev.

"Yeah, but they're not as creepy-cute as yours, Sam." Rocky gestured to one of several cupcake platters on the table. Sam had made and rolled out his own colored fondant—orange, green, and white—then, after utilizing "monster" cookie cutters, molded the designs over the top of the cupcakes, using dark-chocolate frosting as his *glue*. "Jack-o'-lanterns, Frankenstein, and Ghouls. How great is that?"

"Can't take the credit. My kids inspired me."

Ben and Mina, eight and five, respectively.

"Still," Rachel Lacey said, "who makes their own fondant? Not me. I've never mastered the technique."

"I'd be happy to give you some tips," Sam said. "Maybe some afternoon . . ."

Rocky held her breath as did the other ladies seated around the table. Sam, a widower of two years, had joined the club months ago. He'd claimed he'd wanted to broaden his horizons, to break out of his morbid funk. Maybe that was part of it, but everyone knew he had a crush on Rachel. Well, except for Rachel.

How the young woman could be so oblivious was a mystery to all. Or maybe she simply wasn't interested and was too polite to say. Rachel, a day-care center's assistant, was beyond polite. Still . . . Sam was former military, a master furniture maker, a really nice guy, good with children, and he *baked!* How could Rachel not be attracted? And why was *he* tiptoeing around his infatuation? Why not just ask her out on a date? But no, every once in a while he threw out these vague offers that Rachel kept sidestepping.

Not that Rocky was any expert in the romance department.

Okay. She sucked in matters of love. And all right. Fine. Maybe she sucked at relationships in general. She'd certainly screwed up the perfect friends-with-benefits arrangement she'd shared with Adam Brody, a hunky, sweet-natured guy who freelanced as a recreational sports instructor. But that wasn't her fault.

She blamed Jayce Bello.

Her first love. Her first *lover*. A physical and emotional firestorm that had warped Rocky's perception of love and caused a severe rift between her and Jayce for thirteen years. Thank God he'd gone back to New York, after his recent and disastrous visit to town, so that she could get on with her life. Such as it was.

"That's sweet, Sam," Rachel said. "But I wouldn't dream of imposing on your valuable time."

Rocky blinked back to the present debacle: Sam's lame attempts to ease his way into Rachel's life and her shy reluctance to give him a shot. Rocky wanted to shake them both.

"Oh, for goodness' sake, Sam," Gram said. "Just ask her out already. Life's short!"

The seventy-five-year-old woman's motto for the past year and a half, the one that caused her to do foolish things like taking Rocky's snowmobile for a joyride or, most recently, veering off of a bike path and cycling down a hill at full speed. Both incidents had ended in a crash. Gram had yet to recover fully from the latter, still wearing a cast on her broken ankle and leaving her wearing only one trademark metallic sneaker at the moment. Her current motto also caused her to speak her mind when maybe she shouldn't. Although in this instance, no one, including Rocky, hushed her. Nope. Everyone waited for Sam to get off his duff and take action while Rachel sat wide-eyed, her cheeks burning brighter by the second.

"Oh, the suspense." Casey Monahan, part of the younger half of the club and as close to a buddy as Rachel allowed, elbowed Sam, who was doing one of his best silent glares at Gram, who just smiled.

Rocky, who was sitting on the other side of her cousin, nudged him with her knee.

Sam shifted his gaze to Rachel, though he at least ditched the death glare, just one of the intimidation skills he'd learned in the Marines. "This is awkward."

"You want to go out with me?" Rachel's voice was a disbelieving whisper.

"I was working my way up to asking."

"Meanwhile," Gram said, "hell was freezing over."

The senior CLs snickered.

Casey and Monica rolled their eyes.

Rocky's frustration shifted to sympathy. For her cousin, who'd lost the love of his life to cancer and hadn't dated, even casually, since. And for Rachel, who was painfully shy and, when it came to her looks, infuriatingly insecure. So much so she'd refused to participate in a CL photo session a few weeks back. Why did love or even just plain dating have to be so damned complicated?

"Maybe you could go out for drinks?" Monica suggested.

"Why not dinner?" Judy asked.

"You should take her someplace nice," Ethel said.

"But not too fancy," Gram said. "Then you feel pressured about how dressed up to get and which fork to use."

"Yeah." Rocky slid her cousin a teasing look, hoping to ease the tension. "Wouldn't want Sam obsessing on that."

He grunted. "I know which fork to use."

"Take her to the Sugar Shack," Casey said, getting in on the action. "Comfortable surroundings, great food."

Rocky agreed. Plus Luke, who co-owned and ran the place, would give their cousin and his date the star treatment. "Good idea."

"What are you doing Saturday night?" Helen asked Rachel.

"Nothing. That is—"

"Sam will pick you up at six," Gram said.

He shot the Monroe matriarch another one of those glares. "What if I had plans?"

Gram pushed her rhinestone-studded glasses up her nose and glared back. "Do you?"

"No, but—"

"I'll be happy to babysit Ben and Mina," Casey said with a smile.

"This is whacked." Sam dragged a hand down his rugged face. Rolling back his broad shoulders, he adopted what was probably supposed to be a charming smile. His seduction skills were rusty at best. "Rachel, would you like to go out to dinner with me on Saturday night?"

Rachel smiled back, sort of. "Okay."

Not an enthusiastic yes, Rocky thought, but not a rejection. As the president of the club, she used her position to move things along, saving Sam and Rachel from further embarrassment. She hoped. "Now that that's settled, let's get back to the Spookytown event. Which cupcake should we focus on as the giveaway for the kids?"

"I vote for Sam's," Casey said. "No offense, everyone. All entries were delish, but like Rocky said, Sam's are just too creepy-cute. Totally appropriate."

Rocky looked around the table. "All in favor?"

Everyone, including Sam, raised their hands.

"Settled," Rocky said. "To be on the safe side, we'll need approximately two hundred cupcakes for the Spooktacular goody giveaways."

"The pumpkin spice cupcake recipe itself is simple," Sam said. "As for the fondant . . ."

Gram, Helen, Ethel, and Casey volunteered.

"Great," Rocky said. "So along with Sam, you four will tackle the monster fondant. Which leaves Monica, Rachel, Judy, and me to bake the cupcakes."

"What about Tasha and Chloe?" Monica asked.

"Wild cards," Rocky said while pouring everyone a fresh cup of Sweet Apple Chamomile Tea. "Wherever they want to focus their efforts is great."

Chloe Madison, the new love of Rocky's brother Dev, had recently graduated from a New York City culinary arts school. Although she specialized in cooking more than baking, her overall skills were incredible. In fact, she'd recently partnered with Gram to open a quaint café, which was why she wasn't here yet. Detained on business.

As for Tasha . . . When it came to community and charitable events, Rocky tried to put aside her personal dislike of their former club president. At odds since high school, Rocky and Tasha had a long and ugly association. Complicating matters further, after the botched seduction of Rocky's oldest brother, Dev, Tasha had set her sights on Randall Burke, a man thirty years her senior, the flipping town mayor. Last year, in a match that had set the town afire with gossip, Tasha had married into the Burkes, the most influential family in Sugar Creek, aside from the Monroes, intensifying her already bossy, arrogant, manipulative, and sometimes downright *mean* personality.

That said, Tasha made kick-ass cupcakes and had a history with the club that stretched back to her great-grandmother. Big on tradition and holding fast to the hope that maybe someday the thirty-year-old woman would mature into a kinder, gentler being (like her deceased mom and grandma), the club endured Tasha Burke like one endures a perplexing infection while awaiting a miracle cure.

Shaking off thoughts of Tasha-the-Pinhead Burke (as nicknamed by Gram), who was uncharacteristically absent from their weekly Thursday night meeting, Rocky set aside the teapot and reclaimed her seat.

She waited until Sam finished passing around his recipe cards, another tradition, before proposing her next idea. "I was thinking, since we'll have our own booth at the Spectacular, in addition to the free cupcake treats for the kids, maybe everyone could contribute a dozen or so cupcakes, utilizing the pumpkin theme, which we'll sell—proceeds earmarked for the day-care center."

"Great idea," Sam said.

"Dandy," said Gram. "Put me down for two dozen of my Pumpkin Walnuts."

Smiling, Rocky penned a list as everyone chimed in.

Rachel cleared her throat. "Wait. That's a lovely thought, but Gretchen's sort of touchy about contributions. She has her own way of doing things and she's keen on obtaining a grant."

Gretchen Tate, owner of Sugar Tots and Rachel's boss.

"Those things take time," Rocky said kindly, "and from what you've told us the center could use some immediate upgrades. We can at least contribute to the playground fund you mentioned."

"I think Gretchen intends to reach out to local businesses."

"Smart," Helen said. "Meanwhile, let us help a little, Rachel, honey. That's what we do."

It was what Rocky loved most about Cupcake Lovers—their camaraderie and charitable efforts. Founded in 1942, the social club had gathered weekly to share sweets, tea, and news from their loved ones who'd gone off to fight in WW II. As a way to boost morale and to share a taste of home, the group began shipping cupcakes to soldiers. Over time, the club evolved and, in addition to spreading joy overseas, they also started organizing local charitable events.

"It's settled then," Rocky said. "A week to prepare and—"

"Sorry I'm late, Sweet Peeps, but wait until you hear my news!"

Sweet Peeps? Rocky rolled her eyes at the pretentious greeting, then turned and frowned. Decked out in four-inch heels and a formfitting dress that highlighted her curves—some cultivated by a personal trainer, others, like her big, pert breasts, compliments of surgery—Tasha blew into the room, commanding everyone's attention. As always.

"Did you just walk into my house without knocking?" Gram asked.

"I knew I was expected." Tucking her sleek, black hair behind her diamond-studded ears, Tasha took a seat at the head of the table. There were two other empty chairs, but oh no, she assumed a seat of authority.

I should have sat there, Rocky thought. If for no other reason than to rob Tasha of the opportunity. "We were discussing our efforts for next week's Spookytown Spectacular," Rocky said, vying for control.

"I vote for whatever everyone else voted for," Tasha said with an *I-couldn't-care-less* smile. "Now for my news! Brett called. The collective powers-that-be at Highlife Publishing loved our proposal for *Cupcake Lovers' Delectable Delights—Making a Difference One Cupcake at a Time.*" She squealed and applauded. "We're going to contract, Sweet Peeps!"

Rocky bristled. *If she calls us that one more time . . .*

"Incredible," Judy said.

"Unbelievable."

"Seriously?"

"Wow."

Similar sentiments followed, including Sam's, "Freaking A."

Rocky remained skeptical. A brainchild of Tasha's, this project reeked of disaster. That it was actually one step closer to realization only amped Rocky's misgivings.

Three weeks ago, at the urging of Tasha, who at the time had been their leader, the club had submitted a proposal for the recipe book—enhanced by photos, the history of the club, and heartwarming accounts—to Highlife, a New York publisher specializing in nonfiction. The entire process had been a hassle, complicated by Tasha's controlling nature and rabid quest for fame that had resulted in the members demanding she relinquish her role as president. Rocky, who'd been appointed as the new president, had secretly hoped the self-absorbed witch would quit the group entirely.

Ha.

If Rocky were paranoid, she'd think the woman had retained her membership solely to make Rocky's life hell. Not that her life had been a picnic lately even without Tasha's influence, but that wasn't the point. Clearly the main reason the narcissistic woman had swallowed her pride was because she was banking on this publishing deal. Apparently, marrying the town mayor (who was stinking rich and influential) hadn't quenched Tasha's thirst for power and glory. Not that there was much glory to be had in their small town.

Sugar Creek, Vermont. Population 1,355. A quaint tourist destination for Flatlanders visiting the Green Mountain State in search of stunning scenery, relaxation, or assorted outdoor recreation. Home of Cupcake Lovers, an association with a long and notable history that, in addition to their delicious recipes and the current popularity of cupcakes, had apparently landed the club a book deal.

"I don't know why you're all so stunned," Tasha said with a haughty tilt of her chin. "I told you we'd get an offer. Brett called me this afternoon with the good news."

Brett Pearson, the senior editor she'd been wooing on behalf of the club even though she was no longer president. They'd all agreed Tasha should remain the liaison in this instance, mostly because she'd established contact. Partly because no one else wanted the job. Especially Rocky, who was up to her eyeballs in renovations with the Red Clover.

Gram frowned. "You've been sitting on this news all day?"

"Don't get your granny panties in a twist, Daisy. I wanted to tell all of you in person and we were meeting tonight anyway. What's a few hours?"

"Don't get your reconstructed nose out of joint," Gram fired back. "I'm just saying this is exciting stuff."

The front door opened and shut, followed by rushed footsteps. "I apologize for being so late, everyone. It took longer than anticipated for Devlin, Luke, and me to hang the signage and shelves that just came in. You're going to love it, Daisy! Looks even better than it did in the online catalogue!"

Rocky grinned at Chloe, who'd blown into the room and sucked the wind right out of Tasha's sails. The petite woman with an adventurous spirit that matched Gram's had originally moved into town and this house to work as Gram's companion, specifically as a chauffeur and cook. Chloe still did those things, temporarily, but she was now also Gram's business partner. Rocky had known Chloe less than two months but already loved her. She also loved that Dev, her overprotective, sometimes-pain-in-ass brother, loved Chloe. The icing on the cake? Tasha hated the highly motivated and cute-as-hell culinary whiz kid. Partly because Chloe had landed Dev. Mostly because, after living in New York City for fourteen years, Chloe trumped Tasha big-time in life experience and accomplishments.

Long chestnut hair pulled back in her signature sloppy ponytail, Chloe peeled off her vintage leather jacket and trendy scarf and plopped into a chair next to Judy. "What did I miss?"

The older woman leaned into her and winked. "Sam asked Rachel out on a date."

"We got a book deal," Monica said.

"Um . . . wow. On both counts."

"I'm flying to Manhattan tomorrow to seal the deal," Tasha said, grappling for the limelight.

Which earned a universal, *"What?"*

"We agreed that if this happened," Sam said, "Dev would be our business advisor. He needs to look over those contracts, Tasha."

"You can't just sign an agreement without us knowing specifics," Monica said. "We're all involved."

"Settle down, Sweet Peeps. I wasn't going to sign anything."

Chloe blinked. "Did she just call us Sweet Peeps?"

"You really need to drop that, Tasha," Rocky said.

"Why? It's catchy. If I'm going to promote us on Facebook and Twitter, we need a catchy name."

"We have a catchy name," Helen said. "Cupcake Lovers."

Sam shot Tasha one of his death stares. "Don't ever call me Sweet Peep in public, and that includes online."

Tasha huffed. "Whatever. Back to my trip to Manhattan. In one of our conversations Brett had expressed interest in sampling our cupcakes firsthand. He also thought it would be helpful if the publicity department could speak with me in person, to get in touch with the human side of the club."

Gram opened her mouth, only Chloe spoke first. "Maybe Rocky should go with you."

"What?" Rocky blurted.

"Why?" Tasha snapped.

"She *is* the acting president of Cupcake Lovers, plus she could add some interesting insight."

"Plus, she's human," Gram said.

"I agree," Sam said. "Rocky should be involved in those meetings. As for the cupcake samples—"

"I spent all afternoon whipping up a batch of my Death By Maple cupcakes," Tasha said. "Consider Brett and his team smitten at first bite."

"No denying that recipe is to-die-for," Monica said, "but a variety might be nice." She gestured to the platters on the table. "Plenty of fresh cupcakes here and a broader representation of the club's talents."

"I'll wrap you up a nice care package," Ethel said.

"It's a plan," Sam said. "Rocky will join Tasha in New York and together they'll present a sampling of our cupcakes to Highlife. All in favor?"

Everyone, with the exception of Rocky and Tasha, raised their hands.

"Settled," Gram said. "You'll both go."

Rocky could think of a dozen reasons why she shouldn't go. A dozen and one. But as acting president and a longtime member and, even more so, as everyone's friend, she couldn't allow Tasha to represent them unchecked. God knew what she'd say or do while grabbing for the brass ring.

Rocky looked at the woman who, three weeks ago during a down and dirty bar brawl, had tried to shove an olive up Rocky's nose. "Why tomorrow, Tasha? Why so soon?"

"Because they had an unexpected opening in their publication schedule and, given the current red-hot popularity of cupcakes, they're putting our recipe book on the fast track."

"How fast?" Rachel asked.

"I'll find out," Tasha said, then smirked at Rocky. "I booked a private charter."

But of course she did. Tasha, or rather her husband, was loaded.

"Be at the airfield by seven o'clock a.m. As for hotels, I'll be staying at the Waldorf Astoria." She smiled. "Might be a little pricy for you."

"I have some contacts," Chloe butted in. "Don't worry, Rocky, I'll hook you up with something affordable. I'd come with, but the grand opening of Moose-a-lotta is on Saturday."

Tasha snorted. "Charming name."

"We thought so," Gram said. "It's a themed café," she told everyone. "Wait until you see!"

"Can't wait," Rocky said.

Tasha raised a professionally shaped brow. "Did I mention I'm not flying back until Sunday?"

Meaning Rocky would miss the opening of Moose-a-lotta. "What publisher does business on Saturday?"

"Our publisher."

"Don't worry about it, sweet pea," Gram said. "Better you're in the big city looking after our best interests. If you run into any hassles, you can always call Jayce."

Rocky's chest ached at the mention of the man who'd stolen and crushed her heart more than a decade before—not that Daisy knew. That walking Adonis of supercharged testosterone was the number one reason she did *not* want to go to Manhattan. Jayce lived a stone's throw away in Brooklyn. Too close for Rocky's comfort. After years of tense avoidance, they'd shared a week of volatile arguments. Every confrontation sizzled with sexual awareness. Heady stuff. Irritating, too, since Rocky wasn't in the habit of sleeping with men she despised. When they'd parted three weeks ago, Jayce had melted her brain cells with a scorching kiss. *Good-bye,* he'd said. *For now.*

Since then those words had haunted Rocky. They had sounded like a threat. Or maybe a promise. It scared the hell out of Rocky. She did not under any circumstances want to see Jayce again. Her freaking vulnerable and mangled heart couldn't take it.

"Rocky's a scrapper," Helen said. "She won't run into any hassles."

"But if she does," Gram said, "she can count on Jayce. Always been fond of that boy. He's like a third big brother to my Rocky."

Rocky traded a look with Chloe and Monica, who knew her deepest, darkest secret.

Big brother, my ass.

That tore it. Her trip to the city would just have to be 100 percent hassle free. In the words of Gram: *hassle, schmassle*. In order for Rocky to call on Jayce Bello, it would have to be one flipping huge catastrophe.

She couldn't imagine.

CHAPTER TWO

Even though Chloe and Monica had offered to take Rocky out for a drink, she'd opted to drive straight home. She knew they wanted to give her the opportunity to talk about Jayce, something she hadn't done since she'd blurted her secret and barfed up her bitter heart for the two of them to see.

As someone who typically kept her personal life, most especially her romantic liaisons, private, Rocky was embarrassed she'd shared so much. A mistake she'd vowed not to repeat. Thus, all her two friends knew was that she'd broken off with Adam Brody and tried making peace with Jayce. The latter hadn't gone according to plan. At all.

For the last three weeks Rocky had worked hard to push that torrid kiss and the feelings Jayce had rekindled from her mind. She wanted to move on with her life. Past her ancient grudge. If she let go of the resentment, maybe she could let go of the infatuation. Warped puppy love magnified a zillion percent. Maybe with a clean slate she could have a second chance with Adam or a new shot at a relationship with someone equally wonderful and safe. Instead, she still craved cocky and dangerous.

It had been so much easier to smother that attraction when Jayce had been hundreds of miles away. The few times he'd visited Sugar Creek over the years, she'd kept her distance.

Until this last time. This last time he'd rented a room at her inn and ransacked her life.

Okay. It wasn't Jayce's fault that her B and B needed major repairs. He wasn't to blame for her appliances going on the blink or her Jeep's engine crashing. He had nothing to do with her flagging business or dismal bank account. But he *had* pushed her over the emotional edge.

Now Jayce was gone and Rocky was regaining focus. She'd even sucked it up and asked Dev for a little—okay a lot of—financial advice and support. But she was going to pay it back. And she was going to hang on to her dream—the Red Clover.

As she neared her countryside Victorian home, the one she'd lovingly converted into a bed-and-breakfast, the one she'd decorated with antiques and filled with eclectic knick-knacks in a fashion that mirrored Gram's home, Rocky's heart swelled. It wasn't the swankiest B and B in the county, not even close, but it sat on three acres of gorgeous land with Thrush Mountain as a backdrop and it had a history. Rocky was all about history and tradition. As for the Red Clover, with her brother's help—and it had cost her pride dearly to ask—the B and B would at last prosper. Or at least stay afloat.

Rocky parked her Jeep, now running like a charm thanks to Monica's husband, Leo, and hustled inside the house. She tossed her keys in the vintage stoneware pottery bowl sitting on the circa-1880 mahogany parlor table—just two of the cherished bargains she'd picked up during one of her antique-hunting sprees. The familiar *chink* was muffled by thick plastic. Everything in most of the downstairs rooms was draped with plastic and tarp. Aside from the house's needing a new roof, the front and back porch had started to list and warp. There were cracks in the ceiling and several other interior flaws. She hadn't realized how many until the consulting contractors had talked her and Dev through their findings and recommendations. She'd been living in chaos for two weeks now, feeling out of sorts and restless. *Bored.*

"Maybe a couple of days away will do me good."

Readjusting her attitude, Rocky beelined to the kitchen and stored the cupcake care package in the fridge. Then she sailed upstairs and dragged her rolling duffel bag out of her bedroom closet. She suddenly regretted not asking Chloe's advice on what to pack for a weekend in New York City. Tasha had made a crack about Rocky's wardrobe, which mostly consisted of jeans, layered T-shirts, and sneakers.

I don't suppose you have a dress and heels in your closet. Something professional or at least semi-stylish?

A bit of a tomboy and comfortable in her skin, Rocky had never cared or worried about style.

Until now.

She was frowning down at her collection of sneakers, clogs, and boots when her phone rang. "Yo," she answered.

"Are you *insane?*"

"Hello to you, too, Dev." Android wedged between her ear and shoulder, Rocky rifled through her clothes in search of a dress. "Wondered how long it would take you to call."

"Chloe just told me. I'm floored she suggested you go with Tasha and that Gram, of all people, agreed."

"You're just worried because I've never been to the Big Apple."

"You've never been to any big city. Not alone."

"I won't be alone. I'll be with Tasha."

"Like I'm supposed to trust *her?* I'm surprised you do."

"I don't, but I'm a big girl, oh worrywart brother. Almost thirty. I can take care of myself."

"What if you get lost?"

"I'll ask for directions."

"What if you get mugged?"

"I'll chase the guy down."

"Christ."

Rocky rolled her eyes—at her brother and at the modest black dress she'd worn to at least three family funerals. "Kidding. I'm not stupid, Dev. If some idiot has the nerve to snatch my purse, I'll call the police. Not that that's going to happen. What are the chances? I'll be there for two days. Chloe lived in Manhattan for years and she never got mugged."

"She was lucky. And city savvy. Maybe I should come with you."

"You're joking, right? Do you really want to spend the weekend away with Tasha? She'll be all over you."

"I can handle Tasha."

Rocky snorted. "That would make her day."

"Rocky—"

"Forget it. You're not coming." She gave up on the dress hunt and moved to her pine bureau—a sturdy yet romantic piece handmade and painted by Sam. "Besides, what are you thinking? The grand opening of Moose-a-lotta is on Saturday. Day after tomorrow. *Hello?* Gram and Chloe's big day?"

He blew out a breath. "You're right. I can't go." It had to be killing him, being the overprotective control freak Dev was. "I'll enlist Luke."

Rocky gritted her teeth while rolling underpants and bras into a side pocket of her duffel. No doubt she was overpacking, but even though she'd never admit it, she was nervous about this trip. "Luke has a business to run," she said, tossing in two pairs of jeans and assorted T-shirts—go with what you know . . . or have. Hell, she could always buy a dress in New York. "The weekend is the busiest time for the Sugar Shack. You should know since you do the accounting."

Though her brothers co-owned the popular bar and restaurant, Luke handled the day-to-day management as well as acting as host and bartender while Dev operated behind the scenes, handling the books, payroll, banking, et cetera. Luke had never been a numbers guy, whereas Dev, who also ran the family's department store, had a master's degree in business and finance.

"Oh, and whatever you do," she added, cheeks burning, "don't call Jayce."

"This mysterious rift between you two is a pain in my ass, Rocky. You're my baby sister and Jayce is my oldest, most trusted friend. I'd feel better about you frolicking around Manhattan if—"

"I won't be *frolicking* and I don't need a babysitter."

"Do you at least have his number programmed in your phone? In case something happens?"

"Nothing will—"

"Yes or no, dammit."

"Yes." Not that she'd use it. "Is Chloe there?" she asked, desperate to steer the conversation away from Jayce.

"Sitting at the other end of the sofa, casting me annoyed looks in between surfing the Net on her laptop. She thinks I'm nagging you."

"You *are* nagging me. Ask her if she contacted her friend about a hotel room. She said—"

"Done. You'll be staying at the Hotel Chandler. Grab a pen. I'll give you the address. Never mind. Chloe said she'll e-mail it to you, along with her friend's name."

"Great. I'll print out the information later. Is it within walking distance of anywhere neat?"

"There are lots of *neat* places in Manhattan," he said with a smile in his voice. "Hold on. What, honey?" he said off to the side, then into the phone, "Chloe said the hotel's two blocks from the Empire State Building and three blocks from Macy's."

Rocky grinned, more excited now than nervous. "Cool. I mean I may as well do some sightseeing while I'm there, right?"

"Chloe said don't look like a tourist."

"What's that supposed to mean?"

" 'Don't gawk. Be aware of your surroundings.' "

Rocky rolled her eyes and gave a two-fingered salute. "Got it."

"Call me when you take off and call me when you land. And when you get to the hotel. How are you getting from the airport into the city?"

"Tasha hired a car."

"Good. About this meeting, hon—"

"I know. 'Don't sign anything.' Listen, Dev. It's late and I need to finish packing. Plane leaves at the crack of dawn."

"Want me to pick you up and drop you off?"

"Starlight Field? Fifteen-minute drive? I think I can manage."

"Right."

She smiled. "Back in three days. You'll barely know I'm gone. Love you, big brother."

"Love you, too, Sis. Sleep tight."

Rocky disconnected and tossed her phone on the bed, an image of Jayce kissing the holy hell out of her smoking through her mind. She was pretty sure she wouldn't sleep at all.

* * *

Rocky woke with a start, squinted at the blurry red numbers on her bedside digital clock.

5:45

No freaking way!

She thought she'd set the alarm for 5:00 a.m. She'd been tired and must've screwed up, setting it for p.m. instead. Thank God she'd woken up on her own, albeit forty-five minutes late, not that she'd ever fallen into a deep sleep. Bleary-eyed, Rocky showered and dressed, bemoaning the fact that this early flight messed with her morning routine. She typically kick-started her day with a few swigs of orange juice and a run along Pikeman's Trail, weather permitting. This morning all she got was the juice.

At six thirty Rocky set the cupcake care package on the passenger seat, tossed her rolling duffel into the back of her Jeep, and set off for Starlight Field—a private airport for private aircraft and home of the Sugar Creek Hot-Air Balloon Company. Although she'd never had reason to fly out of Starlight, she often provided directions to B-and-B guests who'd booked a balloon ride. Also, her cousin Nash Bentley, a licensed charter pilot, operated out of Starlight. Too bad Tasha hadn't booked *him*. An ally on the flight would've been nice.

Glancing in her rearview mirror, Rocky took a final peek at her beloved home. Last night after printing out the information Chloe had sent, Rocky had e-mailed Luke. Normally she would have called, since Luke wasn't big on e-mails or texts, but she didn't want to risk rehashing the discussion she'd had with Dev. Instead, she'd typed a succinct note informing Luke of her weekend plans and asking if he could check on the Red Clover while she was gone. Just to make sure the workers didn't want for anything. No doubt Dev would check up, too, although he might get distracted and waylaid by the opening of Moose-a-lotta. She hated that she was going to miss Gram and Chloe's big day, but it would be worth it if she could prevent Tasha from misrepresenting the club in any way. Rocky honestly had no idea what she was in for. She knew nothing about the publishing business, but she did know cupcakes and the mission, history, and heart of Cupcake Lovers. It would have to be enough.

Even though it was brisk outside, Rocky rolled down the window, breathing in the fresh, crisp air tinged with the scent of wood smoke. She knew without ever being there that New York City wouldn't smell this good. The sun had yet to rise, so she couldn't drink in the beauty of the lush green valley or the rolling mountains bursting with last remnants of vivid autumn foliage. Still the images burned bright in her heart and mind. Connecting with nature had always been a source of inspiration and serenity, part of the reason Rocky enjoyed her morning runs.

Her sense of calm scattered to the brisk October winds the moment she arrived at Starlight and spied a small plane with blinking lights on its wings sitting on the tarmac. She wasn't afraid of flying. She didn't have enough experience to be scared. She'd only been up in the air once in her twenty-nine years. That had been a long time ago, a family vacation to Disney World when she was seven. As for other family vacations, they'd always opted for driving. Personally, Rocky loved to drive. She liked being in control. Yeah. She liked that a lot.

She glanced at her cell. Six forty-five. Fifteen minutes from now she'd be giving up control for the next forty-eight hours. Daunting, yet stimulating. So *this* was the rush Gram got out of taking risks and facing the unknown.

Braced for whatever crap Tasha slung her way, Rocky locked the Jeep and rolled her burgeoning duffel toward the hangar where she was told to proceed to the DriftAir private jet—the sleek plane with the blinking lights. Crossing the tarmac, Rocky told herself not to obsess on how small the plane was. Surely the lighter the plane, the easier to stay aloft.

A middle-aged, stiff-postured, suit-wearing man took her bag and helped her aboard. Although the interior was confined, it was certainly luxurious. Plush leather and polished wood. Soft gathered drapes shielding the windows instead of those hard plastic shades.

Tasha was already seated in a roomy leather club chair, looking as stylish as her surroundings. She frowned at Rocky's casual attire. "That's the best you could do?"

"Don't worry," Rocky said, setting aside the care package and dropping into a seat. "I'll dress up for the meeting."

Tasha, who was sipping a glass of champagne, smirked. "To be honest, I was hoping you'd bail and let me handle this. But of course you showed. You're just dying to pee in my Cheerios."

Rocky ignored the dig and buckled in. Yes, she was coming along to preserve the integrity of the club. If that somehow ruined Tasha's agenda, so be it.

Pulling the latest *Martha Stewart Living* magazine from her messenger bag, Rocky settled in for the ride, praying she wouldn't get airsick. Just one more thing for Tasha to rib her about. They settled into a tense silence, but Rocky's mind screamed with excitement. In less than two hours she'd be in the freaking Big Apple. She had a short must-see/must-do list of her own and an additional list from Gram, who'd delighted in the thought of living vicariously through her granddaughter. Rocky hated the thought of Tasha potentially raining on *their* parade.

Digging deep for diplomacy, Rocky smiled. "I know this is difficult given our strained history, but for this weekend at least, could we set aside our differences? For the club? For the book deal?" she added, hoping to strike a mutual chord.

Tasha-the-Pinhead Burke rolled her eyes. "Whatever."

CHAPTER THREE

Brooklyn, New York

Jayce Bello stood on the steps of the prewar limestone town house and watched as the moving van drove off with the contents of the one bedroom co-op he'd lived in for the last nine years. He'd spent the past three weeks working up to this decision. No turning back now.

Hands stuffed deep into the pockets of his cargo pants, he tilted back his head, closed his eyes, and absorbed the scents and sounds of President Street and beyond. Park Slope, a fairly upscale neighborhood in Brooklyn, was ripe with historic buildings, top-notch restaurants, bars, and shopping. It was also close to the Brooklyn Botanic Garden, the Brooklyn Museum, and Prospect Park—three of his favorite haunts. Various images and memories slid through his mind, some pleasant, some gritty, all vivid.

He was going to miss this place.

And he wasn't.

Jayce opened his eyes just as a desperate driver tried wedging an SUV into a parking space that would barely accommodate a compact car. Made Jayce think about all the times he'd driven around the block trying to cop a space. There was a reason residents jokingly referred to this area as "*No* Park Slope." He definitely wouldn't miss the lack of on-street parking. Lately, he'd been craving wide-open spaces, along with a few other things.

Tend to your soul, his friend and former neighbor, Mrs. Watson, had said more than once. It had, in fact, been the last thing she'd said to him—her final words. Jayce wondered if he'd ever adjust to the loss of their unique friendship. Since moving to New York, he had elected to keep new acquaintances at arm's length. He didn't trust easily, and he'd always been intensely private. Most people respected his boundaries. Mrs. Watson, rest her soul, hadn't been most people. She'd been as close as he'd had to a confidante in this city, and now she was gone.

Not yet ready to face the bare walls of his co-op and therefore the enormity of this move because, Christ, it was daunting, Jayce sat on the stone steps of the historic building and made the call he'd been putting off until his plan was in motion. He didn't think twice about calling his oldest friend at 7:00 a.m. Dev had been getting up at the ass crack of dawn since they were teenagers. "Hey, man. Free to talk?"

"You called me."

"I know."

"No. *You* called *me.* Not the other way around. Just want to be clear on that."

Amused, Jayce dragged a hand though his longish hair. "What are you smokin', dude?"

"Need that distinction in case Rocky tries to tear me a new one."

"Lost here."

"She told me not to call you. I didn't. You called me."

"We've established that. So what did I just give you the freedom to tell me?"

"Rocky's en route to JFK."

A major airport within minutes of Jayce. His heart slammed against his chest like a steroid-shooting linebacker. *Jesus.* "Why?" The thought of her coming to her senses after thirteen years and coming after *him* made him rock hard and slightly light-headed.

"Cupcake Lovers got a book deal and she's flying in with Tasha to meet with the publisher."

Jayce blinked, the words almost Greek to him because, hell, that wasn't what he'd expected to hear. He took a second to respond. Or maybe it was five.

"You there?"

"Yeah. I just . . . What the hell are you talking about?" Jayce breathed the crisp air, trying to snap out of his disappointment as Dev explained.

"She's staying at the Hotel Chandler until Sunday. Could you just . . . be available in case she needs you?"

So much for starting his road trip within the hour. "Sure." He didn't feel any more comfortable about Rocky being alone in the city than Dev did. Yes, she was tough and smart, but not big-city smart. She didn't know this town. Jayce did. Rocky was Hollywood gorgeous. She typically wore her long blond curls in two braids. *Easier that way,* she'd once said, but the tomboyish style just looked plain sexy to Jayce. As did her sultry blue eyes, high cheekbones, lush lips, milky-white complexion, and the generous curves that would make a dead man drool. The thought of Rocky Monroe walking the streets of Manhattan, unaccompanied, chilled his bones. Stunning young woman. Unsuspecting innocent. She didn't have a clue. He did.

"I'm not asking you to tail her—"

"On it."

"Thanks."

"Sure."

"So why did you call?"

Jayce rolled back tense shoulders. "I'm moving home."

Now it was Dev's turn to pause. "To Sugar Creek?"

"Remember when I said I couldn't decide whether to lease out my parents' house again or to sell?"

"Yeah."

"I'm not doing either. I'm moving in."

"Really. Huh." Another awkward pause. "I mean . . . I'm thrilled you're coming home. It's just . . ." Dev lowered his voice. "You're not exactly fond of that house."

"Something I'd like to come to terms with."

"Well, hell, Jayce, that's great. That's . . . It's about time."

The heartfelt sentiment, in addition to Mrs. Watson's gentle nagging, reinforced Jayce's decision to slay his demons in a bid for peace of mind and a slice of heaven. Jayce's personal paradise included a certain blond hellion, three or four kids, and a couple of dogs. Maybe a cat. The amount of kids and animals was negotiable. The woman was not. He was also keen on surrounding himself with the most caring brood he'd ever known—the Monroes.

Jayce had grown up with Dev, best friends since grade school. Dev's mom and dad had been a guiding force in Jayce's life. Daisy Monroe had treated Jayce like any one of her many grandchildren. Luke had been like a sometimes annoying, always entertaining younger brother, and Rocky . . . Yeah, well, that's where things got complicated. "Do me a favor," Jayce said. "Don't spread the news just yet. Let me ease into it."

"Not to dissuade you, but there's not a big market for private detectives in Sugar Creek."

"Got that covered. I'll explain later."

"When should I expect you? Please tell me not until after Sunday."

Jayce thought about Rocky, naïve and vulnerable, had-him-by-the-balls Rocky. "Not until after Sunday."

* * *

Rocky was damn proud she didn't hurl when the plane hit turbulence. She even kept her cool during the harried transfer from charter jet to private limo. John F. Kennedy International Airport was a frenzied center for hordes of travelers, many of whom were short on patience and manners. Holding her tongue around so much obnoxious behavior was nothing short of a miracle. Or maybe she was too floored to comment.

Mostly she was impressed with herself when she didn't climb over the seat of the hired limo to commandeer the wheel because, damn, the chauffeur Tasha had enlisted to drive them from the airport to Manhattan was insane. To be fair, he wasn't in the minority. So many cars, so much congested traffic. So many morons who ignored the speed limit and didn't signal when changing lanes. Which might have been endurable if Rocky was in control. But she wasn't.

She'd been so distracted by the white-knuckled ride she'd been unable to enjoy the thrill of seeing the Manhattan skyline for the first time. Tasha seemed oblivious to their perilous journey. Then again she was, yet again, sipping champagne. Rocky might've joined her if she wasn't allergic to sulfites.

Then they were *in* Manhattan and surrounded by blocks and blocks of skyscrapers, endless jaywalking pedestrians, mind-boggling traffic, and taxi drivers with a death wish. By the time the chauffeur dropped her at her hotel, Rocky was so overwhelmed, she couldn't think straight. She numbly thanked the driver and told Tasha she'd meet her at the publisher's address at the appointed time of 2:00 p.m. and, yes, she'd be wearing a flipping dress. If she weren't so in awe of the Big Apple chaos she might've curled into an overly tired ball of stress until one thirty. Instead, she checked into her room, a small but really nice room, then, after calling Dev for the third time this morning, set off to do some shopping.

Even though it was probably a really touristy thing to do, Rocky had her heart set on buying something at Macy's. When she was growing up, one of her favorite movies had been the old black-and-white version of *Miracle on 34th* Street. Yes, it resonated simply because it was a Christmas movie and Rocky loved Christmas, but it also represented the power of childhood dreams. Of wishing for and wanting something so badly that, via magic or faith or whatever, that dream came true.

Rocky had set her sights on the Red Clover when she was ten. Her daddy had encouraged that dream by co-signing on the initial loan, and Dev was helping to keep that dream alive.

Another reason Rocky was so intent on seeing Macy's was because of her own ties with a department store. J. T.

Monroe's Department Store—family owned and operated for six generations. In her lifetime, her Grandpa Jessup had run the store and, after him, her dad, Jerome (Jerry to a select few) Monroe. Her dad had surprised everyone by retiring to Florida this past year, and now Dev ran the place, although their dad still had a voice, a big, freaking, insistent voice, in the overall operations, which drove Dev, a mega control freak, nuts. J.T.'s was small potatoes compared to bigger chain stores, but it had heart. Rocky wanted to know if Macy's had heart.

After acquiring walking directions from the concierge, Rocky made it from the Hotel Chandler to the famous department store—hassle free. After losing herself on multiple floors and trying on several dresses, she left Macy's after two hours with her booty—hassle free. Shopping bags looped over one arm, she dipped into the pocket of her over-the-shoulder messenger bag and snagged her Android. She wanted to take a picture of the storefront to text to Dev. He was planning to renovate J.T.'s, and she thought he might be inspired by some of the imaginative window displays. As someone with an intense love of decorating, *she* was duly impressed.

Phone camera in hand, Rocky pushed through the revolving door and was assaulted by a barrage of chaotic noise, pungent scents and odors, and crowds of hustling, bustling people. Disorienting and exciting at the same time. Shaking her head, she jockeyed for a prime position, aimed her camera, and—*BAM!*

"Sorry," a man mumbled.

Unlike at JFK, at least this person had apologized for knocking into her, but then Rocky looked down and noticed her messenger bag was gone. *What the . . .*

She looked up and saw a man rushing away through the crowd, caught a glimpse of her bag peeking out from under his flapping coat. "Stop! *Thief!*" Outraged, she took chase. The gall! The nerve! The freaking *horror!* Her financial life was in that bag. Wallet, cash, credit cards, ID. She spotted the mugger's sorry ass darting across the street.

Incensed, Rocky darted, too. Unfortunately, she didn't look both ways first.

* * *

Jayce was nearing the Flatiron District when he got the call. He recognized the number and swore. Rocky wouldn't call to shoot the shit. Something was wrong.

"Jayce?"

"What's up, Dash?"

"I hate it when you call me that."

"Not always."

"Just since."

She sounded shaky. *Christ.* "What's up?"

Silence, then an aggrieved sigh. "I need your help."

Given the bad terms they'd been on for years, and especially since the additional falling-out last month, he'd never expected to hear those words. Oh yeah. This was bad. "Where are you?"

"NYU Medical Center."

Christ. "Narrow it down, Rocky."

"I think the paramedics called it Tisch. Tisch Hospital?"

"Got it." His pulse raced as he veered toward the East Side.

"Aren't you going to ask what I'm doing in New York City?"

"More interested in why you're at Tisch."

"I was sort of hit by a car."

"Sort of?" Jayce muscled his Volvo through a gridlocked intersection.

"It was more of a tap. Rolled right over the hood. It's nothing but—"

"I'll be there in ten, fifteen minutes, depending on traffic."

"You're that close?"

"In the area on business." Which wasn't wholly a lie. Running a red light, Jayce swerved and dodged traffic, crossing over Third Avenue. "Are you in the emergency room?"

"Yeah. I have to say, it's a little scary here." She lowered her voice to a whisper. "The guy on the other side of the partition? I think he was stabbed."

"Are you with a nurse? A doctor?" *Tasha?*

"Doctor just came in. I have to go."

"Almost there, Dash."

"Jayce?"

"Yeah, babe."

"Whatever you do, don't call Dev."

In spite of his dark mood, Jayce smiled.

* * *

Jayce was the last person Rocky wanted to call. But she'd first called, then texted Tasha, only to get the response: *Do u know what I paid to get an appt w/this hair designer?*

Tasha wouldn't be coming.

Rocky couldn't, wouldn't, call Dev. He'd anticipated trouble. He'd even freaking predicted the purse snatching! If she called, he'd panic and demand she return home. *Now.* As the acting president of Cupcake Lovers, as someone with a personal, heartfelt interest in the members, Rocky needed to be at that publisher's meeting. So she'd called Jayce and now he was on his way. She didn't want to admit it, but she was relieved.

Rocky had been living on her own, in a remote area no less, for years. She was an avid sports enthusiast—snow skiing, snowmobiling, hiking, biking, and boating. One of the reasons she'd gotten along so well with Adam. There wasn't much that intimidated or scared Rocky, but having her purse snatched and being hit by a car in the space of two minutes was rough. The scene after had been almost worse. Everyone hovering, telling her not to move, curiosity seekers, well-meaning passersby, the poor guilt-ridden driver whose hood she'd rolled over, the paramedics, the police. Tasha would've loved being the center of attention. Rocky had not.

Her shoulders sagged with relief when the doctor gave his last instructions, then left. She was changing out of the hospital gown and back into her clothes when someone knocked on the door. "Just a sec." Frowning at her ruined long-sleeved T-shirt, she pulled it on anyway, careful not to touch the wound on her forehead, then called out, "Okay!"

She turned just as Jayce moved into the small room, filling the space with a palatable intensity. As always, her heart fluttered and pounded at the sight of him. Tall, lean, and mean. Physically perfect in her book. He wore his dark-golden hair longer these days and had grown a devilishly sexy goatee. Bad boy to the bone, he was dressed in neck-to-toe black. Baggy pullover shirt, cargo pants, a wool peacoat hanging open, and a pair of rubber-soled boots. He looked to-die-for handsome. He looked . . . angry.

"You said it was nothing."

She realized his gaze was fixed on her shirt—stained with copious amounts of mostly dried blood. "It looks worse than it is." She gestured to her forehead, feigned nonchalance. "Just a tiny cut, but it bled like a mother. It's not that bad. Didn't even need real stitches. Just this butterfly strip."

Jayce dragged a hand down his face. "What else?"

Her body trembled when he moved in for a keener inspection. Her temperature spiked. Her brain glitched. Everything—her senses, her emotions—was magnified. She blamed her shaky state on the mugging, the accident, the meds, but no amount of rationalizing curbed her intense reaction to the reassuring presence of this man. "Just some bruises," she croaked, swallowing hard when he smoothed messy curls from her face. She'd had a crush on Jayce since she was a kid. She'd finally seduced him on the night of her seventeenth birthday. It had been perfect . . . until the next morning, when he'd broken her heart. Every time she saw him, which was hardly ever, a lifetime of memories and emotions battered her soul. Every time she saw him, she fell a little harder instead of digging her way out. "I shouldn't have called."

His gaze flicked from her head wound to her wounded eyes. "Don't shut down on me, Dash."

Her cheeks warmed at the nickname, *his* nickname for her. Self-conscious, she backed away and sat on a chair to pull on her socks and sneakers. "It's just that creep stole my purse and now—"

"Someone stole your purse?"

Focusing on the thieving rat instead of the rogue who'd stolen her heart was a welcome distraction. Rocky vibrated with indignant rage. "Snatched my bag right off of my arm in broad daylight! Took it and ran. The creep. I chased after him and—"

"Hold on. You chased a *criminal?*"

"That's how I got hit by the car. Only to be fair, it was technically *me* who hit the car. The driver was turning the corner and I didn't see. I had my eyes on that good-for-nothing *thief.*"

"For Christ's sake, Rocky, what were you thinking?"

"That that bastard had my bag!"

"He also could've had a gun or a knife!"

"Don't yell at me!"

"I'm not . . . It's just . . ."

"He screwed me over big-time, Jayce." Laces tied, Rocky bolted to her feet and paced. "He got my credit cards, my cash, driver's license, insurance cards. *Everything!* The police offered little hope of getting my stuff back. I didn't see his face, couldn't offer much of a description. How am I supposed to function the next few days without any money or ID? I can't just go home. I have to be at an important meeting. I have to—"

Jayce smothered her rambling with his mouth. One moment she was pacing and venting. The next she was in his arms, under his spell. He kissed her softly, sweetly, but the kiss lingered and . . . she melted. At once she was seventeen and aching with all the fierce desires of a lovelorn teen. Her brain shut down. Her girly parts revved. When Mr. Supercharged-Testosterone Man eased back, Rocky grappled for her wits. After what seemed like a sappy-ass eternity, she licked her tingling lips and willed her voice not to crack. "Why did you do that?"

"You were hysterical."

"No, I wasn't." She swallowed hard, clawing her way

through the sensual fog. "Even if I was, a slap would've been the traditional response."

His expression said, *Get real*. Realistically Rocky knew Jayce would never raise his hand to a woman, hysterical or otherwise. "I'll get you to your meeting on time," he said, "and we'll address the stolen-ID situation together. As for the money, I've got you covered." He cut her off with a raised hand. "You can pay me back later. We'll work it out, Dash."

"All right," she said, feeling overwhelmed and out of sorts as he helped her into her bloodied coat. "Just don't call me Dash. And don't kiss me again."

His eyes sparked and his palm burned at the small of her back as he escorted her to the door. "Don't count on it."

CHAPTER FOUR

While Rocky showered, Jayce contacted the precinct that had handled her case. He tried not to think of her naked while his call got put on hold, then bounced from one officer to another. Tried not to envision steam swirling around that smoking-hot body or water streaming over those badass curves or soap bubbles sliding over those toned limbs.

While the second officer, someone he knew, gave him the not-so-promising status and realistic projection regarding the mugging, Jayce tried not to think about how good Rocky had felt in his arms when he'd kissed her at the hospital or how she'd melted against him, or how amazing she'd tasted. He purposely pushed away the thought of her in that bloodied shirt. He wasn't squeamish—far from it—but the thought of Rocky suffering harm turned him inside out. There'd been another close call a few weeks back when she'd rushed toward her damaged sports shed in a fierce thunderstorm. If he hadn't tackled her, chances were she would've been crushed along with her recreational equipment when the roof collapsed.

"Yo, Bello."

New York's Finest. Jayce scrambled to focus. "What?"

"Just asked you a question."

Only Jayce had been distracted by Sugar Creek's hottest. He forced his gaze from Rocky's duffel bag, the clothes strewn on the bed she'd be sleeping in. He leaned back in one of the two club chairs in the cramped though tastefully decorated hotel room. The Chandler was affordable by New York standards. Not so much by Rocky's. Was Dev footing the bill? He would sure as hell want to know about the accident, but Jayce had promised Rocky he wouldn't call her brother. Another secret. *Christ.*

"Damn, Jayce. Are you there?"

"Sorry, Arnie. Bad day. What was the question?"

"I asked about your connection to this Monroe woman."

Jayce eyed the bathroom door, heard the water shut off, and tried not to think about Rocky toweling her beautiful body dry.

"Carson said she's a real looker with a mouthwatering set of—"

"Tell Carson to keep his opinions to himself and his dick in his pants."

"Easy, man. Didn't know you two were an item."

"Now you know." Jayce shifted and tempered his tone. "Do me a favor, Arnie, give me a heads-up if you guys get something on the mugger or Rocky's belongings."

"You'll owe me."

Jayce disconnected, still burning over Carson's lewd observation. Not that it wasn't true, but that wasn't the point. Ever since Jayce had knocked heads, then locked lips with Rocky in Sugar Creek three weeks back, he'd developed a fierce need to finish what they'd started thirteen years ago. That entailed an exclusive relationship and, if he had his way, marriage.

He dragged a hand over his face, wondering how long it would take to repair thirteen years of bad blood and where to begin, since he wasn't even sure where he'd gone wrong. How could he know, when Rocky refused to talk about it? Thinking about the way he'd offered his heart, his *hand*, only to be told to *piss off* riled him as if it happened yesterday. Except a lot had happened between then and now. If Jayce had learned anything, he'd learned life was short and he'd wasted too much of it.

"Still out there?" Rocky called from behind the closed door.

"Not going anywhere." *Even if you tell me to piss off.*

Just then her cell phone blipped.

Jayce glanced at the Android lying on her bed amidst a pile of colorful T-shirts. Message from her ex-boyfriend? New boyfriend? *Grow up, Bello. Jesus.* "You've got a new text."

"Who's it from?" she called back. "What does it say?"

No secrets? No hesitation? Jayce thumbed the screen, smiled. Not Brody. Not any man. "It's from Chloe." He paraphrased, "Wants to know if you're okay."

"Oh! Tell her . . . Tell her I'm great. Tell her thanks for the room rec. Perfect. And the dress rec. Awesome. And . . ."

"Everything's peachy," Jayce said as he texted: *All's well. More soon.*

He tossed the phone back on Rocky's bed and crossed to the window. He looked down on the kinetic sidewalks and streets of the city, yearned for the quiet of Sugar Creek. It hadn't always been like this. Just lately. A slow burnout and an unexpected call to arms.

"Did you reply?" Rocky called out.

"Done."

"Thanks. Be out in a sec."

"Take your time." Meanwhile Jayce ached to fast-forward. Summoning patience, he dropped back into the club chair. He wasn't one for philosophizing. He didn't sit around analyzing his life. He didn't wallow in self-pity or stress about the future. He rolled with the punches—a coping mechanism he'd honed over the years. As a kid he'd survived some tough breaks. As an adult he'd dodged some bad shit. In all his thirty-five years he'd only been blindsided twice. The night of his parents' death and the night he'd fallen in love. The first had scarred him for life. The second had put all he cherished at risk. A surprise attack that had coldcocked his conscience and left him for buzzard bait.

That weapon of destruction had a name: Rochelle— *Rocky*—Monroe. His best friend's little sister. Five years

Jayce's junior. Not a shocking age difference except she'd been jailbait when he'd nailed her. Just seventeen, her birthday in fact. He'd been twenty-two and spontaneously besotted and seduced by the beautiful girl who'd crawled in through his bedroom window and peeled off her clothes. At first he'd thought Rocky was drunk. But, damn, she'd been sober and aggressive and frickin' irresistible.

Jayce shook off the past and focused on the woman who emerged from the hotel bathroom. Curvier than the girl he'd bedded thirteen years prior. He'd gotten a prime view of Rocky's bodacious figure three weeks ago when they'd faced off in her bathroom at her inn. At the time she'd been wearing a sheer cami and skimpy underpants. Now she wore a long-sleeved, knee-length, black-and-white-patterned dress and tall black boots. Nothing racy about this ensemble, yet his pulse revved.

"How do I look?"

I'd like to lick you head to toe. "Not bad."

Rocky frowned. "This meeting is important. I need to look great." She unknotted the sash-belt and tied it in a bow. "Better?" She turned before he answered, kicked shut the bathroom door to see for herself in a full-length mirror. "Too frilly. Maybe it's supposed to tie in the back."

"It was fine before."

"Then what?" she snapped, fixated on her reflection. "Too short? Too long? Too clingy? Not clingy enough?"

Okay. This was a side of Rocky he'd never seen. He'd never heard, let alone witnessed, her fretting over her appearance. Never known her to ask anyone's opinion. Unlike most of the women Jayce knew, Rocky didn't obsess on fashion. She opted for comfortable. Casual. Jeans and T-shirts never looked so good. Sneakers never so sexy. He chalked it up to confidence. One of Rocky's most alluring and irritating qualities. She was definitely off her game.

Jayce remained seated, although he did lean forward, bracing his forearms on his knees. He locked on to her nervous energy, her uncharacteristic insecurity, and considered that gash on her forehead. She'd just been mugged, then hit by a car. Rocky was tough, but was she really up for a corporate meeting? What if she got dizzy? Or sick? Though she'd downplayed the head wound, there'd been a lot of blood on her shirt. Enough to stop his heart. He'd spoken to the doctor who'd declared her fit enough to leave. But that overworked resident had also been dealing with various other crises. Could Jayce really trust the man's, *She'll be sore, but fine*?

The more Jayce thought about it, the less inclined he was to let Rocky out of his sight. "Maybe you should call Tasha and ask her to postpone the meeting."

"Seriously? I look that bad? Dammit!" She fussed with the deep-V neckline, frowned. "Chloe said this wraparound style was a good fit for my figure and business appropriate. I called her from Macy's and—"

"It's not the dress."

"Is it the boots? Too clunky? Should I go with the pumps?" She bent over, flashing her generous cleavage as she unzipped the boots and kicked them away, treating Jayce to her shapely calves. The woman had kick-ass runner's legs and she accentuated them by slipping her pretty feet into a pair of pointy-toed, three-inch-spike-heeled pumps. *Christ.*

She straightened. "Better?"

Jayce shifted to hide a boner. "Only if you want the marketing department to be distracted by your legs." He dragged his gaze from her killer gams to those lethal eyes. "Sexy."

She flushed, holding his gaze for a second before grunting in exasperation. "I don't want to look sexy. I want to look stylish. Professional. Tasha said . . . Oh, what does she know?" Rocky turned her back and rooted through her shopping bags. "I bought a new blazer. Maybe I should just wear my jeans—"

"The dress looks great, Dash." Jayce pushed out of the chair. "Go with the boots. Business appropriate. Stylish."

"You sure?"

"Positive. Although if you're opting for stylish over sexy you might want to reconsider your hairstyle." The tousled mass of soft blond curls looked just-rolled-out-of-bed enticing. He should know. She'd rolled out of his bed after that one night of lovemaking, backlit by moonlight and looking like a young and sassy version of the legendary bombshell who shared her last name.

Boots zipped, Rocky whirled back to the mirror. "I'd go with a ponytail, but I don't want to expose my forehead. That butterfly strip looks like a freaking badge of stupidity and the bump is starting to discolor."

"Let me see." Jayce turned her around and gently inspected the wound. "It's swollen now, too." Plus, flecks of dried blood caked one edge of the butterfly strip. *Damn.* "How do you feel? Dizzy? Achy?"

"Stressed." She batted away his hands and glanced at her watch. "I'm supposed to meet Tasha in forty minutes and I look like freaking Frankenstein."

"Not quite that bad," Jayce teased. "And I'll get you there in plenty of time." He moved into the bathroom, inspected the vanity strewn with toiletries. Powder, deodorant, lotions, hairbrush, blow-dryer, elastic bands, hair clip. "Where's your makeup?"

"Why? Aren't I wearing enough? Jesus. I'm going for a book, not a modeling, contract. There's something to be said for understated, you know."

"Relax. Just looking to camouflage that bruise."

"Oh. Right. Well, I don't wear foundation, if that's what you're looking for. Just mascara and tinted lip balm."

A natural beauty, Rocky didn't need makeup to enhance her looks. Still, most women he'd known kept an array of beauty products even if they only used them for special occasions. Rocky wasn't most women. He spied a nail file and a pair of manicure scissors. "How do you feel about bangs?"

"What?"

He rounded the corner—comb, towel, scissors, and hair clip in hand. "I dated a hairstylist once."

"That qualifies you to cut hair?"

"Let's just say I was subjected to enough fashion hype to know what qualifies as stylish."

"You're kidding, right?"

"Sit." He motioned her into one chair, placed the towel

over her lap, then pulled over the other chair and sat across from her. "Lean forward."

She blew out a breath and did as he asked. "Fine. Chop away. Just . . . not too much."

"Just enough." Jayce concentrated on the task, thankful that Rocky lowered her lids so he didn't have to gaze into those feisty baby blues. Breathing in the tantalizing scent of her shampoo and body lotion was torture enough. "Followed up with the police," he said. Which seemed wiser than his first thought: *I want you flat on your back and writhing.*

"Did they catch the mugger?"

"No."

"Recover my bag?"

"Wouldn't hold my breath."

"Great." She sighed. "Thanks anyway."

"I'll keep on it."

"And thank you for reminding me to cancel my credit cards. The officer mentioned that earlier, but I was frazzled and then, well, whatever. It's done. Not that the bastard thief could do much damage anyway. I've only got the two cards now and they're pretty maxed out. Dev consolidated—" She looked up, then away. "Never mind."

"Dev's managing your finances?"

"Not forever," she snapped, ever prideful. "Just for now. It was that or lose the Red Clover."

Jayce had witnessed Rocky's financial struggles first-hand. He'd itched to help, not that she'd let him, so he was relieved she'd reached out to family. Dev had always had a gift for numbers. While other kids had devoured the Sunday comics, he'd studied the financial pages. No surprise that he'd excelled in math and majored in business. The man was a genius with finances. He'd even advised Jayce on a few investments. Part of the reason Jayce could afford to abandon his lucrative investigative business in favor of a new endeavor. "Not judging, Rocky. Deducing. If Dev's handling your finances, he'll learn about your canceled credit cards."

"Oh, right. Damn."

"You have to tell him about the mugging. The sooner, the better."

"After the meeting. But just about the purse snatching, not the accident. You know Dev. Biggest worrywart in the world. He'd get Nash to fly him here ASAP so he could look after me and I don't want that. He needs to be home for Gram and Chloe. Tomorrow's their big day."

"Grand opening of their café." Dev had told him all about it. Jayce set aside the scissors, smoothed her newly layered bangs to the side, admired her thick lashes, milky complexion, lush mouth . . . "Surprised you're missing that."

"Unfortunately, the club elected me as Tasha's watchdog." Rocky blushed when he brushed the pad of his thumb over her cheek. Shivered when he lightly blew wisps of hair from her face.

Time froze as Jayce focused intently on the woman he'd set his sights on. A woman he'd known all his life yet barely knew. This was the longest conversation they'd had in more than a decade, and before that, before that night, exchanges had been no more than playful banter between a restless young man and his best friend's cocky little sister. Jayce had spent years waiting for Rocky to grow up and address their history, to banish the secret that had distanced Jayce from the town and people he loved. He was tired of waiting.

Sitting stock-still, gaze lowered, Rocky licked her lips. "Are you done yet?"

His shaft twitched at the nervous catch in her voice. He hadn't even begun. As always a raw sexual heat burned between them. She was as turned on as he was, not that he'd act on it. Not now. *Let it simmer.* "Good to go."

She cleared her throat, eased away. "How do I look?" she asked, forcing her gaze to his. "If you say, *Not bad,* I'll sock you."

Good enough to eat would at the very least earn him a glare, so instead he went with, "Almost perfect." He raked his fingers through her silky curls—yeah, boy, *heaven*—then twisted and secured an updo with one of those hair gadgets that reminded him of a potato-chip bag clip. "There."

Even though Rocky scrambled toward the mirror, the heat lingered. The air sizzled. Visibly shaken, she focused on her reflection, blinked. "Wow. I never considered bangs. They not only cover the bump, but they're . . . flattering. And this style . . . nice. How—"

"Man of many talents," he said, coming up behind her. They locked gazes in the mirror, and Jayce felt something beyond the heat. A shift. An added element. Swimming in Rocky's vivid blue eyes, alongside resentment, lust, and hurt, he spied curiosity.

"It occurs to me that I really only know the Jayce Bello of my youth," she said, breaking eye contact. "I'm still angry with that man. I'd like to get past that, move on. Maybe we could do something about that while I'm in town."

"Meaning you're ready to talk about the infamous morning after?"

"No," she said while nabbing a baker's box from the mini-fridge. "Meaning I'd like to know more about the big bad private dick who just cut and styled my hair like a seasoned pro."

Primed for the challenge, Jayce glanced at his watch, then formulated a plan as he helped Rocky into her coat and out the door. "It's a start."

CHAPTER FIVE

Sugar Creek, Vermont

Women.

Luke Monroe had never been book smart. He wasn't good with numbers like his older brother, Dev. Didn't have a flair for aviation or gambling like his cousin Nash. Or a gift for woodcrafting and art like his cousin Sam. Luke hadn't inherited his dad's razor-sharp managerial skills. However, when it came to women, Luke was an expert.

So when Lizzie Ames strode into the Sugar Shack with that look in her eye, he knew what was coming. He just hoped she didn't cause a scene. Not that there were a helluva lot of customers haunting the local gourmet pub just now. Postlunch, predinner, two hours until Happy Hour.

Luke continued wiping down the bar, smiling when Lizzie perched her cute butt on one of the burgundy-cushioned bar stools. "What's up, honey?"

"We need to talk."

The standard opening line for an ultimatum. "My office?"

"No, here. In public. Where you can't seduce me into forgetting my gripe."

Luke smiled at that. He could seduce Lizzie anywhere. "What did I do?" he asked while pouring her a glass of Chablis.

"You slept with Bridget."

"Honey, I've been seeing Bridget on and off for two months. Along with Connie. I don't do exclusive. You know that. And you knew about Bridget and Connie." He'd always been straight up with his women. Always.

"Yes, but you *slept* with Bridget. *All night.* As in woke up with her the *next* morning."

Ah. Damn. "How—"

"She was bragging about it at the gym. Running her mouth while running on the treadmill. Guess she thought I couldn't hear her with my earbuds in, but I turned the sound down on my iPod and heard just fine. *You should see how sexy Luke looks in the morning,*" she mimicked in a high-pitched voice. "*Scruffy stubble. Messy hair.*"

"I can explain."

"You told me you don't do sleepovers."

"I don't."

"That it's your way of keeping things casual."

"It is."

Lizzie bolstered her shoulders, nabbed her wineglass. "So it's true. You're serious about Bridget."

"No—"

She tossed her drink in his face. "We're through, Luke Monroe." Sliding her cute butt off the stool, she flipped him the bird, then left.

"Damn." Luke toweled wine from his face and shirt, rinsed his hands, and dragged damp fingers through his now sticky hair. He'd assumed trouble loomed but didn't anticipate the clichéd drink baptismal. He glanced to the end of the bar where the Brody brothers (Sugar Shack regulars and two of Luke's sports buddies) nursed beers while watching ESPN on one of two plasma screens hanging over the bar. Only Adam and Kane weren't watching sports. Or at least not the televised kind. Luke shrugged. "At least you two were the only ones to witness that unfortunate display."

Adam raised a brow.

Kane pointed.

Luke turned. *Oh, hell.* "What are you doing here, Connie?"

"Nell asked me to trade shifts."

He knew that look. "Been standing there long?"

"Long enough."

Damn.

She unclipped her name badge and tossed it on the bar.

His best waitress. *Shit.* "I can explain."

Connie waved him off and walked out.

"Oh, for Christ's . . ."

Kane laughed.

Adam, who'd been on the glum side lately, crooked a grin.

Luke gave them the finger, which only hiked their amusement.

Just then Chloe, his big brother's sweet-faced, sexy-as-hell girlfriend, strode in. "What's so funny?" she asked, taking Lizzie's former seat.

Luke shot a lethal glance at his smirking buds. "Two of my girlfriends just broke off with me in the space of a minute."

"Fail to see the humor."

"That makes two of us."

"Except given your wet hair and the splotches on your T-shirt . . ." She glanced at Lizzie's empty wineglass. "I suppose at least one of the showdowns might have been comical."

"Hilarious." Luckily, he had a supply of clean shirts in his office.

"So now you're down to what? One steady girl?" Chloe asked with a teasing gleam in her eye. "How awful."

"Annoying, considering I now have to break off with Bridget, which means I'll be down to no steady girls."

"Why . . ." Chloe raised a hand. "Never mind. I'm sure there's a method to your philandering madness."

"There is."

"Of course there is."

Chloe Madison. A fairly new addition to Sugar Creek. A woman he'd never been able to charm. Not even a little. Nope. Dev had hooked her at *Hello*. Luke poured the petite dark-haired beauty a coffee. "What can I do for you, Chloe?"

She glanced toward the Brodys, Adam in particular, then leaned in to Luke and lowered her voice. "Rocky's in New York."

"I know."

"Devlin asked Jayce to look after her."

"Not surprised."

Another side-glance at Adam. "Jayce is moving back to Sugar Creek."

Luke lowered his voice as well. Unbeknownst to everyone in town aside from Luke, Chloe, and her friend Monica, Adam and Rocky had had a friends-with-benefits arrangement. Jayce had recently rocked that clandestine boat, and now he was moving home? "That's news." Considering Jayce operated a highly successful business in New York and considering his and Rocky's ancient *secret,* Luke was shocked. "You sure about that?"

Chloe nodded. "Jayce called Devlin this morning. Asked him to keep it quiet for now, only Devlin told me, thinking I'd keep it quiet, which I will, except for you." She sipped java and eyed him over the rim. "What are we going to do, Luke? Don't look at me like that. I know you know."

Three weeks ago during a monumental funk, Rocky had confessed two things to Luke. One: She'd been hooking up with Adam for weeks. Yeah, man, *that* had been a real blower, but not nearly as shocking as Two: Thirteen years prior, Rocky had lost her virginity to Jayce Bello—Dev's best friend since grade school, a member of the Monroe family in all but blood. Luke had been stunned and pissed—not only by the decade-old secret but also by the fact that Jayce, a guy he'd always admired, had taken advantage of his seventeen-year-old (just) sister and broken her heart. Luke hated that Rocky had warned him off coldcocking the bastard and even more that she'd sworn Luke to secrecy. Secrets were dangerous, hence his full-disclosure policy on the dating field. "I'm surprised you're keeping a volatile secret like this from Dev."

"Rocky made me promise."

"Me, too."

"This stinks."

"Yeah."

"I don't like keeping secrets from Devlin."

"I hear you."

"But I don't want to betray Rocky."

"Me either."

"I just . . . I thought you should know." Chloe tugged at her messy ponytail, looking flustered and concerned and obnoxiously pretty. "Any ideas on how to proceed?"

"Not one."

"Great."

"I'll think on it."

"It's going to make Rocky miserable. Jayce living here. The rift between them . . . Well, you know."

"What I know is that Dev's going to freak when he finds out about that one-night stand. And he *will* find out. It's inevitable at this point."

"Maybe you're underestimating your brother's capacity to understand and forgive youthful . . . folly."

"It's not the deed so much," Luke said, keeping his voice low. "I mean, yeah, Rocky was jailbait at the time and Jayce should have known better, but the real whammy at this point is the long-ass lie. Dev's spent the last thirteen years wondering why his sister and friend were at odds. We *all* wondered. But it ate at Dev. Talk about a frickin' snowball effect."

"Which means our efforts to protect Devlin and Jayce's friendship, not to mention honoring Rocky's privacy, will backfire."

"Dev's going to feel betrayed on multiple levels."

"Damn."

"Yeah." Luke drummed his fingers on the bar.

Chloe sipped more coffee and surreptitiously eyed Adam and Kane to make sure they weren't eavesdropping. Fortunately, the freelance sports instructor and independent logger had focused back on the television. Luke had thumbed up the volume via the remote as enticement.

"Okay. Here's the deal. We need to get Rocky to come

clean with Dev," Luke said. "Or for her to get Jayce to come clean with Dev. Fess up and face the music. Get it over and get on with life."

"The sooner the better."

"The longer they wait—"

"The worse it will be. For all of us," Chloe added with a frown.

"What a mess," Luke said.

"Compounded by the fact that Rocky's still in love with Jayce."

"She told you that?"

"Freudian slip."

"Yeah, well, it's not a healthy kind of love. It's the obsessive kind."

"And you know this because?"

"I know women."

Chloe's lip twitched as she eyed his stained shirt. "Ah."

Luke ignored her sarcasm. Granted, he'd believed Bridget when she'd promised to *forget* he'd spent the night. He'd misjudged her sincerity. His mistake. Now he'd have to break off with her because obviously she didn't believe him and actually *did* think things were serious. Which they weren't. Not on his end anyway. Luke shook off his own troubles and focused back on his sister's. He wished to hell she hadn't blown off Adam. Adam was a hard worker, devoted to the community, good-humored, and straight-ahead. What you saw was what you got. Jayce was . . . complicated. "Why is Jayce moving back to Sugar Creek anyway?"

"Devlin didn't say." Chloe's Android chimed with an incoming message. "Sorry." She read and smiled. "It's Daisy. She's waiting for me at Moose-a-lotta. Needs me to pick up some lightbulbs."

Luke raised a brow. "You taught Gram to text?"

"Except she keeps spelling everything out. Some of her messages are eons long. At this rate I'm going to need an extended texting plan." Shaking her head, Chloe slipped the phone back in her pocket. "So that's your solution to our predicament?" she said, focusing back on Luke. "Getting

Rocky to come clean with Devlin ASAP? Doesn't seem like much of a plan."

Luke shrugged. "It's a start."

"Speaking of . . ." Keeping her voice low, she leaned in again and smiled. "Did Sam call you about tomorrow night?"

"Reservations for two. Finally got off his ass and asked Rachel out. Amazing."

"Mmm. Well, he was sort of pushed into it and she sort of reluctantly agreed. Not the most promising of beginnings. Plus they both seem, I don't know, awkward and nervous about it. Do you think you could—"

"Give Sam some pointers?"

Chloe smirked. "I was going to say '*make sure they have a special dining experience,*' but a refresher course on dating etiquette might not be a bad idea. From what I understand, Sam's been out of the game a long time."

"Yeah." Losing his wife, the love of his life, to cancer had crushed Sam. Luke envied his cousin for a lot of reasons, but he didn't envy that heartache.

Chloe slid off the stool. "Thanks for the coffee, Luke, and the advice, such as it was. See you in the morning at Moose-a-lotta?"

"Wouldn't miss it." Luke watched her cute butt go, reminding himself that cute butt belonged to his big brother. *Hands off. Thoughts clean.* Right. He glanced down the bar at Adam and Kane, who toasted him with empty mugs.

"If Connie was here," Kane said with a teasing grin, "I'd ask her for a refill. But she's not."

"Didn't you lose a waitress last week?" Adam asked.

"Marla," Luke said. "Moved to Pixley." Next town over. And lately Nell, his newest waitress, had become unreliable.

"Between the weekend crowd and the tourists that'll be coming in for the Spookytown Spectacular," Kane said, "you're gonna be shorthanded."

Adam pushed off his stool. "Toss me the sign."

Luke reached under the bar. He hadn't used this in a while. In fact, lately Dev, who handled the accounting for the Shack, had been nagging Luke about having too many employees on the payroll. Luke had a hard time turning away pretty ladies in need of a job. Unfortunately, they also frequently came and went. Luke passed Adam the laminated sign. "Put it—"

"I know where it goes. Front window. Bottom left corner."

"If you want my advice," Kane started.

"I don't," Luke said. He handed the cocky logger the phone book. "Do me a favor. Look up the number for the *Pixley Tribune*. I've got the *Sugar Creek Gazette* in my speed dial." Android pressed between shoulder and ear, Luke nabbed two Buds from the fridge and set them in front of the brothers.

"Yeah, hi," Luke said when the local newspaper's receptionist answered. "This is Luke Monroe over at the Sugar Shack. I need— Uh, that's right," he said, rolling his eyes when his two regulars chuckled. "Another 'Help Wanted' ad."

CHAPTER SIX

Manhattan, New York

Maybe it was the shock of the mugging and subsequent accident. Maybe it was the bump on her noggin or the fact that she was completely out of her element. Rocky preferred to blame any single one or combination of these things for the slight daze that had dogged her all through the meeting, rather than the way Jayce had kissed her at the hospital. Or the way he'd looked at her in her new dress and heels. Or the way he'd fussed with her hair. (Talk about a shocker of a turn-on.) She didn't want to admit that the man she'd been so intent to forget still had the power to mesmerize her. Instead she blamed everything from A to Z for her distracted mind-set, including the way Tasha had flirted with their future editor as well as the attending publicist.

"Don't you think you were a little overly friendly?" Rocky asked Tasha as they squeezed into the cramped elevator of the pre–WW I building.

"It's called networking."

"It's called flirting."

"Can I help it if I'm interesting and attractive?"

"If not modest."

Nonplussed, Tasha pressed a button on the brass panel, then inspected her French manicure. "I wanted to prove that at least one of us would be effective as a public spokesmodel for the group. You heard Michael. The publicity department will be targeting magazines, newspapers, and television outlets regarding possible features and interviews."

"Yes, but they're promoting the recipe book, not Tasha Burke."

"You bragged plenty, Rocky."

"About the members of the Cupcake Lovers and our accomplishments."

"Which bordered on tedious after a while. Didn't you see Brett's and Michael's eyes glazing over? I simply interjected a little fun—"

"Flirting."

"—into your dull dissertations."

"They *asked* me about the history of the club."

"A blurb would have sufficed."

"Blurb?"

"That's publishing speak for a snippet, an extremely condensed description."

Rocky rolled her eyes as the doors opened and they stepped out of the elevator into the semi-bustling lobby. As if one book offer made Tasha an expert on publishing.

"You're just jealous because Brett and Michael only had eyes for me."

Dream on, Pinhead. Although Rocky had been focused on business and reeling from the aftereffects of Jayce, she'd still picked up on her own share of male appreciation. Thing was, Rocky couldn't care less, whereas Tasha cared more than she should. Being doted on and adored by her rich and influential husband wasn't enough? Talk about pathetic.

"I feel for you, Rocky; I do," Tasha went on as they shrugged into their coats. "You couldn't even attract interest with that revealing dress and tousled hairstyle. Talk about overdoing it."

Revealing? Tousled? "I wasn't trying to attract—"

"No wonder you're hopelessly single," Tasha said. "You don't know how to play the game."

"Yeah, well, you shouldn't be playing at all," Rocky said as they stepped outside and into the crush of a thriving city.

"You're married. Does Randall know you're meeting that publishing suit for dinner this evening?" Rocky had overheard that tidbit just before she'd exited the editor's office.

"It's business."

"Then why wasn't I invited?"

"Envious?"

"Hardly."

"Poor Rocky," Tasha said, primping the haircut that had cost a small fortune—not that it looked all that different from her usual style. "Your first night in the Big Apple and you'll be spending it alone."

"Actually," Jayce said, stepping in from out of nowhere, "she'll be spending it with me."

Tasha blinked up at the tall, broad-shouldered, and darkly dressed man. "Jayce Bello?"

"Tasha," he said, unsmiling. "Burke now, right? Married to the mayor of Sugar Creek. Designer clothes, private jets, chauffeured limos. Moving up in the world."

"Yes, well—"

"Now you've snagged the attention of a New York publisher. What next? The Food Network?"

"I—"

"Impressive." He smiled down at Rocky. "Ready for dinner?"

The sexy tilt of his mouth shanghaied Rocky's thoughts. *Who am I and why are we standing here talking to Pinhead Burke when we could be alone doing the nasty?* "Dinner," she managed. "Sure." Just as that killer smile rendered her weak in the knees, Jayce looped a possessive arm around Rocky's waist.

"By the way, smart move," he said to Tasha. "Ditching your wedding ring while in the city. Flashing expensive jewelry attracts unscrupulous attention."

Rocky blinked out of her daze and glanced to Tasha's bare left hand—something she hadn't noticed during the meeting—then to the woman's burning cheeks. At least Tasha had the decency to blush, or maybe that was anger, because, man, did Jayce have her number.

Tasha gave a tight smile. "Don't let me hold you up."

"Call me. Text me. Let me know about tomorrow's plans," Rocky said to the woman as Jayce maneuvered her away and into the burgeoning sea of pedestrians. Sidestepping a metal grate and an unidentifiable glob of food, Rocky gawked up at her escort. "You totally dissed Tasha Burke."

"Still can't believe Dev dated that conniving bitch."

"The two worst months of my life." Rocky shook off the memory. Before Chloe, Dev had had sketchy judgment in women. Although his most mind-boggling relationship had been with the bane of Rocky's existence. "By the way, nice catch on the missing wedding set. I can't believe I didn't notice. She always wears those gaudy diamonds."

"Even in the tanning bed. Hence the lighter skin around her ring finger, which I wouldn't have noticed—"

"If she'd been wearing the rings." Rocky smiled. "Way to observe."

"Part of the job."

Another dazzling talent. Along with making Rocky's blood sizzle and her senses hum. Not to mention his ability to kiss her into a blissful stupor. She tried not to think about the kissing part. They were not a couple. They weren't even on friendly terms. There would be no more kissing or . . . "Hey. Hey, wait a minute."

Rocky stopped in her tracks, tripping up the person behind her.

"What the hell, lady?"

Jayce placated the man while Rocky frantically checked her coat pocket to make sure the person who'd rammed into her hadn't stolen her phone. Haunted by this morning's purse snatching, she trusted no one. Jayce, meanwhile, finessed her against a storefront. "You can't stop like that in the middle of foot traffic, Dash."

Still in possession of her Android, Rocky tamped down the panic and fury of being violated a second time. She couldn't believe how easily she'd been rattled. Cheeks hot, she latched on to her former concern. "You made it sound like we were hooking up."

"What? When?"

"Back there. You told Tasha I'd be spending the night with you."

"So?"

"You mentioned dinner."

"And?"

"Made it sound like a date. What if she says something to Randall and it gets back to Dev?"

"What if it does? Knowing Dev, he'll be glad his best friend, who knows Manhattan like the back of his hand, is looking out for his little sister who got mugged on day one. Incidentally, did you tell him about that yet?"

"Not yet and don't change the subject."

"You're the one who brought it up and don't pick a fight."

"I'm not . . ."

Jayce raised a brow.

"It's just . . . You . . ." *Damn.* She'd fallen back on ancient anger like a safety net. Easier than managing her whacked-out libido. Preferable to acknowledging the emotional collateral damage of the mugging and subsequent accident. Both had made her feel skittish and vulnerable. Add to that being unfamiliar with Manhattan and overwhelmed by Jayce . . . Okay. Yeah. Maybe she'd been a little overdramatic.

Jayce moved in, ramping her sexual awareness like an airborne aphrodisiac. "Do you want to know more about this big bad private dick or not?"

Rocky's heart raced; her inner thighs tingled. Raging lust. Better than panic. Far better than vulnerability. *Focus on sex. Sex, not assault. Aggressor, not victim. Control. Take control.* Knowing Jayce better might eviscerate her obsessive desire once and forever, or . . . it could backfire. "What did you have in mind?"

"How's your head?"

"What? Oh." Rocky palmed her bandaged forehead. "It's tender, but other than that, I'm good."

"In that case, let me show you around. Dinner. Drinks. First time in the city. Anything special you'd like to do? See?"

Aside from you, naked? "I did have a list. It was in my bag. You know. The one that got swiped? Anyway, I had a few 'must-sees,' but mostly there were things that Gram asked me to do. Things she'd always wanted to do, and I admit they seemed sort of fun."

"Okay."

"You'll think they're touristy. Boring. Maybe even stupid."

"I'd endure boring and stupid for Daisy."

Rocky considered the man, his past, and his genuine affection for her eccentric grandma. She sighed. "Yeah. You would."

"Let's start with dinner. I bet you haven't had a good meal all day."

"You'd win that bet."

"Italian? Thai? Mexican? French? Name your poison."

Rocky eyed the vendor on the corner. The portable silver cart with the heating and refrigeration units, and a striped umbrella to protect food and server from the elements. She'd spied similar food vendors on practically every block, and it was the one city aroma that actually appealed. The devil in her was also tempted to test Jayce's patience regarding touristy ventures. Embracing the moment, if not the man, Rocky cocked a challenging brow. "I'll name the poison *and* the place."

CHAPTER SEVEN

Hot dogs in Central Park.

Jayce had looked forward to treating Rocky to a sampling of New York's finest local food. Pasta and cannoli in Little Italy. Dim sum and lo mein in Chinatown. Hell, even something touristy like the contemporary cuisine of Sardi's. Purchasing hot dogs and a couple of cans of soda from a street vendor and then parking their asses on a cold, hard bench fell short of his expectations. Then again, watching Rocky dressed up and chowing down on a dog smothered in mustard and relish was a bit of a warped turn-on. "Everything you dreamed of?"

"Not bad," she said around a mouthful, "but not spectacular either."

"You expected spectacular from a street vendor?"

"There's one on every other corner. You see them in the movies and on television all the time and people always clamor around them. Figured they had to be pretty good."

"Grab and go," Jayce said, biting into his own dog. "Fast. Convenient."

"Satisfying."

"Really?"

"Sampling native food was on Gram's and my must-do list."

And this counted? He didn't argue. "What else was on that list?"

"Let me think." She polished off her hot dog, sipped soda through a straw.

Jayce watched as he ate. Christ, she was beautiful. And fearless. Down-to-earth, yet complex. Part of what had hooked and intrigued him the night he'd lost his senses and taken her virginity. The same qualities that had haunted him all these years.

"Observation deck of the Empire State Building, Times Square, Statue of Liberty."

"Daisy's list?"

"No, mine. Gram wanted to go dancing in a nightclub and speed-cruising on the Hudson River. Oh, and we both wanted to see a Broadway show. I know it's a lot to squeeze into two days, especially if you have work—"

"I'm free. Anything else?"

She glanced at the horse carriages lined along Central Park South. "A hansom-cab ride though the park was on Gram's list. Romantic, she said." Rocky shook her head. "In the movies maybe. In theory. But not in real life. Horses don't belong in big cities. The traffic. The noise. Look at them. They're miserable."

"The city's steeped in controversy over whether or not to ban horse-drawn carriages. You're right. Harsh life for the animal." He appreciated Rocky's sensitivity. Then again, she was a country girl. Used to seeing animals in a more natural environment.

"Mentally crossing hansom-cab ride off the list." Rocky stood and tossed her trash in a nearby bin. "Can we walk instead? Just enough to get a flavor? That way I can at least share a partial experience with Gram."

"Sure." Been a long time since he'd strolled Central Park. Typically Jayce got his nature fix in Brooklyn's Prospect Park. Smaller yet brimming with picturesque scenery. Woodlands. Lakes. Trails.

Rocky took off down a path in her sleek black boots.

Jayce kept stride. The air was cool, the sun bright. Branches and leaves rustled in the autumn wind. The colorful foliage reminded him of the intense beauty of Vermont this time of year. Walking among nature with a girl from his hometown, a girl from his past, filled Jayce with an unsettling mix of contentment and longing.

"I'd love to jog through here."

"Bad idea."

"Why? The park's like an oasis in a desert. A serene bit of nature amidst steel and chaos."

"Do you know how many rapes, muggings, and murders occur in Central Park each year?"

"No. But it can't be that dangerous, especially if you stick to populated areas and stay aware. Look at all these people. Families, couples, loners. It's not like I'd go running in the dark."

Jayce wished he could see the dense wooded areas, lush grounds, and multiple trails through Rocky's naïve eyes, but headlines, statistics, and personal experience tainted his perception. Instead of expanding on his dark thoughts, he held silent. Why spoil one of the "must-dos" on Rocky's wish list? It was not as if he was going to let her out of his sight.

Rocky glanced his way, then focused back on the path. "Must be tough. Living day after day surrounded by crime. It's either develop a thick skin or live in fear."

"Or make a difference."

"Which is why you pursued a career in law enforcement. Only you left the NYPD after just a few years. You never said why."

"You never asked." She'd spent years shutting him out, obsessing on a grudge he didn't fully understand.

Rocky's cheeks flushed. "I should've said Dev never said why."

"Did you ask him?" Jayce watched as her flush deepened. Of course she hadn't asked. Her way of dealing with their one-night affair and the morning after was to build a wall around herself where Jayce was concerned.

"Fair enough." She licked her lips and stared straight ahead. "If I ask you now, will you tell me?"

Fortunately, her cell rang, saving Jayce from expanding on a conversation he didn't want to have. Not now anyway. His reason for leaving the force was complicated and could be construed as either selfish or indolent. He didn't want to spend the afternoon defending his actions, nor did he want to look like a pompous ass in Rocky's eyes. Bottom line, he didn't feel comfortable enough with the woman to share intimate details of his life. Navigating their complex relationship was like navigating a minefield.

"It's Dev returning my call," Rocky said, jolting Jayce out of his thoughts. He watched as she stared at the screen for another two rings.

"Get it over with, Dash."

She blew out a breath, connected. "Hey, big brother. You got my message?"

Jayce slid on his sunglasses and pretended not to listen. Meanwhile he stayed aware of their surroundings, unlike Rocky, who kept walking while talking.

"Yep. The meeting went great. Our cupcakes were a hit. Tasha's Death by Maple won the honors. Like she needed a bigger head. Overall, Tasha focused more on herself than she should have, but you know Tasha. Anyway, please pass this on to Gram and Chloe so they can keep the club in the loop. In a nutshell," she rushed on, "we met with our editor and publicist and discussed the proposal the club submitted and how they wanted us to expand on that. Also touched on marketing, publicity, and deadlines. It was interesting, I suppose. I just hope it doesn't interfere with our charity efforts. I could see . . ." She shook her head. "Never mind. Don't get me started. . . . No, we didn't sign anything. We told them to send the contracts to our business advisor—which would be you. Speaking of you and business . . ."

Rocky veered off the path and started pacing along the edge. "You might be hearing from my credit-card people. No, I didn't overspend! That's the least of your worries. Hard to spend without the plastic. No, I didn't lose my purse. I . . . It . . ."

Standing on the sidelines, Jayce geared up for the impending meltdown. He didn't have to hear to know Dev had switched into overbearing-caretaker mode.

"Listen, don't overreact," Rocky said to her brother. "It was nothing. Well, it was something, but I'm fine. My bag was sort of stolen. Some bastard snatched it off my arm when— Yes, I'm fine. I told you— Would you please stop shouting. I'm fine. I'm with Jayce." Fuming, she passed him the phone. "Dev wants to talk to you."

"She's fine," Jayce said.

"What the hell?" Dev snapped.

"Like Rocky said, someone snatched her bag. The police are on it. I'm on it. Don't worry."

"Don't worry? My sister's been in New York less than a day and she got mugged!"

"It happens. Meanwhile I've got her covered." Jayce kept his voice calm and low, hoping his friend heard between the unspoken lines: *I'll look out for Rocky, like you asked. I'll keep her safe.* It's not like Jayce was in a position to speak freely. Not with Rocky pacing in front of him, listening to every word, and signaling him *not* to tell Dev about the car accident.

Dev blew out a breath. "You're sure she's okay?"

"You know your sister. Tough as nails." *Obstinate as a mule.*

"I'll wire her some money."

"I've got that covered, too."

"Keep the receipts."

"Don't insult me." Jayce never took money from friends he considered family. Dev knew that, but they still went through this song and dance on occasion. Like last month when Dev had asked Jayce to do a background search on Chloe. Something that had backfired on Dev but thankfully righted itself. Jayce had witnessed the chemistry between Dev and Chloe firsthand. They belonged together. He recognized a similar spark between himself and Rocky. Although it wasn't a spark as much as a raging inferno. Potentially hazardous but impossible to ignore.

"Is Rocky standing within earshot?" Dev asked.

"You bet."

"So you can't talk."

"Not really."

"Did you tell her you're moving home?"

Jayce glanced at Rocky, who'd stopped pacing but was now glaring at him and chewing her thumbnail. "Not yet."

"Maybe you should hold off," Dev said. "Considering her less than stellar attitude toward you, I'd hate to see you alienate her more when I need you to stick close."

"Taking her on a whirlwind tour of Manhattan," Jayce said, throwing a placating smile Rocky's way.

"Unobtrusive way of sticking close," Dev said. "Smart."

"That's why they pay me the big bucks."

"But you won't take my money."

"Finally getting that, are you?"

Dev grunted. "Put Rocky on."

Jayce passed back the phone.

"Happy now?" Rocky asked Dev while frowning at Jayce. "I have a babysitter. Does this mean I don't have to check in with you again tonight? . . . Thank God. . . . Tomorrow? I don't know my precise plans yet. A tour of some local bakeries was mentioned, but— Yeah. Okay. Sure." She rolled her pretty blue eyes. "Shouldn't you be helping Gram and Chloe prepare for the café's opening? . . . Uh-huh. Give them my love. . . . Right. Stick close to Jayce. Got it." Another eye roll. "Pinky swear. Love you, too."

She pocketed her phone and fussed with the buttons of her peacoat. "Yeah. *That* wasn't too painful."

"Dev means well."

"You don't have to tell me. I know my brother's heart. I just don't like being bossed."

"You don't have to tell me." Jayce flashed back on when he'd tried to stop Rocky from rushing into her collapsing sports shed. She'd punched him in the damned jaw. "Had enough of the park?"

"Ready for my whirlwind tour if that's what you're asking." Rocky looked over his shoulder at the towering skyscrapers, then to a nearby family playing catch with their dog on a patch of grass. She touched her bandaged forehead, frowned. "Like Gram says, life's short."

That statement resonated with Jayce more than Rocky could possibly know. His mood inched toward somber, prodded by fresh and ancient memories. Yeah, life was short, but it was also what you made it. He'd been spinning his wheels for far too long, looking for validation and contentment in all the wrong places. With that in mind, he looked hard at the beautiful woman who'd seduced him, then tortured him with rejection and disdain for more than a decade.

He'd managed their irrational feud until this last visit to Sugar Creek. Until he'd gotten an up-close-and-personal dose of the adult Rocky for a full week. He'd thought he'd put their relationship, or lack thereof, in perspective, but then he'd learned she had a fuck buddy and his world as he'd created it imploded. Jealously and envy ate at his gut. Regret, lust, and genuine affection screwed with his head. He'd been set to leave Sugar Creek forever—turning his back on everything he loved . . . and hated. Then Rocky had come running with the news that she'd broken up with Brody, followed by some half-assed attempt to put her past with Jayce to rest. Instead, she had challenged Jayce's priorities and ignited his fighting spirit. That good-bye kiss had cinched his suspicion: Rocky still burned for him. And, God help him, he burned for her.

Tend to your soul.

All roads to validation and contentment led to Sugar Creek.

"About the tour," Jayce said, steering Rocky back toward Fifth Avenue. "This is my city. My comfort zone. For the rest of the day and night, I'm in control."

Rocky sucker punched him with a look that gave him an instant erection. "Dream on, Bello."

"I could drop you back at your hotel, alert Dev you refused

my company. He'll either wire you some money or get Nash to fly him—"

"All right, all right. You call the shots, but just until midnight, Cinderfella. After that I turn back into a pumpkin with a mind of my own."

"Your gratitude is overwhelming. So what's first? Empire State Building? Statue of Liberty?" He quirked a sardonic smile. "Why am I asking you? I'm in charge."

She pursed those lush lips. "I never realized you were so irritating. Oh, wait, yes I did."

Jayce laughed at that. "Wait'll you get to know me better."

CHAPTER EIGHT

Growing up with an old-fashioned dad, two older brothers, and a slew of protective male cousins, Rocky had learned early on to speak up and speak out. Otherwise she would have been treated like a delicate, helpless girl. She was not delicate, nor was she helpless. She was outgoing and athletic, like her brothers. Strong-minded like Dev and sociable like Luke. She had dreams and goals and a strong desire to make her own way.

Whatever it took.

Sometimes it meant invoking a hard, confident stance, brazening her way through an argument. Sometimes it entailed a covert approach, batting her baby blues, playing the vulnerable or coy card. She wasn't fond of the latter, but she wasn't above it either. That approach always worked with her dad. The only man who had ever left her completely clueless and flustered was Jayce.

Five years her senior, Jayce had been around as long as Rocky could remember. Dev's best bud, thick as mud. He spent so much time at their house he was practically a member of the family. He'd even joined the Monroes on a couple of vacations and almost always shown for picnics and parties. Things had been spiffy and okay, and then Rocky had started feeling all wobbly kneed every time Jayce was around and that hadn't been okay. That had been weird. She'd been ten at the time. Over the years things went from weird to worse. By thirteen she was so head over heels in love with Jayce Bello, she could barely breathe when he entered her space. Her heart pounded and her girly parts tingled. By sixteen she was certain she would die if they didn't "do it." She'd lain in bed late at night touching herself, thinking about kissing and stuff. Specifically with Jayce. So handsome. So muscular. So kind, but fierce. One of those guys, like her brothers, who always stood up for the underdog.

She was also attracted to Jayce's mysterious side. An only child of two working parents, he didn't talk a lot about himself. Unlike with her brothers and cousins, Rocky didn't know much about Jayce's likes and dislikes or his dreams and goals. He had a way of making the conversation about you or someone else but never himself. He hadn't changed much in that regard over the years. Even though Rocky had agreed to this personal sightseeing tour in order to get to know Jayce better, so far today the conversation had revolved around Rocky and Manhattan.

Since Rocky had yet to hear from Tasha about a timetable for Saturday, Jayce had suggested combining (and augmenting) Gram's speed-cruising wish and Rocky's desire to see the Statue of Liberty. On the ferry ride across the Hudson River to Liberty State Park, Jayce had pointed out buildings and areas of interest along the Manhattan skyline. Later the conversation had centered on the Statue of Liberty, mostly because Rocky had been so impressed and in awe, then on 9/11 because of a sudden surge of patriotism and a pang of sadness when Jayce had pointed out where the Twin Towers should have been.

Wanting to lighten the mood on the ferry ride back, Jayce had asked Rocky for an update on all things Sugar Creek, and she'd lapsed into a ramble about the upcoming Spookytown Spectacular and Sam's foray back into the dating scene. Before she knew it they'd taken the subway to Times Square, where she had gawked at the fantastic weirdness and glitz of the theater district and Jayce had scored tickets to a Broadway musical she'd never heard of but would never forget. The old theater, the live orchestra and astonishing voices!

Now they sat in a famous little restaurant finishing off the desserts that had followed their posttheater supper. Rocky was exhausted yet buzzed on the whirlwind day and, okay, a little high on the gorgeous man sitting across from her. She realized suddenly that she'd yet to ask pointed questions about his life. *Where had the day gone?* She'd meant to ask Jayce why he'd left the police force, about his home life in Brooklyn, and then the waiter brought the check and Rocky got distracted. *Again.* "How much?"

"Don't worry about it."

"I'm not worried. I just want to know what my half is." As far as she was concerned, there was a fine line between enjoying someone's hospitality and taking advantage. "I've been trying to keep a mental tab throughout the day, but you're not making it easy. Those theater tickets, for instance. They had to cost a fortune. And now this big dinner at Sardi's?"

"I'll mail you an itemized tab."

"No, you won't."

"You're right. I won't." Jayce slipped a credit card into a small leather folder along with the bill. Then he glanced up and smiled a little at Rocky, who couldn't decide if she wanted to punch or kiss him. "You're family, Rocky. My city. My treat."

She narrowed her eyes. "You know what? I'm not going to argue."

"Good."

"I'll just estimate and pay you back after I get home. Better yet, I'll call Dev in the morning and have him wire some money."

"You hate asking Dev for money."

"I hate owing you worse. Besides, I can't go another day away from home without any cash."

"I could—"

"Forget it." Rocky forked up the last bite of her New York

Cheesecake. Yes, she'd gone for the most clichéd item on the dessert list. Just stamp a *T* for "tourist" on her forehead alongside the butterfly strip. Reminded of the mugging, she touched her fingertips to her wound. She felt like such a fool.

"Head hurt?"

"What?" Rocky blinked. "Oh. No. Well, not as much as my pride anyway and not as bad as my feet. I'm not used to spending an entire day in spiky-heeled boots hoofing it all over God's asphalt city."

Jayce pushed away his half-eaten Tiramisu. "No dancing then." He glanced at his watch. "Too early for the best clubbing anyway."

Rocky glanced at her own watch. "It's almost midnight."

"It's also New York City."

It may as well have been another planet. Rocky had felt like an alien all day. Out of sorts. Out of step. She'd never thought of herself as a country girl or a hick, but this city had given her new perspective. It had also made her think about the publishing contract for the Cupcake Lovers on a new level. What if the recipe/memoir book did as well as the editor and publicist anticipated? What if it did mean media interviews? Tasha would light up in front of a TV camera. She'd parry with a reporter and strive to charm viewers. Rocky would fuss with her neckline and fidget under the spotlight. She'd bore the pants off of everyone with background on the founding of Cupcake Lovers and details regarding their charitable efforts, whereas Tasha would at least be entertaining. Tasha probably *was* the better spokesperson for the club. Not an easy thing to admit.

"You okay?"

"Don't I look okay?" Rocky raised an apologetic hand. "Strike that." Unsettled, she'd fallen back on snark. "I just . . ." She leaned forward a little and lowered her voice. "I'm not much of a dancer. And honestly? I'm not into the whole flashing-lights, earsplitting, club-mix-music, couples-basically-humping-on-the-dance-floor scene." She raised a brow, seizing an opportunity to know Jayce better. "Are you?"

"Only when I have to be."

Which wasn't really an answer.

"Ready?" he asked.

"Sure." Rocky ignored a wave of disappointment. Yes, she was exhausted. She'd been up since before dawn. She'd been mugged, hit by a car, challenged by a business meeting, and overwhelmed by a day of sightseeing alongside the man who haunted her dreams. Still, she didn't want this night to end. "I didn't learn anything about you today."

"Then you weren't paying attention."

Rocky pondered that as Jayce escorted her out into the kinetic night. She thought back on the last several hours and realized that although Jayce hadn't talked about himself, he'd shown that he was thoughtful, generous, and protective. He knew New York City inside and out—both historically and geographically. He was not easily flustered or intimidated. He liked Broadway musicals, Cobb Salad, and seafood and tolerated street-vendor hot dogs. He had a soft spot for carriage horses and was cynical about crime.

A few other things came to mind, and Rocky realized she'd learned quite a bit about Jayce today. She'd also enjoyed their time together. When Jayce visited Sugar Creek, it was impossible for Rocky to forget their sketchy past and prickly situation. Here in New York, it was almost as if they were meeting for the first time.

Pulse racing as he guided her through the bustling and brilliant chaos of Times Square, Rocky caught sight of the Empire State Building, its steepled top illuminated by three shades of color. "Look how beautifully it's lit up."

Jayce looked to where she pointed, then squeezed her waist. "You good for another hour or so?"

Rocky's heart nearly burst through her ribs. Another hour with a man who fried her brain cells with the most innocent touch? *Hell, yeah.* "Why?"

"Your wish list. I know a way to kill two birds with one stone."

* * *

As far as touristy events went, visiting the Empire State Building ranked high. When he'd first moved to New York City, Jayce had checked out the view from the 86th-floor observatory. He'd also climbed higher to the 102nd-floor observatory, but he'd never visited at night with a date. Had never even contemplated the romantic boon of a live jazz saxophonist who strolled the deck three nights a week playing standards and the occasional requested song. Jayce remembered reading about the added attraction in one of the city guides—"especially popular for marriage proposals, anniversaries, and special events such as Valentine's Day." He remembered wondering what kind of sap fell for that sort of schlock. He never imagined he'd be said *sap*.

"Beautiful," Rocky said as she devoured the 360-degree view of the city that never slept.

Jayce agreed. The view was magnificent. But he wasn't looking at the sparkling landscape; he was looking at Rocky. The observatory was open-air and, eighty-six stories above ground level, prone to gusty winds. Many of Rocky's curls had been blown free from the loose, tousled style Jayce had created earlier in the day. He watched as she pocketed the hair clip and allowed her long hair to whip unchecked around her gorgeous face. He absorbed her natural beauty, illuminated by the moonlight. Breathed in her clean, flowery scent. Sensed a shift in her mood as he crowded her space.

"I can't decide if that music's annoying or a unique touch," she said, moving away and along the security wall. "It sort of ruins the serenity of a breathtaking view. On the other hand . . ." She glanced at a couple snuggling a few paces ahead. "I suppose music has its perks, depending on the circumstance." She stopped then and looked over her shoulder at Jayce. "Bring a lot of women here, do you?"

"You're the first."

She blinked at that.

"Considering the circumstance," Jayce said, moving toe-to-toe with the blue-eyed beauty, "the music's a perk." The lone saxophonist segued from an unfamiliar rambling song to a melodic version of a Cole Porter ballad, and Jayce took Rocky into his arms.

Her spine stiffened. "What are you doing?"

"Fulfilling your wish list." He held her close and slowly swayed. "Not the same as dancing in a club."

"No," she said in a soft, tense voice. "But it'll do." She relaxed against him a little, wrapped her arms around his neck.

Jayce swallowed hard as she rested her head against his shoulder. What do you know? This *was* romantic. But where did he go from here? He'd never second-guessed his actions with a woman, but Rocky wasn't the random date. She was his best friend's little sister. Jayce had taken her virginity. He'd proposed marriage. He'd distanced himself from the people he loved in order to protect Rocky's virtue and his reputation with her family. Alienating the Monroes would have been akin to cutting out his heart.

Leaving had been all too easy.

It hadn't occurred to him at the time, but Rocky's disdain had afforded Jayce a prime reason to escape the crushing guilt associated with his parents' deaths. He knew that now, and the knowledge was troubling.

Resisting dark thoughts, Jayce splayed his hand across the small of Rocky's back and focused on a hopeful future. Should he share his plans? *I'm moving home. Starting fresh. That includes pursuing a relationship with you.* Would she be angry? Intrigued? He could definitely count on shocked.

"This is weird," Rocky said, but she didn't push away. "This whole day, I mean. Us. Together. No tension."

"Not the resentful kind anyway."

"Yeah. The sexual pull. It's pretty intense."

Direct as always.

"I don't want to go home feeling like this, Jayce. I need to . . . I *want* to be over you."

Well, hell.

"I want to move past my resentment, to let go of this silly, girlish infatuation. I'm almost thirty years old. Time to grow up."

His heart pounded like a mother. Just this morning he'd shipped his belongings off to Sugar Creek. He'd given up his rent-controlled office. He'd made a mental transition. Moving back to a small town. Renovating his parents' house and dealing with the memories trapped within those walls. Reinforcing old relationships and making new ones. He knew it wouldn't be easy, but leave it to Rocky to push his patience and restraint to the limit.

"So we're going to ignore the obvious."

At last she shifted and looked up into his eyes. "I was thinking it might be smarter to scratch the itch."

He raised a brow.

"Once satisfied . . ."

"The craving will vanish?"

"Exactly."

He didn't believe that, but he did see another way, a damned pleasurable way, to advance his intention of winning over the woman in his arms. "Fair warning, Dash. You're playing with fire."

She nipped his lower lip and wiggled her lower body brazenly against his erection. "I'll take my chances."

CHAPTER NINE

Rocky had never been promiscuous, but she wasn't celibate either. She had a healthy sexual drive and had indulged in a few noncommitted liaisons. Relationships had never been her forte. She had a dominant personality and a mind of her own, a turnoff to most of the men who'd shown interest in her. Plus, she was fiercely dedicated to the Red Clover. Building and maintaining her business took up most of her time. She was, after all, a one-woman show—hostess, cook, housekeeper, and recreational advisor. She was also devoted to her family and to Cupcake Lovers and their charitable efforts. She didn't have the energy or the desire to cultivate and nurture a serious monogamous relationship. That's why her arrangement with Adam Brody had been so perfect. Great sex with no strings. Then Adam had gone all screwy on her after Jayce had boarded at the Red Clover for a week. Or maybe Rocky had been the one to go screwy on Adam. Bottom line, Adam had developed genuine feelings for Rocky and Rocky was still hung up on Jayce.

She hoped to extinguish that ancient fire by letting it burn wild for one weekend. A fantasy weekend far from Sugar Creek where no one would be the wiser. *What happens in Manhattan stays in Manhattan.* She mentally chanted that mantra on the two-block walk from the Empire State Building to the Hotel Chandler. She didn't want to think beyond her "scratch-the-itch-and-it-will-go-away" decision. If she did, another kind of logic might intrude. She didn't want to be cautious or sensible. She wanted to seize the moment. The sexual pull was too dynamic, too tempting, to ignore. Who wanted to ignore the possibility of erotic utopia?

They walked in silence, and with every step Rocky's stomach coiled tighter. She couldn't remember the last time she'd been this insanely hot for a man. *Wait.* Yes, she could. The night she'd crawled through Jayce's bedroom window with the express intention of having sex. She'd been young, naïve, cocky, out-of-her-gourd horny, and hopelessly in love. Now she was older, wiser, cocky, out-of-her-gourd horny, and . . . curious.

She'd only made love with Jayce that one time. She'd been inexperienced. Now she wasn't. Maybe she'd find his lovemaking skills less than spectacular. Maybe he'd be selfish and deprive her of an orgasm. Or maybe she'd go frigid under his touch. Either one of those things would shed new light on an old infatuation. Great sex wasn't everything, of course. But the physical attraction was what had held Rocky prisoner all these years. Lust, pure and simple. Okay. Maybe not so simple. But at least she recognized its power. If she couldn't move past this, if she couldn't break the spell, conquer the addiction, she'd never find complete happiness.

Take control, she thought as Jayce slid the key card home and opened the door to her hotel room. *Control your destiny.*

Then the door shut and he was all over her. An aggressive kiss that shut out rational thought.

Holy hell.

His hands—in her hair, shoving off her coat, stroking her curves.

His mouth—taking possession, working magic on her lips, her tongue.

For a moment she thought she'd been blinded by passion, but then she realized neither one of them had turned on the lights. "Want to see you," she managed while shoving his coat from his broad shoulders.

"Feel me." He spun her around, placed her hands on the wall. "Don't move."

She could scarcely breathe. She heard Jayce disrobing, imagined what she was missing, and groaned. Then she felt him unzipping her boots. She stepped out without him asking. Shivered as he smoothed warm palms over her calves, up her dress, and over her quivering thighs. When his fingers snagged her panties, she panicked. She needed to take an active part. She needed to be the aggressor. Control was her weapon of defense. Otherwise she was . . . vulnerable.

"Tell me to stop," he said, planting his hands over hers and pinning them to the wall, "and I'll go. Otherwise, don't fucking move."

The crude order shot through her like an erotic stimulant. As much as Rocky ached to squirm with desire, she stood stock-still. She didn't want him to go. She sure as hell didn't want him to stop. Starving for his touch, Rocky let Jayce have his way.

He untied her sash, slowly opened the wraparound dress, and peeled it from her trembling body. The fabric slid over her skin; the cool air stimulated. Jayce rained soft kisses over her shoulders and down her back while stroking her curves with a featherlight touch.

Sweet, god-awful torment.

Bra and panties gone. Sane thought obliterated.

When Jayce ordered Rocky to part her legs, she complied. When he pressed his naked body against her and slid his fingers over her feminine folds, she whimpered with desperate need. *Take control, Rocky.* "Take me, Jayce."

"Not yet."

He continued to stroke, igniting a fierce orgasm that started at her toes, working its way up, working Rocky over. She quaked and shivered and screamed graphic exclamations as her body exploded with a mind-numbing climax. Her lungs seized and her knees buckled.

Jayce swooped her up, yanked back the bedcovers, and laid her in the middle of the pillow-soft mattress. Dazed, Rocky fought to catch her breath as he switched on the bathroom light, illuminating the bedroom with a muted glow. Standing next to the bed in all his naked splendor—*good God, is that muscled body for real?*—Jayce skimmed her bare flesh with his hot gaze, an intimate inspection that affected Rocky as strongly as a skilled lover's touch.

He raised one brow in appreciation. "The body that taunts my dreams."

He'd dreamed about her? Naked? She'd always thought the longtime physical fascination had been one-sided. Knowing Jayce had dreamed about her made Rocky ache for the man even more. As if that were possible!

Vibrating with desire, she stared up at her seducer—breathless, speechless. So handsome. So sexy. His body was ripped and his shaft hard. *For me,* she thought. She nearly climaxed a second time just contemplating what they were about to do. Her barely functioning mind gave one last feeble cry. *Take charge. Own the moment. Own your life.* But then Jayce straddled her and pushed her hands over her head. He held her wrists with one hand, using his free hand to caress her breasts. He kissed her, a deep and wild kiss that stirred raw lust.

Rocky writhed beneath him, delirious and aching for more.

Jayce stroked, kneaded, licked, and nipped.

She wanted to touch him back, but he held her captive. It was . . . exhilarating.

He shifted and she felt the tip of his erection graze her slick folds. "Tell me what you want," he said close to her ear.

Was he dense? "I want you to take me." Her voice sounded hoarse and foreign to her ears.

He pulled away, then teased her by barely breaching her. "Try again." He suckled her earlobe. "What do you want, Rocky?"

What the hell? She was dying of want. "Your cock."

He released her hands, caressed her face. "Try again."

Rocky met his intoxicating gaze. A lifetime of longing knocked her breathless. "You."

Jayce plunged deep and Rocky saw stars. She wrapped

her arms and legs around him and lost her mind as he rocked against her with astounding intensity and skill. She came and came, a seemingly endless wave of gratification. She rode the wave, body trembling, mind reeling, and realized suddenly that Jayce had eased away. She frowned. "But you didn't—"

"That's because I'm not through with you yet."

The taunt sensitized her pliant body. As sated as she was, every nerve ending pulsed with excitement.

Jayce nipped her lower lip and rolled her onto her stomach. "Told you you were playing with fire."

CHAPTER TEN

Sugar Creek, Vermont

Saturday morning. D-day. Do or die. Flourish or flop. Chloe
Madison stared at the dopey-eyed moose standing proud for
her inspection. If she weren't so nervous about the grand
opening of her first business, she'd laugh.

"So?" the furry beast asked. "How do I look?"

"Your antlers are crooked."

"Give them a tweak, will you, kitten? Hard to do anything
with these hooves."

"Actually, they're more like paws, but I see what you
mean." Chloe reached up and twisted the molded yellow
fabric until the cartoonish antlers were even. The full-body
moose costume was a little big on the woman inside. Daisy
Monroe, a seventy-five-year-old half-pint with the free spirit
of a teen. Chloe's former employer and new business partner. And, for one day only, the mascot for their café: Moose-
a-lotta. "I can't believe you volunteered to do this, Daisy."

"A shot at showbiz? Are you kidding?"

Chloe smothered a smile. As someone who'd dabbled in
several creative careers, including theater, she didn't consider a few hours as a costumed mascot much of an acting
gig. Several years ago, in an effort to earn extra money,
Chloe had appeared as a tutu-wearing gorilla passing out

flyers for a novelty shop in Times Square. The cheap costume had been hot, itchy, and stunk like BO doused with Febreze. She'd been ignored, ridiculed, and snagged for several photo ops—most of them embarrassing. Nothing glamorous about it. Daisy, however, was giddy with anticipation.

"Yes, well, still thirty minutes until we open the doors," Chloe pointed out.

"I'm getting into character."

"Can you get into character without the head? Seriously, Daisy. Aside from the grid eyes and nostrils, there's zilch ventilation. If you pass out, Devlin will kill me."

"He'd have to get past me first."

"Easy to do if you're in a dead faint."

"Point taken."

Chloe helped Daisy remove the moose head and set it gently aside. The woman's normally springy curls had wilted, and her blingy cat-eye glasses had steamed over. "I'll get you a glass of water."

"I'd prefer a cocktail."

Of course she would. Daisy had a fondness for wine and exotic drinks. But after Chloe had discovered the woman was on various prescriptions for anxiety and a heart problem, Devlin had convinced Daisy to curb her drinking. Special occasions only and not mixed with meds.

"I could use a drink myself," Chloe said, noting the eclectic décor and wondering what their customers would think. From Victorian to contemporary to folksy, everything was intentionally mismatched—chairs and tables, lighting fixtures, plates, and utensils. The only constant was the image of a moose—on pillows, clocks, lampshades, paintings, and knickknacks. What if the locals thought Moose-a-lotta was too kitschy? What if tourists preferred the simple Georgian charm of the Pine and Periwinkle Inn? "Maybe we can indulge after," Chloe said. "Especially if there's cause to celebrate."

"Of course we'll be celebrating," Daisy said as she eased into the velvet Queen Anne wingback they'd scored at Maple Molly's Antique Barn. "A themed café that specializes in flavored coffees, gourmet snacks, and scrumptious desserts. A setting that offers a small collection of used books for trade and free Wi-Fi. Moose-a-lotta is unique to Sugar Creek, kitten. Our combined vision. Don't second-guess yourself. I'm not."

You haven't failed at a dozen other careers, Chloe wanted to say but didn't. Voicing her insecurities might dampen Daisy's enthusiasm. Chloe refused to rain on her partner's parade. Daisy had reminded her of the importance of taking chances and living life to the fullest. She'd given Chloe, who'd just graduated from culinary school, her first job as a personal chef. Treated her like family. Introduced her to the Cupcake Lovers and rekindled her love of desserts. Daisy had encouraged and supported Chloe's infatuation with her grandson and, knowing Chloe was strapped for cash, had offered to foot the entire start-up cost of Moose-a-lotta. Not that Chloe had agreed to the latter. Making her own way financially was a huge issue. Maintaining control over her career decisions was also personally vital to Chloe. Something she'd had to impress upon Devlin, a born and schooled genius when it came to business and finance. As much as she loved the man, he was an opinionated control freak. Overprotective, too.

"Earth to Chloe: Here comes our temporary staff. I'd let them in, but between my ankle cast and this bulky costume—"

"On it!" Chloe's heart and heels kicked at the sight of her best friend, Monica, and one of Daisy's oldest friends, Ethel, peering in through the storefront window, grinning and waving like idiots. Chloe waved back while scrambling to unlock the door. "Right on time!"

The two women, one in her thirties, one in her seventies, burst over the threshold.

"Reporting for duty," Ethel said.

"Smells great in here," Monica said. "Oh . . . my . . . God. *Daisy!* Your costume! What a hoot!"

"Wait'll I put my head on."

"Not yet," Chloe cautioned.

"How do you breathe in that thing?" Ethel asked, pointing at the moose head.

"Through the nose," Daisy said. "Ready for a mob? Because I plan on bringing in a herd!"

"Are you really going to stand outside and wave down customers?" Monica asked.

"She's going to *sit* outside and entice interest," Chloe said to her friend. "We'll drag one of these comfy chairs onto the sidewalk a couple of minutes before we open. Daisy promised she'd do her acting from a throne."

"I'm not an invalid," Daisy groused.

"No, but you do have a cast on your ankle," Ethel put in. "What if you aggravate that injury? The sooner you're in tip-top form, the greater help you'll be to Chloe and the café. Right, Chloe?"

Chloe smiled at the older woman, thankful for her subtlety. "Absolutely, Ethel."

"The Cupcake Lovers' display looks wonderful," the older woman went on. "It was really sweet of you both to set aside space for our charity efforts."

"Chloe's idea," Daisy said.

"Our pleasure," Chloe said. "And it's not like Moose-a-lotta won't benefit. Anyone who buys a cupcake will probably purchase a beverage as well. Besides, I love sharing the scrumptious cupcakes of our members."

Everyone had jumped at the chance to share a batch of cupcakes on different days of the week. A chance to show off new recipes and edible decorating ideas. All proceeds, as was dictated in the club's mission statement, would go to someone or some place in need. In this case, for the next four weeks proceeds from Cupcake Lover sales via Moose-a-lotta would go to Sugar Tots. Surely they could at least kick-start the new playground fund.

"When our recipe book comes out," Daisy said, "we'll sell those, too."

"How's the publishing deal going anyway?" Monica asked. "Any more news from Rocky?"

Chloe blushed with a half-truth. "Not today."

"Only what we relayed to the club yesterday," Daisy said. "Don't know what's on the agenda today."

Just then Chloe's and Daisy's cell phones chimed in tandem with a text message.

Daisy pointed to the counter. "Ethel, would you grab my phone out of my purse?"

"Sure does blip loud," the woman said.

"That's so I can hear it," Daisy said.

"It's from Rocky," Chloe said, reading her own screen. *"Thinking of you. Viva Moose-a-lotta!"*

Daisy squinted at her own phone. "Mine says the same. I'll text back and ask what's happening with the publisher."

"Why don't you just call Rocky?" Ethel asked while Daisy diligently typed in her question.

"Really, Ethel. Get with the times."

Monica laughed and Chloe made a beeline for the kitchen. "I forgot your Moose-a-lotta aprons. Be right back." While she was at it she'd text Rocky in private. Using abbreviations, something Daisy had yet to master, Chloe quickly thumbed that Devlin had mentioned Jayce took Rocky under his wing. "How's that going, girlfriend?"

"How's what going?"

Chloe gasped. "Jeez, Monica. Don't sneak up on me like that."

"Who's sneaking?" She followed Chloe into the compact kitchen, gestured to the phone. "Spill."

"All right," Chloe said in a hushed voice. "But only because I'm dying to talk to someone about this and, given the circumstances, only you and Luke qualify. You're here. You win."

Monica's eyes widened. "Must be about Jayce."

Chloe filled her friend in about the mugging and how Jayce had assured Devlin he'd look after Rocky for the rest of her visit in New York. "He took her sightseeing."

"Get . . . *out!* Jayce and Rocky spent the day together? How did that work exactly, what with them being at odds?"

"I don't know. I'm hoping . . . Well, I hope Rocky took the opportunity to make peace with Jayce. Especially since . . ."

"Since what?"

Since he's moving back to Sugar Creek. Chloe had promised Devlin she wouldn't say anything to anyone. "I'm sick to death of secrets." Bad enough she was keeping things from Devlin. Equally bad, or worse, he was keeping things from her. Something about his dad. Or mom. Or both. Something that caused Devlin great angst. Something that caused him to work more hours than he should. Frustrated, Chloe whirled away and nabbed two new moose aprons from the linen closet. "I hate that I know about Rocky and Jayce's . . . *fling* and that Devlin doesn't. And I hate that Devlin . . ."

"What?"

Cheeks hot, Chloe thrust a custom-made apron at her oldest friend. "Never mind. Just suit up. We open in . . ." She glanced up at the moose clock (one of three in the café). "Oh, God, ten minutes."

Monica looped the yellow-and-green polka-dot apron over her neck. "I'm not leaving this kitchen until you finish that train of thought. What about Dev?"

Chloe tightened her ponytail, then smoothed her hand over the embroidered logo of her matching apron. "There's something going on between him and his dad."

"Yeah. The ongoing feud about renovations on the family's department store."

"No. Something else. Something he won't talk about."

Monica raised a brow. "A secret?"

"Not that Devlin's obligated to tell me whatever it is. We're not even engaged."

"Yet."

"Don't jinx it—us," Chloe snapped, hot faced and flustered. Even though she'd known Devlin less than two months, she knew they were both thinking in terms of forever. They'd weathered a rocky start, and their love intensified with every day. Even so, they were still adjusting . . . and managing family secrets and dynamics. "I just . . . Devlin seems really tense and I wish I could help."

"Dev's not the only one who's tense. Polish that counter any harder and you'll wear a hole in it."

Chloe hadn't even been aware she'd picked up the dish towel. Not that the counter needed a scrub. She'd tidied and cleaned after her predawn baking spree. The kitchen gleamed. Stomach aching, Chloe looked at Monica with her heart in her eyes. "I don't want to screw up."

"Are we talking about Dev or Moose-a-lotta?"

Chloe's voice caught. "Both."

Monica pulled her into a hug, smiled against her cheek. "You won't fail, Chloe. Not on either count. I've said it before and I'll say it again. When you put your heart into something, you're unstoppable. Speaking of a formidable force, where is Dev anyway?"

"I needed space to do my thing in preparation. Then I worried if he came right at eight I'd feel pressured if we didn't have a mob by eight ten. I asked him to stay away until at least half past."

"I'm surprised he agreed."

"Me, too."

Just then the man who enriched Chloe's colorful world pushed through the kitchen door. "What's wrong?"

"Just a case of nerves," Monica said, pushing away from Chloe with a wink. "I'll drag a chair outside and help Daisy get her head on straight. The moose head, that is. Five minutes and counting!"

Monica rushed out and Devlin moved in.

Chloe's already-racing pulse pounded. "You were supposed to stay away until we got past opening."

"Tried. Failed."

"I'm glad." Chloe saw the compassion in those blueberry-blue eyes. The man was so intensely gorgeous he stole away Chloe's breath. Or maybe this was a panic attack. "Can't breathe."

Devlin held her close and smoothed a strong hand down her spine. "I know I had my doubts about this venture, Chloe."

"And rightly so. I have no experience—"

"You have heart. Imagination and determination. Not to mention you're a gifted chef."

"Daddy co-signed—"

"And you'll make good."

"Daisy—"

"Is the happiest I've ever seen her. Anything else?"

Chloe's heart warmed, her spirit soared. With Devlin holding her in his arms and looking at her with bone-deep love, it was hard to fret about secrets and failures. She couldn't predict Rocky and Jayce's future, but she could imagine a happy-ever-after for herself and the man she'd jumped off a bridge with. Holding tight to that mind-set, Chloe gazed at Devlin. "I could sure use a good-luck kiss."

"Luck has nothing to do with it, hon. You and Gram worked hard for this. It's all good."

She smiled a little, confidence stoked. "I could still use a kiss."

"Anytime, Chloe." Devlin stroked a thumb over her cheek, nipped her lower lip as a sensual prelude. "Anywhere."

Chloe wiggled against his arousal. "Hold that thought," she said with a playful grin. "I've got a dream to debut."

CHAPTER ELEVEN

Manhattan, New York

"Your stamina's pretty impressive, Bello."

"So's your insatiability." Jayce fell back on the mattress, heart pounding from another intense round with Rocky. He'd ended up spending the night, not that they'd slept much. Every time he thought he'd sated her cravings, she got another itch. Not that he was complaining.

She rolled onto her side—a smokin' naked goddess—and stared down at him, her lush lips curved in a cocky smile. "Too much for you?"

Brow raised, Jayce trumped the goddess's arrogance. "If anyone cries uncle, it'll be you, Dash." He noted the spark in her gaze, the flare of her nostrils, and the quickening of her pulse at the base of her throat. Though she'd never admit it, Rocky liked being dominated. At least in bed. He'd sensed it the moment he'd pressed her against the wall and taken control. He also sensed she'd never allowed another man to be the aggressor, not wholly. Every time she tried to shift roles, Jayce twisted the moment, ultimately "telling" her to do what she "wanted" to do. The more he dominated, the greater her need. He wasn't even sure if she was aware of how he manipulated her in bed—which made him a bit of a bastard.

He was finding it hard to care.

"I keep waiting to feel awkward about some of the things we did last night."

"Why?"

"Some of it was a little adventurous, even for me."

"I don't recall anything out of the ordinary."

"So you do stuff like that with all the women you take to bed?"

"I don't have a stock playlist when it comes to sex. Depends on the woman."

She raised a brow at that. "What kind of woman am I?"

His lip twitched. "The adventurous kind."

She narrowed her eyes while shoving a mass of disheveled curls over her bare shoulder. "This isn't working according to plan."

"Meaning?"

"I thought if I indulged in a carnal carnival, the fantasy would fizzle."

Jayce clasped his hands beneath his head and stared up at Rocky with mock concern. "Should I be flattered or insulted?"

"You were supposed to be a selfish or clumsy lover."

"Sorry to disappoint."

"No, you're not."

"You're right. I'm not."

Rocky grunted, rolled onto her back, and nabbed her phone. "No word from Tasha," she said, frowning at the Android. "Something tells me she's blowing me off today."

"Is that a bad thing?"

"Only if it affects Cupcake Lovers." She set aside the phone, sighed. "I think she's flirting up our editor."

"Of course she is. He's a man of power, isn't he?"

"She's a married woman."

"She's Tasha." Jayce cast his bed partner a curious glance. Getting to know the adult Rocky was a fascinating rush. "You're provincial."

"If you mean I think a person should honor their marriage vows, then that would be a yes."

The heat in her voice warmed his heart. Adventurous *and* old-fashioned. Talk about an enticing mix. "Sweet."

"Sweet?" She playfully lobbed her pillow at his head. "I'm going to shower."

"I'll join you."

Rocky rolled out of bed—lush and naked—and sauntered into the bathroom. "The hell you will."

Jayce smiled. *The hell I would.*

* * *

Rocky wasn't surprised when Jayce joined her in the shower. She wasn't annoyed either. She couldn't get enough of him, which posed a problem, since tomorrow she'd be getting on a plane and flying back to Sugar Creek. Once she was there, life would go on. Without Jayce. She kept telling herself that by that time she'd have this carnal craving in check. But she didn't really believe that, so she decided to focus on the sexual part of the obsession. Taking the emotional aspect out of the equation somehow eased Rocky's ancient misery. She was no longer in love with Jayce Bello. She was in lust. It was a freeing and empowering notion.

"You look beautiful," Jayce said as she weaved her damp hair into two braids. "And smug."

"I was just thinking how excited Gram's going to be when I share my sightseeing ventures," she lied as she shimmied into her jeans. "Because of you, I accomplished everything on our Big Apple wish list in one day."

"It's after nine. Why don't you give Tasha a try?" Jayce said while pulling on fresh cargo pants. At some point during the night, he'd retrieved an overnight bag from his car. *In my line of work, you never know when you'll need a change of clothes.* Forgoing an iron, he pulled a slightly wrinkled brown T-shirt over his head and dragged his fingers through his shaggy hair. Even rumpled, the man was sexy.

"After we know your obligations with the publisher," he went on, "we can explore some of the city's more obscure points of interest."

"Sounds good," Rocky said while speed-dialing Tasha,

not that she expected the woman to answer. Rocky always ended up leaving messages, and Tasha always took her time returning the calls. As if her life were more important than Rocky's. "I thought we could venture to Brooklyn," she said as the phone rang once, twice. "I'd like to see where you've been living all these years. Your office, your apartment—"

"About that—"

Rocky cut him off when Tasha unexpectedly answered. "Really?" she said, sounding hungover and cranky. "You couldn't wait until I contacted you?"

"I waited all night, Tasha. All morning, too."

"It's not even nine thirty."

"And I'd like to know how to plan my day."

"You're asking me for suggestions?"

"No. I'm asking where and when I'm supposed to meet you and Brett or whoever from Highlife Publishing. What about the tour of the bakeries specializing in customized cupcakes?"

"That got put off until Monday."

"*What?* We're supposed to fly home *Sunday*. I have responsibilities in Sugar Creek, Tasha. A business. A family. Preparations for the Spookytown Spectacular."

"So go home. Buy a ticket on a commercial flight or call and ask Nash to fly down and get you. I'll stay here and take one for the team."

"I *bet* you will." Phone braced between her shoulder and ear, Rocky buttoned a floral blouse over her snug tee. "Did you sleep with our editor last night?"

"Did you sleep with Jayce Bello?" Tasha barked a cruel laugh before Rocky could deny or brag. "As if! You pined for Jayce all through junior high and he never even gave you a second look. And yesterday? All I saw was a man looking out for his best friend's little sister. Jayce wouldn't indulge in a one-nighter with you. He's too loyal to Dev. Besides," she said with a judgmental sniff, "you're not his type."

Oh yeah? Rocky wanted to say. *Then why did he take me every which way including on all fours? Why did he kiss me head to toe and lick me to orgasm? Why did he tell me to—*

"No pithy comeback?"

"Not wasting my breath." In truth Rocky ached to rub the woman's face in every sexy detail of her erotic marathon with Jayce, but she held her tongue and, to her amazement, her temper. Instead of blowing her top, Rocky paced. "Is there anything on the agenda today for Cupcake Lovers and Highlife?"

"No."

"If you screw up this book deal—"

"I thought you didn't care about the deal."

"I don't. Not really. But it's important to several members of the Cupcake Lovers and to the club in general. Or rather the soldiers and charities that benefit from our work."

"So you finally admit my idea has merit."

She'd rather die. "We've come this far. Might as well see it through."

There was a tense moment of silence, then, "Listen, Rocky. Contrary to what you're thinking, I had nothing to do with the cupcake tour being delayed until Monday. There was a conflict on Highlife's end. Also, contrary to what you're implying, I'm not sleeping my way to a publishing contract. The club earned the deal with our proposal. As soon as Dev signs off on the legalities, it's official. Unlike you, I have a life beyond Cupcake Lovers and a run-down bed-and-breakfast. I intend to enjoy my unexpected extended weekend in New York. When you figure out if you're going or staying, text me."

Rocky halted in her tracks as Tasha disconnected in anger. "What the hell?"

"Working off a one-sided conversation," Jayce said, "but I assume you're free for the day."

"And all of tomorrow." Rocky tossed her phone on a chair and perched her hands on her hips. "I'm not sure, but I think I hurt Tasha's feelings."

"Pretty sure that's impossible."

"She was definitely upset."

"Given your tense history with the woman, I'm surprised you care."

"Whether we get along or not, accusing her of sleeping her way to fame and fortune is pretty rough. Especially if it's not true."

"Asking and accusing are two different things."

"Not always. Implication can be just as damning."

"When did you get so wise?"

"I grew up when you weren't looking."

"Did you?"

Rocky blinked at his odd tone. Was that censure? Sarcasm? Warped humor? "What's that supposed to mean?"

Jayce held up his hands in surrender. "I've usually had three cups of coffee by now. I'm a little off."

"I've usually had a glass of OJ, a morning run, and a full breakfast by now. I'm a lot off. Plus I'm stuck here now until . . . I don't know when. Tasha said she's meeting again with Highlife on Monday, but she didn't say when she booked the charter plane for the return flight. Monday night? Tuesday morning? Hell, I've got things to do at home."

Frustrated, Rocky dropped in a chair and pulled on her sneakers. No pub business, no sense torturing herself with heeled boots. She watched as Jayce buckled on his watch and a thick leather bracelet. She'd noticed that bracelet yesterday and sneaked a closer peek while he'd lingered in the shower. A simple brown band imprinted with black-and-tan dog paws.

"What's the significance?" Rocky asked, momentarily distracted.

He glanced from the bracelet to her. "Homeless-animal awareness."

Rocky raised a brow, but Jayce didn't elaborate. Huh. Rugged, street-smart, cultured, and kind. A champion of people *and* animals in need. How could she not know about his soft spot for animals? Her stomach fluttered in a troubling way. "How much do you think a last-minute one-way ticket on a commercial flight would cost?"

"A lot."

"I figured. I'm not going to ask Dev for that kind of

money." She chewed on her thumbnail. "I suppose I could ask Nash for a favor."

"I'll drive you."

"What?"

"I'll drive you home. When do you want to leave? Tonight? Tomorrow?"

Rocky shot to her sneakered feet. "You're offering to drive me from New York City to Sugar Creek, Vermont? That's gotta be . . ."

"Six, seven hours."

"Why would you do that?"

"Because I want to and because it's on my way."

Rocky stared; her mind spun. "You were planning another trip home?"

"As a matter of fact . . . yes."

"Something to do with the sale of your parents' house?"

"You could say that."

"Don't you think it would be a little awkward? Seeing Dev so soon after we . . ." She gestured to the rumpled bed. "I assumed you wouldn't make it back to Sugar Creek for another, I don't know, few months. If that. There have been times where you've gone a year or two without visiting. It would be easier to pretend—"

"I'm done pretending."

Her insides twisted.

"I'm moving home, Rocky. For good."

She didn't react at first. She was too stunned. Her vision blurred and her hearing buzzed. Her brain slowed, then raced. Jayce living in Sugar Creek. How would that work exactly? Obvious answer: It wouldn't.

"I've been fighting the inclination for months," he said, addressing her wide-eyed silence. "Out of respect for you and our secret. In deference to my friendship with Dev and the sincere fondness I feel for your parents. Thing is, I'm no longer content living a lie."

The buzz in her ears grew louder. Rocky gripped the edge of the desk to stabilize her wobbly legs.

Jayce moved toward her.

"Don't," she choked out. She couldn't think straight as it was. If he touched her . . . "Why?"

"The life I've built in Brooklyn isn't the life I want."

"But you could go anywhere, live anywhere."

"I know."

"But Sugar Creek—"

"Done deal, Rocky. Shipped my belongings yesterday morning."

A slow, furious burn started at her toes and sizzled throughout her body. The buzz in her ears intensified to a roar. "You knew and you let me . . . let us . . ."

"Don't argue the inevitable."

"But it wasn't inevitable!" Rocky threw her arms wide, gestured to the bed. "I never would have . . . If I'd known you were moving home . . . Bastard!"

"So you just planned on having a weekend fling and then blowing me off? Again?"

She blinked. "If you're referring to that morning thirteen years ago—"

"I am." Jayce stood his ground, crossed his arms. "The morning I asked you to marry me. To which you replied, *Piss off.*"

Rocky marveled at the subtle resentment in his tone. "You didn't *ask* me anything. You *told* me we should get married. 'Should' as in it was the right thing to do. 'Should' as in it was your duty as a stand-up guy to make an honest woman out of the virgin seducer who also happened to be *jailbait!*"

"You blew me off and harbored a grudge all these years over semantics?"

"I *loved* you. I . . . I worshiped you for *years.* Every day you didn't touch me, I died. When you went away to go to college, I was miserable. Then I thought, if we could just be together, if you could just be my first, and then it happened! It was wonderful and romantic and perfect. I had no expectations, just this wonderful sense of loving and being loved— even if only for that one perfect moment. Then you *ruined* it!"

"*This* is what's been festering inside you all these years?"

He was angry. No, he was furious. He didn't move. He didn't blink, but Rocky felt a shift in Jayce that muted her own temper and filled her with confusion and dread.

"Do you or don't you want me to drive you home?"

"I'm not going anywhere with you." Not because she was wary of his anger, but because she couldn't get past her own stupidity. Scratching the itch had only aggravated the constant craving. How was she supposed to co-exist with Jayce in Sugar Creek without wanting to jump his bones every time they crossed paths? That she was still attracted to him boggled her mind. She'd just poured out her heart, shared her deepest feelings, her longtime affection, and he made it sound so insignificant.

This *is what's been festering inside you all these years?*

As if it were no big deal! She folded her own arms, hiked her chin. "You need to leave. I'll find my own way home."

Without a word, he gathered his things.

Rocky's blood pressure spiked to the moon and back. "If you tell Dev about that night just to clear your conscience—"

"I was thinking more about Dev's peace of mind. Do you have any idea how much he's struggled with the tension between us?"

"Of course I know." Her brother had been pressing her to confide in him for years.

"Yet you'd leave him puzzling rather than risk an uncomfortable confrontation."

"*Uncomfortable?*"

"Knowing Dev, he'll be shocked and pissed. But he'll get over it. Your dad's not going to hunt me down and shoot me and he's sure as hell not going to disown you." Eyes sparking with fury, Jayce snatched up his duffel. "I can't believe I let this drag out for so long."

"You speak as if we broke curfew or filched a couple of beers from Gram's fridge," Rocky ranted. "We had *sex*. I was barely seventeen, Jayce. You were *twenty-two*. A trusted member of the family. Mom and Dad will never look at you the same way. Or me for that matter." His silence incited panic and fury. Trembling, Rocky held her ground rather than pounce and pummel. "How can you be so selfish?"

"I could ask you the same." He spared her a glance while walking out the door. "That bit about you growing up while I wasn't looking? You were wrong."

CHAPTER TWELVE

Sugar Creek, Vermont

Good food, good drink, good vibes.

Luke scanned the lively crowd, his heart full and his hands busy as he opened a fifth bottle of champagne—on the house. *This* was why he'd been inspired to buy the Sugar Shack. He loved the rush of fostering a business that inspired good times and the occasional celebration. Celebrations involving friends and family were a special bonus. Like this impromptu gathering following the first day of business for Gram's and Chloe's new café.

Even though it was only 4:45, the Shack was fairly crowded. Luke's chef, Anna, and her team were in the kitchen preparing for the dinner rush. In the pub, a fire crackled in the cobblestone hearth and a melodic mix of classic rock provided unobtrusive atmosphere. Some patrons nibbled on party mix while watching the televised college football game. Others were engrossed in conversation. Several ladies from the Cupcake Lovers sat around one table chatting about their special display at Moose-a-lotta, while the owners and staff of said café had crowded into a nearby window booth. On one side—Gram, Chloe, and Dev. On the other—Ethel, Monica, and her husband, Leo.

Once Luke and Nell—the only waitress on the clock for

the next half hour thanks to Connie quitting—distributed glasses to one and all, Luke raised his sparkling flute in a toast. "To Moose-a-lotta!"

"Moose-a-lotta!" Everyone drank to the café, then resumed their personal conversations.

"I'll watch the bar," Nell said to Luke. "You celebrate with your family."

Luke smiled at the woman, a pretty thing, although a bit shy for his personal taste. "Thanks, hon. I'll just be a minute or two." He pulled up a chair and felt a kick in the shin.

"Don't go there," Chloe warned Luke as Nell hustled toward the bar. "You can't afford to lose another waitress."

Gram squinted at Luke as though he were a dim bulb. "Didn't anyone ever tell you it's bad business to mattress dance with the help?"

Mattress dance?

"Yeah," Dev said. "Me."

"Sometimes big brother knows best," Monica said.

"Hell hath no fury," Leo said

Gram turned to Chloe. "I think we should hire Connie to work at Moose-a-lotta."

Like everything else in Sugar Creek, news that Lizzie and Connie had given Luke the royal kiss-off had spread like wildfire within moments of the unfortunate double whammy.

"Always liked that girl," Ethel said. "Smart and fast. Pleasant, too."

"I'm hoping Connie will come back to the Shack once she cools off," Luke said.

"Then why did you post the *Help Wanted* sign?" Dev asked.

"Because we lost Marla last week and if Connie doesn't come back that means I'm down two waitresses. Nell's sweet, but she's been a little unreliable lately, and Sadie just informed me she's pregnant, so—"

"Sadie Thompson is pregnant?" Monica asked.

Luke froze at the woman's stricken expression. Everyone in the booth shot Luke a not-so-subtle death glare. *Nice go-*

ing, Monroe. Common knowledge: Monica and Leo had been trying to have a baby for months. So far, no luck, and according to gossip, their marriage was feeling the strain.

"Uh . . . yeah," Luke said. "Sorry. Thought everyone knew."

"Not everyone," Leo said.

"I'm thrilled for Sadie and Paul," Monica said. "Just married and newly pregnant. They must be over the moon."

"I think they're in shock," Luke said. "It was an—"

Someone gave him a hard kick.

Leo glared.

"An accident." Monica jammed her hand though her spiky short hair. "Huh."

"I need something stronger." Leo pushed aside his champagne glass. "Anyone else?"

Gram raised her hand. "I'll take a Blue Hawaiian!"

"Nell wouldn't know how to make that, Gram," Luke said.

"Then I'll have glass of chardonnay. Thank you, Leo. And stop frowning at me, Devlin Monroe. Vincent has been monitoring my medication. I'm fine."

Vince Redding. Proprietor of Oslow's General Store and Gram's devoted friend. If the bearded old guy had his way, he and Gram (both widowed) would be more than friends, which struck Luke as cool and weird at the same time.

Dev, who had yet to fully forgive Vince for keeping him in the dark about Gram's heart condition, frowned. Then he turned that frown on Luke. "About the staffing situation—"

"Can we talk about this later?" Luke glanced at Monica, who was looking across the bar at Leo, who was smiling at Nell. *Oh, Christ.* "This moment's about Moose-a-lotta," Luke said, trying to draw the attention to something positive. "Can I just say that was the best Mocha Latte I've ever had? You've got a magic touch, Monica."

"It was the Café Latte Maker. All I did was push a button."

"You did more than that," Chloe said. "You and Ethel were amazing today."

"Can't thank you ladies enough for filling in until we know exactly how much help we'll need on a steady basis," Gram said.

"And how much we can afford to pay on a steady basis," Chloe added. "Although if today was any indication . . ." She beamed a thousand-watt smile. "I can't believe how many people dropped in and how many vowed to return!"

"I can," Dev said. "Never had a doubt."

"Me neither," Gram said. "Although I do believe I enticed more than a few oblivious passersby with my moose antics."

Chloe smiled. "You were adorable, Daisy, and I agree, Millie Moose is a valuable marketing tool. But to optimize the effect I think we should reserve her presence for special occasions."

"Yeah," Monica chimed in. "Makes Millie all the more special. Like a reclusive celebrity."

"I see your point," Gram said. "Speaking of special occasions, I have an idea that will benefit both Moose-a-lotta and the Cupcake Lovers booth during the Spookytown Spectacular."

The women sipped champagne while Gram launched into a vibrant pitch.

Luke took the opportunity to grab his brother's attention. "Talk to you for a minute?"

Dev brushed a kiss over Chloe's cheek. "Be right back."

The dark-haired beauty smiled at Dev, and Luke's heart gave a funny jerk. Women smiled at him all the time but not like *that*. He couldn't pinpoint the difference, but it was sun and moon, worlds apart. *Huh*. One thing was certain: Luke liked Chloe a lot. She loved his brother, good and true, faults and all. Not for his bank account or what he could do for her. As smart as Dev was, over the years he'd made some dumb-ass choices in women. Especially and foremost his ex-wife—not that anybody in the family ever mentioned Janna. Talk about a sore spot.

"Is this about the staffing problem?" Dev asked as Luke shut them inside his small office.

"No. It's about our sister. Nash called."

"Shot me a text an hour ago."

"So you know he flew down to New York to bring Rocky home."

"I know."

"Why isn't she flying back with Tasha? I phoned and left Rocky a message, but she didn't return my call. Just texted: *Business concluded. New York sucks. Coming home.*" Luke dropped into his desk chair. "I hate texts."

Dev crooked a smile. "And e-mails."

"I just happen to like the personal connection of a phone call." Luke had been accused of being a Luddite for years. It was not that he was adverse to technological change. It was that technology proposed a special challenge that taxed his patience.

"For what it's worth," Dev said, "Rocky didn't return my call either and the text she sent me was similar to the one you got. I did, however, get the scoop from Jayce."

Luke listened as Dev relayed news about a glitch with the publisher and about Tasha staying on through Tuesday. When Dev segued into announcing Jayce was moving home, Luke pretended to be surprised so as not to rat out Chloe.

"When Rocky mentioned she wanted to return home today," Dev went on, "Jayce broke his news and offered to drive her back to Sugar Creek."

"Let me guess: Rocky freaked out about Jayce moving home and they ended up having a fight."

Forearms braced on knees, Dev leaned forward and regarded Luke with a raised brow. "You once said you suspected the cause of the rift between those two."

And now Luke knew for sure. "Not my story to tell."

"Someone's going to talk. I don't intend to spend every day of the next several years playing mediator between my sister and best friend at family and social gatherings. Whatever it is, it can't be that damn bad."

Luke stifled a grunt. It was, in truth, pretty damn bad. He couldn't decide which was worse, the ill-timed tumble itself or the fact that Jayce and Rocky had kept it secret for thirteen years. Big on loyalty and honesty, Dev would see this as a big-ass betrayal. Their parents would be shocked and hurt. Hell, Luke had been shocked and he was royally pissed at Jayce, whom he'd yet to see face-to-face since learning the truth. He couldn't promise he wouldn't lose it on the man. Any way you cut it, things were going to get messy. Even so, Luke intended to urge Rocky to come clean with Dev pronto. Clear the air and move the hell on.

"Whatever you do, don't ride Rocky too hard on this. I'm worried about her. She's had more than her share of bad luck over the past few years. She puts on a tough front, but she's only human. I checked up on the Red Clover after I left Moose-a-lotta this morning and . . . I don't know, Dev. Do you really think the renovations will save her business?"

Dev shrugged. "In these economic times any small business is a crap shoot. But I do know those renovations will save Rocky's *home*. Which qualifies the investment. She loves that property and it was falling apart around her ears."

Luke arched a brow. "Putting sentiment before business? What's happening to you? Not that I mind."

"Let's just say I've had a recent lesson in priorities."

"Spurred by Chloe?"

"In part."

Luke sensed he'd hit a raw nerve. Sensed a shift in Dev's mood. Something was troubling him beyond Rocky and Jayce. "Care to expand?"

"I wish I could. I—"

Someone knocked on the door.

Luke frowned. "Yeah?"

A woman peeked in—a veil of limp, blah-blond hair obstructing a good portion of her pale face. "I . . . Oh. Sorry. I didn't realize . . . I was told I'd find you in your office," she said to Luke. "I didn't know—"

"I was just leaving, Rachel," Dev said. "He's all yours."

Luke watched as his brother left, feeling as though their conversation had been cut off at a crucial mark. He couldn't help resenting the intrusion. Rachel Lacey, of all people. What could the meek day-care teacher want?

"So is there a formal application?"

Luke jammed a hand through his hair, his thoughts still with his brother. "Sorry?"

"The sign in the window," Rachel said in a soft voice. "*Help Wanted.* I'd like to apply."

A recent lesson in priorities? Did it have something to do with Dev going head-to-head with their dad over store renovations? Their parents had retired to Florida, but Luke's brother had been duking it out with their old man long-distance.

Rachel cleared her throat.

Luke shook off his musings and focused on the mousy woman who'd somehow snared his cousin's affections. "I'm sorry, Rachel. What?"

"There's a *Help Wanted* sign in your window. I'd like to apply."

"For a job?" *That* snagged his full attention. "Don't you work full-time at Sugar Tots?"

"Gretchen cut back on my hours. So is there an application?"

"Not a formal one. Have you waited tables before?"

"No."

"Ever worked in a restaurant or bar in any capacity?"

"No. But I'm a quick study."

She was also on the frumpy side. Her hair was clean but lifeless, the drab locks falling forward and masking her expressions. It didn't help that she looked at her feet or the floor most of the time. From what he could see, she wasn't wearing a stitch of makeup. Rocky could pull off a totally natural look, but Rocky was gorgeous. Rachel was, well, plain. As for her figure . . . Did she *have* one? Hard to tell. Her wardrobe seemed to consist solely of what Chloe called peasant dresses. Shapeless dresses that hung below Rachel's knees or to her ankles. She was also fond of those flat-soled sweater boots. There wasn't one single sexy thing about Rachel Lacey, and yet Sam had been mooning over her for several months. Luke didn't get the fascination. But he did pick up on a hint of desperation.

A woman in need.

Shit.

"Okay. Sure. I'll give you a try. Two-week trial."

"Seems fair."

Barely, but he needed to get his act together as far as a reliable staff. Especially with Spookytown Spectacular on the horizon and the upcoming winter season. High tourist season for Sugar Creek, booming business for the Shack. "You supply the uniform basics—black pants, white top. I supply the Sugar Shack apron."

"When do I start?" she asked the stapler on his desk. At least that's where her gaze was directed.

"I'd say tonight, but you've got a date with Sam."

"I can break it."

"No. God, no." Sam would kill him. What was he saying? The whole of the Cupcake Lovers would kill him. Death by muffin-pan beating. Luke shuddered. "What about a short training session on Monday? A lay of the land. If you're still interested, we'll talk scheduling after."

"I work noon to five at Sugar Tots, but I could do before or after."

"Will eleven work for you? It won't take long."

Rachel nodded. "Anything else I should know? Any paperwork?"

"Nope. We're good." He glanced at his watch. "You should get going. Sam made reservations for six thirty. Not much time to run home and doll up."

She glanced down at her dress, blushed.

Oh, Christ. Was she dolled up? *Shit.*

"Thank you for the opportunity, Luke. I appreciate it." She pushed out of the chair and tripped over her clunky booted feet in her haste to blow out of the office.

When the door shut, Luke thunked his hand to his forehead. He could see it now. Overturned serving trays and lots of broken dishes. At least he wouldn't be tempted to do any mattress dancing with his newest employee.

"Buck up, Monroe. Maybe she'll put Connie's serving skills to shame."

In which case, Rachel Lacey would be a blessing in frumpy disguise.

CHAPTER THIRTEEN

"I owe you, Nash."

"You don't owe me anything, Rocky. That's what family's for."

The tornado of emotions swirling inside of Rocky for the last several hours ratcheted to an F3—severe. The mention of family, now that she and Nash had landed on home turf, weakened the dwindling starch in her spine. Nash was just one of several cousins living in the area—although he was definitely one of the closest to her heart. Would he think less of her when he learned about her long-buried secret? She'd snuck out of a friend's house on the night of her seventeenth birthday, crawled in through Jayce's bedroom window, slowly stripped, and . . . Oh, God. She'd *so* been the instigator. Never mind Nash. What would her aunts and uncles think? What about Gram?

Rochelle Leigh Monroe: the Virgin Slut.

Shudder.

Rocky had been so focused on surviving the impending shitstorm with Dev and her parents, she hadn't thought about the wider family scope.

As if sensing her mounting frustration, Nash gently gripped Rocky's elbow as he rolled her duffel across the tarmac of Starlight Field. "Just wish you'd share whatever's eating you," he said. "Gotta say, flying from New York to

Sugar Creek with you fuming in sizzling silence was un-
nerving."

"You? Charter pilot of private planes and hot-air bal-
loons? Poker player extraordinaire? Rattled? Didn't think
that possible."

"Yeah, well, I'm full of surprises."

"You're not the only one." Even though she'd blasted
Jayce after he'd shaken her world with his mind-blowing
news, the man had covered her hotel bill and left her an envelope at the front desk on his way out. An envelope containing two hundred bucks and a short note.

You can pay me back later.

Even though he'd been pissed, Jayce knew she'd need
money for incidentals, including cab fare to the airport.
She'd spent as little as possible and planned to pay him back
whether he liked it or not first thing tomorrow. Tonight she
needed to get her head on straight.

"Maybe I should give you a lift home," Nash said.

"My Jeep's right over there."

"You don't have a driver's license. Stolen. Remember?"

How could she forget? "Pretty sure I can manage a fifteen-
minute drive without getting pulled over."

"It's not just that." He cast her a worried look. "You're
distracted."

"I'm fine."

"Liar."

"Okay. I'll *be* fine." Rocky breathed in the frosty, fresh
air, noted the silhouetted mountains and peaceful silence of
the remote field. Unfortunately, reconnecting with nature
did not mean instant serenity.

Rounding her Jeep, Rocky reached under her front bum-
per and snagged the little magnetic box that contained an
extra key. Her regular car key—along with the keys to her
house, sports shed, gym locker, and such—was in her stolen
bag, which was probably in the bottom of some New York

City Dumpster by now. The list of things she needed to re-place was pretty long—*damn that bastard thief.*

Hopped up on outrage, Rocky unlocked the doors, and Nash hoisted her bag into the back. Before he could reissue his offer, Rocky kissed her bighearted cousin on his scruffy, chiseled jaw. "Thanks for coming to my rescue, Nash."

"The kiss-off, huh? All right. I'm done prying. And you're welcome. Anytime." Nash quirked one of his infectious smiles as Rocky climbed up behind the wheel. "See you tomorrow at Gram's."

Rocky's stomach churned. Sunday dinner at Daisy Monroe's. A family tradition. Not that all of the family made every Sunday. Except for Rocky. She rarely missed a date. "Sure thing," she lied. In truth, she wasn't sure if she'd be up to face time with whatever family showed. Depended on how she felt by tomorrow. Depended on whether or not Jayce went straight to Dev when he rolled into Sugar Creek. It would be so like Jayce to try to square things with his oldest friend before embarking on this new phase of his life. He'd moved away so he wouldn't have to "lie" to Dev's face every day.

Which was exactly what Rocky had done.

Dammit.

"If you want to talk later," Nash said, reaching through the window and squeezing her hand, "give me a holler."

Rocky forced a smile and keyed the ignition. "Sure thing."

Ten minutes later, five minutes from home, Rocky heard the staccato blurt of a siren. She glanced in her rearview mirror and cursed the whirling cherry of a black-and-white. Seriously? The SCPD rarely patrolled these back roads. *Of all the rotten luck!*

Irritated, Rocky pulled her Jeep to the side of the road and reached for her bag. *Oh, right. Stolen.* Along with her license. "Damn."

Someone tapped on her window. Billy Burke. Son of Randall Burke, the freaking town mayor, and therefore, techni-cally, Tasha's stepson. Which was sort of weird considering Billy was older than Tasha by two years. Whenever Rocky saw those two together, her skin crawled, mostly because of a story Chloe had shared with her. Of all of the cops on the small SCPD payroll, why did it have to be the one cop who was always a bastard to the Monroes? Then again, his hostility made sense considering the Burkes and Monroes had been at odds for decades.

"Evening, Billy," she said as pleasantly as possible while rolling down the window.

He shined a flashlight in her face, then on the badge pinned to his uniform.

On duty. Right. "Sorry, *Deputy* Burke. What's the problem?" She knew for certain she hadn't been speeding.

"You have a broken taillight."

"No, I don't."

"Want to step out and see for yourself?"

Yeah. She did. But instead, she sat tight. Last month Billy had frisked Chloe after pulling her and Gram over for reckless driving. Gram had beaned him with her purse after he'd touched Chloe inappropriately, and both Gram and Chloe had ended up in jail. He'd never gotten frisky with Rocky, but she didn't trust that he wouldn't. It wasn't about sex with Billy; it was about control. Considering they were out in the middle of nowhere, alone . . . "I'll take your word for it."

He smirked. "Driver's license and registration please."

Oh, hell. More irritated by the moment, Rocky snagged her registration from the pocket of her sun visor and passed it to Billy, who was still shining that damned flashlight in her face. "My license was stolen in New York."

"Likely story."

"Call your stepmom and ask," she gritted out. "Or check with the NYPD. There'll be a report."

"I'll take your word for it." He pulled a pad and pen from his back pocket. "Broken taillight and driving without a license."

"Oh, come on. Seriously? It's not my fault if—"

"Should've gotten a lift from a friend," he said as he continued to write.

She narrowed her eyes on the bastard weasel. "A warning would have been nice."

"Okay. Don't think just because you're a Monroe your shit don't stink. Watch your ass, Rocky. I am." He passed her the ticket. "How's that for a warning?"

Stunned, she gawked as he touched the brim of his hat, told her to "drive safe," then returned to his patrol car. *Dickhead.* "Welcome home, Rocky."

* * *

"Pathetic."

"Excruciating."

Luke looked to where the Brodys looked. Sam and Rachel, seated at the most romantic booth in the house, drinking and dining in awkward silence. Luke had been trying not to watch as the disaster date unfolded, but it had that train-wreck vibe. Hence, Adam and Kane rubbernecking from their seats at the far end of the bar and Luke stealing peeks in between filling drink orders for Janie and Nell.

"You gotta save him, dude," Kane said to Luke.

"Sam's a grown man. Former Marine. He can take care of himself."

Adam shook his head. "Nope. He's goin' down."

"Hurts to watch." Kane shifted away and motioned to the tap. "I need another beer."

Luke complied only to get a frown in return.

"How can you leave your cousin twisting in the wind like that?" Kane asked.

Luke served him the foaming draft. "What do you want me to do? Slip him a cocktail napkin with scribbled suggestions on seduction?"

"Couldn't hurt."

"I feel for Sam," Adam said. "Women are tough."

Luke was pretty sure Adam was thinking about Rocky. She'd messed with his head big-time. So much for the uncomplicated friends-with-benefits package. Thinking about his own relationships, or lack thereof, Luke was beginning to rethink his own dating style. "I don't know what Sam sees in Rachel anyway."

"She's sweet," Adam said.

"In a shy, insecure way," Luke said. Qualities that had never raised his flagpole.

"She's good with kids," Kane offered. "Must be tough on Sam, raising Ben and Mina on his own. He can't dick around with just any woman. She's gotta be mom material."

"I get that," Luke said. "I want my young cousins to have a kind stepmother. God knows they're missing out on a mother's love and influence. And sure, yeah, I guess Rachel would be good with them. But she has to be a good fit for Sam, too."

"In bed you mean," Kane said.

"He may be nearing forty, but he's not dead. He's got needs. I assume. Then again, he's been celibate for a couple of years now." Luke uncorked a bottle of Merlot. "Can't imagine."

"That's because you haven't loved a woman the way Sam loved Paula," Adam said.

"I've loved plenty of women."

"Not like that."

Luke didn't argue, but as he poured two glasses of wine he did take stock of Adam's body language. Did Adam feel the same kind of love for Rocky that Sam had felt for his wife? Luke hadn't considered the true-love angle. He wasn't privy to Adam's feelings for Rocky. Hell, Adam wasn't even aware Luke knew about the secret affair. Rocky had told Luke in confidence and, truth told, Luke didn't give the secret affair a hell of a lot of thought. If he dwelled on the fact that his high-school bud had been having no-strings-attached hot and wild sex with his sister, he'd have a hard time getting past it. If, on the other hand, Adam and Rocky were to explore a serious relationship, Luke would be all for it. Adam was a great guy. Top-notch brother-in-law material. Luke wasn't sure he could say the same for Jayce.

"They're leaving."

"Show's over."

"Sam's not getting any tonight."

Luke felt coldcocked by the Brodys' exchange. He'd been at the other end of the bar filling Nell's order, settling up a tab, and lost in his own thoughts. How much time had passed? Five minutes? Seven? Sam and Rachel were leaving? "Did they even have dessert?"

"Shortest date in history," said Kane.

Adam shook his head, guzzled beer. "I feel for Sam."

So did Luke. *Damn*. He thought about what a good soul Sam was. All he'd done in his life and all he'd done for Luke. He thought about how much Sam had loved Paula and how he'd mourned her death. He thought about his young cousins, Mina and Ben. Rachel *would* be good with them. "I should've helped."

"No shit, Sherlock," Kane said.

"There's always tomorrow," Adam said.

New day. New chance to put his expertise to good use. Luke knew Sam. Rachel—not so much. But Luke knew women, and he knew how to charm them into bed. Tomorrow he'd take his first shot at matchmaking. Why not? Just because Luke's, Adam's, and Rocky's love lives were in a depressing black hole, no reason Sam couldn't strike romantic gold.

Smiling, Luke topped off the Brodys' mugs and poured himself a beer. "To second chances."

CHAPTER FOURTEEN

Crappy life circumstances, including that damned run-in with Billy Burke, had caused Rocky a restless night's sleep. Mostly she'd stared into the dark, dreading a phone call from Dev.

Just had a visit from Jayce . . .

Jayce just called. . . .

What the hell were you thinking? . . .

That call never came. Not in the middle of night and not at the crack of dawn. It would, though. Jayce was primed to spill. Every time Rocky thought about their blowout, her pulse spiked.

A headache and a bad attitude threatened to ruin her day, so she'd kicked off her morning, as was her routine, with a glass of OJ and a four-mile run along Pikeman's Trail. Unfortunately, it didn't rouse the anticipated meditative bliss. Strange given the blissful atmosphere. Yesterday she'd awoken to a cacophony of big-city noise . . . and the steady beat of Jayce's heart.

It had been jolting, unsettling. *Exhilarating.*

Today had arrived on a gentle hush. The familiar. The only sound in her room the thwacking whir of the ceiling fan. No beating heart, other than her own. Waking in her own bed should have been comforting, but she'd never felt more restless.

Or lonely.

As angry as she was with Jayce, she missed him.

Even now as she jogged through the woods, something she normally loved, her thoughts turned to walking in Central Park with the charismatic Adonis. She didn't need to go back there, but she did want to turn back time. *No.* Capture *time.* Just that one day and night. The easy conversation, jovial moods, genuine smiles, and laughs.

The sizzling sex.

That day represented the life she'd imagined with Jayce in her wildest dreams.

How cruel that fate had doled out a slice of that dream only to rip it away. Rocky had tossed and turned all night trying to spin circumstances to her favor. Maybe her family wouldn't care that Jayce had been her first lover. Maybe they'd shrug at the jailbait issue. Maybe they'd brush off thirteen years of lies.

Maybe the sun would rise in the west.

No matter how hard she tried, Rocky couldn't think beyond the lie. She couldn't accept that maybe, just maybe, she and Jayce had a solid chance at a normal relationship. A loving relationship that would lead to marriage and babies. Not that she wanted marriage and babies right now. She was too busy trying to resurrect her dream, her *other* dream—the Red Clover. She was too busy trying to make sure Tasha didn't sully the reputation of the Cupcake Lovers and that the efforts of the club didn't suffer as they pursued the recipe/memoir book.

Rocky stopped in her tracks and braced her hands on her knees as she fought to catch her breath. She rubbed her aching chest. *Overwhelmed.* She was drowning in a flood of responsibilities and expectations. *Chaos.* She needed to take control. Control was the key to contentment.

Sunbeams cut through the thick foliage, taking the edge off of the frosty morning air. A bird chirped, and the nearby creek, honest to God, babbled. The tension in Rocky's shoulder's eased; her temples ceased to throb. Her mind wasn't totally clear, but she had at least one constructive thought.

Control.

Basking in a chilly breeze, the smell of pine, and the sounds of nature, Rocky turned her face to the sun and considered her options. Five seconds later, Jayce's voice rang in her ears.

This *is what's been festering inside you all these years?*

Her stomach churned with doubt.

Had she overreacted to his proposal? *Had* she been an insensitive bitch all these years? If she hadn't been so hostile toward Jayce, Dev wouldn't have suspected a rift. He wouldn't have worried over the why. He wouldn't have coaxed Jayce into staying at the Red Clover three weeks ago in order to mend bridges with Rocky.

And quite possibly, she wouldn't be in the position she was in now.

Screw it.

Instead of living in dread, wondering when Jayce was going to come clean with Dev, and obsessing on the fallout, she'd take matters into her own hands. Contrary to what Jayce had intimated in New York, she was not an immature chickenshit. Wary, yes. Nervous, yes. But she'd be damned if she'd allow Jayce to call the shots concerning her damned life.

Hopped up on adrenaline, Rocky plucked her phone from her sport armband and seized the day.

* * *

It had taken Dev twenty minutes to get to the Red Clover. That meant twenty minutes to go over her story, pick and choose her words, and practice her tone of voice.

Twenty minutes to lose her nerve.

Rocky forced a smile when her brother crossed the threshold bearing a paper bag stamped with the logo from Moose-a-lotta.

"You promised coffee," he said with a smile that didn't reach his eyes. "Figured I'd bring Danish. Chloe made them. Apple," he added.

Rocky waved Dev inside and led him into the kitchen.

Christ, he was as tense as she was. Although you wouldn't know it to look at him. Dressed in business casual, he affected a confident and calm demeanor. Aside from their dad, Dev had always been the rock of the family.

"So what did you want to see me about?" he asked, getting to the point as she set out plates and poured them each a cup of banana fudge java. "I assume it's not about the publishing contract or your stolen purse," he said as she struggled with her opening line. "Otherwise we could have had this discussion over the phone."

Rocky resisted the urge to pace. Instead, she sat across the kitchen table from her older brother. The protector. The stand-up guy who always did the right thing. "I need to talk to you about Jayce."

"Okay."

"I need you to listen and not interrupt. Just . . . let me get it out."

He nodded, then placed a gooey Danish on her plate.

"It's about the rift." His gaze flicked to hers, and she felt the force of his curiosity and concern mixed with relief. As if he was thinking, *Finally*. Rocky broke his gaze, stared at her pastry. "Jayce and I . . . He was my first."

Silence.

"Lover," she added, risking Dev's gaze.

Dev raised a brow.

Rocky wanted to die. "It was all my doing. Well, not all. I mean it takes two. Obviously. But I started it and made it pretty damned hard for him to refuse. I mean he's a guy after all and I was naked—"

Dev cut her off with a raised hand. "*When* was this exactly?"

She flushed. "The night of my seventeenth birthday." She saw Dev do the math, saw his jaw clench in anger. "For what it's worth," she rushed on, "Jayce proposed marriage the morning after. Sort of. Said we should get married. So he tried to do the right thing, I guess, only it felt all wrong. Who wants to marry a man out of old-fashioned duty? Not me. I told him to piss off."

Dev stared.

"Harsh, I guess."

"You think?"

Rocky's temper flared. "I *loved* him. Heart and soul. Blinding passion. Jayce offered to marry me out of guilt and a sense of obligation. Why doesn't anyone, aside from me, see the insult?"

Dev dragged a hand down his face.

"He crushed my heart and I put up a wall. A huge wall of seething resentment. I didn't think he'd actually move away, but I was glad when he did. It made things easier. Sort of. He wanted to tell you a long time ago, but I urged him not to. What was the point? I knew you'd be angry and I didn't want you to think less of me or Jayce. I certainly didn't want to jeopardize your friendship." Rocky's throat clogged; her eyes teared. "I'm sorry we weren't honest with you, Dev. I just . . . I couldn't see past my mangled illusions."

Her brother sat stock-still, his expression enigmatic. What was he thinking? What was he feeling? She couldn't take the suspense. "Aren't you going to say anything?"

"I'm trying to figure out when and how I failed you."

"What?" Rocky furrowed her brow. "You think my seducing Jayce was somehow your fault?"

He barked a humorless laugh. "God, no." He pushed out of the chair, braced his hands on the wall, and dropped his head. In frustration? Denial? Fury?

Five seconds of tense silence seemed like an eternity, and when he turned back around Rocky's heart ached so bad, she could scarcely breathe. She couldn't remember the last time she'd seen Dev look so *hurt.*

"It kills me that you didn't feel you could share something with me that weighed so heavily on your heart and mind, Rocky," he said in a grave voice. "Given the situation, maybe at first, but a year or two after? You struggled with this for thirteen years because, why? Did you ever think that it might've helped to mend your heart, your pride, and anything else that needed tending by confiding in someone who could be objective?"

"*Could* you have been objective, Dev?"

He looked her dead in the eye. "After I got over the initial shock and considering my own history regarding marrying out of guilt and obligation . . . yes."

He was referring to his high-school sweetheart, his first wife . . . until she'd miscarried and run off to reclaim her freedom. Rocky's heartbreak had been nothing compared to her brother's. For some reason, that hadn't resonated until now. Never had she felt so childish, so petty. She fought to rally but was stumped for words.

Dev moved toward her then, and Rocky's heart pounded even harder. He rounded the table, cupped the back of her neck, and kissed the top of her head.

She blinked, panicking when he turned suddenly and left the room. The embrace had been gentle, but the air vibrated with turmoil. Rocky jumped to her feet and followed. "Where are you going?"

"I need to clear my head."

Did he mean that? Was he going for a brisk walk? A fast ride? Or was he heading over to Jayce's for a showdown? She hated that Dev was so calm, so quiet. That was never a good thing with him. It meant he was stewing and when he blew . . .

"Point of interest, why tell me this now?" Dev asked, pausing on the threshold.

"How can I persist with the lie with Jayce living here? Also . . ." She looked away, shamed because she probably *would* have tried to live with it if she'd trusted Jayce to stay quiet. "I know he intended to tell you, but I wanted it to come from me." She blew out a nervous breath. "What are Mom and Dad going to think?"

"Why would you tell them? You think Luke and I had a heart-to-heart with Mom or Dad about the first time we had sex?"

"But it was with Jayce."

"Yeah, I got that." He braced his hands on his hips, glanced toward Thrush Mountain as if gleaning serenity from the rustling foliage. "Speaking of Luke, something tells me he already knows about this."

Rocky blew out a nervous breath. "Don't take this personally—like you're the last one to know, because you're not. And believe me I hadn't planned on spilling to Luke."

"But you did." Dev met her gaze. "Just want to be clear on who knows what."

"I had a meltdown a few weeks ago," Rocky admitted. "Luke pressed at a vulnerable time. Please don't blame him for keeping quiet. I swore him to silence."

"Anyone else?"

"Promise me you won't hold it against her."

"Chloe?"

"Chloe and Monica," Rocky blurted, cheeks flushing. "That damned meltdown. I'd kept everything—the seduction, the proposal, my crushed feelings and resentment—bottled up for all those years; then that one day . . . it all gushed out. I begged them both to keep my secret. I know Chloe felt weird about it, but she promised anyway. She's a good friend, a good soul. She didn't want to hurt me or to put a strain on your friendship with Jayce."

"You don't have to defend Chloe's actions," Dev said in a calm tone. "I get it. I get her."

So there it was. She'd told her big brother, her overprotective, mega-controlling brother, everything about the past. Filled him in on who knew what. The world didn't end. It didn't even shift. Rocky hugged herself feeling all sorts of stupid. She'd wrestled with her secret for thirteen years and this was the extent of the fallout?

"Rocky."

She met her brother's gaze. "Yes?"

"Thank you for telling me."

* * *

Jayce's homecoming had been a dismal affair. Rolling into Sugar Creek just prior to midnight, he'd parked in front of the chalet he'd grown up in, staring into the darkened overgrown lawn twenty minutes before having the balls to cross over the threshold. Crossing that threshold represented the meshing of his past, present, and future. It meant dealing with some shitty-ass memories instead of locking them behind a mental armored door. Purchasing another property would've have been easier but would've entailed admitting defeat.

Screw that.

Because of his time on the force and his years as a private investigator, Jayce had witnessed people battling demons far greater than his own. Yet whenever he visited Sugar Creek, in particular this house, the past seemed insurmountable. How could a grown man feel like a vulnerable kid? Why couldn't he believe what Dev and Dev's dad had told him that one terrible night—that it wasn't his fault? Normally he kept the painful memories at bay, but by God they thrived inside the four walls of 241 Lark Lane. He hated the power this house had over him. That his parents had over him—even after death.

Time to come to terms.

Jayce had spent the night bunking on a bare mattress in his old bedroom, alternating between nightmares and insomnia.

This morning, he stood in the shower—hands braced on the tile, head lowered—trying to snap out of a bad mood while the pulsating water pounded his tense shoulders and back.

He was wiped.

Not so much from the long drive or the restless night of sleep but because he was being haunted by a whole new set of memories. Twenty-four hours chock-full of Rocky. Rocky at the hospital—mugged, rattled, and bloodied. Rocky striding into a publishing house with kick-ass confidence and curves. Rocky eating hot dogs in Central Park and bemoaning the treatment of carriage horses. The list went on. He couldn't purge the sound of her laughter or the smell of her shampoo or the sight of her naked luscious body. He couldn't shake off the memory of her writhing beneath him in bed, begging for more, screaming his name. *His* name. He kept reliving one moment after another, knowing they were meant to be together.

If they could just get past the bullshit.

Jayce gave up on the shower, slaking water from his body and stepping out onto a folded towel. Somewhere, in the dozens of boxes stacked in the living room, dining room, and kitchen, was a bath mat. The house was in chaos. Dev had gone above and beyond, meeting the moving van and getting all of Jayce's furnishings and belongings inside. Mostly everything was crammed into the three larger rooms of the fairly small house. Which was fine. Jayce had had the walls repainted and the hardwood floors refurbished, but there were still a lot of details left undone. He wasn't quite ready to set up house. Not that he was stalling.

Jayce stepped into a pair of jeans, eyeing his cell when it rang. *Dev.* "Mornin'."

"You up?"

"You coming over?"

"Just pulled into your driveway."

Beautiful.

Dev hadn't been happy when Jayce had called from New York with the news that he and Rocky had quarreled and that she'd be returning to Sugar Creek on her own. The man was fed up with the bad blood between his sister and friend and their constant reluctance to fill him in on the crux of their hostility. Jayce fully expected Dev to call him on the mat today. He just wished they could've duked it out somewhere else. Just what this house needed—another ugly scene.

Resigned, Jayce pulled a baggy long-sleeved tee over his head and raked wet hair from his face. Barefoot, he trekked over cold hardwood floors, kicked up the thermostat on his way through the living room. The end of October in northern Vermont. A good twenty degrees colder than Brooklyn. Bracing himself for the frigid air and a cold reception from his friend, Jayce opened the front door and got a fist in his face.

Pain exploded in his jaw, knocking him back two steps. *"Damn!"*

"She was sixteen."

"Seventeen."

"Barely. You were fucking *twenty-two*."

Jayce worked his offended jaw and contemplated the moment. The secret, thank God, was out. "I can't believe Rocky told you."

"Disappointed?"

"Impressed." He'd expected Rocky to hold out, not to rush forward. "Although I would've preferred to tell you myself or at least together. How much hell did you give her?"

"Not much. Figured she'd suffered enough."

"Me, on the other hand." Jayce welcomed the throbbing pain in his jaw. This had been a long time coming and maybe was the first step in moving beyond. "I have no excuse. I should've known better."

His friend hovered on the threshold.

Jayce didn't know what chilled him more—the frigid wind blowing through the open door or Dev's frosty glare.

"Rocky claimed she was the instigator."

Jayce didn't respond.

"Said you offered marriage, tried to do the right thing."

"Yeah, well, that's when things *really* went wrong." He still couldn't believe that his proposal had been the reason behind Rocky's fierce resentment all these years, but lamenting the fact to Dev, or anyone for that matter, wasn't Jayce's style.

"What really gripes my ass," Dev went on, the cold fury in his eyes melting down a notch, "is that you kept me in the dark for so long. Thirteen years of wondering why my best friend and little sister were at odds."

"Are you going to be able to get past this?"

"Eventually." Bearing a paper bag Jayce hadn't even noticed until now, the man moved into the house without an invitation. "Coffee's getting cold."

Jayce shut the door, feeling as though he'd been coldcocked a second time. "You brought coffee?"

"Wasn't sure if you'd unearthed a coffeemaker. Brought Danish, too. This will be my third attempt at breakfast this morning." Dev weaved through a maze of packing boxes on his way into the kitchen.

Shaking his head, Jayce followed. Apparently they were going to "get past this" over coffee and Danish. Trying to adjust to the new kink in their friendship, Jayce pulled two mismatched stools up to the breakfast bar while Dev produced two ceramic traveling mugs and neatly wrapped pastries. The mugs were stamped with a moose head—a cartoonish bull wearing blingy cat-eye glasses and a chef's hat—and the name Moose-a-lotta. "Customized coffee mugs? Looks like Daisy and Chloe went all out."

"You have no idea. Wait until you see the place." Dev draped his jacket over a box and took a seat. "I have to say, I'm impressed and proud. Great location, concept, and food. Sure to be a hit with locals and tourists."

"Didn't know Daisy had a business streak in her."

"Gram's been full of surprises lately. Sort of like you." Brow raised, Dev handed him one of the mugs. "I know Rocky blew you off, Jayce, but you were the adult. You should have addressed the situation, considered her romantic illusions, reasoned with her, struck a compromise or truce. Something. *Jesus.* Instead, you escaped to New York and fostered the angst of her melodramatic youth. It goes against everything I know about you. Why the easy way out?"

Jayce met his friend's puzzled gaze. "Not easy," he said. "Convenient. Deep down, I think I was looking for an excuse to leave Sugar Creek. Rocky gave me one in spades."

Dev glanced around the kitchen, and Jayce knew he was thinking about Jayce's shitty childhood and that one unbelievably shitty night.

"When . . . if you need to talk about it, I'm here."

In that moment, Jayce felt the full force of Dev's sincere friendship. All Jayce managed was a nod.

"So here's how we're going to get past the jailbait issue and thirteen-year cover-up," Dev went on, smoothing over a painful memory with talk of an awkward misstep. "We're going to shelve this topic and never touch it again, because what's the point?"

While Jayce contemplated his response, Dev's phone rang.

Dev glanced at the caller ID, then glanced back at Jayce. "It's Chloe," he said, then took the call. "Yeah, honey. What's up? . . . No, I didn't kill him." He glanced at Jayce. "Yeah. I know. Working on it. Talk to you later." He disconnected, then sipped coffee.

Jayce toyed with his cup, feeling exposed. "So you told Chloe."

"Rocky told Chloe. And Luke and Monica." Dev cocked a brow. "You didn't know?"

Jayce scraped a hand over his whiskered chin.

Dev quirked a smile. "I think that's the extent of it. For what it's worth, Chloe and Monica sympathize with you, whereas Luke . . . You might want to steer clear of his right hook for a while. Anyway," Dev plowed on. "I was worked up when I stopped by Moose-a-lotta for the second time this morning. Chloe talked me down."

Jayce massaged his jaw. "That punch came *after* you cooled off?"

Another grin. "So, what prompted you to leave Brooklyn?"

The question caught Jayce off guard. He'd expected Dev to ask for an update on the mugging incident or on the current status of Jayce and Rocky's relationship. Aside from the blowout, wasn't Dev curious about the time they'd spent together this past weekend? "It's a long story."

"I've got all day."

"I was restless."

"That's your long story?"

Jayce shrugged. He'd never been big on sharing his intimate thoughts and feelings. A building sense of discontentment coupled with the death of his friend Mrs. Watson had made him itch for another life. Rocky had merely given him direction. He wasn't in the mood to discuss either motivating factor. "On my last visit, I realized how much I miss Sugar Creek. Wide-open spaces. Laid-back pace. That day I pitched in with your family to build a new shed for Rocky? It felt good."

"Being surrounded by the people you love and who love you."

Jayce raised a brow at his friend's choice of words. "When did you get so pansy-ass sentimental?"

"New outlook on life."

"Because of Chloe?"

"Partly."

Jayce eyed his friend over the rim of his steaming mug. Of the two of them, Dev had always been more forthcoming. Mostly because he was an opinionated control freak. "Something you want to share?"

"No. What about your career plans?" Dev prompted after finishing off his apple pastry. "You said you had something in mind."

Again, Jayce was surprised. Still no mention of the weekend in New York with Rocky. "Starting a new venture. A cyber detective agency. I—"

Dev's phone blipped. "Sorry." He checked the screen. "Text from Gram: *'Vincent got detained,'*" he read aloud. *"Need a ride to church. Rocky not available. You? Or I could drive myself."* He shook his head. "Like hell."

"Thought she still had an ankle cast."

"She does. Even without, she's a menace on wheels," Dev said while thumbing in a return message. "Told her I'd be right there."

"Why didn't you just call her?"

"She wouldn't answer. Ever since Chloe taught her to text, she's been as addicted as a teenager. Except she doesn't abbreviate," he said while zipping up his jacket. "Guess I'm going to have to increase her data plan before she drains her bank account."

Jayce followed Dev to the door, feeling more awkward by the minute. No interrogation or, hell, slight interest in how Jayce and Rocky had gotten along during the daylong sight-seeing tour? How they'd spent their time? What they'd talked about? No prying at all?

"Sorry to cut this short," Dev said. "I'm curious about the new agency. You can fill us in tonight."

"Us?"

"The family. Or some of us anyway. Dinner at Gram's. Sunday tradition, remember?"

He remembered. It used to be one of his favorite things. Sunday dinner with the Monroes. Jayce had always had a standing invitation, just like a member of the family.

Guilt needled his conscience. It wasn't just the past. It was the fresh tumble with Rocky in New York. Not that Dev needed intimate details, but he did deserve to know Jayce's long-term intentions. Then again, so did Rocky. Jayce dragged a hand through his hair, knowing they wouldn't be having that conversation anytime soon. Not until she cooled off. "I'm not sure—"

"No excuses. You said you wanted to ease back into Sugar Creek. What better way than to start with the family?"

Showing up for dinner, catching Rocky off guard in the wake of their latest fight, struck Jayce as a bad idea. On the other hand, skipping dinner to avoid an uncomfortable scene would be taking the easy way out. Again. "Five o'clock?"

"Four thirty. Gram tweaked tradition by adding a cocktail hour. See you then. Oh, and Jayce," Dev said as he crossed the front porch. "Word of advice: Make peace with Rocky before dinner."

Coldcocked, chastised, supported, and manipulated by his best friend over coffee and Danish. In spite of his unsettled mood, Jayce's lip twitched as he watched Dev drive off. "Welcome home, Bello."

CHAPTER FIFTEEN

Cocoa powder, baking powder, brown sugar, canned pumpkin.

Chewing her thumbnail, Rocky studied the multiple ingredients lined across her counter. Something was missing. She glanced at the vintage recipe she'd printed off the Internet. Peanut butter! She rifled through her pantry and snagged a jar of smooth. Or should she use chunky? No, smooth. Definitely smooth. She was already using ground almonds.

Nervous energy fueled Rocky's restlessness. She'd been zipping around her kitchen for a good two hours. Poring over recipes, sorting through ingredients. At last she'd settled on a baking project. Something productive to keep her from obsessing on her emotional confrontation with her brother. Something to distract her from the fact that she hadn't called and warned Jayce.

You might get a visit from Dev. FYI, I told him about the jailbait hookup.

On the other hand, she had texted Luke, Chloe, and Monica:

CONFESSED ALL 2 DEV ABT JAYCE. SORRY IF I PUT U IN AWKWARD POSITION. ☹

Chloe texted back within seconds: *THANK U!* ☺

Monica texted: *Movin' on!* ☺

Typically, Luke had called. *How bad was it?*

Not that bad. Which makes me feel worse.

Want to talk about it?

No.

Okay, Luke said. *Visiting Sam today, but I can swing by after. Give you a lift to Gram's for dinner.*

I'm not sure—

Pick you up at four.

Instead of arguing, Rocky had sucked it up. It's not like Dev, Luke, or Chloe was going to bring up her indiscretion over dessert. Rocky was fairly certain they'd never mention it again. Still, she felt self-conscious.

What was Jayce feeling? Thinking? Was he going head-to-head with Dev this very minute? A warning from her would have been courteous, but dammit she was still angry with the man for misleading her in New York. He should have told her he was moving home *before* they hit the sack. Because of that incredible one-nighter—their *second* freaking amazing one-nighter—Jayce had her more twisted up than ever, not that she intended to admit that to him. She wasn't sure *what* she was going to say when they next met— which she hoped wouldn't be for a few days at least.

She glanced at her phone, snuffed a flash of guilt. If Dev *did* confront Jayce, the cocky PI could handle himself, and besides, this was what he'd wanted. No more secrets.

Where do we go from here?

Pushing Jayce from her mind for the zillionth time, Rocky focused on her supposed distraction.

A new Creepy Cupcake treat.

The Spookytown Spectacular was five days away. She had plenty of time to prepare and her Gingerbread Pumpkin Cupcakes had already gotten the thumbs-up from the Cupcake Lovers. Not as the featured giveaway, but as cupcakes to be sold in order to benefit the Sugar Tots playground fund. Thing was, Tasha planned on selling her Death By Maple cupcakes and everyone in town knew how incredible those cupcakes were. Tasha's famous DBMs would sell out long before Rocky's GBCs. Honestly, aside from the twist of crystallized ginger, her Gingerbread Pumpkins were pretty standard. Any baker with a lick of talent could whip up the same delicious concoction. She hated to admit it, but she'd been a tad irritated when the editor and publicist of Highlife had fawned more over the Death By Maples than any of the other cupcakes they'd tasted from the CL sampler. The more she thought about it, the more it bugged her. She wasn't about to let Tasha show her up at the Spooktacular.

Hence a new recipe.

Rocky had experimented with banana and pumpkin, but while pouring batter into the cupcake liners she'd remembered Monica saying something about using that combo. Desperate for unique inspiration, Rocky had skimmed a few baking sites online. That's when she'd run across a recipe that had been handed down from one Turlington generation to another. Not that Rocky knew the Turlingtons, but she was a sucker for tradition. She took it as a supreme challenge to put her own spin on a traditional recipe while staying true to the original concept. Hence a mere variation on measurements and spices. Maybe an adjustment on texture. A unique topping design. Something to make it her own.

Caught up in a creative blitz, she cursed when someone knocked on her front door. It had to be Dev.

Or Jayce.

Chloe was manning Moose-a-lotta solo. Gram was at church along with most of the other Cupcake Lovers. Luke was visiting Sam.

Oh, hell. What if it was Adam? Nice, reliable, always reasonable Adam, coming to bury the hatchet. She'd been hoping to mend their friendship. Just not today.

Rocky moved quickly, wanting to slay the suspense.

Don't let it be Jayce. Don't let it be Jayce.

She straightened her spine and opened the door.

So much for wishful thinking.

Rocky stared at the Adonis standing on her front porch, her heart bucking like a wild stallion. Faded blue jeans, black peacoat, black boots. How could basic casual wear be so sexy on a man? His longish hair was raked back from his chiseled features. His goatee neatly trimmed. His killer eyes hidden behind those damned aviator sunglasses. She hated that she couldn't see his eyes, read his intent. She hated that she wanted to jump his infuriating bones.

"Nice play," Jayce said.

Her fluttery insides churned. "Dev came to see you." Narrowing her eyes, she noted a slight discoloring along the Adonis's jawline. "Oh, God. Did Dev *punch* you? Did you hit him back?"

"Why would I do that?"

Because it was the natural thing to do? Reflex? Pride? "If someone hit me, I'd strike back." She flashed on the knockdown drag-out she'd had with Tasha a few weeks back. It's not that Rocky was violent, but she wasn't a door-mat either. "So what happened? Did he tear you a new one? Brand you a disappointment? Lecture you? Threaten you?"

"He brought coffee and Danish."

"What?"

"He may have dropped a curse word or two; then he asked about my new business venture."

"What?"

"Secret's out. Guilty parties admonished. Moving on," Jayce said.

Rocky gaped. "It can't be as easy as that."

"Maybe it is."

Was that supposed to make her feel better? It didn't. It intimated that she'd made a mountain out of a molehill—for thirteen freaking years. Torn between mortification and fury, Rocky struggled not to slam the door in Jayce's face. "Okay. Well, I'm glad Dev didn't shoot you. You're right. Secret's out. No one died. Moving on. Good luck with your new venture."

She gaped as Jayce ignored the brush-off and stepped inside. Fidgeted as he pocketed his shades, scanned the tarp-covered furniture, the stripped walls, and the sanded banis-ter and newel post of the stairway. She prided herself on maintaining a picture-perfect interior. Currently every room, including the back porch and roof, was in the process of upgrades.

"I'm not sure who's living in more chaos," he said. "You or me."

Rocky couldn't think straight, so she clung to his observation. "Makes me batty. The upheaval," she clarified. "But the contractors promised they'd be done soon. Two weeks more. Approximately."

"Even in the chaos, your flair for decorating shines through. I could use some decorating advice," Jayce said, knocking her even more off balance. "Since the last tenants moved out, I had the walls repainted and the floors refurbished, but other than that . . . I'm thinking the kitchen could use an overhaul. New cabinets, appliances."

Rocky blinked. Were they really talking home renovations? *What the hell?* "I can suggest some home décor magazines."

His lip twitched. "I'd prefer your hands-on expertise."

She scrunched her brow. "You want me to decorate your house?"

"I shipped up a few of my furnishings and essentials like cookware, linens, sentimental belongings, but for the most part I'd like to start fresh. I want to transform my parents' house into a home. My home."

She had to admit, she was intrigued. She'd only been inside Jayce's house a couple of times, and she'd always left with the same impression. No sense of warmth. No sense of him. "Have a particular style in mind?" she heard herself asking.

"Not really. But I am partial to comfort and character." He gestured to her living area. "Something like this or similar to Daisy's décor. Something that feels like . . ."

"Home."

"I need help."

Rocky's heart pounded. The look in his eyes. The tone of his voice. *Vulnerability?* "As it happens, I do have some time on my hands." Renovating Jayce's place would keep her occupied and out from under the construction crew's feet here at the Red Clover. Plus, it would be fun. "And I do like to decorate," she reasoned out loud. "I'm a hell of a bargain shopper, if I do say so myself." Channeling Gram's reckless zest for life, Rocky took the plunge. "Have a budget in mind?"

Smiling a little, Jayce pulled his wallet from his inner coat pocket and passed her a credit card. "The balance is clear and the limit's high."

"You're trusting me with a platinum card?"

"I'm trusting you with my home."

Huh. That was kind of hot. And scary. Rocky contemplated the financial responsibility, the thrill of the task, and the danger of spending a *lot* of time with Jayce.

"What's cooking?" he asked with a sniff.

The trial batch of cupcakes she'd made before she'd decided to give the Turlington recipe a whirl. Rocky glanced at her watch. "Crap." *Two minutes too long.* She pocketed Jayce's credit card, beelined to the kitchen, and opened the oven door. The heat and combined scents of pumpkin and banana overwhelmed. Using a pot holder to slide the muffin pan closer, she stuck a toothpick in the center of the toasty-topped cupcake. "Done. Way done." She deposited the piping-hot pan on a cooling rack, scowled. "Damn."

"They look fine to me," Jayce said.

"Shows what you know about baking."

"I know nothing about baking." He moved in behind her, crowding her space, making her nerves jump and her skin tingle. "Maybe you can give me a lesson sometime. Seems a fair trade when I taught you a thing or two."

He was referring to their sexual escapades in New York. Rocky's cheeks burned, and her girly parts ached. She pushed away the memories. Unfortunately, desire lingered. She didn't want this. *Or do I?* She'd just agreed to redecorate his house. Which meant she'd be spending a lot of time *at* his house. With . . . him. *Jesus.* "If you think you can erase that argument in New York by distracting me with sex, you're wrong."

"I should've told you sooner that I was moving home. I apologize."

She blinked over her shoulder. "You do?"

He nodded. "I'd also like to revisit that discussion regarding our past."

"That makes one of us."

"I'm sorry if I was insensitive, but—"

"Let's leave it at that for now." She wasn't ready for another heart-to-heart. She'd had enough of that for one day. At the same time, she gave him credit for trying. Desperate to redirect the conversation, she gestured to the Banana Pumpkin Cupcakes. "As soon as these cool you can taste one. If you like, you can have. Just let me frost them first." Anything to get rid of the man who scrambled her thoughts and senses.

Coming clean with Dev had been akin to wiping the slate clean. Jayce seemed intent on rushing forward, while Rocky was still trying to catch her breath. Her mind and heart hadn't caught up to her new reality—whatever that reality was.

Mouth quirked in a tender smile, Jayce motioned to the mixing bowls, the flour, sugar, and assorted other ingredients. "Making another batch?"

"Different recipe. As soon as I put the Banana Pumpkins in the oven, I realized Monica had said something about utilizing that combination for her Spooktacular cupcakes. I could stick with my Gingerbread Pumpkins, but I'm of the mind to knock Tasha down a notch," Rocky said as she nabbed a package of cream cheese from the fridge. "I found this other recipe . . . never mind." She was babbling. "Don't take this the wrong way, but I'm busy, Jayce." *Go away.* "I'm hoping to try out my new cupcakes tonight on Gram and the gang. And—"

"Dev invited me to dinner."

Rocky bobbled a jar of honey. "What?"

"Thought you should know."

Gripping the jar tight, she poured honey over the cream cheese, then opted for her portable mixer over her stand mixer, anything to keep her trembling hands busy. "You turned him down, right? Made some excuse?"

"He didn't give me that option."

"That cinches it then," Rocky said as she mixed the icing. "I'm begging off. I'll say I'm exhausted from the trip."

"Are you going to beg off next Sunday and the Sunday after that? Avoid J.T.'s on the off chance I might be shopping there? Shun the Sugar Shack in case I drop by for drinks or dinner? If you think I'm going to boycott Moose-a-lotta, think again. Aside from the Burkes, the Monroes are the most influential family in Sugar Creek. Your relatives are everywhere and they're an important part of my life. I won't be a hermit and I'm not leaving town," he said calmly. "You're going to have to live with that. With me and what's burning between us."

Rocky spun so fast she neglected to switch off the mixer. Icing splattered everywhere! On her. On Jayce. The counter and floor. Flustered, she cut the power and returned the beaters to the bowl. Heart pounding, she turned to give Jayce hell, only his intimate proximity stole away her breath.

"If I taste and like," he said, cupping the back of her neck and pulling her close, "can I have?"

Her inner thighs tingled. *Oh no.* She tried to object when he licked icing from her cheek, but all that came out was a low, lusty groan.

"Tasty."

"Honey–cream cheese," she said in a breathy voice.

"Rocky Monroe."

Oh, God.

Jayce licked and nibbled her chin, her ear.

Rocky could feel herself slipping under Jayce's spell. *Control. Take control!* She licked a splatter of icing from the corner of his mouth, bit his lower lip in order to warn him off, break the spell, but the aggressive move backfired. A sensual thrill shot through her when he winced, then counteracted with a punishing kiss, a kiss that melted the last of her feeble resistance.

They were all over each other. Grappling. Kissing.

Next thing she knew half their clothes were in a puddle on the floor. She should care, but she didn't. She should stop, but she couldn't.

"Upstairs," she said.

"Here," he countered.

Delirious with lust, she dropped her head back as Jayce trailed hot kisses down her neck, over her shoulders. Her breath caught as he smeared gooey icing over her breasts, then licked and suckled.

Can't . . . breathe.

She felt his warm, sticky hands on her bare thighs. Jeans, gone. Panties, gone. Naked in her kitchen. *Wrong, wrong, wrong.* Yet, she heard herself begging for more. Felt Jayce lifting her, laying her on the table. More icing. More tongue and teeth. More delicious delirium as every muscle tensed, her stomach coiled. Then his head was between her legs and one breathless aching moment later . . . she was done. Spent. Sprawled naked on her kitchen table, senses reeling in the aftermath of a mind-bending orgasm. Not that she was a prude, far from it, but Jesus. "You should go."

"Nice try."

Jayce hauled her off the table, into his arms, and carried her upstairs. Hadn't she suggested that in the first place?

"We're sticky," he said, bypassing her bed and heading for her modernized bathroom.

"Whose fault is that?" Just thinking about the way he'd licked honey–cream cheese icing from her body sent an erotic shiver up her spine. "If you think you're going to have your way with me in the shower—"

"I'd be right."

They were barely soaked before he had her against the tiled wall. His muscled front to her slick back, Jayce took her from behind. Rocky gasped at the feel of him, trembled, and moaned. A word whispered at the back of her foggy mind. *Control.* Oh, Jayce was definitely in control. Although that wasn't exactly right. "Wait."

In answer he suckled her earlobe, plunged deeper. Oh, hell, did she *squeal?*

One arm around her waist, Jayce intensified the rhythm, the pressure, and Rocky's body responded—wanting more, needing more. They came as one and she swore she saw stars. Just like the first time. How sappy, but there it was. Freaking galactic stars. "You realize you've made matters worse," she managed as her heart thudded and the water pelted.

He held her close. "I'm not running from this, Rocky."

"You could at least slow down."

"You've kept me waiting long enough."

She turned in his arms, stared up into his hypnotic eyes. "What does that mean?"

He studied her long and hard. "Means I'm righting a wrong."

"Between you and Dev?"

"Between you and me."

Rocky froze, her mind and body still reeling from Jayce's erotic assault. "I don't want this."

Jayce, damn his gorgeous, naked self, caressed her cheek. "Yes. You do."

CHAPTER SIXTEEN

Luke had started skipping church as soon as he'd gotten his driver's license. Organized religion wasn't his thing. But he still tried to live life in a godly way and still treated Sunday as a special day—a day of reflection, relaxation, and good deeds. After a leisurely breakfast and some reflection, he'd settled on his good deed. Coaching his cousin Sam on the finer points of wooing a woman.

Maybe Luke should've called first, but that seemed sort of formal and he wanted this talk to be off-the-cuff. Natural. Two guys shooting the shit. Otherwise Sam might feel insulted. He was, after all, several years Luke's senior.

"I knocked at the house. You didn't answer, so I came around." Since Sam's truck was in the drive, Luke knew he was at home. Luke's cousin spent a lot of time in his spacious backyard and the pole barn he'd converted into an impressive workshop a few years back. Sure enough, there he was, surrounded by power tools and stacks of lumber, intent on some sort of blueprint for a new project. Luke moved in beside Sam and eyed the drawing. "What is that? A new jungle gym for Ben and Mina? Where are they anyway?"

"With Charlie and Sue."

Their maternal grandparents. Luke pocketed his keys, more certain than ever he was doing the right thing. Sam needed, *deserved,* to move on with his life. Amazing he'd gone two years without a woman. Luke hadn't had sex in three days and he was already twitchy.

Sam pulled a pencil from behind his ear, erased a couple of lines, and readjusted some measurements. "Building this for Sugar Tots."

Connecting with Rachel through her kids. "Beautiful." Luke smothered a pleased grin. "I mean, that's thoughtful."

"Rachel mentioned Gretchen's touchy about monetary contributions. She didn't say anything about actual equipment."

"Part swing set, part monkey bars, and fort. The kids will love this."

"Ben and Mina put in their two cents," Sam said with a proud smile.

"Miss those rug rats. Haven't seen them in a while."

"You should come around more often."

"Yeah, I should." Luke felt a rush of shame. He'd always looked up to Sam, hung on his coattails even, but then Paula had died and Sam had grown somber and remote. Luke had felt awkward, not knowing what to say or do. He'd spent a lot of time dodging one-on-ones, not that Sam was forthcoming with his personal feelings. Still, Luke could've been more present. Just in case.

Sam cut him a curious glance. "Why are you here now?"

"It's about last night," Luke blurted, feeling the urgent need to help his cousin pronto. "Your date with Rachel. I don't want you to be discouraged."

"Why would I be discouraged?"

He was kidding, right? "Not that I was watching—"

"Everyone watched. The pathetic widower and the timid day-care assistant. Will they or won't they? Sugar Creek's own reality show."

Well, hell.

Sam chucked his pencil and moved to a mini-fridge wedged under his workbench. "Beer?"

"Sure."

They twisted off the caps of the longnecks in tandem. Sam sat on an old pickle barrel. Luke plopped on a crate. He reveled in the taste of local ale, the smell of sawdust, and Sam's confident manner.

"All I know about Rachel is what I've learned through Cupcake Lovers meetings and events," Sam said. "Which isn't much. Part of the charm of the club is when everyone shares news about loved ones in the military or when they open up about some difficulty in their personal life or announce good news. We commiserate. We celebrate. And, naturally, we gossip. Some more than others. Rachel . . ." Sam shrugged. "She rarely speaks."

Luke raised a brow. "This from someone who's famous for being a man of few words."

"I participate. You'd be surprised."

"You like baking. *That* was a surprise."

Sam chugged beer, then grinned. "Who knew? Amazing what we learn about ourselves when we step out of our comfort zone."

"So what did you learn about yourself last night?" Luke asked. "Dating. That's out of your comfort zone, right?"

"I learned that I'm attracted to Rachel even more than I thought."

Huh. "No offense and no disrespect to Rachel, but what do you see in her?"

"A tortured soul."

"Sounds complicated and depressing. Wouldn't you rather be with an upbeat free spirit?"

"What? Like one of the Kelly twins? Blond, buxom, and giggly? No."

"There's a middle ground, you know. Take Chloe."

"Dev already did."

"Hypothetical," Luke said with a snort. "What about Casey Monahan?"

"Casey's great. You should give her a call."

"All right, all right. You're attracted to Rachel. I get it."

"Do you?"

Luke sipped beer and mulled that over. Was it the soldier in Sam? The desire to rescue a lost soul, to protect the vulnerable? Or was it because he hadn't been able to protect or save Paula from cancer?

"You're thinking too hard," Sam said with a teasing glint in his eye. "Here's the thing: Rachel may be damaged and repressed, but her actions hint of a warm nature. She's generous and kind. That's appealing. She isn't self-absorbed or shallow. Also appealing. And when she smiles . . ." Another shrug. "My heart does this funny jerk. I thought my heart was dead, Luke."

Shit. "So how did you leave things when you dropped her at home last night?"

"No good-night kiss, if that's what you're asking. It was awkward and tense, but I blame myself more than anything. Hell, it took me six months to ask her out, and even then I was prodded into it by Daisy. Rachel was put on the spot. We both were. There were expectations. That's a lot of pressure for the first date."

Luke raised a brow. "So there's going to be a second?"

"I asked. She said she'd think about it, which, in Rachel's very polite way, meant 'no.'"

"But you're not giving up."

"No."

"Do you have any common interests?"

"Kids and cupcakes. Plus, she's got a brother in the military. He's stationed in the Middle East."

"Know much about him?"

Sam shook his head. "I know she loves him and worries about him. Period."

Luke scratched his head, trying to think of a way to get Rachel to loosen up. "Rachel's only lived in Sugar Creek, what? A year?"

"Something like that."

"What do you know of her life before here?"

"Next to nothing. She doesn't talk about herself. When she does talk it's about Sugar Tots or Cupcake Lovers."

"Did she tell you Gretchen cut back her hours and that she asked me about a waitress position at the Shack?"

"No." Sam angled his head. "Did you hire her?"

"She seemed sort of desperate."

"That would be a yes."

"Maybe I could pry a little. Not that I'm bragging, but I'm pretty good with getting to know women."

"You are bragging, you arrogant shit," Sam said in a teasing tone. "But do me a favor and don't."

"She's friends with Casey, right? Maybe you could pump her—"

"I don't want to pry. Not like that."

"Then how—"

"Patience."

"I'm more of a go-getter myself. Man of action."

"I know." Sam's mouth quirked. "How's that going for you? As far as someone special?"

Now it was Luke's turn to shrug. "Guess you heard about Connie and Lizzie."

"Everyone heard. You know Sugar Creek. What I don't understand is why you broke off with Bridget."

"Because she thought she was special and she wasn't."

"But you broke one of your cardinal dating rules and spent the night with her. All night into the next morning."

"Heard that, too, did you?"

"Everyone heard."

Luke rolled his eyes. "I was exhausted due to a long dogged day, plus I had too much to drink."

"Ah. So instead of leading Bridget on, you ended the relationship." Sam toasted him with his half-empty bottle. "You may be a hound, Cuz, but you're a hound with a conscience."

"Thanks. I guess."

"Imagine if you directed all that charm on one woman."

"One woman couldn't take it."

Sam laughed.

Luke smiled. It was good to hear Sam laugh. Anxious for them to part on an up note, Luke polished off his beer and stood. "See you at Gram's for dinner?"

"Nah. The kids will be at their grandparents' until later

this evening. I want to take advantage of the free time and make as much progress on the jungle gym as I can."

Luke eyed the lumber and tools. He'd sort of tanked with the dating advice, but his heart was still in the "good deed" game. "Can I help?"

"Sure." Sam slapped him on the shoulder. "Just watch yourself with my buzz saw and don't cut off anything important. The women of Franklin County would never forgive me."

Smiling, Luke consulted the penciled drawing and listened to Sam's instruction, basking in their unexpected reconnection. More than ever Luke wanted to help his cousin in his quest to win over Rachel. "Patience, huh?"

Sam grinned. "It's not just a virtue; it's a secret weapon."

* * *

"What's wrong?"

"Nothing."

"You look tense."

"Just focused," Chloe lied. She was wound tighter than a trussed turkey.

Devlin moved in and massaged her shoulders as she cut two-inch rounds of biscuits and transferred the dough to a pan. "Can I help?"

Chloe smiled at his offer. Until he'd met her, the financial wiz and CEO of J.T. Monroe's Department Store had relied on ready-made foods and his microwave. Even now he was a bit of a menace in the kitchen. Not that she planned on booting him out. Daisy's home kitchen was enormous, a slice of deluxe-appliance heaven to Chloe and normally a place of bliss. Today, however, she was on edge.

Yes, she was relieved that Rocky had confided in Devlin about her teenage folly with Jayce, *hugely* relieved, and Chloe counted her lucky stars Devlin hadn't made a stink about her keeping Rocky's secret. But Chloe expected more fireworks from Rocky and Jayce, suspected a possible bomb from Daisy, and worried about whatever was brewing between Devlin and his dad. Not to mention her own personal potential crisis.

Stomach queasy, Chloe glanced over her shoulder at the man who lit up her life. "You can help by keeping me company. I've missed you."

Devlin wrapped his arms around her waist and pressed a kiss to her temple. "We'd be together more if you moved in with me."

"We've discussed this." Shoulders bolstered, she slipped Devlin's embrace and placed the biscuits in the oven, then returned to finish prepping the vegetable platter for Daisy's cocktail hour. Chloe had learned that fresh veggies helped to offset the zany or toxic flavor of her former employer's featured drink. "I need more time to prove that I can make it on my own," Chloe said. "Even living here with Daisy isn't ideal. Now that I'm no longer officially working for her, I should be paying some sort of rent, but she won't let me. I've been meaning to look for a place of my own, but between preparing for the opening of Moose-a-lotta and interviewing new companions for Daisy, I don't know where the time goes." She realized suddenly that her hands were trembling and her throat was tight.

Devlin grasped her shoulders and finessed her around and into his arms. "You've been working too hard."

She quirked a feeble smile. "This from a self-professed workaholic."

"I've been trying to cut back. But between J.T.'s, the Shack, and various other investments . . . Like you said, I don't know where the time goes." He stroked a thumb over her cheek. "Move in with me, Melon Girl, and we'll make the most of more time together."

Every time he called her that, Chloe regressed to the moment they'd initially bumped into each other at Oslow's General Store. Her pulse skipped as keenly now as the first time she looked up into his blueberry-blue eyes. "You're nothing if not persistent."

"And you're charmingly proud if not stubborn. Moving

in with me does not equate to taking advantage of me financially," Dev said.

"Would you let me pay rent?"

"You're my lover, not a boarder."

"I need to be a partner, Devlin. An equal partner."

"The house is paid for, honey. I can't take your money."

"What if I paid half of the utilities?"

"I don't feel right about that."

"Then I can't move in." She turned back to the raw vegetables and concentrated on slicing a cucumber. Yes, she was prideful, dammit. Her dad had funded her lifestyle for years and then Ryan—the man she'd mistakenly thought she'd had a future with. She'd moved straight out of his apartment into this house with Daisy. Moving into Devlin's house without contributing financially in any way *was* taking advantage and detrimental to her vow to take charge of her life. How did Devlin not see that?

He grasped her forearms, stilled her angry chopping. "Okay." He kissed the back of her head, held her close. "We'll figure out something. Divvy up the utilities, household chores. Whatever it takes. Partners."

Chloe's heart pounded and tears pricked her eyes. It was not as if Devlin had proposed marriage, but it felt just as romantic.

"Sure smells good in here." Nash Bentley, one of Devlin's many cousins, blew into the kitchen and ruined the moment. "Ham?"

Chloe caught Devlin's eye and mouthed, *Okay*. Then, basking in his beaming smile, she glanced over at Nash. "Baked ham with my special glaze."

"Can't wait," Nash said, then sighed. "Don't suppose there's any way to ensure Daisy's new companion has a culinary degree like you?"

"Sorry, but that's not a priority," Chloe said.

"Sunday dinners won't be the same," Nash complained while filching a beer from the fridge.

"Unless Daisy allows me to claim Sundays as my night to cook."

"Start of a new tradition," Devlin said. "I like the sound of that."

"Best news I've heard all week," Nash said, eyeing the triple chocolate cake cooling on the counter. "Speaking of news, how about Jayce moving back into town? What's he gonna do? Join the Sugar Creek police force? Even that would be boring compared to what he's used to."

"Wouldn't mind if he took Deputy Burke's place," Chloe mumbled as she arranged a colorful display of veggies and dip.

"Better yet," Nash said, "Sheriff Stone's up for reelection next month. If Jayce ran against him, he'd win for sure. Then we'd have one of our own keeping the Burkes in line. Father *and* son."

"Not a bad idea, but Jayce has other plans," Devlin said to Nash, then turned a troubled gaze on Chloe. "Did Billy hassle you again?"

"No, no. Haven't seen him in over a week," Chloe said, sorry she'd brought up the name. "He just . . . he gives me the creeps." Billy Burke, son of the mayor of Sugar Creek. Tasha's stepson. Tasha was closer to Billy's age than her husband's, which was sort of weird, but worse, Chloe had caught Billy leering at his stepmother in a wolfish way and Tasha flirting back. *That* was icky. Not to mention wrong. Billy, like Tasha, was married to someone else. Clearly he didn't take his vows seriously. Not long after Chloe had moved into town, Billy had felt her up during a supposedly official frisk—not that she'd been able to prove it. Still, Devlin believed her. The only reason he hadn't retaliated was because Chloe had begged him not to. The Burkes were in a position to make life difficult for the Monroes. She didn't want to stoke the family feud.

"Here." Chloe shoved the colorful vegetable platter into Nash's empty hand. "Take this into the living room, will you, please? Who else is here?"

"So far just me. Luke drove over to pick up Rocky, who, as you know, is temporarily without a license. Sam begged off. I think he's embarrassed about his bomb date with Rachel. The whole town's buzzing about that one. And Jayce isn't here yet."

"What about Vince?"

"Gram said he'll be a few minutes late."

"All right, well go out there and keep Daisy company," Chloe said while shooing Nash. "Otherwise she'll try to hobble in here and help."

"Or indulge in too many . . . What's the featured cocktail?" Devlin asked.

Nash grimaced. "Screaming Fuzzy Navel."

"Disgusting ingredient?" Chloe asked.

"Peach schnapps."

"That doesn't sound so bad."

"It does if you're a hard-core beer drinker." Scowling, Nash disappeared over the threshold with his bottled brew and the veggie tray.

"Sunday dinners are usually reserved for family," Devlin said.

Wary, Chloe moved to the stove to check on the simmering Potato Leek Soup. "Meaning?"

"Vince Redding isn't family."

Here we go. "No, but he's Daisy's friend. Monica and Leo occasionally attend. And what about me? I'm not family."

"You're as good as family," Devlin said, reaching into the fridge for a bottle of chilled wine. "Vince is . . ."

"A nice man."

"They've been seeing an awful lot of each other, Gram and Vince."

"You should be glad. He chauffeurs her around when I need to be at the café, and since she's being stubborn about hiring a new companion—"

"Okay, okay." Devlin passed Chloe a glass of chardonnay and smiled. "You win."

"I know you don't approve—"

"I'll be pleasant; I swear."

Chloe clinked her glass to his, then casually set it aside. "While we're on the subject of being pleasant," she said, "please go easy on Rocky and Jayce tonight."

"What do you mean?"

"Don't push. I know you want them to get along, as if nothing ever happened, as if you harbor no gripes about the . . . indiscretion and secret, but—"

"I won't push."

Chloe blinked. "Really?"

"I've got a new tactic where those two are concerned. Now that Jayce is living here they'll be forced to work out their differences. I'll just hover in the background, in case I need to step in and mediate."

Chloe's lip twitched. "I'm not sure hovering is much different than pushing."

"Big difference," Devlin said. "Trust me."

"What if working out their differences means getting together romantically?" Chloe asked. Rocky had made a Freudian slip during her tell-all meltdown. "Your sister will deny it, but she's still hung up on Jayce."

Devlin nodded. "She's got Jayce twisted up, too."

"He admitted that?"

"Jayce doesn't give up much, if anything, about his personal feelings. Let's just say I can read him. Most of the time," he added, then sipped wine.

"So if they hook up," Chloe ventured, "you're all right with that?"

"I just want them to be happy. Whatever that entails."

Enchanted by Devlin's devotion to family and friends, Chloe moved into his arms. "Is it any wonder that I love you, Devlin Monroe?"

"No wonder at all," he teased. "So when are you moving in?"

When Daisy hires a companion? When it feels right?

"Soon."

Blue eyes sparking, he leaned in and brushed his mouth over hers. "Maybe you could use some incentive."

"Maybe I could," Chloe said, then welcomed her lover's enticing kiss.

CHAPTER SEVENTEEN

"Are you sure nothing weird happened in New York?"

Rocky slid Luke a look as he steered his V-6 Explorer over the potted back road leading into Sugar Creek. "You mean aside from getting mugged by a thief and nicked by a car?"

"I can't believe you didn't tell Dev you got hit. As soon as he sees that bandage—"

"My bangs will cover it."

"I saw it."

"The wind blew my hair off of my face. There will be no wind inside Gram's house."

"Just a lot of hot air."

Rocky rolled her eyes. "Can we change the subject?"

"It's just that you look different. And I'm not talking about your new hairstyle. Or the relief you must feel after coming clean with Dev. You look . . . happy."

"You say that like I'm always a sourpuss."

"Not always, just lately. And not sour so much as, um, subdued."

"Depressed and cranky, you mean."

"Not that you haven't been entitled. Troubled finances. Tense relationships—Tasha, Adam, Jayce. A run of shitty luck with your Jeep, appliances, and house."

"Gee. To think I was in a good mood ten seconds ago."

"Anyone would be frustrated."

"In my defense, I think I've been optimistic and pleasant these last couple of weeks."

"Yeah, but then you spent a weekend with your two least favorite people—Tasha and Jayce. Dev said you flipped when Jayce told you he was moving home."

"Jayce's timing sucked, that's all."

"Nash said you were fuming the whole flight home. Now you're willingly attending a family dinner with Jayce? And what about the fallout from your confession to Dev? I mean, okay, Dev didn't rip your heads off. Still, things must be tense. Awkward. Can't blame me if I'm surprised by your good humor."

"I told you Jayce and I talked earlier today and agreed to mend bridges."

"Just like that?"

"Just like that." Cheeks burning with the lie, Rocky turned to look out the window. At her insistence, Jayce had left the Red Clover soon after their latest sex-a-pade. She hadn't been ready to discuss their past or present, or possible future. She couldn't think straight when he was around. Did she really want to pursue a sexual relationship with him? Yeah. She was pretty sure she did. Would it, *could it,* lead to something more serious? She didn't know. Their face-off in that New York hotel room was only one day old. Even though he'd tried to make peace, the verbally inflicted wounds were fresh. His shallow reaction when she'd confessed her bone-deep hurt regarding his "dutiful" proposal still stung. His parting jab regarding her *questionable* maturity rankled.

Yet she couldn't wait to see him again.

You're warped, Monroe.

Rocky took a deep breath and reminded herself to play it cool. Jayce had agreed not to make their current physical attraction public—not even to her family—until they'd had a day or two to adjust and decide whether or not the attraction was long-term or fleeting. Strictly sexual or compounded by genuine emotion. Rocky had never been in a serious romantic relationship. It wasn't a prospect she took lightly. Especially when it involved Jayce.

"For the record," Luke said, intruding on her thoughts, "I'm still pissed at Bello."

"Ancient history," Rocky reminded him. "Movin' on." Her new motto.

"Don't suppose moving on entails moving past Jayce and back to Adam."

Rocky frowned. "Adam's a nice guy—"

"Exactly."

"But not for me."

"Sorry to hear it," Luke said as he parked his rugged Explorer behind their big brother's luxury Escalade.

"Do me a favor and please be civil to Jayce," Rocky said. "I've had enough drama for one day."

"Civil. Got it. Movin' on." Luke tossed his sunglasses on the dash. "Do me a favor and go easy on the PDA. I'm not up for it yet."

"I don't do PDA," Rocky said, then tamped down a flutter of panic. What if Jayce looked at her all smoldery eyed and she got flustered thinking about the way he'd licked icing from her body? Or what if he said something that set her off and she blasted him regarding their issues? *Get a grip!* "How do I look?"

"I told you. Different. You might want to douse that glow."

"Get real." Still, Rocky stole a look in the visor mirror. *Did* she look different? Granted she'd fussed over her appearance more than she usually did, forgoing braids and opting for a half-up, half-down do, applying an extra coat of mascara, changing her clothes three times before settling on black jeans, a V-necked black tee, and the bright teal corduroy blazer and funky scarf she'd bought in New York. So she looked a little more polished than usual. She certainly was *not* glowing. Although she had to admit (to herself anyway) there was a giddy spring in her step. That last lovemaking session with Jayce had turned her inside out and hopeful. Maybe they did have a chance at a romantic relationship. Maybe it would work out.

Or maybe it would be a disaster.

"Earth to Rocky."

"Sorry." Nervous excitement surged through her blood. Reality check: Given all the rows and revelations over the past forty-eight hours, dinner *was* going to be tense and awkward. Rocky squared her shoulders and pushed open the car door. "Let's get this over with."

"The quicker the better."

* * *

Asking Rocky to decorate his house had been a spontaneous decision, but one that worked on several levels for Jayce. It would afford them time together based on a mutual cause, time to build and shape their relationship beyond the physical attraction. He'd be paying her for her services, which meant he'd be helping her financially without denting her pride. And she'd be instilling 241 Lark Lane with a sense of charm and comfort. It was up to Jayce to banish the ugly memories within those walls, but at least Rocky could pave the way superficially. Every room in her B and B screamed whimsy, nostalgia, and good taste, offering Jayce a dose of old-fashioned contentment. Even a touch of that in his parents' house would go a long way.

He got the same easy feeling the moment he pulled into Daisy Monroe's driveway. Stepping into the eccentric woman's three-story Colonial Revival was akin to leaping back in time for Jayce. Not just because of the antique furnishings and overabundance of nineteenth-century collectibles, but because of the wealth of memories the eclectic and cozy rooms inspired.

Growing up, he and Dev had been inseparable, so when Dev had visited his grandparents Jayce usually tailed along. Sunday dinners had been the highlight of many a week. A rotating guest list of the Monroes and extended relatives, including the McClouds and Bentleys. Charged conversation and a lot of laughs.

Although when he'd been alive, Daisy's husband, Jessup, hadn't been the source of ribald fun. A powerful town figure and head of J. T. Monroe's Department Store, the old man had been a stern, overbearing soul. All work, no play. Daisy had been reserved though kind. Jessup's death had affected her deeply and in a way that had surprised everyone, including Jayce. He'd expected her to wither and flounder, unable to navigate the world on her own. Just the opposite. Over the last few years, Daisy had blossomed into an outspoken free spirit. Her newfound sense of adventure extended to an outrageous wardrobe and accessories. The newest twist— purple hair. He'd managed to stifle his shock. Unfortunately, he'd had a more difficult time hiding his reaction when he'd tasted her version of a Screaming Fuzzy Navel. Running low on vodka, she'd substituted coconut rum. Fortunately, Chloe's amazing vegetable platter had purged the nastiness of that botched cocktail from his tongue.

For the most part, conversation over drinks and then on into dinner had flowed like old times, mostly due to Daisy and Nash. Those two were full of gossip and questions. Luke cast Jayce an occasional irritated look, and Chloe seemed a little uptight. Dev was in a surprisingly good mood, although he did tense every time Vince Redding treated Daisy with affection.

As for Rocky, instead of ignoring Jayce or keeping her distance, as had been her practice for the last several years, she'd conversed with him as easily as Nash. She even sat next to Jayce at the dinner table—a blessing and a curse. He knew she was working hard to keep the overall tone casual. It was all he could do not to reach under the table to squeeze her thigh in reassurance. Or to brush her loose curls over her shoulders every time they fell forward obstructing his view of her beautiful face. He ached to lean closer, to connect physically. But surely even the most innocent touch would betray his screaming lust for this woman. He sensed the same restrained passion in Rocky, saw it in her eyes—whenever she dared to meet his gaze. Granted, they'd agreed to allow the dust to settle on their past before making waves with the present. Still. How was it no one else noticed the sexual tension raging between them? No curious looks or ribbing. No prying. Talk remained focused on the success of Moose-a-lotta and Jayce's surprising move home.

"I don't get it," Daisy said. "How do you solve crimes on a computer?"

"It's a specialized service," Jayce explained. Daisy wasn't the only one seated around the table who'd looked confused when he'd announced his intention to open a cyberinvestigation agency. "Data breaches, identity theft, cyberstalking, asset tracing and recovery. I'm particularly interested in Internet defamation."

"Still lost," Daisy said as Vince loaded her plate with another potion of garlic mashed potatoes.

"Do you know what a blog is?" Jayce asked.

"Sure," Daisy said. "Chloe and I surf cooking blogs all the time."

His mouth quirked. Daisy Monroe, sporting Kool-Aid hair color and a geriatric boyfriend (if the gleam in Vince's eyes was any indication), texting and surfing the Net. Time had not stood still in Sugar Creek. "By targeting blogs, Web sites, e-mail, social media—"

"Places like Facebook and Twitter," Dev interjected.

"—an anonymous poster can bring a business to its knees or malign a person's reputation within minutes by spreading slander and false information across the cyberworld."

"Cyberbullies," Chloe said with a look of disgust. "You hear more about them every day. Especially those cases involving teens. More severe cases end up with the victim taking their own life."

"Suicide?" Daisy railed. "That's awful!"

"Agreed." Just one of the many injustices that pushed Jayce's buttons. "Other variations include scammers and corporate hackers. Part of my job will be to ID these attackers, assist in stopping them, and also devise a plan to permanently remove all damaging materials from the Internet."

"Sounds technically challenging," Luke said.

"Sounds noble," Daisy said with a righteous sniff.

"I'm with Luke," Rocky said. "Sounds like a severe deviation from standard detective work. Won't you need some sort of IT training?"

"What's IT?" Vince asked.

"Information Technology," Dev said. "Jayce completed a course several months ago."

Rocky glanced at her brother. "You knew about this career change?"

"Just about the new interest in computer science."

"Won't you miss the cloak-and-dagger stuff?" Nash asked Jayce. "You know. Tailing suspected adulterers. Bugging apartments. Sniffing out dirt on crooked politicians."

"As glamorous as it sounds, no." He'd had more than his fill of the tawdrier aspects of his former business. The day-to-day exposure to the senseless and heinous crimes of the big city had taken its toll. He'd grown cynical and unmotivated. Not that he'd been consciously aware until his friend Mrs. Watson had gently pointed out his increasingly pissy attitude over the last year. The first chime of his wake-up call.

"Not that it would be all that exciting," Nash said, "but I think you should run for town sheriff."

"Now there's an idea!" Daisy said. " 'Sheriff Bello.' I like the sound of that. Stability. Respectability. Plus you wouldn't have your nose up the Burkes' butts like Stone."

"Elections are next month," Nash added.

"The town would benefit from some new blood on the force," Dev said. "Not that I'm pushing," he added after a quick glance to Chloe.

Jayce felt the force of everyone's attention, including Rocky's. "The stability aspect is tempting." Especially for someone hoping to start a family. Health insurance. Pension. *Tend to your soul.* "But I think I can do more good on the outside."

"A do-gooder rebel," Rocky noted. "Interesting."

"Are cyberinvestigators in great demand?" Vince asked.

"The good ones are," Jayce said, pulling his attention away from Rocky's gorgeous face.

"Knowing you," Dev said, "you'll be one of the best."

"Man of many talents," Rocky said more to herself than anyone else, but everyone heard. It wasn't what she said so much as hint of a secret smile as she stirred sweetener into her iced tea.

That's when Jayce felt it. The first ripple of awkwardness.

* * *

Crap.

Rocky realized her mistake a second after the words escaped her mouth. She glanced up and saw Gram eyeing her with a bemused grin, saw Chloe rise a little too quickly from her seat.

"Almost time for dessert," Chloe said, shooting Rocky a perturbed look. "I'll put on the coffee. Excuse me."

Dev watched Chloe go, then looked back to Rocky, one brow raised.

Luke redirected the conversation with the worst segue of all time. "Speaking of injured reputations, I'm worried about Sam's. He's fast becoming the topic of conversation around town."

"The Eternal Widower." Nash shrugged when Luke glared. "Just sharing what I heard."

"There was talk at church," Daisy said in a conspiring tone. "Well, after church. Ethel heard it from Helen, who heard it from her cousin who dined at the Sugar Shack last night around the same time as our poor Sam and Rachel. She said they both looked miserable. No love match there, I'm afraid."

"I heard about it, too," Dev said to Luke. "Was it really that bad?"

"It was bad," Luke said. "But like Sam said, they were under a lot of pressure to hit it off. I spent the afternoon with him and—"

"I'll help Chloe with dessert and coffee." Desperate for a moment alone with the woman, Rocky gathered her plate and utensils.

"Don't you want to hear about this?" Nash asked.

"Luke filled me in on the ride over. Honestly," she snapped. "Why can't people mind their own business? So they got off on a bad foot. Doesn't mean they won't hit it off on the second try."

Another curious look from Dev.

Dammit!

Jayce's boot knocked against hers as if to say, *Easy, Dash.*

Smiling, Rocky stood. "Excuse me." It was all she could do not to sprint into the kitchen. As it was, she pushed through the door with a little too much zeal. "Are you mad at me?" she whispered to Chloe, who was in the process of grinding java beans.

"Why didn't you tell me you and Jayce slept together again?"

Rocky's cheeks burned. "Why would you think that? Are we that obvious?"

"So it's true. Happened in New York, I assume."

"And this morning at my place."

"So, it's like a thing? A serious, steady *affair?*"

"I don't know about the 'serious' part. Unless you mean serious sex. Adventurous sex. The kind—"

"I don't need details, Rocky." Chloe flipped the deluxe coffeemaker to Brew, then hustled toward the frosted cake on the counter.

"Why are you so pissed?"

"Because you're doing it again. You're fooling around with Jayce behind everyone's back. Behind *Devlin's* back. Why didn't you just tell him this morning when you came clean about the past? You and Jayce are an item."

Rocky's heart pounded. "It's not that simple. We may be hot for each other, but we may not be long-term. It's complicated, Chloe. Jayce is as good as family. If we pursue this and screw it up, it could be messy. Hard-to-live-with messy."

"I never took you, of all people, for a wimp," Chloe said. "And Jayce? I'm sorry. Family or not, I seriously wonder about his character."

Rocky gawked, stunned at her gentle friend's outburst.

Even if Rocky had wanted to push the issue, the booming voices from the dining room proved a distraction. Her heart pumped as dread flooded her entire being. "Oh no. Do you think Dev figured it out? Do you think—"

Chloe blew out of the kitchen and Rocky hurried after. It was Dev all right. Red faced and shouting at Gram, who was shouting right back. Luke and Vince kept trying to interrupt, which added to the chaos.

"What in heaven's name?" Chloe asked.

Panicked, Rocky dropped into her chair next to Jayce. "Is it—"

Jayce hushed her by squeezing her thigh. She was about to say *us*. Leaning in, voice low, he nodded toward their indignant host. "Daisy just dropped a bomb. Apparently, she's moving in with Vince."

CHAPTER EIGHTEEN

"Did you try calling Daisy?" Chloe asked as she came out of the bathroom toweling her hair dry.

Devlin, who was lounging on the bed in his sweats and a wrinkled tee, looked up from the publishing contract he'd been reviewing since yesterday. "Three times. No answer."

"Did you text?"

"*That* she answered. To quote: *I'm not talking to you. Buzz off.*"

Heartsick, Chloe sat on the edge of the mattress. "She told you to buzz off?"

"She texted me to buzz off. Swear to God, she's growing more eccentric by the day. How am I going to keep Dad from hearing this latest bit about Vince?"

"Why would you keep it from him?"

He glanced back to the multi-page contract. "Never mind."

"According to Monica, your dad tried to get Daisy to downsize years ago. Maybe he'll be thrilled about this move. A smaller house *and* someone to look after her."

"Dad's never been one to make a radical change on a whim. He's a planner and he's conservative. He'll see all sorts of complications, including lewd gossip. Have to say I'm with the old man on this one. If I can save him the aggravation—" Devlin broke off, worked his jaw. "Maybe Gram will change her mind after sleeping on it."

Chloe frowned. Why did he always tense up or shut down at the mention of his dad? She almost dreaded meeting the senior Monroe. Was he that much of a judgmental bastard? "It's not a whim, Devlin. Daisy meant it. She's moving in with Vince. Accept it. Get over it. Move on."

"What's gotten into you?"

"Why are you being such a prude?"

"We're talking about my grandmother, honey."

"A grown woman who deserves to be happy. Vince makes her happy. Which should make you happy, because the man dotes on her. He monitors her medication, drives her around, keeps her entertained, and tries to curb her reckless ways."

"Deserting her beautiful home, her family home, and risking scandal to move in with a man of modest means seems pretty reckless."

"I never realized you were a snob."

"I'm not a snob, Chloe. I'm logical and I'm concerned. If Vince had offered marriage that might be one thing, but—"

"He did."

"What?"

"He asked Daisy to marry him and she turned him down."

Devlin blinked. "Why didn't this come up at dinner? And why are you just now telling me?"

"Because Vince told me on the sly. He wanted me to know his intentions were honorable."

"Would've been nice if he would've told me."

"How could he? Between you and Daisy arguing like lunatics, he couldn't get in a complete sentence, and besides, the man has pride. Can't be easy to announce to the world that the woman you love rejected your proposal."

Devlin dragged a hand through his hair. "My seventy-five-year-old grandmother chose a friends-with-benefits arrangement over marriage."

Chloe snorted. "I don't think Daisy knows the true meaning of 'friends with benefits.' She hears these terms and uses them thinking she's being hip. She thinks of Vince as a friend and the benefit is his companionship."

"Not sex?"

"I haven't asked specifically. It's not something I really want to know. Besides, it's none of my business." She leveled him with a look. "Or yours."

He shook his head. "Can't wrap my mind around it. What if it doesn't work out?"

"What if it does?"

"What about the financial aspect? Will they pool their funds? Will he have access to her bank account? What about health insurance?"

"Can we sort that out later and focus on making peace?"

"Are you and I at war?"

"No, but you and Daisy are."

"While we're on the topic of friction," Devlin said, "what's going on between you and Rocky?"

They'd barely spoken to each other while hurriedly clearing the table, which was all they'd managed as far as cleaning up before Daisy had booted everyone, including Chloe, out for the night. "Surprised it took you this long to ask."

His lip quirked. "I didn't want to push."

Chloe appreciated Devlin's effort to lighten the mood, but it didn't help. "Let's just say that I'm puzzled by her furtive lifestyle. First Adam. Now Jayce."

"She's extremely private—"

"To the point of being deceptive."

Devlin angled his head. "I think she's scared. As independent as Rocky is, she's also old-fashioned. Committing and failing isn't an option, so she's treading lightly. Trust me, hon. Everyone in that room felt the attraction between my sister and Jayce. She's not deceiving anyone. Except maybe herself."

Again, Chloe marveled at Devlin's compassion. "Why can't you be that tolerant of Daisy's choices?"

"Good question."

Chloe pressed a hand to her queasy stomach. "I can't stand any more family drama."

"Sweetheart, this family is huge and . . . colorful, for lack of a better word. There will always be drama." He set aside the contract and opened his arms. "Come here."

Upset and exhausted, Chloe hooked the towel over a doorknob and crawled across the king-sized bed in her cotton pink jammies. Even a hot shower hadn't soothed her tense muscles. Her stomach hurt and her head ached. She snuggled against Devlin with a weary sigh. "So what do you think about the contract?" she asked by way of distraction. "Everything look legit?" Highlife had overnighted the paperwork for the Cupcake Lovers recipe book and Devlin had been assessing the details in his spare time.

"A lot of legalese, but yes, it looks legit. I'll have my lawyer look it over tomorrow morning, and if he agrees we'll sign." He smoothed a hand down her back. "Now back to what's troubling you."

A lot was troubling her. "I just want everyone to be happy."

"So do I."

"Then make peace with Daisy and her decision."

"How about if I promise to have a calm discussion with her and Vince concerning logistics?"

She blew out a breath. "That's something, I suppose. Just remember Daisy and Vince living together isn't much different from you and me living together and you're all for that."

He tensed, smoothed a thumb over her cheek. "You're still moving in, right?"

The vulnerable look in his eyes tugged at Chloe's heartstrings. She palmed his cheek. "I love you, Devlin. I want to be with you. Always."

"Good to know."

She smiled when he finessed her beneath him, reveled in the feel of his hard body, in the knowledge that he loved her heart and soul. Pulse skipping, she took a leap of faith. "When the dust settles a little, I'll make these overnighters permanent."

He raised a brow. "Considering the varied dramas just now—Gram and Vince, Rocky and Jayce, Sam and Rachel, Luke and his damned revolving door of waitresses—"

"You and your dad."

"That's a separate issue."

"But part of the sandstorm."

"Considering all that," he pressed on, "your timetable is pretty vague."

"It's the best I can do."

He smiled then. "At least it's a yes. You're moving in. Eventually."

She smiled back. "Yes."

*   *   *

"Are you alone?"

"It's one in the morning, Dash. What do you think?"

"I think someone's watching the house."

Jayce bolted upright in bed, switched on the bedside lamp. "The Red Clover?"

"I know it sounds crazy. It is crazy. It's just . . . I heard a car but didn't see any headlights and then there was silence and . . . I can't explain it. Sixth sense? Paranoia? I shouldn't have called. Jesus, I'm a mess."

"Are your doors locked?" he asked, stabbing his legs into a pair of jeans.

"They are now."

"Sit tight. Stay away from the windows. And for Christ's sake, if someone knocks, don't answer."

"But what if it's a traveler? This *is* a B and B."

"With a *Closed for Renovations* sign in the yard. Don't open the door. I'll be there in ten."

"It's a fifteen-, twenty-minute drive."

"See you in ten."

*   *   *

Rocky forced herself not to pace. She always paced or hurried about like a nitwit on speed when she was anxious. It had been her coping mechanism since she was a kid. Hence the reason Jayce had nicknamed her Dash.

Pacing, although the natural thing to do, would be stupid in this circumstance, making her a visible target if someone was prowling around and peeking through windows. She got that. So instead, she hunkered down in a corner of her darkened living room, behind her tarp-covered Queen Anne wingback chair, a cast-iron meat mallet in one hand, her phone in the other. Shivering with an inexplicable chill, she checked the time via her cell. Five minutes since she'd spoken to Jayce. It seemed like five days.

She kept telling herself she was being silly, childish. She'd lived in the country—alone except for when she had guests—for years. She'd never been nervous or scared. Tonight she'd been creeped out to the point of calling Jayce. Was her mind conjuring a sinister scenario to justify calling him just because she missed him? Just because they'd parted from Sunday dinner at Gram's without a private moment to talk? She hoped not, because that would be really pathetic.

After a restless night of cleaning her pantry, surfing the Net, then getting sucked into some campy vampire flick, Rocky had given up and gone to bed. Craving fresh air, she'd cracked open her bedroom window, and that's when she'd heard the sound of tires slowly crunching over gravel. That's when she'd gotten spooked. She would've blamed the movie, but it hadn't been scary, just stupid. And it was not like she'd heard flapping bat wings. She'd heard a car. An invisible car. The ominous feeling of being watched had been potent.

Socked foot jiggling, Rocky checked the time. Only one minute later than when she'd last checked. *Damn.* Maybe she should have flicked on every light in the house. Maybe she should've blasted the radio and every television. Instead, she'd gone into hiding, throwing the Red Clover into silence and shadows. She listened for any movement outside, but all she heard was the pounding of her own heart and the soft, thudding tick of a wound-up Victorian mantle clock.

Tick. Tock. Tick. Tock.

She couldn't take the suspense. She jammed her phone into the pocket of her zipped-up hoodie and, clenching her makeshift weapon, scurried to the living-room window on hands and knees. She'd just take a peek.

Riiiiiiing.

"Jesus!" She'd forgotten to turn the volume down on her phone. Back against the wall, chest heaving, Rocky looked at the screen. *Jayce.* "Where are you?" she asked in a brittle whisper.

"On property. Skirting the perimeter. Clear so far."

Naturally. Rocky thunked her palm to her forehead. "I feel like an idiot."

"Don't. There's something to be said for sixth sense and paranoia. I'm pulling around back. Let me in."

"Jayce—"

"Don't argue." He signed off.

Crap. Rocky rolled back her shoulders and forced herself to stand. Her knees wobbled. She told herself it was because she'd been tensed up for so long. Not because Jayce had come to her rescue. *Liar.* Would she ever outgrow her romantic vision of him?

The breath whooshed from her lungs when she heard the knock on her kitchen door. The same door he'd chased her through on that night of the terrible storm that had destroyed her sports shed. The same night he'd tackled her to save her from rushing into a dangerous situation. She'd hated and loved him for that. She flipped on the light over the stove and opened the door. "I'm sorry."

"I'm not." Jayce moved into her kitchen looking rumpled and dangerous. "Don't ever hesitate to call if you feel threatened, Rocky. Even if it's a salesman trying to sell you some souped-up vacuum."

She laughed at that, even though the laugh was shaky.

He grasped her forearms. "Tell me exactly what you saw, heard."

Ignoring the sensual tingle his touch inspired, she rattled off her tale, feeling more ridiculous with every word. "It could have been Dev or Luke, I guess. Checking up to make sure I was okay. Or to make sure you weren't here. I sort of botched dinner, after all."

"Your brothers wouldn't stoop to spying on you, Rocky. You know that. Dig deeper."

"So either I was hallucinating or someone was really stalking me. The latter makes no sense. So, what? Am I experiencing posttraumatic paranoia from that damned mugging? Or maybe my subconscious is doing a number on me. Guilt manifesting itself in threatening ways?"

Instead of commenting, Jayce locked the kitchen door. "I want to do a walk-through. You stay here."

Rocky stiffened. "You think someone's in the house?"

"Not really." He shot her a glance. "But better safe than sorry."

"Which is why I'm coming with you. Not partial to being a sitting duck, thank you." She'd cowered long enough behind that chair, dammit. Blood pumping, she raised her mallet in defense.

Jayce tugged her braid—a tender gesture that made her heart flutter—then flashed the shoulder holster under his coat. That freaking big semi-automatic would do a hell of a lot more damage than her gourmet cast-iron meat tenderizer.

"Yeah, well," she said with a nod to his gun. "I'm packing regardless."

He surprised her by grinning and smacking a kiss to her forehead before moving ahead into the sitting room.

Rocky's pulse raced as she shadowed Jayce. He flicked on light switches and she refused to allow him to shut them off as they progressed to the next room. This month's electric bill be hanged. Jayce moved confidently and effortlessly through the first floor and then the second and, in spite of the circumstance, Rocky found herself a little turned on. This man had been a cop and then a private detective. He'd faced down criminals and protected innocents. That was admirable. That was . . . hot.

"All clear."

She blinked, meat mallet poised. She felt embarrassed for lusting after him in a crisis situation, and stupid that it hadn't been a *real* crisis. "Better safe than sorry," she muttered.

"Absolutely." He squeezed her shoulder. "Stay here."

"Where are you going?"

"The Clover's lit up like a Christmas tree." He left her standing in her bedroom, backtracked through the second floor, then traipsed downstairs. He was shutting off the lights, which meant he thought she, *they*, were safe. So why was she still on edge?

Rocky placed the mallet on her bedside table, shook out her cramped hand. She crept to the partially opened window and peered into the darkness. Nothing sinister or eerie. Just the normal black of night.

"I imagined it, didn't I?" she asked as she sensed Jayce moving back into her bedroom.

"Maybe. Maybe not. Let's talk."

She turned and saw he'd nabbed two beers from her fridge. Which meant he was staying for at least one drink. Her tension eased. Assuming he was okay talking in her bedroom, the only room in the house aside from the kitchen that wasn't covered in tarp, Rocky crawled into bed with her beer.

Jayce shrugged out of his coat and draped his holstered gun over a chair. He settled in beside Rocky and crossed his feet at the ankles.

They were both clothed. Jeans and a wrinkled tee on Jayce. Rocky in her sweatpants and zippered hoodie. Only their shoulders touched. There was nothing inappropriate about Jayce lounging in her bed, yet her face burned red and her stomach fluttered. She nabbed the remote and turned on the television, surfed three channels until she landed on The History Channel. Some show about Medieval warfare. Nothing romantic about that.

Jayce stole the remote and thumbed down the sound. "What about the guys on the crew?"

"What?"

"The guys doing the renovations. Anyone overly friendly? Any lewd looks or remarks?"

"No."

"Did one of them ask you out? Anyone linger after the others were gone?"

"You think one of the construction guys rolled through

here with a pair of binoculars, hoping to catch a glimpse of me parading around naked or something?"

"I don't know what to think. Just fishing."

Rocky sipped beer, shrugged. "Some of the guys flirt. That's what guys do," she said matter-of factly. "But no one crossed the line and I sure as hell didn't encourage anyone."

"Don't bite my head off, Dash."

"Sorry. I feel foolish and I'm taking it out on you." She sipped more beer, then, cheeks hot, cut Jayce a glance. "You don't think it was a subliminal freak-out, do you? My mind playing tricks to get you over here even after I said we should play it cool?"

His mouth tilted with a wry smile. "That would be flattering, but that's not how you're built."

"Know me that well, do you?"

"Not as well as I'd like to."

"Just because we're good together in the sack doesn't mean we'd be good together in life."

"Chickenshit."

"I'm not . . ." She tamped down her temper. "You're a pain in my ass, Bello."

"You love it."

She did. She blew out a breath and cursed a mental blue streak as Jayce flipped channels and landed on Animal Planet. All sorts of gushy, mushy young-girl feelings flooded her body as he smiled at the sight of a couple of mutt dogs interacting with seniors in a rest home. She worried she'd never fallen out of love with Jayce. She worried she was hopelessly, passionately *in* love with Jayce. It scared the hell out of her, because she'd never wanted anything so bad and her greatest and grandest desires always seemed to flounder.

"About our fight," Jayce said, still focused on the screen.

"Which one?"

"The one in New York."

She cast him a suspicious look. "Which part?"

"The part about my proposal."

"And my immature reaction?" She blew out a breath.

"That was snarky. Sorry. You're right. Let's clear the air." Otherwise she'd harbor a grudge, which was detrimental to moving on.

"Until yesterday," Jayce said, holding her gaze, "I didn't realize you'd misconstrued my intentions."

Her back went up, but she willed an even tone. "I didn't misconstrue anything. You said, and I quote: '*We should get married.* 'Should' as in 'it's the right thing to do.' Dev married Janna out of honor and look how that turned out."

"Let's keep the focus on us, Dash. I know what I said that morning. I know what I didn't say. I confess I'd been blind to the depth of your infatuation, so the seduction took me by surprise. You, us together—how powerful it was blew my mind." He met her gaze. "The feelings you inspired knocked me on my ass. I may not have phrased it right, but I meant what I said. We should get married in that we'd be good together. As in I wanted to be with you. I sure as hell didn't want any other man to have you."

Heart pounding, Rocky stared. "The fact that I was underage had nothing to do with it?"

"Hell, yes, that factored in. It also mattered that you were, *are*, my best friend's sister. It was damned complicated and I was twisted up good." He reached over and wrapped his hand over hers. "But I never would have proposed solely out of duty. I cared about you too much to play false."

Cared, not loved. *Still*. Rocky knocked the back of her thick noggin against her headboard. "I feel like an idiot."

"Same here."

"Why didn't you say something before now?"

"You wouldn't let me."

Her entire body flushed with the truth of that simple statement. She'd shut him down, pushed him away . . . for thirteen years. "I don't know what to say."

"Say we've made peace with the past. Say you're ready to approach our attraction with a clean slate."

A clean slate sounded like heaven. Like somewhere she'd never been where the possibilities were endless. She flashed on Gram's reckless approach to life. Nothing ventured, nothing gained. *Chickenshit, my ass.* "I'm ready."

He kissed the back of her hand, winked. "Good."

Heart pounding, Rocky finished off her beer, set the bottle on her nightstand alongside the mallet. She felt flustered and wonderful and a little self-conscious. "So where do we go from here?"

"Forward."

"How's that work exactly?"

"We'll find out together."

She tingled with anticipation and, wow, *contentment?* "So this is us at peace, huh?"

Grinning, he sipped beer and squeezed her hand.

Her pulse raced. "I guess *something* good came out of my bizarre freak-out. Thank you for coming tonight, Jayce."

"I've seen too much to dismiss sixth sense, babe. Just because I didn't spot anyone, that doesn't mean someone wasn't there."

"It could've been two teens stealing away for a hookup for all I know. Why did I think the worst?"

Jayce didn't answer, but he did open his arms.

Rocky snuggled close. "Thanks for not making me feel like a paranoid twit."

He kissed the top of her head, flipped off the bedside light.

Together they watched some show about adoptable pit bulls.

Rocky thought about Jayce's devotion to homeless animals and his new commitment to combat cyberbullying. For as long as she'd known him he'd championed the underdog. For the first time ever she wondered what fueled that passion. Exhausted from the whirlwind day and content in the moment, she decided to pursue that discussion another time. Moving forward entailed more nights like this, right? Not to mention the time she'd be spending at his house. Transforming every room would take time. More than ever, she relished the challenge of making that stark house a warm home.

Rocky tugged at Jayce's collar, bade him to meet her gaze. "Feel like sleeping over?"

He smiled—a smile that wrapped around her heart and pumped through her system like freaking sunshine. Pulling her closer, he brushed a possessive kiss over her lips. "Thought you'd never ask."

CHAPTER NINETEEN

Rocky didn't remember falling asleep. She didn't hear Jayce leave, but when she woke up the feeble light of morning illuminated her room and he was gone. She remembered then that he'd said something about a 9:00 a.m. meeting. She glanced at her bedside clock.

9:45

For real? The construction crew would be here in fifteen minutes. *Get your lazy rear in gear, Monroe.* She never slept this late. Amazing she'd slept at all given her scare, but instead of having nightmares about a potential vampire stalker, she'd dreamed about puppy dogs and Jayce.

She looked to see if he'd left a note but didn't see anything. She checked her phone. He'd sent a text at 8:00 a.m.

CALL IF U NEED ME

She smiled and hugged the phone to her chest. A second later, she rolled her eyes. *Sap.*

Still wearing her sweats and a cami, Rocky rolled out of bed shivering as cold air brushed over her bare arms. She moved to the cracked open window to close out the chilly breeze. Dark clouds loomed, and thunder rumbled in the distance. Maybe the construction crew wouldn't come after all. Although there was plenty to keep them busy inside.

Flashing back to the night before, Rocky stared out at the vast lawn, the distant mountains, the nearby road. Everything looked normal. So why couldn't she shake that icky feeling of being watched?

"You're being ridiculous," she told herself. Still, maybe she'd forgo her run through the woods this morning. Running with the willies, dodging shadows, and enduring heart palpitations at every unexpected sound did not appeal. Not to mention a storm was brewing. Considering the late hour, she'd do better to shower and race over to the DMV in Pixley, replace her license, and . . . Rocky froze halfway to the shower. She couldn't race anywhere. Not on her own. Not without her driver's license.

Watch your ass, Rocky. I am.

She reeled with a troubling notion. Was it possible? Anything was possible, she supposed, but why would Billy spy on her? She hadn't thought to mention their run-in to Jayce because she'd pretty much pushed the incident from her mind. It's not like Billy hadn't had legal reason to pull her over. Her taillight *had* been broken. Knocked out, she assumed, by a careless driver in the airport parking lot. Not that she thought she deserved a ticket, but Billy had been a jerk to Rocky and her brothers ever since she could remember. Their dads were longtime rivals, and Billy had an inferiority complex that had manifested into shifty arrogance. She'd chalked up his *warning* to his normal dickhead behavior.

Just then her cell phone rang. Speaking of dickheads or, rather, *pinheads.* "Morning, Tasha."

"I need you to call everyone and schedule an emergency meeting of the Cupcake Lovers," she said in a rushed, hushed voice. "I'll touch down at Starlight around four. To be on the safe side, make it for five."

"What's going on?"

"I can't go into it right now. I'm in the middle of that cupcake tour with Brett. I slipped into the restroom to give you a heads-up."

"Are they canceling the book?"

"God, no. They're sending a video crew to shoot footage of the club in action. Footage for a documentary and a book trailer."

Rocky blinked. "We haven't signed the contract yet."

"Dev got it, right? Brett said Legal overnighted three copies."

"He got it and he's looking it over."

"I'm sure everything's fine. If not, he can haggle. Meanwhile Highlife wants to take advantage of our involvement with the Spookytown Spectacular. A small film crew's been booked to fly up and cover the event. There'll be interviews and random shots and . . . I'll fill everyone in when I get home."

Rocky's head spun. "I'm not sure everyone will be available on such short notice."

"Just gather as many members as you can. It's important."

"Why?"

"Because it's crucial I impress upon everyone the importance of being on our best behavior. Highlife thinks the Cupcakes Lovers are squeaky-clean, all-American do-gooders."

"Last I knew there weren't any ax killers in the club."

"Would you be serious?"

"I am."

"We, everyone, need to be on our best behavior. No bickering or backstabbing. No scandal. No freaking drama."

Rocky sank down on the bed. Drama like her possibly being stalked? By the town's deputy, no less? Drama like Monica not being able to conceive and suspecting Leo of having a roving eye? Or Chloe being ticked at Rocky for keeping her attraction to Jayce under wraps? Scandal like Gram getting ready to shack up with Vincent? "Well, hell."

"You see what I mean," Tasha said, still whispering. "We need to clean up our act. That includes you and me."

"Did hell just freeze over?"

"We don't have to be best buds; we just need to be civil. At least while the film crew's in town."

Rocky smirked. "You must want the deal even more than I thought."

"You have no idea. I have to go. Arrange the meeting. Text me the location."

Tasha disconnected, leaving Rocky with mixed feelings of dread and joy. Highlife's commitment to this project was impressive, and no doubt most of the members would be ecstatic about the potential rocket to fame. Nowadays who didn't want their slice of televised glory? Well, except maybe Rachel. However, having to police their personal lives . . . the thought was daunting, not to mention annoying.

Irritated, Rocky dialed Jayce.

"You okay?" he asked, answering midway through the first ring.

"Annoyed."

"At me?"

Her mouth twitched. "For once, no."

"What's up, Dash?" Jayce asked with a smile in his voice.

Squaring her shoulders, Rocky took what she hoped was a step forward in their relationship. "I need a favor."

* * *

"Is this a bad time?"

Luke glanced up from the inventory list to the woman peering in through his partially opened office door. The veil of dull blond hair hiding three-quarters of her face was a dead giveaway. *Rachel.*

"I knocked," she said in a tentative voice, "but when you didn't answer . . ."

"Sorry. I was concentrating." Trying to make sense out of the jumble of numbers and words in front of him. Distracted, Luke waved her inside his office without maintaining eye contact.

"Nell asked me to tell you that the delivery guy is getting impatient. He's only midway through his route and—"

"Like I don't have other obligations? Tell him I'll be right there," Luke snapped. "No, wait. Sorry, Rachel. Bad day." Chest tight, he passed her Pete's clipboard. "Do me a favor and rattle off the liquors and quantities listed while I find the damned file for the Sheffields' birthday party. It's a multitasking Monday."

Luke listened as Rachel quietly relayed the detailed list. She read quickly and with ease. He committed every word to focused thought. Meanwhile he rooted through a file cabinet, looking for the file that included all the anal details for Amy Sheffield's sixteenth birthday party even though he knew precisely where the file was.

When Rachel finished, Luke took back the clipboard and signed off at the bottom. "Ask Nell to tell Pete everything looks great. Sorry for the wait."

Rachel nodded, taking back the clipboard and leaving Luke's office without another word.

"Shit." Rattled, he sleeved sweat from his brow. Normally Anna signed off on these things, but she'd called in sick and her assistant, Danny, was running around the kitchen prepping to do the work of two people. When Anna wasn't available, Luke had been able to rely on Connie or one of his regular patrons to convey specifics. Amazing how creative he'd grown over the years. He almost always found a way to pass off anything involving reading in a way that didn't betray his dilemma. Mostly under the guise that he couldn't be bothered. He had other things to do. It was not like he couldn't read an inventory list or the phone book or e-mails or texts . . . it just took time. Time to sort out the letters and to make sense of the gibberish his eyes saw. Only today he'd been rushed and Rachel had caught the brunt of his frustration.

He blew out a breath when she rapped softly on the door and peeked back inside. "Pete said, *No problem.*"

"Thanks, Rachel. Sorry I bit your head off. Like I said, bad day." The glitch with the inventory list and his lead chef's absence were mere drops in the troubled waters. Rocky and Jayce. Gram and Vince. Dev and Chloe. Sam and Rachel. And what the hell was up with his parents? He would've thought that retiring to Florida would have been relaxing, yet whenever they spoke on the phone Luke sensed tension. As did Rocky. He was pretty sure Dev knew something that the rest of them didn't, although he pretended otherwise. Luke didn't press because he honestly didn't want to know if his parents were having marital problems. He wanted to believe they'd work it out. Meanwhile the rest of his love-struck family struggled with their issues right in front of his eyes. Last night's dinner had been a freakfest of repressed feelings, except for Gram, who'd let it all hang out. Currently free of any romantic entanglements himself, Luke felt compelled to make sure everyone skated through these awkward times unscathed. *A round of happily-ever-afters, please.*

"Maybe I should come back tomorrow. For training, I mean."

"What? Oh, that. I forgot." He caught a flicker of hurt in her eyes. Were they hazel or brown? He couldn't tell. She averted her gaze before he got a good look. "Not entirely," he clarified. "Lost track of the time. Let me show you around, describe the basics, and we'll take it from there."

Twenty minutes later and Luke had a deeper understanding of what his cousin saw in meek, mousy Rachel Lacey. She was smart. Whip smart. Kind and patient. Probably part of the reason she was so good with the kids at Sugar Tots. And when she smiled, she was sort of pretty in a bland vanilla way.

"Still interested in the job?" Luke asked.

"I think I can handle it. Do you?"

Was that a hint of sarcasm? He tempered a smile. Maybe not so meek after all. "We'll see."

"When do I start?"

"Let's go into my office and talk about a schedule. Want some coffee or a soda?"

"I'd love a beer."

Really? Not that he hadn't indulged in a drink before noon on occasion, but . . . "I thought you had to go straight to Sugar Tots."

"So did I," she said with a frown. "Gretchen called early this morning and said she'd miscalculated her new budget. Instead of cutting back my hours, she's cutting me loose."

"Oh, shit. I mean, sorry." *Shit.* "Surely she can't run the day-care center on her own."

"We, *she*, has a couple of loyal volunteers. Sugar Tots will get by."

"I didn't realize things were that bleak for the preschool."

"Yes, well . . . It's complicated."

Unsure what to say, Luke went with what he knew. "Domestic or imported?"

"Domestic is fine."

He nabbed two longnecks from the cooler. The way his day was going, he didn't mind joining her. "Glass?"

"I'm good. Thanks."

Huh. He twisted off the cap, handed her the chilled beer, then clinked his bottle to hers. "Welcome to the Sugar Shack."

"Here's hoping I last longer than a week."

As if he'd fire her on the heels of losing her other job. *You're stuck with her now, Monroe.* In tandem, they took a sip and then moved into his office. Luke sprawled in the chair behind his desk, whereas Rachel sat primly on the edge of the vintage sofa Rocky had picked up dirt cheap on one of her antiquing sprees. With Rachel and Luke alone together in his office, she seemed to fade a bit, turning in to herself. Gaze averted, shoulders hunched, the toes of those clunky suede boots turned inward. As if she was hiding from life. Considering her life as he knew it, he almost understood. He thought about Sam's impression of the woman. A tortured soul. Damaged and repressed. *What's your story, honey?*

"About my schedule," she said, fidgeting under Luke's scrutiny.

"Right." He swigged more beer, then set aside the bottle and studied the calendar on his desk. "I definitely need coverage on the weekends."

"Weekends are perfect."

"Not this weekend," Luke said. "Not for you. The Spookytown Spectacular runs Friday through Sunday."

"So?"

"Aren't you already committed to the Cupcake Lovers booth?"

"They can do without me."

"But that camera crew . . . Didn't you hear? Rocky told me Tasha called this morning. Said the publishing company's sending some freelance video crew to shoot footage for a documentary."

"So?"

"Don't you want to be in the video?"

"No."

"But you're a member of the Cupcake Lovers. A contributor to the recipe book."

"So?"

He was beginning to hate that word. "So don't you think you should be involved?"

"It's not about me. It's about the Cupcake Lovers, the club, and how the club's baking benefits the community, the military, and various charities."

"Yeah, but—"

"I don't mind missing the shoot, Luke. I'll square my absence with Rocky and she'll square it with the other members. I'd rather work. I need the money."

"Okay." He got that. She'd lost her other job. Her steady income. But hadn't she saved enough to sustain her for one week? Most young women these days would kill for a sliver of fame. Apparently Highlife was hoping this video would go viral, giving the Cupcake Lovers a leg up on instant popularity. Why was Rachel so adverse to exposure? Not too long ago, she'd bowed out of a group photo shoot. Was she that insecure about her looks? That shy? He understood self-esteem issues, but she was supersmart and kind. Why was she so damned antisocial? Aside from the Cupcake Lovers and Sugar Tots, she kept to herself. Luke was the exact opposite. What was life if you couldn't share it with others? Lots of others? Not to mention the Shack was known for its cheerful, easygoing, friendly atmosphere. Timid Rachel-stick-up-her-butt-Lacey was all wrong for this job, yet he kept that thought to himself. He'd never been one for turning his back on a person in need, plus he felt compelled to look after her for Sam's sake. "I'm strapped for help on the night shift."

"I don't mind working nights."

"It'll put a damper on your social life."

"I don't have a social life."

"Pretty sure Sam would like to change that." Okay. That came out of the blue and, seriously, it was none of his business, but Luke couldn't help meddling. Sam was crazy about Rachel, and Rachel . . . *Well, hell.* In spite of her issues, Luke sensed she'd make a great mom for Ben and Mina. He could see it. What he couldn't see was her happily, or successfully, waiting tables at the Shack.

She fidgeted on the sofa, fussed with her shapeless dress. "Sam's a nice guy. A really nice guy."

Luke raised a brow. "Just not your type?"

"Something like that."

What the hell *was* her type? Sam was former military. A successful independent furniture maker. A great dad and, like she said, a really nice guy. Good-looking, too, if you asked just about any female in town. And he baked freaking awesome cupcakes! How could she not be attracted to Luke's cousin? Unless . . . *Oh, hell.* Was Rachel gay? Not that there was anything wrong with that. *It's just . . . Wow. That would explain a lot.* Unless, she wasn't. Maybe there was no spark because Sam was radiating an *I'm-looking-for-a-mother-for-my-children* vibe or a *Let-me-save-you* vibe rather than an *I'm-looking-to-get-off-with-a-hot-chick, let-me-rock-your-world* vibe. Maybe Rachel was more interested in sex than commitment. One of those shy women who, once in bed, morphed into wildcat. Maybe if Sam were more aggressive . . .

"So about my schedule," Rachel prodded.

"Right." Luke cleared his throat, tapped his finger to the calendar. "How about Tuesday through Saturday? Night shift except on Thursday."

"Because of the weekly Cupcake Lovers meeting?"

"I may not belong to the club, but I support and believe in the cause."

"You're a good man, Luke."

"Not as good as Sam." *Way to sound confident, Monroe.* But it had slipped out and he'd meant it. Sam deserved Rachel's praise, not Luke.

"Tomorrow then." She stood looking as though she couldn't escape fast enough. "Thanks for the beer."

She'd barely touched it. "Sure." He stood as well, wishing he knew more about her. The more he knew, the more he could help Sam. "About your uniform—"

"I supply the black pants and white shirt. You supply the apron."

"Right. As for your hair—"

"A ponytail or bun, I assume. As long as it's off of my face, away from the food."

"Yeah. And, not that I'm recommending you going for slutty, but a formfitting top might invite bigger tips from the male customers. Smiling is good, too. For both genders."

"Not to mention good service."

Well, damn. "Absolutely." Luke stuffed his hands in his pockets, rocked back on his heels. "I'm sure you'll do fine."

"No, you're not. But I'll see you Tuesday anyway."

Luke blinked as the door shut between them. He'd never felt so inept with a woman in his life.

CHAPTER TWENTY

"Well, *that* was embarrassing." Rocky buckled herself into Jayce's car, then pushed back the hood of her rain jacket and slaked water from her face. She didn't need to look in the visor mirror to know her cheeks burned red. Being irritated with the man when he was doing her a favor by driving her to Pixley to get her license, in a sleet storm no less, was beyond petty, but dammit, he'd rattled her chains big-time.

"Just wanted to meet the guys working on your house."

"Meeting is one thing; scrutinizing is another." Rocky glared as Jayce raked wet hair from his obnoxiously gorgeous face. She cursed her fluttering heart. *Sap.* "Surprised you didn't ask them for character references."

"Didn't have to," he said, tweaking the windshield wipers as he pulled onto the road. "I got their names. The Internet will do the rest."

"You're going to poke into their lives?"

"Just peek around the fringes."

"There's something smarmy about invading someone's privacy."

"Not if it's for the greater good."

"So when you did that background check on Chloe . . . that was for the greater good?"

"It was meant to protect family, so, yeah."

Chilled from the icy rain, Rocky reached over and cranked

the heat a notch, telling herself to let that particular incident drop. Dev had had his reasons for asking Jayce to pry, and Chloe had forgiven them both. Dredging up old dirt was definitely petty. "Sorry. I know some people deserve to have their privacy invaded, especially those with wicked intent, like the cyber bullies you mentioned last night. But snooping into the lives of harmless folk—"

"There are plenty of people who appear innocuous yet, in private or on the sly, commit devious or sinister acts."

"That's pretty cynical."

"Life as I know it."

She thought back to when he'd pointed out the crime rate in Central Park—rapes, muggings, and murders. "Is that why you left the NYPD? Because of all the ugly stuff you saw?"

His lip twitched. "'Ugly stuff' covers a lot of ground, Dash. Saw plenty of ugly as a PI."

An opportune moment to gain insight on Jayce's life. The question she'd never asked. At least not directly. "Why did you leave the force, Jayce?"

"Too much out of my control."

An answer that blindsided. Control was Rocky's thing, not that she seemed to have much of it anymore. "Can you elaborate?"

He flexed his hands on the wheels and, for a moment, she thought he was going to refuse. Instead, he shrugged. "I hated being restricted by regulations and laws when it came to righting wrongs."

"If there's any truth to what's portrayed in television shows and movies, cops bend the rules all the time."

"Fine line between bending and breaking."

"So you threw up your hands and quit the game? Doesn't sound like you."

"You mean it doesn't sound like your romanticized version of me."

She focused on the windshield, the steady thwacking of the wipers. The slow thudding of her heart. All those years of secretly crushing on the man followed by thirteen years of pushing him away. Did she really know Jayce at all?

"Bottom line, I wasn't happy on the force, so I moved on. Tried to make a difference in my own way. Which worked okay for a while." He paused, gaining Rocky's full attention, then cut her an intense glance. "But then I wanted more."

Holy smokin' hell. The sexual vibes rolling off of the golden Adonis nearly melted Rocky into a puddle of raw desire. She wanted to jump his bones. She wanted to kiss him blind. Lethal moves considering he was navigating an icy mountain road.

Rattled, Rocky redirected the conversation. "Saturday night, when I was driving home from the airfield, Billy Burke pulled me over for a broken taillight. He gave me a ticket, warned me to watch my ass because he was."

"Son of a bitch."

"I thought it was just one of his stupid power plays, and maybe it was. I don't know that it was Billy lurking outside the Red Clover. I don't know that it was anyone. But my gut says I have nothing to fear from the men working their butts off to resurrect my B and B."

Jayce reached over and squeezed her hand. "That your way of telling me to snoop in another direction?"

His touch amped her physical awareness. Like her libido needed a boost. "Yeah. I guess it is."

Jayce continued to hold her hand, driving one-handed into the pelting rain. He stroked a thumb over her knuckles while seemingly deep in thought.

Rocky squirmed in the tense silence, her mind racing with erotic thoughts about Jayce rather than working the puzzle of her stalker. *If* she had a stalker.

"Billy's a spoiled rich kid," Jayce said matter-of-factly. "An insecure prick."

"I know."

"He's always been a prick."

"I know."

"Chances are this was just another case of him being a douche."

Now Rocky smiled. "I know." She interlaced her fingers with Jayce's. She'd never been big on holding hands. For the life of her, she couldn't understand why. Holding hands was intimate, intense. Squeezing her tingling thighs together, Rocky focused on the conversation. "Soon after Chloe moved to town, Billy pulled her and Gram over for reckless driving. Billy got fresh with Chloe during a frisk and Gram ratted him out to Sherriff Stone. Even though Stone didn't believe Gram, I'm pretty sure Billy holds a grudge. Also, Dev's trying to renovate and expand J.T.'s, which amplifies the power struggles between the Monroes and Burkes. Then there's Tasha."

"What about her?"

"Billy seems to dote on her. A lot of men do. She's like a walking sex magnet."

"Except most men lose interest when they get to know her."

"Her husband's still attentive."

"Randall Burke's self-absorbed and power hungry. Two peas in a pod."

"What if there are three peas in the pod?" Rocky voiced an ugly suspicion. "Chloe thinks Billy's sniffing after Tasha."

"That could get fifty shades of ugly."

"Tasha wouldn't fall for a cheating weasel like Billy. She wouldn't risk her high-profile marriage. But that doesn't mean she doesn't bask in Billy's adoration and that he wouldn't try to impress her by hassling her nemesis."

"You."

"Tasha and I have never gotten along. Ever. Plus, I pretty much got her demoted as president of Cupcake Lovers. She hates me for that. What if Billy's trying to get on her good side by hassling me, spooking me?"

"What if Tasha asked him to?"

Rocky crinkled her brow. She hadn't thought of that. "I suppose it's possible. Actually, I wouldn't be surprised. Tasha's not above a little warped revenge. Except . . . if that's the case then last night will be the end of it."

"Why do you say that?"

"Her phone call this morning. The film crew. She called

an end to any drama. Called a truce between us." Rocky rolled back her shoulders and smiled. Relief cut through the gloomy weather like a bolt of sunshine. "I feel so much better. I can't believe how freaked out I was last night over a prank. By Billy-the-Dickhead Burke, no less."

Jayce smiled, too, although the tender gesture failed to reach his eyes. "You're probably dead-on in your scenario, Dash."

"It's totally logical."

"Nevertheless, be aware of your surroundings and call me if you're troubled by anything at all."

"Maybe you should move in and be my private bodyguard," she teased. Only her voice was husky rather than sarcastic, making the jest sound more like an invitation. *Crap.*

"About that promise I made to you over the phone," he said, skating over her flub. "I don't mind trying to reason with Dev about Daisy and Vince. Avoiding a stink while that film crew's in town aside, I actually think Vince is good for your grandma. But, just so you know, I'll be bringing Dev up to speed on us as well."

Rocky squirmed. "Meaning?"

"I'm not willing to lie low for a test run."

Rocky got the reference and she flushed head to toe. Less than a month ago, Adam Brody had been her secret sex partner, although it wasn't much of a secret now since she'd spilled her guts to Chloe, Monica, Luke, and Dev. *And,* in a drunken moment, Jayce. She didn't feel guilty about Adam. Adam was a great guy; he just wasn't for her. *Jayce* was for her. He had always been for her. Now that he was within reach, she panicked. "So, what?" she asked with a nervous snort. "You wanna be my boyfriend?"

He felled her with a look that sent her heart flying from her chest. "It's a start."

CHAPTER TWENTY-ONE

By the time four o'clock rolled around and Rocky rolled her Jeep into a parking space across from Moose-a-lotta, she was in an insanely sunny mood even though the weather had been dismal all day. Instead of bursting into the café like a freaking fireball of joy, she relaxed against the seat and took a calming breath.

Yes, she'd spent an amazing afternoon antiquing with Jayce, getting a feel for his personal taste, and, yes, she'd been over the moon charmed when he'd stopped by an animal rescue shelter in Pixley to make a donation and to visit with the dogs. One mutt in particular, Brewster, had stolen Rocky's heart, and she'd instantly understood why Jayce donated his time and money to homeless animals. But the highlight of the afternoon was when Jayce had veered off into a wooded area where they'd made out in his car like two horny teenagers. What a ridiculous rush!

Still flushed from the spontaneous interlude, Rocky told herself to get a grip. She needed to ratchet her enthusiasm down a notch. She needed to relay this new development to Chloe and Monica in a nonchalant manner. Rocky was already on shaky ground with Chloe, and Monica was on shaky ground with Leo. Clearly it wasn't the best time for Rocky to tell her friends she was not only having amazing sex with the man of her dreams but that he'd also romanced her off her feet. Clearly it wasn't the time to gush. But she did have to break the news to them before they heard it from someone else. Jayce had made it clear: He wanted to date her—openly. He wanted to be her freaking *boyfriend*. Every time she thought about it she wanted to giggle or sigh or both. "Definite sap."

Just then she noticed Chloe flipping the sign on the door to *Closed*.

No more stalling.

Tossing her newly made keys into her new purse alongside her new wallet containing her new license and the replacement credit card that had come today in the mail, Rocky left her Jeep and crossed the puddled street. At least it had stopped raining.

Nearing Moose-a-lotta, she admired Gram and Chloe's new storefront. The green-and-yellow-striped awning, the custom logo painted on the sparkling plate-glass window. That cartoonish moose with its cat-eye glasses and chef's hat—a reflection of the owners' personalities—made Rocky smile every time. Gram and Chloe had transformed the takeaway confectionery, previously Gemma's Bakery, into an inviting hangout fairly quickly. Dev had offered support and advice on the business end. Rocky had recommended local eclectic shops and decorating advice. Luke and Sam had installed shelves, wall hangings, and such. But Gram and Chloe had been the idea people and had worked tirelessly pulling everything together. Prime location, cozy atmosphere, gourmet treats, flavored coffees, and the only public hang that offered wireless Internet access. Knowing Sugar Creek—the locals and tourists—Rocky had no doubt Moose-a-lotta would be a raging success. A popular and profitable business like the Sugar Shack and J. T. Monroe's Department Store.

The exact opposite of the Red Clover.

Shoving away that dismal thought, Rocky tapped on the glass.

Chloe peeked through the drawn blind, then opened the door and waved Rocky inside. "You're early."

"Hope you don't mind. I wanted a few minutes alone with you and Monica before the other members started trickling in. Thanks again for letting us meet here tonight."

"Seemed the easy solution given the short notice. That way no one had to clean their house in a frenzy. My pleasure."

Rocky skimmed the moderate-sized café—so unique—while reveling in the delectable scents. She'd seen Moose-a-lotta in progress, but the finished product was truly spectacular. "So you've been superbusy, huh?"

"Steady, but not overwhelmed—yet. In the high seasons, I fully expect to be hustling nonstop." Smiling now, Chloe unknotted her apron. "We definitely have to hire a couple of full-timers. Pretty sure Connie's coming on board. I can't impose on Monica to keep filling in when she's already got a part-time job, although she swears she doesn't mind."

"Where is Monica anyway?"

"In the back freshening up. Just as we were closing she bobbled a carton of chocolate milk. Her apron took the biggest hit. Still." Chloe shook her head. "Between the library and Moose-a-lotta she's taking on too many hours, but she said she needs time away from Leo." Chloe glanced toward the back hall. "Trying for a baby should bring two people closer together, not push them apart."

Rocky agreed. Also, it was not like Monica and Leo had been trying for all that long. Rocky didn't fully understand the strife between them, so she felt awkward commenting. "They'll work it out."

Eyes on the closed bathroom door, Chloe sighed. "I hope so."

"As long as we're alone . . . ," Rocky said, shrugging out of her coat. "Are you and I okay? Last night was awkward."

"I'll say."

"I'm sorry if I seemed cagey. It wasn't calculated. I just . . . everything's moving so fast. It's—"

"Scary?"

"A little."

"I understand."

"You do?"

Chloe nodded, sighed. "I overreacted last night. I've been stressed about the café, among other things. Hard to be objective when your wits are out of whack. Anyway, I can see where you'd want to tread lightly where Jayce is concerned. It's complicated."

Rocky nearly wilted with relief. "I've decided to go for it. Nothing ventured, nothing gained, right?"

"Now that's exciting news. Speaking of . . ." Chloe quirked a small smile. "Your brother asked me to move in with him."

Wow. Big honking step for Dev. "Did you say yes?"

"Not before dragging my feet a little. You're not the only one worried about things moving too fast."

"But you're going for it?"

Chloe smiled in earnest. "Life is short."

Just then a door clicked open. Rocky glanced to the bathroom. "Monica knows Jayce moved back, right?"

"Everyone knows. Apparently Jayce is a hometown hero of sorts."

"The onetime golden boy of Sugar Creek. A superjock in high school who was also supernice."

"A man of few words but huge gestures, Dev told me. Always looking out for others."

Rocky nodded; her pulse raced. Selfless and honorable. "Few were surprised when he moved away to fight big-city crime."

"Welcome home!" Monica called to Rocky from the back of the café. "Can you believe this bit about a video shoot?" she asked, smile wavering as she neared. "Am I interrupting something?"

"No," Rocky said. "I'm glad you're here. I just hope I can get this out before anyone else shows." She nabbed both women's hands and tugged them down alongside her on a love seat and chair. "About Jayce . . . Three weeks ago I dumped my private misery on you two and Luke in a moment of deranged weakness."

"You weren't deranged," Chloe said. "More like tortured."

"A lot tortured," Monica said.

"I want you to know I'm sensitive to the fact that I've made you my partners in crime, so to speak. Begging your confidence wasn't fair. I apologize."

"Apology accepted," Monica said.

Chloe nodded. "Absolutely."

"As you know, I filled Dev in, and as far as he's concerned, the past is in the past. I don't care if people, including my parents, find out that Jayce and I had an ancient fling, but I would like to keep the exact when private. Especially in light of the book deal."

"Not that we ever intended to gossip about your 'first time,'" Chloe said. "But how does Highlife figure in?"

"They're not only putting a rush on the production of our book; they're planning a media blitz over the next several months. Tasha said this video shoot is just the start."

"Wow," Monica said.

"What's that got to do with you and Jayce?" Chloe asked.

"This project is important to the members of the club and, as Tasha keeps preaching, if it takes off in a huge way, it will benefit our charitable causes and potentially Sugar Creek itself. As president of the club," Rocky said, "I can't afford a hint of scandal. Cupcake Lovers is supposed to represent small-town, all-American, old-fashioned values. Family. Tradition."

"I'm not sure your teenage seduction—an incident that took place thirteen years ago, mind you—constitutes a scandal," Chloe said.

"I disagree," Monica said. She glanced at her friend. "I've lived here longer than you. The jailbait issue. That qualifies. And the fact that it was Jayce . . . talk about grist for the gossip mill."

Rocky stood and paced as new thoughts took hold. "If Tasha found out, I could see her twisting this to get me to quit the club or to at least resign the presidency. Maybe I should beat her to the punch and step down on my own. For the good of the club."

"You're overreacting," Monica said. "Calm down."

"Tasha won't find out," Chloe said. "Seriously, Rocky.

Put the past out of your mind and focus on the now with Jayce. It's all good."

Monica raised a brow. "There's a 'now' with Jayce?"

Chloe cringed. "Oops."

Rocky smiled. "That's okay. It's not a secret. Or at least it won't be. Jayce is going to break it to Dev this evening."

"Break what to Dev?" Monica asked, perched on the edge of her seat and primed for juicy gossip.

Rocky plopped back down on her chair. "It started in New York," she said, trying to contain her girlish excitement. "In fact . . . We kind of hit it off."

Monica raised a brow. "Meaning you slept with him again?"

"It just sort of happened and it was amazing and, well, there's more."

Monica glanced at Chloe, and Chloe waggled her brows.

Rocky stifled a giddy squeal. "Jayce wants to see me. On a steady basis. As in dating. Exclusively."

"Wow. Zero to ninety in the blink of an eye."

"I have no idea where this, Jayce and I, is going."

"Who cares?" Monica said. "Enjoy the ride. That man is a hunk with a capital *H*."

"Do you think my moving in with Dev constitutes scandalous?" Chloe asked out of the blue.

"Only to someone with extremely conservative views," Monica said.

"Still it might be best to hold off until that film crew leaves town," Chloe said.

"What about Daisy moving in with Vince?" Monica asked. "When's that happening?"

Rocky and Chloe traded a look, shrugged. "They didn't say."

"Just so you know, we're all going to get the riot act from Tasha," Rocky said. "According to her, once that video crew shows up every Cupcake Lover needs to exemplify a wholesome image."

"That's rich," Chloe said. "Coming from a woman who flirts with her own stepson."

"I'll tell you one thing," Monica said. "I don't want the world to know my problems. No way am I risking some camera dude catching me on film boo-hooing about my inability to conceive or my husband's discontent. For the next week call me Miss Suzy Sunshine."

"Vince drove Daisy to the hospital a few hours ago for a checkup regarding her ankle and cast," Chloe said. "Devlin went along so they could all talk after. He's hoping to smooth things over and sort out this bit about Vince and Daisy moving in together. Said he'd fill me in tonight. A few minutes ago I got a text from Daisy saying her cast was off and her grandson wasn't a total stick-in-the-mud, just a pain in the patooty."

"So Dev made some sort of peace with Gram," Rocky said. "That's good. One less drama."

"I just want everyone to be happy," Chloe said with a quick glance at Monica.

Rocky quirked a pleading smile. "I'd be ecstatic if I could breeze through this week sans scandal."

"As long as you don't jump Jayce's bones in public," Monica teased, "you should be okay."

"I've never been one for public displays of affection, let alone flat-out exhibitionism. But I have to admit," Rocky said with a shy smile, "Jayce is awfully adventurous. Yesterday, when I was baking, he—"

"No details," Chloe said with an eye roll.

Monica gaped. "Are you kidding? Leo hasn't touched me in over two weeks. I can at least live vicariously through Rocky. Spill, hon."

Rocky glanced at her watch. If she hustled she could at least cover some highlights before the other members showed. Heart fluttering, she spilled like a smitten teen. "It all started when he asked me to dance on top of the Empire State Building. . . ."

CHAPTER TWENTY-TWO

Jayce breached the doors of J. T. Monroe's Department Store riding high on an afternoon spent with Rocky. Instead of dreading this scheduled meeting with Dev, Jayce looked forward to it. He needed to broach a couple of topics, but his relationship with Rocky topped the list.

Navigating the first floor and fondly remembering the various jobs he'd held at J.T.'s as a teen, Jayce smiled and returned the waves of a few familiar faces. He wasn't sure why Bert Hawkins, owner of a local sports store, gave him two thumbs-up, but Jayce nodded all the same. Just as he reached the stairway that led to Dev's second-floor office, the store's assistant manager stepped in his path. "How you doin', Chris?"

"Oh, you know. Same ol'." The man clapped his palm to Jayce's for a firm shake. "Heard you're back for good. Welcome home."

"Thanks."

"Also heard you're running for town sheriff."

Jayce frowned. "Where'd—"

An overhead speaker crackled, then screeched. "Manager needed in the shoe department," a young man's voice snapped. "Shoe-polish crisis."

"Sorry," Chris said. "A new hire. Gotta go." He rapped Jayce on the shoulder. "Just want you to know you've got my vote, Bello."

"But I'm not—" Jayce cursed as the man raced off. Distracted, Jayce hurried up the stairs and pushed inside Dev's office.

"Doesn't anyone knock anymore?" Dev asked, looking up from his desk.

"The door was cracked and you were expecting me." Jayce shoved a hand through his hair. "Just ran into Chris Bane."

"Not surprising since he works here."

"You tell him I was throwing my hat in the ring for sheriff?"

Dev shook his head.

"Well, someone did." He thought about the dinner conversation the night before. "Must've been Nash or Luke."

"Or Gram. Wouldn't put it past her to make it her personal mission to see you elected." Dev grinned. "She's keen on having one of our own on the force and you're qualified, my friend."

"Qualified, but not interested."

"For what it's worth, Stone's running unopposed."

"Still not interested."

Dev held up his hands in mock surrender, then waved Jayce into a seat.

Jayce felt the man's confusion. *Why so adamant?* He didn't want to get into it, but he felt he owed Dev an explanation, especially since Jayce wanted to pursue a long-term relationship with Rocky and, as Daisy had pointed out, as Sugar Creek's sheriff he'd have stability and a certain amount of power.

"When I first enrolled in that IT class," Jayce said, "it was simply to broaden my horizons. I'd grown bored with my job. Cynical. Thought about specializing in corporate investigations, advanced surveillance. Then a few months ago I had a visit from a teacher who claimed one of her students was being bullied at school. She suspected cyberbullying as well. Thirteen-year-old boy. Teased about being gay, although she wasn't sure that was even true. Came from a broken home. Alcoholic mother who cared more about her booze than her kid."

Dev shifted, making the connection.

"According to the teacher, the boy was severely depressed and she was worried. She'd heard rumors that a compromising photo was being distributed of the boy in a lewd sexual act. A doctored photo. Could I find out where it had originated from?" Jayce repressed a stab of remorse. "I never got to meet Calvin. He hanged himself the next day."

Dev dragged both hands down his face.

"I still did some investigating. Other than that teacher, Dev, Calvin pretty much fended for himself. Except he wasn't very good at it. Made me wonder. What if I hadn't been influenced by you and your family? What if I'd been less likable, less popular? What if, as a kid, I'd only had my parents to rely on?" His stomach clenched at the thought. "I could've ended up like Calvin. Or ended up a two-bit thug. Or a useless piece of shit."

"But you didn't."

"No, I didn't." He looked his friend in the eye. "It's important to me to help kids like Calvin and anyone else who's being bullied or persecuted in some way. No matter the family structure or support system. And that's just one facet of cyberinvestigations that I intend to explore. I'm good at it, Dev, and I can help a lot of people in a specialized way."

"If I can help you to get the business up and running in any way—"

"I'll let you know." Jayce relaxed against the chair, knowing that was Dev's way of saying he approved and trusting he wouldn't pry further. Jayce smiled a little, hoping to lighten the heavy tone. "That was damned exhausting."

Dev smiled a little, too. "Especially for someone who never shares his feelings. Anything else you want to get off your chest?"

"As a matter of fact . . . I need to talk to you about Rocky."

"Okay."

"About me and Rocky."

Holding Jayce's gaze, Dev dummed his fingers on his desk. "Wanna drink?"

"Couldn't hurt."

"Think I'll join you."

Jayce's mind raced as Dev moved to an old sidebar installed by Jessup Monroe more than fifty years before. Owned and operated by the Monroes for six generations, J. T. Monroe's Department Store brimmed with history, trivia, and assorted tales. Growing up alongside Dev, Jayce knew a good many of those tales by heart. He also knew that Dev was running this place more out of duty than passion. Jayce hoped he wasn't about to add to his friend's headaches.

Dev passed him a glass of scotch straight up. Then instead of settling back behind his desk, he pulled up a chair across from Jayce. "Shoot."

"I'm in love with your sister."

Dev stared.

"Shit." Nothing like easing into the discussion. Jayce downed the scotch in one swallow.

Dev followed suit.

"Yeah. Okay. *That* came out of left field."

"Does she know?" Dev asked.

"No. At least, it's not something I've verbalized."

Dev took their empty glasses, stood for a refill, and returned. "I knew there was something between you two—an attraction, chemistry—but this is serious."

"Not to revisit a taboo subject, but it was serious from the get-go."

"You're going to have to give me a minute."

"Take your time." Jayce sipped more scotch, reveling in the slow burn down his tight throat. He'd been living with this for thirteen years. He'd fallen in love with Rocky the moment she'd crawled into his bed. Yeah, he'd been young and randy and she'd been beautiful and naked, but the unexpected connection when he'd breached her cherry had gone beyond lust. She'd stirred his senses and soul. She'd ruined him for other women, and then she'd sent him packing. A seventeen-year-old smart-ass tomboy. His heart and pride had taken a lifelong hit. In hindsight he cursed himself for running instead of fighting. He cursed the young man who thought he didn't deserve Rocky Monroe. And all because of his parents.

Dev drank deeply, then blew out a breath. "Okay. So what's the deal?"

Jayce shook off the past, focused on now. On Rocky the twenty-nine-year-old smart-ass tomboy. "She agreed to see me exclusively."

"Forgive me for being blunt, but Rocky had a similar arrangement with Adam Brody not too long ago."

"I know about Brody. This is different."

"Because you love her." Dev rubbed the back of his neck. "She feel the same about you?"

"I think so, but it's not something we've discussed."

"Huh. So . . . what?"

"We date, officially, publicly, and take it from there."

Dev nodded, finished off his drink. "Okay."

"That's it? No reservations? No lectures? No threats?"

"What? Like hurt her and I hurt you? I assumed that was understood."

Jayce smiled at that. "My intentions are long-term, Dev."

"As in marriage?"

Jayce nodded.

"Jesus. Okay." Dev shook his head, smiled. "Good to know."

Jayce set aside the glass. "I didn't expect you to take it this well."

"Don't get me wrong; I'm still processing. And there are certain aspects of your relationship I don't care to dwell on."

"Smart."

"On the other hand, selfishly, I'm relieved. I worry about Rocky. She's had it tough with the Red Clover, and even with the renovations I'm not sure it will be a big money-maker. She's too independent for her own good and, swear to God, I can't think of many men in the area suited to her strong personality."

"Good to know."

"You're right," Dev said. "This was out of left field, but I think it's a good play. Easier to let go and move on with my own life knowing my sister's in the hands of the man I trust most. I'll try not to interfere and hope for long-term."

"You always interfere and I'll do my best."

Dev smiled. "At least you didn't call me a tight-assed buttinski like Gram."

"Speaking of your grandmother." Jayce finished off his scotch.

"I spent all afternoon mending that bridge."

"This mean you're okay with Daisy moving in with Vince?"

"Let's just say I have fewer reservations."

"Rocky asked me to speak with you regarding those two. She thinks you're being unreasonable."

"So does Chloe." Dev angled his head. "And you?"

Jayce shrugged. "Vince Redding's a good man."

"I know. And he's good to Gram. Good with her. Somehow he manages to keep her out of trouble. Since Gram's against hiring a new companion, someone has to monitor her reckless inclinations. Chloe's going to be moving in with me, so, hell, I guess Vince is a godsend."

"You asked Chloe to move in?"

"I'd marry her tomorrow if I thought she'd agree, but she's touchy about proving she can stand on her own two feet. Between that and the fact that we've known each other less than two months, the timing seems off."

"How do you pinpoint the right time?" Jayce asked. "To propose, I mean."

"No clue." Dev raised a brow. "If you figure it out before me, let me know."

* * *

"So that's the deal." Tasha, who'd been sitting rigid in one of the most comfy-looking chairs in the café, bolted to her designer heels and cinched the coat she'd never taken off.

Gram glared at the glossy woman through her blingy cat-eye glasses. "That's it? I interrupted my celebratory date with Vincent for a ten-minute lecture on decorum?"

Rocky, too, was surprised at their former president's brevity. She'd expected Tasha to relay the events of Friday's meeting with Highlife in nauseating detail, to brag about how she'd wowed the publicist, and to rub everyone's noses, especially Rocky's, in her private dinner with their editor as well as the personal tour of Manhattan's most popular cup-cake bakeries. Instead, Tasha had skated over the entire weekend, focusing on the arrival of the video crew and the importance of everyone being on their best behavior. During her fervent but short lecture, Tasha must've gotten five texts. Not that she replied, but she did glance at each incoming message, growing more agitated with every ping. Was it her husband checking up on her? A persistent Sugar Creek citizen vying for her attention? Tasha didn't have a lot of true friends, if any, but as she was the wife of the mayor her influence was often in high demand: *Could you speak at this function or support this cause?*

Another loud ping set off Ethel. "At the risk of sounding like a fuddy-duddy," the elder woman said, "from now on I think we should agree to silence all phone calls and *whatchamhoozits*—anything that dings, pings, sings, or rings—from all Cupcake Lover events. These constant interruptions are irritating."

"So is the fact that less than half of the members showed for an emergency meeting," Tasha snapped with an anxious glance at the door.

Rocky was in a hurry to leave, too. The sooner she got out of here, the sooner she could check in with Jayce regarding his meeting with Dev. Still, she felt obligated to fulfill her job as club president, which included defending the absent members. "Casey had an important business appointment," she told Tasha. "Sam—an after-school function for the kids. Judy's away visiting relatives, Helen's laid up with the flu, and Rachel bailed for personal reasons." She gestured to Chloe, Monica, Ethel, and Gram. "Not a bad turnout for last-minute, if you ask me."

"Don't worry," Monica said to Tasha. "We'll make sure

everyone knows"—she hooked her fingers in quotes—"*the deal.*"

"No drama," Ethel said.

"Models of Americana perfection," Chloe added.

"Stepford wives with a cupcake fetish." Monica snorted. "Having a hard time imagining Sam in a vintage dress, apron, and heels."

Ping!

"Dammit," Tasha grumbled.

"At least set your phone to vibrate," Chloe said.

"My phone vibrates?" Gram asked, digging into her purse. "That could be fun."

Chloe rolled her eyes.

"I have to go," Tasha said, making a beeline for the door. The other attending members gawked in her wake.

"She didn't give us any insight into Highlife's plans for that video," Ethel said.

"Do we get to see the finished product before Highlife takes it public?" Monica asked. "What if they edit it in a way that makes us seem ridiculous?"

"Yeah," Gram said. "I don't want to come off like a goofball."

This, Rocky thought, *from a purple-haired senior wearing blingy metallic glasses, crushed velvet overalls rolled up at the hems, and high-top sneakers decorated with colorful cupcakes.* The latter a gift from Vince to celebrate the removal of Gram's cast. "I don't think they'd show us in an unflattering light," Rocky said reasonably. "The goal is to push book sales."

Chloe raised a brow. "You do realize that a lot of people are attracted to train wrecks and freak shows, right?"

Rocky thought about the recent media blitz for a book written by a TV reality-show star. No doubt the pseudocelebrity considered her memoir a work of art while the rest of the world was drawn to her ludicrous lifestyle. Rocky envisioned Highlife twisting her own life to boost sales and shot out of her seat. "I'll get more info."

While she strode to the door, Gram launched into a story about Dev and Vince and her impending move, something she'd kept to herself while Tasha had been preaching the importance of no scandal, no drama, no bickering. Rocky wanted to hear more but needed to nail a pinhead. She hit the street, looked right and left, spotting Tasha a half a block down and striding toward a patrol car on the corner. Billy stepped out, and Rocky slinked back. She watched a tense exchange between stepmom and son, frowning when they both climbed into the patrol car. What the hell was going on between those two?

The car drove off, and Rocky succumbed to a spontaneous itch. She scrambled to her Jeep and gave chase. Following at a discreet distance, she dialed Chloe. "Yeah, it's me. Listen, Tasha took off before I could nab her. I'll get more answers when I can, but for now I need to follow up on something else. Sorry to bail. Make my apologies to the girls? . . . Thanks."

She signed off and texted Jayce.

CAN U TALK?

A heartbeat later, he called. "What's up, Dash?"

She didn't think he'd appreciate knowing she was tailing her nemesis and the man who'd possibly stalked her, so she glommed on to another thought. "Gram said you're running for sheriff." Just one of the things the purple-haired woman had gossiped about before Tasha had launched into her lecture. "Did you change your mind? What about your cyber detective agency?" *Why didn't you tell me?*

"JB Investigations is still a go," he said, sounding a little hassled. "I have no intention of running for sheriff."

"Wishful thinking on Gram's part," Rocky assumed. "Unfortunately, rumors spread like wildfire around here."

"I know."

"Don't be surprised if you get a call from Sheriff Stone. Probably shaking in his boots at the thought of competing with you."

"We've already had that discussion," Jayce said.

"Really? Wow." Rocky focused on Billy Burke's cherry top, three cars ahead of her now. "Wonder if Deputy Dickhead got wind of that rumor yet?"

"Seems like everyone's gotten wind. Speaking of discussions, I spoke with your brother."

Rocky perked up big-time.

"And?"

"He was surprised but not opposed to us seeing one another."

"He didn't flip out? Or read you the riot act? Or—"

"We have his blessing."

"Why don't I feel good about that?"

"Because you're a pessimist."

Her back went up. "No, I'm not."

"Where you and I are concerned, yeah, hon, you are."

She couldn't tell if he was teasing or chastising her. Focused on the distant cruiser and grateful for moderate traffic enabling her to blend, Rocky fidgeted with her seat belt. Part of her itched to pick a fight. It was so much easier to manage her vulnerable heart when she was angry and riled. Instead, she took what she hoped was the more mature route and, even though he couldn't see her, slapped on a happy face. "On second thought, might as well enjoy Dev's blessing."

"That your way of asking me for a date?"

Detecting humor in his voice, Rocky rallied. "I've never been one for dating, per se. Movies, dinner, dancing. Canoodling in public."

"Canoodling?"

"Gram's word, not mine, but you get the picture."

"Not a fan of PDA."

"That and . . . I'm just not, I don't know, a girly girl. I think Luke got the last of the Monroes' romantic genes."

"What about bowling?"

"You're missing my point."

"No, I'm not, but I'll compromise. Canoodling in private. A picnic."

"Seriously?" She couldn't decide which was more out of

character—Jayce using the word "canoodling" or alpha man plopping down on a blanket for fried chicken and coleslaw. Neither one fit her picture of him, but both made her smile.

"Weather's supposed to turn nice tomorrow," he said. "We'll spend the afternoon at Willow Bend."

A woodsy spot on the river. She knew it well. Willow Bend had been a popular hangout for the Monroe family for eons. It was not that she was against an intimate picnic with Jayce, but tomorrow seemed a lifetime away. "What's wrong with tonight? A moonlight . . ." *Oh, crap.* "You know what? Never mind." Rocky scrambled to backtrack, realizing she'd sounded jealous or needy or something. "Just remembered I'm busy tonight."

"Me, too."

Doing what? she wanted to ask, but didn't. "It's settled then."

"You mean it's a date."

The man was teasing her. She tried not to smile and failed. "Whatever. Tomorrow it is. A picnic, huh? I'll pack a basket."

"Just tackle dessert. I'll handle the rest. By the way, Dash," he said in a sexy drawl, "do me a favor and peel off into Maple Molly's before you blow my surveillance."

The monstrous antique barn where Rocky frequently shopped loomed a quarter mile ahead. How did Jayce know . . . *Wait. Surveillance?* "You're tailing Billy?" Stunned, Rocky squinted at the two cars between her and the cruiser, then glanced in her rearview mirror. "Where are you? I don't see you."

"That's the idea, babe. On the other hand, I see you, or rather your Jeep, and unless Billy is a total moron, he'll make you, too. If he hasn't already. Peel off."

"Dammit, Jayce."

"I'll fill you in later."

He disconnected and, gritting her teeth, Rocky slowed and made a left into Maple Molly's. If Billy *had* spotted her, he'd assume she'd headed this way on a bargain hunt. He'd continue on to wherever with Tasha, clueless of being tailed by Jayce, because Jayce was a professional and damned good at his job. Rocky still had no idea what he was driving or where he was exactly. The irritation she'd felt because he had busted her and ordered her away gave way to admiration. And appreciation. He'd taken her concerns about Billy seriously and was following up. If Billy and Tasha were involved in a seedy affair or maybe plotting to make Rocky's life hell, Jayce would find out and report to Rocky. What exactly she'd do with that knowledge she didn't know. This moment, she couldn't think beyond the sexy fact that Jayce was looking out for her.

Suppressing a besotted sigh, Rocky breached the sliding doors of Maple Molly's Antique Barn. God, Rocky loved this place. As always, she marveled at the rows and levels of eclectic and retro furnishings, carpets, lighting, and collectibles. Some of the stock dated back to the eighteenth and nineteenth centuries. The more kitschy items originated in the 1920s through '60s. She could practically smell the history. She thought about Jayce's semi-refurbished home—a rustic chalet that lacked warmth and charm—and the fact that he'd hired her as an interior decorator. As long as she was here and now that she had a feel for his taste, no harm in scouting out some unique and functional treasures. High on the thought of working magic on her *boyfriend's* house, Rocky immersed herself in antiquing heaven.

CHAPTER TWENTY-THREE

"You're not going to believe the day I had."

Chloe sat cross-legged in the center of Devlin's leather sofa watching the love of her life striding into his living room. So handsome, so confident, so intense. Normally she would have risen to welcome him home. A kiss. A hug. Instead, she sat frozen with misery. "Daisy told me you're warming to the idea of her moving in with Vince," Chloe said in a brittle voice.

"Warming is an exaggeration," Devlin said while slipping off his coat. "But I do see some advantages."

"And from something Rocky said I assume Jayce spoke to you about their relationship?"

"At odds for thirteen years and now they're a damned item. Can you believe it?" Devlin jammed a hand through thick brown hair and dropped down on the sofa next to her. "I have to admit, I'm thrilled. As long as they don't blow it."

"Two strong personalities. Probably lots of fireworks along the way, but I think they'll make it." Chloe tried to smile and failed. Her stomach twisted with her own surprising news. She'd suspected but hadn't known for certain until a half hour ago. Home testing wasn't 100 percent accurate, but she knew in her heart she'd screwed up. As always, when driven by passion, she'd been reckless. She hated that she wasn't happy about this unexpected turn. She *wanted* to be happy, but there were too many issues at play. Surely there was a rainbow beyond the thick fog of complications. If only she could catch a glimpse.

"What's wrong?"

"What?"

"You're distracted."

Obsessed with her own dilemma, Chloe couldn't get past the knowledge that Devlin had been down this pregnancy road before. The difference between her and his high-school sweetheart was that Chloe wasn't looking to be saved. Knowing Devlin, she assumed he'd step up, again, and do the honorable thing. Chloe finally understood why Rocky had been so crushed when she'd thought Jayce had proposed out of a sense of duty. Marrying because it was "the right thing to do" battered Chloe's romantic sensibilities, not to mention her self-esteem.

Blue eyes sparking with concern, Devlin smoothed her hair from her flushed face. "I burst in here rambling about my surprising day and obviously something went wrong with yours. Whatever it is," he said with a troubled smile, "it can't be that bad."

Chloe burst into tears.

"What the—"

"I'm sorry."

"For what?"

"The . . . the timing couldn't be . . . be worse." Tears turned into sobs as her mind fixated on the cruel twist of fate. "I . . . I haven't even met . . ."—*hiccup*—"your parents."

"What do my parents—"

"Then there's Daisy and Moose-a . . . Moose-a-lotta. How will I . . . and then there's *you!*" She doubled over with tears and frets, fought to catch her breath.

Devlin pulled her onto his lap, into his arms. "Chloe, hon, calm down. Tell me what's wrong. Whatever it is, I'll fix it."

It was exactly the wrong thing to say. Sick to her stomach, Chloe pushed up and away and bolted for the bathroom. By the time Devlin caught up, she was on her knees, puking into the toilet. Add mortification to her list of miseries.

Instead of pummeling her with questions, Devlin soaked a washrag and pressed the cold cloth to her forehead while holding back her hair. Chloe struggled for calm, absorbed his quiet strength. Nervous stomach purged, she pushed to shaky legs, welcoming Devlin's support as she rinsed her clammy face and washed out her mouth.

"Better?" he asked, one arm around her middle.

"You can't fix this, Devlin."

"Let me be the judge of that." He finessed her around and framed her face with cool, steady hands. "What's wrong?"

"I'm pregnant. I think. I'm pretty sure. According to a home test." The words came out stilted, but at least they came out.

He blinked, then dragged a hand through his hair. "Another lob from left field."

"I haven't been feeling well," she plowed on, "and I've been irritable. I thought I was overly tired. Stressed about the opening of Moose-a-lotta. But then I was late. Really late and I suspected but . . . I sort of went into denial. Until today. I stopped at the drugstore hoping to ease my mind, erase the possibility, but then it showed positive and there was no erasing—just panic." She realized suddenly that she was wringing her hands and that Devlin was staring. "Are you angry? Disappointed? Shocked? Why aren't you saying anything?"

"I'm trying to figure out why you're so upset."

"It should be obvious."

"You don't want children?"

"Of course I want children. Absolutely. I just . . . the circumstances." She swallowed hard, licked her lips. "Aren't you going to ask me if it's yours?"

"Why would I ask you that, Chloe?"

"Because as of two months ago, I was living with another man."

"And since then you've been with me."

"So you'll accept the baby as yours whether it is or not. Just like with Janna."

His expression hardened. "You're nothing like Janna.

We've been through this." He shook his head, pressed a kiss to her forehead, then guided her into the living room, back onto the couch. "How far along are you?"

"I don't know for sure, but I'm several weeks late."

"Weeks." He smiled a little, brushed his thumb over her palm. "Sweetheart, the baby's definitely mine."

"I know that. I'm so sorry."

"I really wish you'd stop apologizing."

"What will your parents say?"

"You mean after, *Finally. A grandchild?*"

"How can you joke?" she snapped.

"I'm not making light. I'm . . . sorry, but I'm thrilled. I wish you felt the same. What's the problem here, Chloe? Are you worried about gossip? The fact we're not married? I—"

"Don't say it." She stiffened her spine and knotted her hair. "Don't propose just because—"

"There is no *just because.* I love you. I want to spend my life with you. Share a home. A family."

Fresh tears burned her eyes. "I don't want it to be like this. How it was with her. I don't want to repeat your past or my penchant for failure. I'm trying not to be superstitious, but . . ."

Devlin's expression softened. "You're not going to lose this baby, honey."

"You can't know that. Janna was five months along when she . . . Anything could happen. I've spent a lifetime screwing up. Bad timing. Bad luck."

"This is different. You're different. You've changed and so have I. You're going to have a beautiful healthy baby and I'm going to drive you crazy because I will, I promise, smother you both with love and protection." He stroked a thumb over her cheek, smiled. "Whether you marry me or not."

Her racing heart bloomed. "It's not that I don't want to."

"It's just that you'd rather wait."

Until she'd had the baby. Until she was certain she wasn't reliving his first wife's fate. Chloe also wanted more time to nurture her relationship with Devlin. She didn't want either one of them to feel pressured into marriage. When he proposed and when she accepted, she wanted it to be solely from the heart and not bound to honor or obligation.

"Be warned," Devlin said, holding her close. "I'd wait a lifetime for you."

She took comfort in his arms, in the slow, hard thud of his big-as-the-world heart. "I won't make you wait that long."

"Thank God." He smoothed his hand down her back. "What do you say we move past shock and worry to optimistically joyous?"

"Monica's going to be crushed."

"Mmm. Probably. At first anyway. But she'll get past it, Chloe."

"I'm not so sure. She's obsessed with having a baby. So much so, she's driving Leo away, which doesn't help her cause. What if she ends up alone and I get her happily-ever-after? What if—"

"What if you think positive? Have more faith in Monica and Leo. In your friendship."

"What about Moose-a-lotta? Daisy and I just launched the business. I don't want to give up our dream, but I don't want to be an absentee mom either."

"We'll work it out."

She glanced up at the man who was famous for trying to control the lives of friends and family. "We?"

"We're in this together." He bade her to meet his gaze, raised a brow. "Any other concerns, problems, or beasts you'd like me to slay? I'm feeling pretty invincible just now."

Charmed, Chloe practically wilted with relief. "You're really happy about this, aren't you?"

"Second-best day of my life."

Her lip twitched. "Best day being?"

"The day you scrambled on your hands and knees for my pork 'n' beans and grabbed my sausage."

"You say the most romantic things." She smiled, thinking about the first time they'd met. The first time they'd kissed. The first time they'd made love. And the night they'd been so hot for each other they'd slipped up on birth control.

Hopelessly in love, Chloe closed her eyes and settled into Devlin's embrace, into their future. Things weren't perfect, but they were certainly looking up. All she had to do was weather Monica's envy. Chloe's heart sang at the glimpse of a rainbow.

Devlin traced a thumb over her sudden smile. "Optimistically joyful?"

"Second-best day of my life."

CHAPTER TWENTY-FOUR

Rocky's spontaneous visit to Maple Molly's had been fortuitous on many levels. She'd not only reserved a few items for Jayce's house; she'd scored a lead on another decorating job as well. According to Molly, a wealthy businesswoman from California had purchased the old Rothwell property as a vacation home and, while trolling for antiques, the woman had intimated the need for a local decorator. Most people refused to step foot in that turn-of-the-century farmhouse given its reputation for being haunted. Rocky wasn't most people. She'd snuck into that old house a few times when she was a kid, enchanted by the multiple rooms and unique design and, okay, jazzed about the possibility of seeing a ghost. The prospect of decorating that creepy old place gave Rocky the shivers, but in a good way.

Intrigued, she'd spent the ride home contemplating the future. She'd never considered a career outside of running the Red Clover, and though the B and B was still her primary concern, Rocky couldn't shake the thrill of branching out. The challenge was invigorating. She wondered if Jayce had gotten that same rush when he'd first considered launching his cyber detective agency. She itched to pick his brain but had refrained from calling since he was *on the job*.

Two hours after they'd last spoken, Jayce finally called.

"Billy drove Tasha home. The long way around, but they didn't stop anywhere."

"Maybe he spotted you following and they nixed their plans."

"Maybe. But I don't think so."

"Then why the out-of-the-way drive?"

"Privacy to talk?"

"About what?" After navigating her darkened yard, Rocky took refuge under the porch light. She wedged her phone between her ear and shoulder as she unlocked her front door while balancing an antique hand-painted globe lamp on her hip. Although she'd been scouring Molly's with Jayce in mind, Rocky had been unable to resist a bargain buy for herself—or rather her Monarch guest room. "Do you think they're plotting something behind Randall's back? Or plotting to advance his career in some devious way? Increased fame and fortune for the Burkes, maybe through the Cupcake Lovers book deal? That would be so like Tasha and Billy. Conspiring for their own gain."

"I don't have enough information to offer a concrete opinion. But I can tell you this: Billy's wife filed for divorce."

Rocky almost dropped the lamp. "You're kidding. When?"

"A couple of weeks ago."

"I had no idea."

"Not public knowledge."

"Then how . . . Oh. You ran some sort of background check on Billy."

"It's what I do, Dash."

"I'm not criticizing." She set aside her booty and flicked on lights, struggling to get a foothold on their new relationship. "In fact, I'd like to hear more about your new cyber detective agency and how you went about launching a new business. Maybe I could drive over, make you dinner, and we could, you know, talk."

"I can think of more pleasurable ways to spend the evening."

A sensual thrill zapped her libido. "Name one."

"Angling for a bout of phone sex, Dash?"

"You wish," she teased, seconds from peeling off her jeans. The mere sound of his voice inspired lust.

"The real thing it is."

"When?"

"After I handle some business."

"Time frame?"

"Don't wait dinner."

He disconnected and Rocky cursed. Phone sex would have been fun, but hooking up in the flesh would fry her senses. Worth the wait if the waiting didn't kill her. She imagined Jayce's smoking-hot body, shivered with erotic memories. She thought about the vibrator tucked away in her dresser drawer.

Her cell phone pinged. A text from Jayce.

BTW DON'T JUMP THE GUN. HAVE PLANS 4 U

"Damn."

* * *

"Okay. I'm here. Where do you want me?"

"I appreciate this, Rachel," Luke said without turning. "Day from hell. First Anna calls out, then Nell. Sadie complained about an upset stomach, so I sent her home."

"There's a flu bug going around," Adam said while Luke served up his draft.

"We were down two guys today on my crew," Kane said. "Not that it mattered much with the heavy rain."

Luke's ears roared with the dueling sounds of country rock, crowd chatter, and the intermittent curses and cheers from a competitive game of pool. It wasn't an overly busy night at the Shack, but it was damned lively.

"Where do you want me?" Rachel asked for the second time.

Focused on multiple drink orders, Luke gathered the ingredients for a Piña Colada and Long Island Iced Tea.

"Moderate dinner crowd. Gemma's a whiz. She can manage the dining area solo. Think you can handle the pub?"

"Guess we'll find out," Rachel said with a twinge of sarcasm. "Apron?"

"On that shelf under the cash register." Luke heard her shift away. Heard one of the Brodys whistle low. "What?" Luke asked.

"Rachel," Kane said. "No wonder Sam's hot for her."

"Who knew?" Adam asked.

Luke measured portions of rum and pineapple juice into the blender, then followed the Brodys' gazes. *Holy shit.* Rachel Lacey had curves. He'd never seen her in anything other than those shapeless peasant dresses. Tonight she wore slim-cut black pants and a formfitting long-sleeved shirt. He stared as she tied the Shack's signature crimson apron around her trim waist.

"Nice rack," Kane said.

Luke reached over the bar and punched his friend's shoulder. "That's Sam's girl. Show some respect."

"Oh, she's got my respect. Wow."

"Sure she's Sam's?" Adam craned his neck to watch as Rachel waited on a table of four seated by the fireplace. "We all witnessed the disaster date."

"Like you've never struck out first time at bat," Luke said while dumping a cup of crushed ice into the mix.

Adam and Kane felled him with arched brows.

Neither had Luke, but that wasn't the point. "Yeah, well, cut Sam a break."

Luke fired up the blender, cursed his own randy reaction to a side of Rachel Lacey he'd never seen. That sweet figure would get a rise out of any man, but Luke was especially intrigued with her face. She'd pulled her lackluster, stringy hair into a high ponytail, exposing her almond-shaped eyes, high cheekbones, small upturned nose, and sensual lips. Not Hollywood beautiful, but unconventionally pretty.

Sam's girl.

Right.

Rachel hurried over, tray and notepad in hand. "Two

glasses of Merlot, one Cosmopolitan, and one Sam Adams Seasonal." She double-checked her writing, then glanced at Luke. "What?"

"Nothing."

"You're staring."

"Your outfit."

"Black pants, white shirt." She gave herself the once-over. "Standard uniform, right?"

"Yeah. It's just . . . tight."

"You're the one who suggested I'd earn bigger tips if I showed a little cleavage."

"I know, but—"

"I need the money, Luke. Am I dressed inappropriately?"

"No."

"Then would you please fill my drink orders? Speedy service prompts higher tips."

Again with her almost desperate need for money. Rachel had been working steadily at the day-care center for months. She drove a beat-up car, owned a limited wardrobe, rented a small apartment, lived a conservative life—as far he knew. How could she be strapped for cash? Was she paying off old debts? Supporting a parent? Saving for a dream house that just went on the market? Luke was intrigued. Not good. When something snagged his interest, he was like a dog with a bone. Obsessed until he grew bored or something else nabbed his attention. Being obsessed with Sam's girl would suck.

Luke poured wine, resisting the urge to ask Rachel why she typically worked so hard to hide her face and figure. Was it because she disliked attention? She was getting plenty of that now from Adam and Kane, and, dammit, himself. While mixing a Cosmo he stole a glance at the mousy day-care aide turned provocative waitress. One thing hadn't changed: her habit of avoiding eye contact.

"Hey, Luke. Frannie's selling sweets. A fund-raiser for the school band. I know I just hit you up for another one of my grandkids' fund-raisers, but I can't play favorites. Know what I mean? Besides, I know how much you love cookies."

Luke garnished the rim of the martini glass with a lime wedge just as Bert Hawkins, owner of the town's most popular sports shop, slid an order form across the bar. The print was minuscule, and there was a lot of it.

"What can I put you down for?" the older man asked.

"Three boxes."

"Of what?"

"An assortment." Luke loaded Rachel's tray with two Merlots and the Cosmo and nabbed a tall glass for the beer.

Bert tapped the order form. "Can you narrow it down? There are twenty different varieties."

"Peanut butter." A safe guess, right? What cookie company didn't hawk peanut butter?

"The Peanut Butter Cashew Cakes or the Peanut Butter Pecan Pinwheels?"

"Pinwheels."

Bert pulled a pen from his pocket and ticked off a space. "That's one box. What about the other two?"

"I like them all," Luke lied as another patron whistled for his attention and pool balls clacked like thunder in his ears. "Just put me down for whatever."

"Wouldn't feel right about that. These are the gourmet kind. Take a quick gander at these descriptions," Bert said, tapping the pen to one of several rows of print.

Luke's head buzzed as the letters swirled.

"I love cookies," Rachel said, moving in beside Bert and nabbing the form. "Let's see. What looks good?"

Luke listened as she calmly and quickly read a few descriptions. He locked on to two. "Put me down for those Double Chocolate Caramels and White Chocolate Maples," he said while setting a foaming beer on Rachel's tray.

"Who can resist decadent?" Rachel asked Bert while flashing Luke a small but kind smile. "I'll take a box of each of those myself plus the Coconut Fudge Creams and . . ." She skimmed the page. "Yes, these. Sugar Doodles. Thanks."

"Thank *you*," Bert said with a toothy grin, then shifted his attention to Luke. "Mind if I hit up your other employees? It's for a good cause."

"Knock yourself out," Luke said, catching Rachel's gaze before she nabbed her tray of drinks and hurried off. His first thought was: *Brown.* Her eyes were brown. Second thought: *She knows.*

* * *

Rocky had never been good at taking orders. That's why she liked running her own business. Sure, guests voiced their two cents now and then regarding their room or the property or her limited recreation equipment—but she was the boss. Making her own decisions, following her instincts and impulses, fed into her need to control her destiny. It also stemmed from a lack of patience. She wasn't one to wait around. Which was why she'd taken the initiative with Jayce thirteen years ago. If she'd waited for him to make the first move they might never have made love. At the least, he wouldn't have been her first. For all the drama, she'd never once regretted that Jayce had been her first. For all the drama, she had no problem imagining him as her last. A lifetime of lovemaking with Jayce Bello. Yeah, boy, she could handle that. What burned her buns was the way he bossed her. No, what burned her buns was the way she *let* him boss her.

Wait.

Three hours ago, Jayce had teased her with the promise of hot and heavy sex. He'd said he'd let her know when and where. She'd showered and changed into low-riding chenille lounging pants and a matching powder-blue lace cami. She'd cranked the heat because the temperature outside had dropped to thirty-six and, because of construction and some drafts, she was freaking freezing. An hour ago she'd given up on baring sexy skin and pulled on a thick robe and texted Jayce.

STILL ON?
YES.
SHOULD I COME TO YOU?
SIT TIGHT.

What the hell did he think she'd been doing? She was more than a little peeved. Partly because her raging libido had yet to cool. *Since when did lust trump anger?* And partly because she itched to talk about the Rothwell property and the possibility of branching out as an interior decorator. She wasn't schooled in the profession, but she had great instincts, an innate talent, and a reasonable amount of experience. She could call and bounce the idea off of one of her brothers or her parents or any one of several friends, but Rocky wanted to dish with Jayce. She was ready to move forward with their relationship, yet he'd put her on hold. Okay. So it had only been for a few hours, but it seemed like forever and his bossy texts rubbed her the wrong way.

Desperate for distraction, Rocky curled up on her sofa with a collection of cupcake recipes, assorted photos, and typed memoirs—all for possible inclusion in the CL recipe/memoir book. If the club's project was on the fast track, she didn't want to fall behind. Twenty minutes passed and then ten more. She checked her cell. No updated texts. No missed calls. Where the hell was Jayce?

The television bleated in the background, a rerun of a bake-off on the Cooking Channel. The mantle clock ticked. The huge house, empty except for Rocky, creaked intermittently as harsh winds battered the façade and tree branches whipped against the eaves.

Rocky had never felt so alone. So frustrated. So impatient. And, okay, a little spooked.

She glanced at the time. Ten thirty. "Wait, my ass."

Too pumped to go to bed, Rocky bolted off the sofa and shoved her feet into a pair of ankle-high UGGs. She traded her robe for a fleece-lined coat and cinched the waist tight. She'd drive to the Sugar Shack. Hang with Luke for a while. Order a beer and nachos and maybe discuss the Rothwell farm. If Jayce thought she was going to spend a lifetime cooling her heels while he did his PI thing or whatever, he was dead wrong. Hopped up on pent-up lust and frustration, Rocky grabbed her purse and blew out the door. The brisk wind stung her cheeks as she trotted down the porch steps and marched through the dark toward her Jeep.

She slammed into someone and screamed.

"Damn, woman."

"Jayce?" Heart hammering against her ribs, Rocky punched his muscled shoulder. "You scared the hell out of me!"

"That's what you get for prowling around in the dark."

"I'm not prowling, you jackass. I'm leaving!" She pushed past him, but he nabbed her arm. She glared even though he probably couldn't tell. Thick clouds muted moonshine, and her porch light was a dim, distant glow. "Tell me to wait," she warned in a low voice, "and you're dead meat."

"I told you I'd be late."

"It's after ten!"

"Early by my standards."

"Well, not by mine and that's not the point. You could have been more forthcoming in your texts. *Wait*? *Sit tight*? I have a life, too, you know." She wrenched away, then vacillated between her Jeep and the house. *Damn.*

Jayce decided for her. He nabbed her by the waist and half-carried her toward the porch. "You're hell on wheels when riled." He cursed when he tried the door and it gave. "You forgot to lock the door."

"I was in a hurry."

"No excuse."

"Don't lecture me."

"Don't tempt me." He flicked on the wall switch, then caught her wrist as she tried to leave. "I'm sorry I upset you."

"Apology not accepted." She balled her fists, acknowledging a new and troubling realization. She'd been worried. Not knowing where Jayce had been exactly or what he'd been doing, deep down she'd harbored ghoulish thoughts. What if he'd tangled with a bad sort—he carried a gun after all—or ticked off Billy and landed in jail or blew a tire and rammed his car into a tree? She wasn't used to worrying about a lover. The only other time she'd gotten this worked up was last month when Jayce had been a guest at the Red

Clover and had stayed out superlate. Her fierce reaction when he'd finally walked through the door had stunned them both. Would it always be like this with him? The possibility made her queasy.

"The business I mentioned, it was personal." Jayce looked away, worked his jaw. "Took longer than I anticipated."

There it was again. *Vulnerability.* And it took the wind right out of her sails. Mostly. "I hate that you're able to twist me up with a simple word or gesture."

"Same here."

"I hate your domineering attitude."

"Not always."

Clinging to her agitation like a lifeline, Rocky struggled with her cinched belt.

Jayce moved in and freed the knot. "Where were you going anyway?"

She wrenched off the coat. "The Sugar Shack."

"Dressed like that?"

Okay. Maybe she could've gotten away with the lounging pants and boots, but the lace cami? "I wasn't planning on taking off my coat."

He raised a brow.

"I was in a hurry."

"So you said."

Why did he have to be so freaking handsome, so charismatic? Blood burning, pulse racing, Rocky glared. "Sometimes I really hate you."

"Back at you, Dash."

Rocky launched herself at the longtime, lustful bane of her existence. She wrapped her arms and legs around the freaking-hot bastard and cursed and thanked God. She kissed Jayce with passion and frustration and he responded with equal fervor. The frenzied clash and mesh escalated to a fever pitch, breaking only to shed layers of clothing.

Quaking with blinding affection, Rocky's mind burst with erotic images as Jayce hauled her into his arms and up the stairs. Next thing she knew she was flat on her back in bed staring up at the only man who'd ever owned her heart.

The word *love* whispered in her head, scaring her, thrilling her. "Take me."

Jayce torched her senses with a soulful kiss while finessing his rock-hard body beneath her. "No." He gripped her hips, then relinquished control. "Take me."

CHAPTER TWENTY-FIVE

"Fix Mama another drink, Jayce-e."

"Get your own damn booze, Angie. Go outside and play, kid."

Jayce looked from his mom to his dad, sick to his stomach, sick to death of being told what to do by two people who didn't give a crap about him.

Chilling out in the worn recliner, his mom shook her empty glass at him, the ice cubes tinkling like a bully's taunt. "Half a glass of bourbon and a splash of water," she said in a slurry voice. Then again, her voice was almost always slurred.

Jayce's dad pushed off of the sofa with his own empty glass and nabbed Angie's, giving her that creepy look he always got just before they disappeared into their bedroom.

Jayce's face burned. He hated the sounds they made in that room. The grunts, the squeals, the dirty words that filtered through the walls. "Dev invited me to his grandma's for dinner."

"Someone going to pick you up?" his dad asked, looking annoyed at the prospect of tearing himself away from his liquor and whatever he had in mind for Angie.

"I'll ride my bike." He headed for the door, not surprised when no one said, Be careful, Have fun, or Don't be too late. Nope. It was the Monroes who said stuff like that to

him. Jayce blew out of the suffocating house and into the fresh air and sunshine. The cramp in his stomach eased as he straddled the banana seat of his most prized possession. Gripping the moustache handlebars of his secondhand bike, Jayce pedaled hard. Daisy Monroe lived on the other side of town. Since he was only eleven, probably he should feel lucky that his parents gave him so much freedom. He didn't feel so lucky.

Someone touched him. Not a slap or a push, but a gentle brush.

"Jayce."

He'd know that voice anywhere. Especially in his dreams. Although not *this* dream. Jayce shoved away the shitty memories of the past and focused on his future. He lazed open his eyes and smiled at the naked woman cuddled against him and cradling his face. "Morning, Dash."

"You were dreaming."

"Talk in my sleep?" He'd been known to mumble when particularly troubled, which sucked. Although past lovers had labeled the mumbling as incoherent.

"No, but you were frowning and restless. Want to talk about it?"

He grasped her hand, kissed her palm. "Nothing to talk about." They gazed at each other for a long moment, and Jayce breathed slow and deep, appreciating the mingling scents of Rocky's herbal shampoo, her flowery-fresh sheets, and some sort of pine potpourri. Country scents, comforting scents. Sunshine filtered through her lacey curtains, illuminating the antique furnishings and eclectic curiosities. Everything from the braided rugs to the framed scenic paintings screamed an appreciation of old-fashioned sensibilities. Basking in the domestic tranquility, Jayce felt the painful remnants of the past fade away. "I could get used to this."

She quirked an ornery grin. "Sleeping with me?"

"Waking with you. Sex is a bonus."

She trailed her fingers over his shoulders, his chest. "The sex is amazing. Know what would make it even better?"

"Got something kinky in mind?"

"Depends on if you consider intimacy kinky."

"Depends on your definition of 'intimate.'"

She rose up on one elbow and studied him with wide blue eyes. He stared back, mesmerized as always by her natural beauty. Her intense gaze promised trouble. Warning bells clanged in his head even as his shaft sprang to life.

"You're awfully private," she said.

"You mean like you?"

"You're worse. Way worse. I've known you all my life, Jayce, and I hardly know you at all. It wouldn't matter except, if we're going to do this, us, I want . . . I need to know you more than anyone else. Even Dev."

That wouldn't be hard, since Jayce had been nearly as guarded with his best friend. Jayce had craved a lot of things in his life, but never sympathy. He pushed up and tried to relax against the pillows. Meanwhile his gut clenched. "What do you want to know?"

"Why do you always refer to your house as your parents' house? They've been gone a long time and, yes, you rented it out for years, but you do own it. You grew up in that house, yet you seem so detached."

"It's never felt like home," he answered honestly.

"Ever?"

"Ever."

"I don't understand."

"I don't expect you to. We were dealt very different lives, Rocky."

"For all the time you spent with us, I never really knew your parents. They weren't very sociable. Is that where you got your independent streak?"

"I'm hoping I didn't get anything from them." He reached out and tucked her messy curls behind one ear. "Why the preoccupation with Angie and Joe Bello?" As Jayce had grown older, more confident, and more distant from his folks, he'd fallen into thinking of them by their given names. "Mom" and "Dad" were too intimate and undeserved.

"Honestly, they were an afterthought. I was fixated on your house. I've only been inside a couple of times and I've always been aware of an emptiness. A lack of personality. *Your* personality." She shifted under the covers and sprawled on top of Jayce, cocooning him in feminine warmth and affection. As she gazed down at him, her expression turned from inquisitive to determined. "I'm glad you asked me to decorate. I think . . . I *know* I can make it into a home. *Your* home."

He smiled a little, thinking it would take a miracle. "If anyone can, you can."

"You don't have to worry about me abusing your credit card."

"I'm not worried."

"I spotted some interesting pieces at Molly's. Some I reserved pending your approval. One I purchased on my own. A housewarming gift. It's being delivered later today."

Jayce's heart jerked. "I'm intrigued. And touched."

She smiled. "Yay."

Moved beyond words, he traced a finger over the healing wound on her forehead. She'd been nicked by a car, but he'd been slammed by a damned Mack truck. With Rocky at the wheel, his life would never be the same. *Hoo-frickin'-rah.*

"So about your dream."

Damn.

"Have anything to do with that personal business that kept you from me last night?"

He thought about distracting her with a kiss, but that wouldn't be fair. She'd asked a valid question. "Yes."

She blinked, looking pleased and surprised that she'd guessed right. Looking curious.

Jayce shifted, rolling her off of him so that they were resting on their sides—face-to-face. "Knowing me entails knowing some ugly stuff, Dash. You sure about this?"

"I'm sure."

No hesitation. Well, hell. "I spent last night tearing down a wall. I asked you to make my house a home, but I couldn't see that happening with certain memories bouncing off certain walls. Specifically the walls that used to be my parents' bedroom."

He took a breath and uttered words that he'd never spoken aloud before. "My mom was an alcoholic and my dad liked her that way because he was a sexual deviant." Jayce saw no reason to cite specifics. "To each his own behind closed doors, but not at the expense of a kid. They never wanted me and that room represented the extent of their rejection. So last night, I rejected that room."

Rocky stared at him a long moment before responding. "Why not just purchase another house?"

"I don't want to give them that kind of power over me. I need to put the past to rest—things they said and did. Things I said and . . . didn't do."

"So you moved back to Sugar Creek to conquer demons? Purge your soul?"

"And to be with you."

She licked her lips, angled her head. "Wow. That's . . ."

"Heavy? Scary?"

"Romantic. The last part, that is. As for the ugly stuff . . . I can't imagine."

"I don't want you to." He stroked his palm down her bare arm, interlocked his fingers with hers. "I don't want the past tainting the future."

She held his gaze, but he caught a flash of panic. "Okay. *That* was sort of heavy," she said with a nervous laugh. "The future thing. Feeling a little overwhelmed here. Between openly *dating* you and the decorating opportunities coming my way . . ."

"How 'bout we approach the future one day at a time? Starting with today." He squeezed her hand and smiled to lighten the mood. "Speaking of gifts, I bought you one, too."

She blinked, then lit up like Times Square—a vibrant, kinetic force. "You did? Where is it? *What* is it?"

Jayce laughed. Her excitement over a present obliterated the last of his gloom. He'd have to remember that. Rocky liked gifts. He kissed her, relishing the taste of her tongue, the feel of her skin, then rolled out of bed with a teasing grin. "The faster we shower, the faster you'll get your present."

She practically knocked him over in her haste to get to

the bathroom. He admired her wicked body and confident spirit, appreciated the fact that she hadn't dredged up their fight from the night before or pushed for more details regarding his parents. He knew he'd piqued her interest, but she seemed to know when to back off. Maybe he'd been a little harsh in New York when he'd labeled her immature. Or maybe they'd reached a new level in their relationship. That thought, and the sight of Rocky soaping up in a frenzy, made Jayce smile.

* * *

Even though she'd grown up in a small town, up until recently Chloe had been living in New York City. Sugar Creek was a stark change from the thriving, congested, sometimes bombastic city. Heart full, she navigated sparse traffic, steering Daisy's big-as-a-boat Caddy past quaint two- and three-story businesses, brick sidewalks, and Victorian-looking street lamps. Trees were abundant as well as expanses of verdant grass. Beyond the town's limits, rolling mountains exploded with the last vivid colors of fall—red, yellow, orange. The autumn foliage was overwhelming in its beauty and a popular attraction for tourists. People came from miles away to witness the splendor, and a portion of those tourists would be mingling with locals this weekend, enjoying the town's annual Halloween festival.

Smiling, Chloe imagined all four seasons and future adventures with Devlin and their child. Raking up, then jumping into heaps of colorful leaves, sledding down snow-covered hills, taking nature walks in the throes of spring, tubing down Sugar Creek—the river, not the town—in the height of summer. She considered the low crime rate and escalated sense of community. Even now the preparations for the Spookytown Spectacular—three days away—were evident. Honeysuckle Street, an offshoot of Main Street, had been stanchioned off. Chloe noted two of what were to be several carnival rides and smiled. Someday she and Devlin would be standing in line with their son or daughter eagerly choosing the specific horse for their spin on the merry-go-round.

Her future was not only bright but also optimistically, fantastically brilliant.

Nearing Moose-a-lotta, Chloe tried to focus on now, on business, but damn, it was hard.

She would've enjoyed nothing more than spending the day in bed with Devlin. In fact, he'd suggested just that, saying they should both play hooky. She was pretty sure Devlin Monroe had never called out sick a day in his life, and she'd bet her cherished Cuisinart mixer he'd never played hooky. Loving that he'd bend his work ethics in order to afford them a leisurely day to celebrate her pregnancy, Chloe had almost relented. But her obligations at Moose-a-lotta were too new and a burst of unexpected energy too welcome to ignore.

Jazzed on the aftershock of a lengthy, passionate, *see-you-later* kiss with Devlin, Chloe approached the café, smiling as she noted Vince Redding's shiny blue four-door rolling curbside. Chloe pulled into a designated *Merchant* parking space and tried not to stare as the robust man walked Daisy to the café's door and said his good-byes. What an odd-looking pair. From the moment Chloe had laid eyes on Daisy, she'd labeled the quirky woman a cross between Whoopi Goldberg and Betty White—although Daisy had recently dyed her white curls purple. Daisy had also given up the majority of her conservative Jackie O wardrobe in favor of bohemian clothing and blingy accessories. Vince, on the other hand, looked like the cliché of who he was— the seventy-some-year-old owner of a small-town general store, complete with baggy pants, plaid flannel shirt, and red suspenders.

The old-fashioned widower and the devil-may-care widow.

Chloe still wasn't sure of the exact nature of their relationship. She'd never seen them kiss or cuddle, although affection shone in Vince's old eyes every time he looked at or talked about Daisy. Unlike with Rocky and Jayce, Chloe knew Daisy and Vince had common interests and goals. They never fought, and talked about anything and everything, according to Daisy. Even their past relationships. They seemed like the perfect couple, although how perfect could it be if the romantic interest was one-sided? What if Daisy only saw Vince as an amiable companion and friend? Was she leading him on by moving into his home? With their being together 24/7, would Daisy start to feel smothered? Would Vince become disenchanted? All of a sudden Chloe understood Devlin's reservation regarding this couple cohabitating, although she was more focused on the personal ramifications rather than the financial.

Chloe glanced at her reflection in the Caddy's rearview mirror. "Mind your own business, Madison."

Easier said than done.

Even though the Monroes weren't technically her family, she'd considered them family since soon after moving to Sugar Creek. The big, sloppy warm family she'd never had. She worried about each and every one of them, including Nash and Sam. She worried about Luke and Rocky but especially Daisy—a woman who indulged in every whim because life was short. Even shorter for a seventy-five-year-old woman with a heart condition.

Daisy waved good-bye as Vince drove off; then she whistled at Chloe.

Smiling, Chloe exited the refurbished Caddy, unlooping her scarf and welcoming the warmth of an unseasonably mild day.

"Shake a leg, kitten. Time to make the donuts."

"You mean muffins," Chloe said as she joined her friend and partner.

"Doesn't have the same ring to it," Daisy said while unlocking the door.

"I need to buy a car," Chloe said while they entered and set about their morning rituals.

"You can't afford a car." Daisy placed her fringed shoulder bag behind the counter. "You put all your pennies into this business."

Aside from draining her own meager bank account, Chloe had relied on her dad to co-sign for a loan, which had dented her pride but at the same time boosted their relationship. She refused to feel bad about something so good. "I know. But I feel like I'm monopolizing the Caddy." A car she'd once wrecked and that, thanks to Monica's whiz-mechanic husband, had been given an extended life. "What if you need it?"

Daisy raised a penciled brow as she shrugged out of her lime-green coat. "I've been barred from driving ever since the reckless-driving arrest. Remember? Besides, I don't need the Caddy. I have Vincent."

"But what if he's unavailable and you need to get somewhere?"

"Then I'll call you or one of my grandchildren or steal a set of wheels."

Chloe blinked.

"Kidding about that last part," Daisy said with a gleam in her eye. *"Maybe."*

She trotted to the kitchen, and Chloe followed. After seeing the woman hobbling around in that ankle cast for weeks, it was good to see her mobile again. Although it also meant Daisy was back in action, as in back to her reckless ways—like stealing someone's wheels.

"You look different," Daisy said while lining up their ingredients for the muffin-of-the-day.

Cheeks flushing, Chloe tied on an apron. "How so?" She wasn't showing. Surely she wasn't *glowing.* That was a cliché, right? Although since sharing her news with Dev, Chloe *felt* different. Lighter. *Excited.*

"You're smiling. What gives?"

Chloe mixed the muffin batter while Daisy attacked the topping. She considered her mood. She *was* happy. Devlin's acceptance and enthusiasm had made all the difference in the world. "Can't a person be happy for happy's sake?"

"Sure, but you've been an Anxious Annie for days. Why the sudden turnaround?"

"Why the third degree?"

"Why the stone wall?"

She didn't want to share her news until a doctor had confirmed the pregnancy. Certainly not until that video crew had left town. Unmarried and pregnant constituted scandal, right? As much as Chloe wanted to confide in Daisy—this would be her first great-grandchild!—Chloe didn't trust the impetuous woman to keep her secret. "I confess I've been edgy lately. Between the book deal and issues with assorted family members, it's a little overwhelming."

"The Cupcake Lovers have survived several wars and decades," Daisy said while melting a hunk of butter. "We'll survive a book deal. Did I ever tell you about the time—" She waved off her words and nabbed a bag of fresh nuts. "Never mind. Long story. Regarding the family, we'll prevail. We always do. Take my son, for instance. . . ."

Devlin's dad. "What about him?"

Daisy chopped pecans with a little too much zeal. "Darn my loose lips. Forget I mentioned it, kitten."

She couldn't. She'd been on pins and needles for weeks wondering about the gloom that settled over Devlin every time he spoke with his father. Yes, they were at odds regarding store renovations. But there had to be more to it.

Chloe added an egg, vanilla extract, and her melted-chocolate mixture into a bowl while contemplating the best way to snoop. "I'm a little nervous about meeting your son and his wife. I want them to like me."

"They'll love you. We all love you."

Chloe smiled at that. She did indeed feel cherished and appreciated by the Monroes. "Rocky said they might be flying up for Thanksgiving."

"More like Christmas," Daisy said. "What with the treatments—"

They stopped working and locked gazes.

Chloe felt the lemon-yellow walls of their pristine kitchen closing in as she noted the haunted look in the other woman's eyes. "What wrong with Jerome, Daisy?"

The senior woman pursed her lips, blinked, then poured premeasured ingredients into her own bowl, forking the topping into coarse crumbs. "Let's talk about what's right. Early diagnosis and aggressive treatments. A determined streak and a supportive wife. He's coming along and by Christmas, and the Grace of God, he'll be fine."

What could it be? Something serious, but not terminal.

By the Grace of God.

Chloe wanted to press for more details, but it seemed invasive. Heart pounding, she poured the chocolate batter into the paper-lined muffin cups. How long had Devlin been burdened with this knowledge? Why wasn't the rest of the family aware? "No wonder Devlin's been so preoccupied."

"Exactly why my son kept his . . . *affliction* a secret. He didn't want to worry family and friends. He didn't want panic or pity. The only reason Devlin knows is because he pried it out of his mom. The only reason I know is because I pried it out of Devlin." Daisy topped the batter with streusel pecan crumbles and sighed. "Jerome's a proud man."

Chloe squeezed the woman's boney shoulder. "He sounds like a thoughtful and courageous man to me," she said with a kind smile. "On second thought, I can't wait to meet him."

Daisy smiled back, and together they slid four muffin pans into the oven.

"My grandson's trying to honor my son's wishes by keeping the affliction under wraps. Don't be angry that he didn't confide in you, kitten. Trust me, keeping this secret hasn't been easy. For my grandson or me."

Secrets. Chloe had never been privy to so many confidences in her life. Although when she thought about it, almost every secret involving a Monroe was based on the desire to save someone else stress or strife. Everyone's secret was rooted in good intentions. Even the personal secret near and dear to Chloe's heart. Yes, she preferred to have a doctor's official confirmation. Yes, she harbored concerns regarding a safe pregnancy. But she was also worried about crushing Monica's heart and perhaps damaging their friendship. On the other hand, sharing this particular news with Daisy would give the woman something positive to obsess on.

The suffocating walls receded as Chloe's heart bloomed.

Smiling a little, she grasped Daisy's flour-covered hands and squeezed. "I have a secret, too."

The woman's penciled brows rose above the rhinestone-studded rims of her glasses. "Are you going to share?"

"I am."

"Do I have to keep it quiet?"

"For a little while, yes."

Grinning, Daisy leaned in and whispered, "Devlin asked you to marry him."

"No. Not exactly. Not yet. But we are engaged in another joint venture." Sensing Daisy's excitement, Chloe pressed her friend's palm to her belly. "I still need confirmation from the doctor, but, well, I'm pretty sure we've got a cupcake in the oven."

Daisy squealed, then performed a comical happy dance. "Zip-a-dee-doo-dah! Strike up the band! Hot diggety dog!"

Chloe laughed.

Daisy jigged. "If anything will give my son more oomph to beat that bastard disease, this is it. A grandchild! But don't worry," she said, coming to a winded stop. "I won't breathe a word until you say it's okay."

"At which time, feel free to shout the news from Grenville's Overlook." The covered bridge where Devlin had joined Chloe in a leap of faith and sealed their love. "We'll be right there with you."

CHAPTER TWENTY-SIX

They would've been out of the house and on the road a half an hour sooner if they hadn't fooled around in the shower, but Rocky had a hard time keeping her hands off of Jayce's hot and hard body. Her fascination with the man had doubled when he'd opened up to her about his crappy childhood. What did it feel like to grow up knowing you weren't wanted? How did a kid who'd been born to, not one, but *two* selfish and addicted parents turn out as compassionate and grounded as Jayce? With such an awful home life, no wonder he'd spent so much time at the Monroes'. Thank *God* he'd spent so much time at the Monroes'.

Every fiber of Rocky's being had wanted to hug and hold Jayce, to curse his parents' monsters, and to bemoan his sad childhood. But Jayce wouldn't want sympathy. She didn't have to know him well to know he wouldn't want her, or anyone else, to feel sorry for him. So she hadn't coddled and she hadn't pried. Considering his private nature, she realized it must have cost him dearly to share as much as he had with her. She cherished that confidence . . . as ugly as it was. And she secretly vowed to brighten Jayce's day, his life, as much as she could. Getting it on in the shower had seemed like a good start. Or at least a pleasant distraction.

Even though her attraction to Jayce now ran deeper than

ever, the physical fascination bordered on obsessive. Whenever he was in her sights, Rocky's thoughts went straight to
sex. Thinking back, she knew even her young-girl crush had
been based on thoughts and desires revolving around Jayce's
drop-dead gorgeous face and to-die-for physique. She'd never
defined the attraction in those terms, but now that she'd pondered the obvious, an uneasy feeling niggled at her gut. "Do
you think I'm shallow?" she blurted while buckling into
his car.

"You're kidding, right?" He slid on his sinfully sexy aviator sunglasses and keyed the ignition. "There's not a shallow
bone in your body."

"Then what do you call a person who's totally enamored
with another person's face and body? Don't let this go to
your head, but every time I see you I want to jump your
bones."

"You're freaking out because you're hot for me?"

"I'm not freaking out. I'm concerned, a little, about my
preoccupation with you and sex."

"Trying to deduce the problem and failing."

"All these years I thought I was in love with you."

"You are in love with me."

Her stomach fluttered with the probability, but she didn't
want to go there. Not yet. *One day at a time.* "Arrogant
much?" she teased.

"Intuitive."

"How can I be in love with you when I've always been
fixated on the physical rather than the intellectual? True love,
real love, should be more meaningful, don't you think? A
deeper connection? Intimate knowledge? What makes you
tick? What makes you you? I'm talking about the adult you,
not the kid you," she clarified. "What do you do for kicks?
What's your favorite book? Favorite movie? Where do you
stand on global warming? Health care? Do you want kids?"

"Yes."

She blinked. "Yes to . . ."

"Kids." He swerved to miss a pothole, then cut her a
glance. "You?"

"Sure. Absolutely. Someday. Although I'm not sure how I'd swing being a mom while running the Red Clover. And now that I'm thinking about branching out into interior design, that complicates matters more. Kids are time intensive." She cringed as soon as the words left her mouth. "At least a parent *should* devote massive time and energy to child rearing. Come to think of it, I'm not sure how I'd manage a marriage, let alone kids." Mind and heart stuttering, she looked away and focused on the quiet beauty of Thrush Mountain. *Way to rush the future, Monroe.* "Not that I'm suggesting anything, just hypothesizing. I never minded having guests in my house—renting rooms for a day or week, allowing them the run of the living and dining area—because it was always just me. I'd be as sociable as needed; otherwise I'd do my own thing. But when my *thing* includes a husband and children . . ."

How would she maintain privacy in a public setting? How would she handle *sex?* In the past she'd only indulged in her own home when there were no guests. She couldn't imagine regulating hot and heavy time with Jayce. She flushed thinking about how he'd pleasured her in her kitchen. Once the Red Clover was back up and running, there'd be a definite kink in spontaneous adventurous sex. "Would you want to live your private life under the noses of strangers?"

He shot her a look, and even though his gaze was shielded by those glasses, she knew his mind. He would not. "When the time comes, Dash, you'll figure it out. There's a solution for every problem."

Talk about clichés. She grinned. "That your motto for your JB Investigations?"

"Still working on a motto for JBI. And stop undressing me with your eyes."

"I wasn't. . . . Ah. Humor. Ha."

"If it makes you feel better, I want to jump your bones every time I see you, too. I'm haunted by your beauty and fantasize about that body."

She ignored a jolt of lust and crossed her arms over her chest. "Great. So we're both shallow."

"Give me your hand."

"Don't tell me you moonlight as a palm reader?"

"Don't tell me you're chicken."

Rolling her eyes, Rocky interlaced her fingers with Jayce's, swallowing hard as their warm palms melded. A delicious heat stole up her arm, shooting straight to her heart. The charged silence made her squirm. *That's it?* she thought, watching the blurring scenery. *He just wanted to hold my hand.* Sweet. Hot.

But then he spoke.

"Given my parents' preoccupation and addiction to sex and alcohol and the fact that they saw me as an inconvenience, I learned early on to fend for myself and to keep my thoughts private. Hungry for love and wary of it at the same time. That's what makes me tick."

Rocky's heart lodged in her throat.

"Nature walks, museums, and working with rescue animals. That's how I get my kicks. Favorite book? Anything by Raymond Chandler or Robert B. Parker. Favorite movie? A toss-up between *The Maltese Falcon* and *The African Queen.*"

A longtime classic movie buff, Rocky had seen both movies and knew the common denominator. "Humphrey Bogart," she said with a small smile. "Tough guy with a soft heart."

Jayce squeezed her hand as he turned onto the road leading into Sugar Creek.

Rocky's blood stirred as he filled her in on a few of his political views. Not because she disagreed, but because she knew what it cost him to share such personal details.

The deeper connection. An intellectual connection. Overwhelming in its intensity. Heartwarming and sexy. As important as his past was to her, she focused on the present. A place where she had some sort of influence. "Here's the good news," she said after an animated debate on gun control. "Apparently, I'm as turned on by your brain as I am by your brawn."

"And I'm a longtime sucker for your ballsy approach to

life. Nothing shallow about this attraction, Rocky. Never has been."

"So the constant fixation on sex?"

"I'm all for it."

"Smart-ass."

"Not a candy and flowers kind of guy. Sorry, babe."

"What kind of guy are you? Should I be worried about my present? Let me guess, a new kitchen gadget? Baking supplies? You seemed awfully fond of my cupcakes," she said with an ornery grin. She'd been on pins and needles, giddy like a kid at Christmas, since the moment he'd mentioned he'd bought her a gift. Although, honestly, she didn't care if he was taking her to pick out a new chain saw. Or maybe he'd sprung for a new TV set for her bedroom. Apparently hers was too small and robbing her/them of the ultimate viewing experience. Adam had made the same comment once, not that she'd shared that with Jayce. What was it with guys and big screens? "You know what? Don't tell me. Surprise me. I'm sure I'll love whatever it is."

"Sure you don't want a hint?" Jayce teased while breaching the town limits.

"Yes. No. Okay. A small hint."

"Think fur."

* * *

"Are you serious?"

Rocky gaped at her gift, brow furrowed, hands on hips. Not the reaction he'd hoped for; then again, Jayce had to admit this gift was assumptive. He took the leash from the vet's assistant, thanked her, and then led the tail-wagging dog outside into the gated front yard.

Rocky followed, looking shell-shocked. He didn't want to force this, but he *would* put up a fight. His immediate intentions had merit even if the big picture was selfish. "When I saw the way you interacted with Brewster at the rescue shelter I thought, *Here's a perfect match,*" Jayce explained.

"He needs a loving home with acreage to run and you'd benefit from a protector. He's a good dog, Rocky. Loyal and affectionate, according to Mrs. Rush, and from what I've witnessed, alert and obedient. I know you feel comfortable living alone in the country, but I'd feel better if you had some security. A watchdog is a good start."

Rocky stooped down and Brewster, who'd been sitting not so patiently, his butt wiggling with the force of his wagging tail, moved forward and greeted her with gentle kisses. "So what?" Rocky asked, petting the mutt's sleek coat. "He'll lick an intruder to death?"

Jayce smiled down at the pair. "Brewster's a Lab-shepherd mix. Highly intelligent. With proper training he'll make an effective guard. Trust me." When Rocky didn't respond, Jayce plowed on. "He's approximately two years old, past the stage of destructive chewing, housebroken. If there's ever an issue with a guest being allergic, I'll take him for however long."

"Why not take him period?" she asked, still focused on Brewster's brown-eyed gaze. "You obviously have a weakness for animals and now that you're not living in the city . . ."

"Like I said, you seemed the perfect match." Even though Brewster had been good with Jayce, the dog gravitated toward Rocky. Watching the two—head-to-head, Brewster's paw on her knee, Rocky kneading the dog's thick neck—made Jayce's heart swell and thump. "I picked him up yesterday, brought him here to the vet for an overnighter. Grooming and a full checkup. He's good to go . . . if you want him."

"You got me a dog," she said in a disbelieving voice.

"Did I screw up here?"

She stood and finally met Jayce's gaze, tears shining in her river-blue eyes. "I haven't had a dog since I was a kid."

"Shiloh. Great dog." He remembered the golden retriever well. He'd wanted a dog just like her. Then any dog at all. His parents had nixed that wish like so many others.

"It'll be a huge adjustment."

"I'll help." He tugged on Rocky's braid. God, he loved her braids. "So did I screw up or score?"

She smiled then, wrapped her arms around his neck, and felled him with a fierce embrace. "You knocked it out of the park, Bello."

* * *

Rocky couldn't remember the last time she'd felt this giddy. "Giddy" so rarely applied to her mood, she almost mistook the dizzy elation for a panic attack. She still hadn't put two and two together when Jayce had pulled up to the Sugar Creek Animal Clinic. Even when she'd recognized Brewster as the dog she'd been so enamored with at the Pixley Rescue Shelter, she didn't get that he was her "gift" until Jayce spelled it out.

Her dog.

My dog.

Her pulse had skipped and raced as the notion sank in.

Losing Shiloh, the dog who'd brightened most of Rocky's childhood, had been so painful, she had shied away from loving and losing a pet again. Plus, she'd been so singular in her determination in making the Red Clover a perfect and profitable inn, she'd never considered the additional responsibility of a dog. It just hadn't been on her radar, but now that Brewster was in her face, she welcomed him with open arms. "How could anyone abandon such a wonderful dog?" Rocky asked, twisting around to stare at her new best friend, who was sitting in the middle of Jayce's backseat looking regal and cute as hell.

"People abandon pets all the time," Jayce said while driving toward his house. "Lack of room. Lack of time. Economics. There are valid reasons to surrender an animal. What I can't stomach is neglect or mistreatment."

Rocky glanced at the man who'd suffered his own brand of neglect, her mind traveling down ugly roads. Had her parents been aware of his god-awful home life? Had Dev? She barely remembered Joe and Angie Bello, but she remembered the night they died. A horrible car crash. And she remembered the weeks after when her own dad had taken a distraught Jayce under his wing. Thinking back and knowing what she knew now, she was surprised at how affected Jayce had been by the loss. His compassion must know no bounds.

"What's wrong?"

Rocky blinked. "What?"

"You look sad."

"Preoccupied." She shook off the past and focused back on Brewster. "Not that I doubt your training abilities, but I can't imagine this dog attacking anyone. He looks more like a teddy bear than Cujo." Mostly he was black, with small patches of brown on his chest and paws. One ear stood straight up, and one flopped halfway over. Half black Lab, half German shepherd, he was fairly large but a little on the skinny side. His big moony eyes killed her, and she'd swear he had a permanent smile on his snout.

"At the very least he'll alert you to someone's presence, maybe scare off an unwanted visitor."

"As in Billy Burke? I really think that was a freaky one-time deal, Jayce. If he's stalking anyone, I'm beginning to think it's Tasha. Did I mention she got several texts during our emergency Cupcake meeting? She looked annoyed. And then who was waiting outside for her? Billy."

"What would you think of having an alarm system installed?"

"I think it would be inconvenient with paying guests coming and going at all hours."

"I'd like to rig the grounds with motion-detector lighting and some security cams."

"I run a bed-and-breakfast, Jayce, not a prison. No." Rocky reached over the seat and scratched Brewster's chin. "Thanks to you, I've got a watchdog now. And there's always my meat mallet as backup."

"We'll revisit this later," Jayce said while pulling into his driveway.

"When did you become such a worrywart?"

"The day I fell for you."

Rocky's hand froze on the door latch as Jayce climbed out of the car.

He opened the back door and whistled for Brewster. "Come on, boy."

She forced herself to join them, stunned for the third time today. One eye on Brewster as he sniffed around the yard, Rocky sidled up to Jayce. "What did you mean by that?"

"By what?"

"That *fell for me* comment."

"Forget I said anything."

"Why would I want to forget—"

"Bad timing."

"Why?" Rocky's heart pounded as Jayce kept his gaze trained on Brewster. Jayce was angry. *What the hell?* "You always complain about me shutting down on you. How is this different? Talk to me, Jayce. Are you saying you . . . you *love* me . . . or something?"

"You're just now figuring this out?"

Rocky flushed, blindsided and confused by the conversation as well as the confrontational vibes. "I know you're attracted to me. I know you care about me. You said so the other night. And I feel it. I do. But as far as love . . . We've been at odds for years. And these last few days, mostly it's been about sex and getting to know one another. How would I know . . . why would I assume you'd fallen in love so fast?"

"Fast?" He shoved a hand through his hair and then, finally, shot her a look. A look tinged with hurt. "Rocky, I fell for you the first time we made love."

She blinked. "Thirteen years ago?" Her stomach churned with a weird mix of elation and anger. "Why didn't you say something before?"

"You wouldn't have believed me. You had it in your head that my proposal was based on duty, period. You rejected me. For years. And the longer you rejected me the more I rejected my own feelings. Pride. Self-preservation. You said I broke your heart; well, honey, you blew a massive hole in mine."

Rocky swallowed hard, trying to put everything in perspective. She hadn't been the only one to reject Jayce. She glanced at the house. *His parents.* She blew out a breath.

"I'm a little overwhelmed just now. Maybe we should set this topic aside for later."

"Good idea."

"Are you still mad?"

He turned then and took her into his arms. "I'm not mad, Rocky. Just . . . give me a damned inch, will you?"

"What do you mean?"

"I worry about you. I want to take care of you. Make sure you're safe. Billy's just one concern. Things happen. Bad things. Unexpected things. I've witnessed more shit than . . ." He closed his eyes, then refocused. "You think you're impervious, hon, but you're not."

She'd never been afraid of living in the middle of nowhere on her own. She still wasn't. But she understood and respected Jayce's feelings. She thought back on how he must've felt when he'd picked her up—bruised and bloodied—at that New York hospital. "Not budging on the alarm system, but I guess some motion-detector lighting wouldn't hurt."

He smiled against her forehead. "I'm thinking that was half an inch, but I'll take it."

Feeling his mood lift a little, Rocky hugged Jayce tight, reinforcing their new connection. Yes, she was still a little unsure about their relationship—this was a first for her—but she wasn't running or pushing him away. "The first time we did it, huh?" she teased good-naturedly.

He glanced at the small chalet. "The one good memory connected with this place."

Before she could comment, Brewster nudged their legs. "He must be thirsty," Rocky said, noting Brewster's panting. "It's warm today."

Jayce reached down and ruffled the dog's ears. "Let's take this inside." He nabbed a mixed bag of dog supplies from his trunk while Rocky led Brewster to the shade of the porch.

"How big of a path should I clear for that delivery from Molly's?" Jayce asked as they scaled the front steps.

"Path?" But as soon as Jayce opened the front door of his house, she understood. The entryway and living room were jammed with boxes and crates. A leather recliner was the only piece of exposed furniture. That and a television and laptop. Stunned, she followed Jayce into the kitchen. More boxes. "You've been here, what, four days? And you haven't unpacked anything?"

"Can't decide where to put anything. Nothing feels right." He pulled a porcelain bowl out of the bag and filled it with water.

Rocky resisted the urge to move in and hug him. His tone had been casual, but she sensed discomfort. This house. The house he'd grown up in. *She* was his only good memory?

Brewster trotted in and made a beeline for the water dish. The tension cracked as Jayce smiled down at the slurping dog, then up to Rocky. "Want some coffee? I did manage to unpack the automatic drip."

She smiled back. "Sure. Then you better start on that path." She thought about the rolltop desk on its way over from Maple Molly's. "A *wide* path. As for deciding where to put stuff . . ." She glanced around the kitchen and back into the living room. "Leave that to Brewster and me. Could take a while," she added after opening a couple of boxes. "How do you feel about overnight guests?"

She'd be damned if she'd leave this house without infusing it with a few more good memories.

CHAPTER TWENTY-SEVEN

Luke was one of those guys who always woke up in a good mood. Not so today. Maybe because he'd tossed and turned all night and when he had slept he'd had crazy-ass erotic dreams about Rachel. Not cool.

Sam's girl, Sam's girl.

Not only that, but Luke would bet the frickin' Sugar Shack she knew about his dyslexia. *How* he didn't know, but it bugged the hell out of him. Made him feel stupid, even though he knew he wasn't. So here he was attracted to his cousin's girl, a girl who knew Luke had a reading problem and either felt sorry for him or thought he was a moron. Worse, he had to work with her. Several nights a week for who knew how long. Firing her wasn't an option. She hadn't done anything wrong. Nope. This was 100 percent his problem—hence his sucky-ass mood.

Luke rearranged the back bar, thankful the Shack had been fairly quiet. The calm before the busy festive weekend. Since Anna was back to work and Gena, the second bartender on staff, had said she wouldn't mind an extra night, Luke was seriously considering taking the night off. Aside from Sunday, he rarely took one. Maybe distance or a good lay would clear his mind.

"Hey, bud. The usual."

Luke noted Adam's reflection in the back bar mirror.

Again with the somber expression. Again with a visit pre–Happy Hour. Luke nabbed a glass and turned. "Don't you have lessons to give somewhere? Horseback riding? Boating? Fishing?" Adam worked as a freelance sports instructor for several local resorts. Skilled and personable, he was always in demand.

"In between seasons. My slow time. So"—he raised an annoyed brow—"no."

Undeterred by his sarcasm, Luke pressed. "I know you have hobbies. If I were you," he said while serving up the beer, "I'd take advantage of the slow time instead of hanging out here crying in your booze over my sister."

Adam shot him a stormy look.

Oh, shit.

"You know about me and Rocky?"

"I caught her at a bad time a few weeks ago and she slipped. It's not common knowledge; trust me."

"*This* is awkward."

"You sleeping with my sister?"

"Past tense."

"Yeah, well, I try not to think about it."

"Me, too." Adam sipped beer, then focused on the bar. "I really care about her, Luke."

"Let it go, man." *Rocky and Jayce have history.*

"Working on it."

Just then Sam walked into the pub. *Damn, damn,* damn.

"Hi, Adam."

"Sam."

"Got a sec, Luke?"

"Sure. My office?"

"No. This is fine." Sam settled one stool over from Adam. "I'll have what he's having."

A freakin' broken heart? Beautiful. Luke poured Sam a Beck's.

"Rachel here?"

"Not yet."

"I've called a couple of times, to check in, but missed her," Sam said.

And she didn't call you back? Shit.

"Just wanted to make sure she's doing okay here at the Shack."

"Only one night under her belt," Luke said, "but, surprisingly, yeah, she's doing okay."

"Who knew?" Adam mumbled.

"Knew what?" Sam asked.

"That Rachel was so—"

"Personable." Luke shot Adam a look. Was he really going to comment on Rachel's sexy figure?

"I was going to say *good with people,* but, yeah, 'personable' covers it," Adam volleyed with a look that said, *Give me some credit.*

"I'm not surprised. If she can handle a bunch of rowdy preschoolers, I suspect she can handle just about anything if she needs to. Living on her own, she *needed* a job." Sam sipped beer. "Still can't believe Gretchen let her go. With no notice, no less. I asked around. A couple of parents mentioned they'd caught a vibe, like Gretchen was jealous of how much the kids loved Rachel."

"I thought she fired Rachel due to budget constraints," Luke said.

"Then why did she hire another assistant?"

Luke frowned. "Thought she was relying on volunteers."

"Who told you that? Rachel?" When Luke nodded, Sam shrugged. "Guess that was her pride talking. I'm telling you if it weren't for the kids I'd stop construction on the jungle gym. Rewarding pettiness or, in this case, Gretchen sticks in my craw."

"You're building a jungle gym?" Adam asked.

"I had the supplies and the time and the kids need new playground equipment. Figured I could donate at least one piece."

"Need some help?" Adam asked. "Apparently I've got too much time on my hands."

"Sure."

"Luke, can pitch in, too," Adam ribbed. "Not like he has any girlfriends to entertain these days."

Great. The Lovelorn Construction Club. "I already pitched in for a few hours." Luke glanced at Adam. *Smartass.* "But sure. Count me in."

The main door opened, letting in a flood of sunshine and, Christ, was that a dog? And *oh no. Oh, hell. Rocky and Jayce.*

Adam must've spotted them in the mirror. His expression hardened just before he lowered his head and grumbled, "Damn."

Sam, on the other hand, turned and smiled. "What's with the pooch?"

"His name's Brewster," Rocky said, beaming. "Isn't he the cutest?"

"He's a dog," Luke said, stating the obvious. "Dammit, Rocky. Health regulations? Get him out of here."

"You don't have to be rude," she said, ruffling the dog's ears. "I just wanted to show him off and—" Her face fell when Adam swiveled around, making his presence known.

"Where'd you get him?" Sam asked, breaking the sudden silence.

"A gift from Jayce," she said, looking uncomfortable.

"Thought she could use some company," Jayce said.

"Other than yours?" Adam asked.

Here we go. Luke braced to bust up a fight. It wouldn't be the first time.

Rocky flushed. "We just stopped in for . . . Jayce ordered . . . That is . . ."

"I called ahead and ordered some takeout from Anna," Jayce said easily, then turned to Rocky and squeezed her hand. "Luke's right about Brewster, hon. Meet you outside."

Luke resisted an eye roll. Hand-holding. Endearments. *We get it, Bello. You and Rocky are together.* It was not that he didn't like Jayce, but damn, Luke felt for Adam.

The air crackled as Rocky and her mutt left the bar.

Jayce turned to Adam. "Problem?"

"Not unless you hurt her." Adam turned back to his beer. Sam followed suit.

Luke jerked a thumb toward the dining area. "Anna's in

the kitchen. Follow me." *Okay.* He was definitely taking the night off. He didn't want to deal with anyone's crappy or complicated, love or sexual, problems.

Including his own.

* * *

Jayce had suggested a picnic as their first official date partly to appease Rocky's discomfort with public outings, partly because he knew Brewster would be in the mix. Adopting the dog only to abandon him on his first night didn't sit right with Jayce. Rocky had noted his soft spot for animals. She had no idea. Dogs especially. Universally they possessed the capacity for unconditional love, a concept that fascinated him. A practice that eluded the majority of mankind.

He glanced at Brewster, sprawled on the blanket, stomach exposed. Trusting and accepting of his new "people," sensing somehow that he was in safe, loving company. Rocky, on the other hand, did not look so comfortable. She'd been subdued on the ride from town to river and even throughout their meal. Not that Jayce had been all that talkative himself. It had been a day of mixed emotions. Jumbled communication. He sucked it up and opened a foul can of worms. "Adam's hung up on you."

"I know. At least I do now."

Jayce raised a brow.

Rocky tossed her half-eaten chicken leg back on the paper plate, rolled onto her back, and sighed. "It was supposed to be sex. Just sex."

Which should have made him feel better but didn't.

"I like Adam," she said, staring up through the rustling orange leaves at the vibrant blue sky. "He's a great guy. Nice. Stable. But I don't love him. I never loved him. And frankly, I don't get why he's so fond of me. I never gave him reason . . . I never led him on. Plus . . . Honestly? I was a controlling bitch most of the time." Another sigh. "Talk about confounding."

"That's the trouble with love," Jayce said. "Makes no

sense." Over the years, every time he thought he had a grip on his own feelings regarding Rocky something would trip him up. A memory. The mention of her name or a brief interaction. Where she was concerned it didn't take much to put him in a tailspin. Even though he didn't want to commiserate with Adam Brody, Jayce did.

Rocky blinked up at the sky, then slid Jayce a wary glance. "I'm thinking if I keep my distance, Adam's feelings will cool and he'll find someone else. I really want him to find someone else. Someone nice. Adam's a great guy."

"So you keep saying."

She scrunched her brow. "Are you jealous, Jayce Bello?"

"Uncomfortable. But I'll get over it." He stroked a thumb over her cheek. "I like to think I'm an enlightened man. Rational. We're adults. We have history with other people. It's just that your relationship with Adam isn't quite history enough."

Rocky's mouth quirked. "This is probably the wrong thing to say, but that's sort of sweet. You're sweet. Brewster. The picnic. Pretending you like the desk when you really don't."

He'd been stunned by the enormity and beauty of the late-nineteenth-century rolltop. An exquisite piece of furniture more suited to Rocky's Victorian home than his parents' contemporary chalet. He'd never been comfortable with receiving gifts, and that desk had been a whammy. Still, he thought he'd done a better job of concealing his discomfort when the delivery guys had unveiled his present. "It's not that I don't like the desk, Rocky. It's beautiful and thoughtful."

"I just thought if you're going to do most of your detective work via your computer you should have an inspiring and comfortable work space."

"I appreciate that."

"But?"

"It had to cost a fortune."

"I shop at Molly's all the time. I got a great deal."

"A *small* fortune."

She pushed up into a sitting position and frowned. "It's a gift, Jayce. You're not supposed to debate the cost."

"I know. And normally I wouldn't. But you have to admit it's an extravagant gift, especially given your financial situation."

"I'm trying not to take offense here."

"I'm trying not to offend." He could see her struggling to keep her calm and her seat. Typically she paced when riled. Interesting that she was tempering old ways.

"Okay. It's not so much that I got a great deal," she said while stroking Brewster's fur. "More like I struck a deal. I agreed to work off some of the cost by helping out at Maple Molly's in my spare time. I just happen to have a lot of that right now."

Jayce raised a concerned brow. "Working at Molly's in addition to decorating my house and the Rothwell farm? Talk about being overwhelmed."

Rocky matched his expression and tossed in a saucy grin. "Worried we won't have enough sack time?"

"Worried you'll wear yourself out." And, yeah, that a heavy workload would encroach on their time together. It was not that he was possessive, but they were just getting off the ground. *Tend to your soul.* He couldn't shake his vision of the perfect life. Wife, kids, dogs . . .

"The Rothwell gig isn't a given. I called the new owner, Harper Day, and left a message, but I haven't heard back yet. As for Molly's . . . Even though the contractors hope to finish up at the Red Clover in another week or so," Rocky said, "I don't have any reservations on the books until late November. Sitting around twiddling my thumbs and obsessing over the lack of business and income doesn't appeal. Working part-time at an antique barn does. Please don't ask me to return the desk. If you really like it—"

"I do."

"Then I want you to have it."

"Okay."

She blinked, smiled. "Really?"

That smile rocked his cockeyed world. "I plan on solving

a lot of cybercases at my new and inspiring work space." He still wasn't comfortable with the financial aspect and the strain on her time, but he was less keen on insulting Rocky's generous heart. "Thank you."

She beamed. "You're welcome."

"And thank you for everything you did at the house today."

"A dent, but a start."

"The wildflowers were a nice touch." Aside from helping him unpack boxes and arrange sparse furnishings, Rocky had picked bunches of wildflowers from the backyard and arranged small bouquets for the kitchen, bathroom, and living room. "But nothing brightens the place like you and Brewster."

Rocky moved closer and climbed onto his lap. She wrapped her arms and legs around Jayce and dazzled his senses with a slow, deep kiss. "I'm thinking we should go back to your place or my place for dessert," she said, coming up for air. "Feeling a little exposed here riverside."

"There's always the backseat of my car," he teased as they scrambled to their feet.

"With Brewster watching from the front seat?"

Sure enough, as soon as Rocky stood Brewster stood. He was fast becoming Velcro-Dog. Jayce smiled. "Looks like you have a friend for life."

"The best gift ever," Rocky said as she packed up the remnants of their gourmet lunch.

Jayce nabbed the blanket and basket, and together they weaved their way through the dense patch of woods. His mind spun with memories of his youth, good memories, picnics and barbeques with the Monroes at Willow Bend. He added this afternoon with Rocky and Brewster to the treasure trove. But then they cleared the trees and his mood faltered.

"What's that stuck on your windshield?" Rocky asked as they neared his car.

Jayce approached first and snagged the note and silky black fabric from beneath the windshield wiper. His gut clenched as he passed the sexy thong to Rocky. "Yours?"

She flushed, frowned. "What the hell?" She nabbed the typewritten note from Jayce's hand and read aloud the words already burned in his brain. *"You crushed my life, now I'll crush yours."*

Fury pumping through his blood, Jayce loaded the picnic supplies and Brewster into the car. Then he took back the thong and note and ushered a flustered Rocky into the car. "Lock yourself in. I want to look around."

"Jayce—"

"Lock the damned door." He waited until she complied, then did a quick but careful sweep of the perimeter. His suspicions had been confirmed. Someone was stalking Rocky. Someone with a personal beef. Jayce had assumed Billy, but now he considered Adam. "Great guy" or not, he'd been burned and the jealousy and anger Jayce had felt emanating from Adam at the Shack had been intense.

"Find anything?" Rocky asked when Jayce joined her in the car.

"Nothing of consequence." He keyed the ignition. "You're moving in with me."

"What?"

"Just until I nail the bastard who's threatening you. It's someone close to you or someone who got close by breaking into the Clover and rifling your belongings."

"Maybe it *is* one of the construction crew," Rocky said in a tense voice. "I mean they have free run of the place and I'm not always there when they are. In fact, I've been gone a lot lately. Between the Cupcake Lovers and you . . ."

"Did you insult one of them? Get one of them fired?"

"Of course not."

"The note says: *You crushed my life.*" He latched on to her troubled gaze. "Aside from ending your affair with Adam, didn't you renege on a business deal as well?"

She gaped.

"He'd offered to invest in the Red Clover, to become your partner, to help you run the place, increase business and revenue, right?"

"Yes, but—"

"He was primed for a business venture. With you. The woman he was sleeping with. In one day, one moment, you ripped the professional and personal ground from beneath his feet. Depending on the depth of his emotional investment, that could qualify as crushing his world."

She shook her head. "Adam's not a vengeful man."

"Then who?"

"That's for you to find out."

Jayce lifted a brow.

"I don't want to go to the police. Not yet. If it's Billy . . . we'll have a hard time convincing the SCPD that one of their own is up to no good. If it's Adam, which it's not, but if it is, I don't want to get him in trouble with the law. Maybe he's just hurt and . . . lashing out. For all I know it's Tasha. Or, hell, maybe it's a couple of teenagers, pulling a prank. What with Halloween around the corner, it's possible, right?"

"Anything's possible." But he highly doubted a Halloween prank.

"Just do what you do and find out who it is and we'll handle it from there. Okay?"

She was putting her trust in him, allowing him an inch.

"In return, I'll move in with you. For a while. Most of the renovations on the Clover are moving upstairs next week anyway."

Jayce reached over and squeezed her hand. *An inch, hell.* She was giving him a mile. "I'll get to the bottom of this, Dash."

"I know. Just please be discreet. That video crew is flying in tomorrow."

Jayce didn't give a damn about that publishing contract and Tasha's "no scandal" decree. But he did care about Rocky and the Cupcake Lovers. "No worries, hon. *Discreet* is my middle name."

CHAPTER TWENTY-EIGHT

Given the multiple surprises and shockers on Tuesday, Rocky had been stunned when Wednesday and then most of Thursday had whooshed by without any major incidents. In fact, things had been so uneventful, she'd almost forgotten about the ominous note threatening to crush her life. She wanted to believe it was a prank. She maintained that anyone could've broken into the Red Clover when she wasn't there. Anyone could have swiped a pair of her underwear and typed up a stupid note. Yes, it was creepy and mean, but unlike Jayce, she wasn't worried about someone causing her actual harm. Not even Billy Burke. Yes, he was a weasel and a bully, but she'd known him all his life and she'd never known him to cause malicious physical harm.

Leave it to Jayce to point out that crushing her life could entail ruining the career or reputation of one or several of her loved ones. It just seemed so over-the-top, she couldn't imagine. Or maybe she didn't *want* to imagine.

Since nothing sinister had happened on the heels of the note and since Jayce hadn't dug up any damning dirt, it had been relatively easy to push the ugly incident from her mind. Instead, Rocky had concentrated on training Brewster and settling in with Jayce. She'd cleaned, and decorated, and cooked up a storm. She'd put in a few hours at Maple Molly's and a couple of hours helping to construct the Creepy

Cupcake booth for the Spookytown Spectacular. When Jayce wasn't with her, Brewster was. Unlike at the Shack, everyone else had welcomed her canine friend with open arms.

Now she was at Moose-a-lotta, along with half of the Cupcake Lovers, gearing up for a private bake-a-thon. She'd joined forces with Chloe, Monica, Judy, and Rachel to make the eighteen dozen giveaway pumpkin spice cupcakes.

Gram, Helen, Ethel, and Casey had joined Sam at his house in order to tackle the fondant. The overall workload was so massive it made sense to divide their efforts and join up later for the actual cupcake decorating.

Tasha and her husband had taken the video crew out for dinner at the Pine and Periwinkle Inn. *We'll meet you at Moose-a-lotta around six thirty,* she'd said to Rocky during a short call. *Start baking on schedule. It will look better if you're in the thick of things when we arrive.* Acting as the club's liaison, Tasha had toured the three-person team around Sugar Creek the day before and then accompanied them when they'd filmed candid interviews with the senior members of the club. Gram had texted Rocky that the "shoot" had been successful and that she'd managed not to embarrass Tasha by spouting anything scandalous. She'd even bleached her purple hair old-lady silver in an effort to conform to Americana standards. Even Gram was doing her best to make sure the CL recipe book got its best shot at record sales. More than ever Rocky was determined to keep that irritating threatening note under wraps until that film crew left Sugar Creek.

"So how's it going at the Shack?" Monica asked Rachel as she opened a new bag of flour.

"Luke didn't ask you to work over the weekend, did he?" Chloe flitted around the café's kitchen making sure everyone had what they needed. "The kids would be so disappointed if you weren't involved in the Creepy Cupcake giveaway."

"I still can't believe Gretchen let you go," Judy said. "The children love you."

Rocky glanced up from her mixing bowl, noting the bright flush of Rachel's pale skin.

"Things are going great at the Shack," Rachel said while

measuring spices. "I've only worked two nights, but everyone's nice and if I hustle I make great tips. I'm planning to hustle big-time this weekend."

Rocky frowned. "So Luke *did* ask you to work?"

"That sucks," Monica said. "What gives? He knows you're a Cupcake Lover and he knows about our booth."

"And the video crew," Chloe added.

"Luke didn't ask me to work," Rachel said. "I offered. He's shorthanded and I need the money, plus . . . honestly, I'm not comfortable with being filmed."

Camera-shy wallflower Rachel Lacey. No one in the room was surprised.

"We'll miss you," Judy said as she, along with Chloe, lined the muffin cups. "The kids will miss you."

"What about you?" Rachel asked, turning the focus on Rocky. "Heard you got a job at Maple Molly's."

"I wish I would've known you were looking for work," Chloe said. "Daisy and I could've brought you on board here at the café."

"It was sort of a fluke," Rocky said, adding spices to her sifted flour—cinnamon, nutmeg, cloves. . . . "Right place at the right time kind of thing, plus you know how I adore collectibles. Not to mention they allow Brewster to tag along. He's fast becoming the antique barn's mascot."

"Not surprised," Monica said. "That dog's adorable. Where is he now? With Jayce?"

Rocky's heart fluttered. "Yeah. Jayce is really good with Brewster. He's good with all animals actually. He volunteered to help out at the Pixley Rescue Shelter once a week. If there was a shelter here, no doubt he'd be there every day."

"He could start a private shelter in Sugar Creek," Chloe said. "Something associated with the animal clinic, maybe. Or what about fostering dogs waiting for adoption?"

"Too much of a commitment, I'd think," Rocky said. "He plans on being pretty busy with the cyber detective agency."

"He's seems pretty busy now," Chloe said while opening several cans of pumpkin puree. "Devlin was just commenting on how he's not seeing much more of Jayce now than when he lived in Brooklyn. What's he up to anyway?"

"Aside from playing house with you?" Judy asked.

Everyone gawked at the older woman.

Judy glanced up. "Oh my. Did I say that out loud? I must be channeling Daisy. It's just we were talking, the senior members that is, about what a good-looking couple you make and how nice it is that Jayce took you in while your house is under construction. Although you could have stayed with your grandma. Since Chloe's living with Devlin now, there's certainly plenty of room."

"And once Daisy moves in with Vince," Chloe said, "that beautiful old home will be completely empty."

"I'm not living with Jayce," Rocky amended. "I'm just staying there awhile. Convenient since I'm also decorating the place."

"But you are a couple," Judy said.

By now, everyone in Sugar Creek knew. Rocky suppressed a besotted smile. At least she thought she suppressed it.

Rachel elbowed her and winked. "You're crazy about him. I think that's sweet. To think you've known him for years and the attraction only just now sparked."

Monica coughed and Rocky blushed. "Yeah, well . . ."

"Maybe there's hope for me after all," Rachel said.

"Are you talking about Sam?" Judy asked. "Surely you know he's crazy about you."

"I—," Rachel faltered, then bobbled her spoon. "Sorry. I . . . Chloe," she said, shifting the focus. "Are you okay? You look clammy."

Chloe stepped away from the cooking island. "Just need a drink of water."

"Casey mentioned she saw you coming out of Doc Worton's office yesterday. Did you catch that bug that's going around?"

"You didn't tell me you went to the doctor." Monica joined her friend at the sink. "What gives?"

"Nothing. I'm fine. Really. Please stop fussing."

"I'm not fussing and you're not fine. You've been shaky for a couple of weeks," Monica said. "I thought it was the stress of opening the café. But that's not it, is it?"

"Let it go, Monica."

"Why? What's wrong? You can tell us. You can tell *me*, for God's sake." Monica jammed a hand through her spiky hair. "Jesus. Is it serious?"

Chloe wrung her hands and Rocky got a bad feeling.

Rachel and Judy abandoned their baking efforts, their attention riveted on the heated scene between two friends.

"I'm not sick." Chloe looked Monica square in the eye. "I'm pregnant."

Rocky gasped—she couldn't help herself—as did Judy and Rachel. Rocky really wanted to squeal with joy, but the devastated look on Monica's face shut her down. *Oh, crap.*

Chloe shifted. "Monica, I—"

Someone banged on the front door of the closed café.

"Must be Tasha and the film crew," Monica said.

"Send them away," Chloe said, seemingly frozen in place.

Monica bolted from the kitchen, and Rocky and the other two women converged on Chloe.

"Dev must be thrilled," Rocky said with a quick hug.

"Congratulations, sweetie," Judy said.

Rachel teared up as she squeezed Chloe's hand. "So happy for you."

Monica burst back in with Tasha and crew before Rocky and immediate friends had a chance to retreat to their mixing bowls. "I was just telling these guys the great news," Monica said, hustling over and hugging Chloe with a big, *ready-for-my-close-up-Mr.-DeMille* fake-ass smile. "My best friend's having a baby."

* * *

"It was awful, Devlin. The way she acted all happy and carefree." Fatigued by an extralong day and the pressure of having to put on a cheery front for Tasha and crew, Chloe fell back on the bed fully clothed. "I know Monica was hamming it up for the camera crew, but even as we cleared out of Moose-a-lotta she gave me another huge hug and smile and told me how happy she was for me."

Dressed down in sweats and a tee, Devlin sat on the bed and tugged off Chloe's shoes. "Maybe it wasn't an act."

"I've known Monica all of my life. It was definitely an act. It's not that I doubt her sincerity. I know, deep down, she's genuinely thrilled for me, us. It's the fact that she's pretending it doesn't hurt."

"Sounds to me like she's putting your feelings ahead of hers. A sign of a good friend."

"But I don't want the pretense between us. I want her to know I feel her pain. I know how badly she wants a child and how disappointed she is that it hasn't happened yet. How frustrating it must be to learn about two other pregnancies in the space of a week, both accidents, one of them being her best friend. We need to talk about this."

"Can I make a suggestion?" Devlin asked as he pulled off her socks.

"Sure."

"Let Monica come to you."

"But—"

"Give her some time, Chloe. Let her process, come to terms, maybe talk to Leo for perspective—"

"That's if they're speaking."

"They're going through a rough time. They'll work it out."

"You keep saying that. Such faith."

The bed dipped as Devlin moved up and stretched alongside her. "That's because I have faith in true love."

She smiled up at the father of her child. So handsome. So strong and kind. "You say the most romantic things."

He smiled back and smoothed her hair from her face. "Setting aside the issue with Monica, how did it feel sharing the news?"

She beamed. "Great. I know the rest of the girls were dying to gush, especially Rocky. I couldn't get a read on Tasha— what was real or fake—because she was 'on' for the cameras. She pretended like she was happy for me anyway. She spun the news in a way that made 'good press' so to speak. A future Cupcake Lover in the making. The tradition lives on. Yada yada. Scandal averted."

"What about the fact that we're not married?"

"That didn't come up."

"Chloe—"

"I was thinking," she said, cutting off marriage talk. "Now that the news is out, I'd like to share it with the world. Especially your parents." She pushed up to one elbow and locked gazes with Devlin, determined to banish another secret from their lives. "I think we should fly down and tell them in person. As soon as possible."

"The timing—"

"Is perfect." She reached over and squeezed his hand. "News of a grandchild might do your dad a world of good."

He raised a brow. "Gram told you."

"I pried it out of her. Part of it anyway. I know your dad's fighting a life-threatening affliction. I don't know what specifically."

Devlin blew out a breath and rolled onto his back.

"Are you angry?"

"Relieved." He jammed his hand through his hair. "You don't know how much I wanted to confide in you, Chloe."

Heart pounding, she snuggled against Jerome Monroe's eldest son and hugged tight. "I understand. You promised your mom and dad to keep his illness secret, and promises are sacred."

"Dad's a proud and stubborn bastard. He didn't want pity and he didn't want family to worry."

"Having to keep this from Rocky and Luke must be killing you."

"I regretted the promise soon after making it. If Dad's health had taken a turn for the worse—"

"But it didn't," Chloe said, feeling his unease. "Your dad's on the mend."

"Thanks to radical treatment and top-notch specialists. He's hoping to come home for Christmas."

"Is he ever going to come clean about whatever he's been fighting?"

"Prostate cancer. I don't know. Puts me in a hell of a spot with Rocky and Luke either way."

"This family's like an artichoke," Chloe said. "You peel away one layer, one secret, only to find another."

Devlin laughed. "Leave it to you to compare my family to food."

"At least it's one less layer between us," she said, playfully tugging up his shirt, then sliding her hand down his sweats.

"Are you trying to distract me with sex?"

"Is it working?"

"Hell, yeah." He rolled on top of her, sliding his hands over her curves, then framing her face and seducing her with a scorching kiss. "I love you, Chloe."

Her heart pounded and her soul sang. "I love you, Devlin." She quirked a gentle, teasing smile. "So are you going to introduce me to your parents, or what?"

"One stipulation."

She braced for a proposal.

"Pack a bikini."

Chloe blinked, then laughed. "You're such a guy."

"You're quite the girl. My girl."

He kissed her again, infusing her with love and hope and a sense of family.

Their family.

CHAPTER TWENTY-NINE

Day by day, little by little, Jayce was making peace with his dysfunctional childhood or at least with the house he'd grown up in. Living within these rooms, rooms Rocky had miraculously transformed with eclectic art and furnishings, infusing the space with the positive interactions between warm, caring people, not to mention an affectionate, animated dog, worked wonders in obliterating any lingering negativity. Facing Jayce's demons head-on had been a wise move, although he'd yet to slay the biggest monster. He'd wrestled with confiding in Rocky regarding the night his parents died—maybe verbalizing his guilt would exorcise that ghost. Although he'd purged his soul to Dev's dad plenty that night and had only felt worse. Bottom line, Jayce didn't want to talk about it. Not yet. Maybe not ever.

Just now he had bigger worries: Rocky's stalker.

To Jayce's amazement, she wasn't concerned or was doing a damned good job of pretending not to be concerned. The night before, she'd talked about anything but—the cupcake video shoot, the news that Chloe was pregnant, and her fear that Monica was heading toward a total meltdown. This morning Rocky had kicked off their morning with a round of hot sex followed by a run with Brewster. The sex had been amazing. Jogging through the woods that ran behind Jayce's house would've been more enjoyable if he hadn't had one eye peeled for a thong-stealing bully. Throughout the run Jayce had been primed to spy some nut job hiding behind a tree. Worse, he imagined the bastard making a grab for Rocky or taking a potshot or . . . Christ, the possibilities were endless and troublesome.

But the run had been uneventful, as had, in truth, the past couple of days.

There'd been no more threats, no evidence of anyone lurking outside Jayce's house. And the whole of Sugar Creek knew Rocky had moved in with him, at least temporarily. Jayce had made sure of it. All it took was a casual mention to Marvin, Vince Redding's son and the acting manager of Oslow's General Store, when Jayce and Rocky had dropped in for groceries. And another mention when he'd visited the hardware store to pick up supplies enabling him to rig the Red Clover with security.

Sugar Creek was a small town with small-town sensibilities. News spread fast and stories tended to mushroom as gossip rolled from one person to the next. Even though Rocky kept telling those who commented that this living arrangement was temporary, just until construction was complete at the inn, most folks already had them married off. Fine by Jayce. Not so fine with Rocky. As much as he admired her independent streak, it irritated him at the same time. Two strong personalities vying for control. The only time and place Jayce truly dominated was whenever and wherever they were having sex. He understood that compromise was the key to any successful relationship, but when the subject of their battle was Rocky's welfare he had a hard time bending. So did she. As much as he loved Brewster and as obedient and loyal as the dog was, Jayce worried he'd instilled Rocky with a false sense of security. As if nothing could touch or harm her with that dog by her side.

Jayce glanced in his rearview mirror as he backed his car onto the road. "You're obsessed, Bello." To the point of pushing her away. He knew it and was trying to get a damned handle on it, but given his past experiences on the force and as a PI working the city, he couldn't dismiss his deep-rooted concerns. That damned note attached to her thong had sent him over the edge. She kept playing it down, but he couldn't. His latest clash with Rocky had happened over breakfast when he'd tried to convince her to allow him to download an app to her phone that would allow him to track her location via GPS.

What, so you'd know when I was in the bathroom or having a beer at the Shack?

It isn't a camera, Rocky. It's a locator. And not so specific as to know what room you're in.

You're smothering me, Jayce.

And with that he allowed her to drive off to Maple Molly's with Brewster but no tracking app. Now Jayce was on his way to J.T. Monroe's Department Store to speak with Dev. Jayce needed some help, and in this instance his friend was the best source.

Pulling into Sugar Creek, Jayce noted more traffic—foot and vehicle. Traditionally, the town always buzzed more on the weekends, but especially during special events such as the Spookytown Spectacular. Honeysuckle Street had been blocked off. Instead of cars, carnival rides took up the length of that road. Food and artisan booths of various sizes crowded the sidewalks of both Honeysuckle and Main Street. Business owners all over town had decked out storefronts with Halloween decorations and, just as they did every year, Sugar Creek Elementary School had converted their gymnasium into the always popular Spookytown Haunted Hall.

On the one hand, Jayce looked forward to this weekend. As a kid he'd always loved the Spookytown Spectacular. The corners of his mouth twitched as memorable "scares" via Haunted Hall flitted through his mind.

On the other hand, it would be harder to protect Rocky during an event that attracted hundreds of people. Yes, she'd be working the Creepy Cupcake booth, but not all the time. Just like most everyone in Sugar Creek, she wanted to enjoy the many festive aspects of the Spectacular. Jayce couldn't deny her that, and he'd stay with her as much as possible.

The chaotic crowds just made it harder for him to spot trouble.

By the time he parked and made his way into J.T.'s, Jayce was pretty worked up. He was heading for Dev's office when a text came in from Rocky.

BREW & I AT MOLLY'S. GOOD 2 GO.

Jayce blew out a breath. At least she wasn't too pissed to check in. He thumbed in a reply, resisting anything that might make her feel smothered. Instead of *I love you* he typed: *Have fun.*

Which earned him a smiley face.

That was something.

He knocked on Dev's door, poked in his head. "You busy?"

"Always. Come on in, stranger." Dev swung away from his laptop and motioned Jayce to sit. "Coffee?"

"No thanks."

"Problem?"

"Couple of concerns." Jayce took a seat and absorbed his friend's easy manner. Hell, Dev almost seemed relaxed. Not his normal aura, especially during working hours. Jayce smiled. "Let's backtrack. Congratulations."

Dev smiled back. "I figured Rocky would tell you. By the time I learned Chloe had spilled the beans, it was a little late in the night and we were preoccupied."

"I can imagine. So you're happy about the baby?"

"Thrilled. Once Chloe agrees to marry me, I'll be the happiest man on earth."

"Did you ask her?"

"She won't let me." Dev waved off the topic. "It's complicated."

"Speaking of complications."

Dev raised a brow.

"Stone called. He heard a rumor about me running for sheriff, asked if there was any truth to it. I said no, and the conversation was short-lived. Regardless, I figured I better address this with Daisy. Took your advice and texted her: *Not running for sheriff. Stop pushing, gorgeous.*"

"Flirtatious compliment. Nice touch."

"Not that it helped. Got two more thumbs-up and promised votes at the hardware store."

Dev's lip twitched. " 'I'll have a talk with her."

Jayce would have seen the humor in Daisy's bulldog campaign if he hadn't been hampered by that monster of a secret. "Candidates typically dig for dirt in hopes of sullying the reputation of the competition," he said, wanting to shed greater light on his concern. "Granted, I told Stone I wasn't running, but if the rumors persist, he may think I'm plotting some sort of last-minute bid. I'm not keen on Stone rooting in my past, Dev. If he finds out about the cover-up regarding my parents' accident . . ." Jayce blew out a breath, blew off the guilt. "I can take the heat, but I'm worried about your dad."

Dev's face clouded. "What the hell's gotten into Gram? First Chloe. Now you. Did you tell Rocky?"

Jayce frowned. "Tell Rocky what?"

"About Dad's illness."

"Jerry's sick?"

"When you said you were worried about Dad, I assumed . . . Damn." Dev rubbed the back of his neck. "Yeah. Dad's been ill. He didn't want the family to know, didn't want us to worry or to hover or show pity. You know Dad."

"Strong and proud." Jayce's heart swelled and cramped as he mentally ticked off numerous other admirable qualities regarding the man who'd treated Jayce like a son. "Thought there was something going on with you," Jayce said. "Are you the only one aside from your mom who knows?"

"I had to pry it out of Mom," Dev said. "Gram pried it out of me and then the other day she slipped to Chloe. I thought maybe she slipped to you as well."

Jayce shook his head. "But now that I know, can't say that I feel right about Rocky and Luke being in the dark. How bad is it?"

"Bad, but getting better. Early retirement was a ruse. Mom and Dad relocated to Florida so he could undergo radical treatment with specialists. Thank God, he's beating this thing. Should be home by Christmas. Maybe sooner."

"So he's going to spring the news on the family over the holidays? Brush it under the rug and never bring it up? Not for anything," Jayce said. "But both of those options suck."

"I know. I'm going to have a talk with him. Do me a favor and sit on this. I want to tell Rocky and Luke myself."

Jayce eyed his friend. "Heavy load you've been carrying. And Jerry . . . Even more reason to keep anyone from rooting in my past. Looking back, I wish I wouldn't have allowed your dad to use his influence—"

"He did what he thought was right, Jayce, and Sheriff Crawford, rest his soul, didn't fight him on it."

"Still—"

"Let it go." Declaring the subject closed, Dev switched focus. "You said *concerns.* Plural. What else?"

Jayce tried to shake off the past, tried to adjust to the knowledge that Jerome Monroe was currently fighting some serious ailment. He rolled back his shoulders and focused on the present. "Your sister."

Dev quirked a brow. "Let me guess. You've only been living together for two days and Rocky's already driving you crazy."

"First of all, if she was here, Rocky would remind you we're not *living together,* she's just staying with me until renovations are complete on the Clover."

"But if you had your way . . ."

"We'd be married."

Dev grinned, a genuine smile that eased the tension in the room. "Have you broached the topic?"

"She's not ready. And besides, knowing her, she'd spin it as a 'dutiful' proposal. My way of protecting her."

The smile faltered. "From?"

"I need to talk to you about something and I need you not to freak out."

"Well, when you lead with an intro like that . . . Hell, Jayce."

"Sorry. Especially since I'm about to heap on your

already-existing worry, but here's the thing. Someone's bullying Rocky."

Dev blinked. "What, like cyberbullying? Sending her rude e-mails or messages on Facebook?'

"I almost wish. *That* I could track. No. It's more elusive than that. I've got three incidents and two suspects."

Without dramatizing, Jayce relayed the events the night Billy pulled Rocky over for the broken taillight. The same night he warned her to watch her ass. Next, the night Rocky heard a car outside the house but saw no headlights. The night she'd called Jayce because she'd been certain she was being watched. Last, and the most concrete of threats, her thong and the damned note promising to crush her life.

To Dev's credit, he didn't raise his voice. "Why am I just now hearing about this?"

"Until Tuesday's note, I wasn't totally convinced there was a serious threat. Rocky's still not convinced. She thinks it's a prank. Or at least, that's what she wants to think. She asked me to try to identify the culprit, which I would've done anyway."

Dev stood and walked to the beverage bar. He poured coffee, then added a splash of whisky. "Want a hit?"

Jayce shook his head, rolled back his shoulders. He didn't blame his friend for needing liquid fortification. By nature, Dev was overprotective of family. Knowing someone meant his sister harm had to be tying his guts in knots. Jayce knew the feeling.

"Obviously Billy is the natural suspect. He's always been a bastard and there's the longtime feud between the Burkes and Monroes."

"He's also tight with Tasha," Jayce said, "and you know how Tasha feels about Rocky. It added up until this latest incident. The message: *You crushed my life, now I'll crush yours.* How has Rocky crushed Billy's life? She can't think of anything. Can you?"

Dev shook his head.

"And the thong. That's intimate, Dev."

"No shit."

"As in personal. What's the significance of Rocky's underwear unless . . ."

"A past boyfriend? Rocky's never been one for relationships. Nothing serious anyway. I'm trying to think who . . ." He glanced at Jayce and frowned. "Adam Brody?"

Jayce shrugged.

"Can't see it."

"What do you know about him?"

"Probably as much as you. Grew up in Sugar Creek. Moved away. Moved back. Successful sports instructor." He raised a brow. "Good friend of Luke's." Dev sat and sipped his spiked coffee. "I assume you did a background check."

"Nothing suspicious or nefarious while living in Sugar Creek. Information on the years he spent in Alaska is sketchy."

"From what I remember, when he was younger Adam was a bit of a geek."

"He's not a geek now." And he'd been Rocky's freaking "friend with benefits." *It was just about sex. Christ.* "His social-networking accounts were pretty innocuous. Mostly posts about sports."

"You hacked into his social networks?"

"His Twitter feed is public and his security settings on Facebook are low. Hey, we're talking about your sister's safety."

Dev blew out a breath. "What about Billy?"

"No social networking."

"E-mails?"

Tougher to crack, but doable. "A lot of racy notes to Tasha."

"His dad's wife. Could be a new low for Billy. She reply?"

"History shows some flirty responses. They taper off, though. No recent replies."

Dev grunted. "So she got bored and blew him off."

"Or wised up and laid off traceable e-mails."

"Think they're having an affair?"

"Haven't found any proof."

Dev leaned back in his chair, absorbed. "Think about everything you've told me today, Jayce. All signs—including his questionable character—point to Billy."

"I'd agree except for that note. Do me a favor and talk to Luke about Adam."

"Accuse one of his best friends of terrorizing his sister? That'll go over well."

"Don't accuse Adam of anything. Manipulate the conversation so Luke offers an opinion on his friend's state of mind."

"And I'm doing this instead of you because?"

Jayce dragged a hand down his jaw. "Luke's aware of some hostility between Adam and me. Not to mention your brother doesn't hold me in the highest regards."

"Since when? Since you took up with Rocky? He didn't say anything to suggest he had a problem with you two dating."

"Pretty sure he's holding a grudge regarding the off-limits topic of the past. Trust me when I say Luke will be more open with you than me."

Dev shook his head. "Fine. But I don't think it's Adam."

"Jealousy can drive a man to crazy things," Jayce said while pushing out of his chair. "I've seen it. Meanwhile just help me keep tabs on Rocky this weekend. As best you can without being obvious. We need to keep this low-key for several reasons."

Dev stood and followed him to the door. "This is hard to take in, Jayce. You realize that, right? We're talking Sugar Creek. Probably the lowest crime rate in all of Vermont. Any chance the underwear and note could've been a warped prank, something unconnected to Billy's taunt or the fact Rocky got spooked one night?"

"Rocky wondered the same thing."

"Considering where you lived, all you've seen and experienced . . . Any chance you're blowing this out of proportion?"

Jayce paused on the threshold and turned. "If you're asking me if I'm paranoid about losing the woman I love, then, yeah, it's possible."

CHAPTER THIRTY

From the time she'd been a little girl, Rocky had been a sucker for the Spookytown Spectacular. She was a sucker for all holidays, especially Christmas, but there was something special about Halloween or, more specifically, the way Sugar Creek celebrated Halloween.

It was always the last weekend of October. A three-day event that officially kicked off on Friday night with food and craft vendors, carnival rides, and Haunted Hall. Saturday and Sunday featured more of the same but with special events like the costume parade, scary storytelling, pumpkin carving and decorating, and horse-drawn hayrides. Family fun and spooky sensations. Something for everyone.

She was actually glad that Highlife Publishing had sent their crew to film this weekend. Yes, the focus of their shoot was the Cupcake Lovers, but she hoped with snippets of the Spookytown Spectacular included as well, the documentary would also benefit tourism—a key source of revenue for Sugar Creek businesses. Even the Monroe family store, J.T.'s, benefited from tourism.

Knowing she had a full night ahead of her and knowing Jayce planned on attending the festival, Rocky had left Brewster with Molly. Not trusting him home alone yet and not keen on putting the dog in a crate—even though Jayce had assured her it was a "safe haven"—Rocky had been overjoyed when her new boss had volunteered to pet sit. Mind at rest on that score, Rocky had packed up the cupcakes she'd baked that afternoon and headed into town.

With his obnoxious trophy wife at his side, the mayor of Sugar Creek, Randall Burke, had kicked off the festivities at 5:00 p.m. sharp, reminding those present that most of the shops and boutiques would remain open until 9:00 p.m. and the way to get free goodies at the food and craft booths was by visiting the shops whose employees had decorated their storefronts. Each shop gave out different "goody" tickets, and all you had to do was ask a salesclerk for one. While collecting "goody" tickets for their kids, a lot of adults browsed the shops and bought merchandise. Rocky had always thought the ticket and goody exchange a clever marketing ploy. As always, the "goody" tickets for the Creepy Cupcake booth were available at J.T.'s.

"So all a child has to do," Tasha said while cheesing it up for the video camera, "is hand a Cupcake Lover one of these numbered orange tickets and they get a free cupcake. This year we're featuring Sam McCloud's creation—Monster-Mash Cakes." She presented a sample to the interviewer—Amber—then passed the cupcake to the kid who'd given her the ticket.

"Where's Rachel?" the little girl asked.

Tasha retained her fake smile. "Rachel's not here."

"But Mommy said she's a Cupcake Lover."

"She is," Tasha said to the girl, then looked to the mom. "But she's not here."

"Can I have my ticket back?" the girl asked.

Tasha blinked. "Why?"

"I want Rachel to give me my cupcake."

"Sorry," the mom said with a self-conscious glance toward the camera. "Laurie attends Sugar Tots and she misses Rachel. We thought . . ." She squeezed her daughter's shoulder. "Just say thank you, baby."

"Can I have my ticket back?"

Red-faced, Tasha handed the kid a ticket. *At least she didn't ask for the cupcake back,* Rocky thought. *Points for Tasha.*

One of Highlife's people stepped over for a word with the mother, and Amber motioned for the camera to "cut" before turning back to Tasha. "Did we meet Rachel last night? Was she on the fondant team or cupcake team?"

"The cupcake team," Tasha said. "Although I don't think . . . Wait. I know I saw her."

Rocky added the last of her Choco PB & Pumpkin Cupcakes to the "Cupcakes for Charity" display, then interceded. Thus far, she'd allowed Tasha free reign with the camera crew. As much as Rocky hated to admit it, her longtime foe had been saying and doing all the right things. But in this instance Rocky worried Tasha would make poor Rachel look bad. "She left early," Rocky said. "Just after you arrived. She wasn't feeling well." Or at least that's what Rachel had claimed when, head lowered, shoulders hunched, she'd made her apologies to Rocky, Chloe, and Judy and scooted out the back door. Rocky had called to check on Rachel this morning, and she'd been better. Good enough to work at the Sugar Shack tonight. *Go figure.*

"That's too bad," Amber said. "But, she'll be working the booth at some point this weekend, right? Brett specifically asked for a cameo appearance, at least, of every member."

"She'll be here," Tasha said.

Rocky shot her a look.

"At some point."

"Hey, Amber!" one of the camera guys called. "That woman wouldn't sign a release form. Doesn't want her kid in the film. Said she was impolite."

"That's a shocker," Amber said. "Most parents nowadays wouldn't care about their kid's manners if it meant getting them some media exposure."

Tasha brightened. "We're going to be an Internet sensation," she said to Rocky.

"That's what Highlife's hoping," Amber said. "Excuse me. I want to get a shot of the line forming and . . . check out the Moose!"

"Millie Moose," Rocky said with a smile. "Official mascot of Moose-a-lotta. Honorary Cupcake Lover."

"Who's in there?" Amber asked. "Chloe?"

"Daisy."

"Your grandma? Oh, this is priceless."

Amber left the small booth, and Rocky breathed a sigh of relief. "Are they going to be here all night?"

"The film crew? On and off," Tasha said. "About Rachel—"

"She's not coming."

"Everyone's working the booth at some point. It's tradition."

"She has her reasons."

"Which are?"

"Her own." A lame snarky-ass reply, but Rocky didn't know why Rachel was so adverse to participating in the video, or being photographed for that matter. Okay. So she was kind of mousy and shy, but she was also a skilled baker and generous soul. Dedicated to the club and the cause. Or so Rocky thought.

Rocky didn't give a fig about personal fame, but she was stinking proud of being a Cupcake Lover. She was a team player, and the team was gung ho for this book project and all it entailed. It kind of hurt that Rachel couldn't or wouldn't conquer her insecurity (if that was the problem) for friends and the cause.

"You need to talk some sense into her," Tasha said.

"What? Why me?"

"Because *you're* the president," Tasha whispered in a hushed voice.

Rocky blinked. How could the woman sound so angry and look so calm? Her fake smile bordered on scary.

"Have I told you, by the way, how much I resent that you stole that title from me? My mom hoped . . . and Randall wanted . . . Oh, what do you care? You'll never be alone."

"Hold on.'"

"Go to hell."

Rocky stood shell-shocked as Tasha walked, not stormed, off. The seeming epitome of grace, Tasha smiled and chatted amiably with a few people waiting in line for cupcakes before disappearing into the growing crowd. Even though she was seething on the inside, outwardly she seemed fine.

No bickering or backstabbing. No scandal. No freaking drama.

Pretending for the camera. Pretending in order to secure a shot at fame.

You'll never be alone.

What did Tasha mean by that? Was her marriage in trouble? When they'd appeared on the podium together, Tasha and Randall had looked like a happily married couple. Were they putting up a united front for the sake of appearances? Was Billy the source of strife? Had Tasha screwed up and gotten in over her head? An affair, with her stepson no less, would be a huge freaking scandal. Randall wouldn't stand for it. Sugar Creek wouldn't stand for it.

What would it be like to lose everything? Rocky wondered. *Your husband, your reputation, your home?* Unlike Rocky, Tasha didn't have a big family. She didn't have any real friends.

"Snap out of it, Rocky," Casey said as she stepped into the booth and tied on an apron. "We've got cupcakes to give away. What were you thinking about?" she asked as they worked in tandem. "You look weird."

"I think I feel sorry for Tasha."

Casey snorted. "Definitely weird."

* * *

Happy Hour had been chaotic, and the reservations list for dinner was booked full. The Sugar Shack was rocking. Luke should have been on top of the world. Instead, he was distracted.

By Rachel Lacey.

Once again, she'd traded her typical baggy dress for a formfitting shirt and pants. She'd brushed her hair into a high ponytail, a style that accentuated her face. When she smiled—something she'd been doing a lot of tonight—Luke got a tight feeling in his chest. It had gotten to the point where just thinking about her gave him an erection. He wished to hell the attraction was simply sexual, but she'd gotten under his skin and he wasn't even sure why.

Luke mixed drinks and chatted up customers just like he always did. Gena worked alongside him at the bar, and a full waitstaff worked the dining area and pub. A hundred things and a dozen people vied for his attention, but his gaze kept drifting to Rachel. He'd been so convinced she'd be a lousy waitress, but she was amazing. Fast and efficient, friendly. He knew without asking that she was focused on impeccable service in order to earn hefty tips.

I need the money.

He sensed a nervous energy beneath her capable façade. He sensed her discomfort when anyone's gaze lingered too long or when a guy openly flirted. Yeah, Luke was watching that closely. And he just happened to be watching when a guy grabbed her ass. Rachel flinched and backed away. The bastard nabbed her wrist.

Luke was around the bar and at her side in two seconds flat. "Let her go." He didn't know the guy. Luke didn't know a lot of people in the Shack tonight. The town was crowded with tourists.

"Relax, dude."

"Luke Monroe. This is my place. My rules. No inappropriate touching of the staff. No touching, period."

The kid raised his hands in mock apology. "Just trying to get her attention."

"You got it. And mine."

The kid's friends shifted in their seats. "Message noted," one of them said.

Rachel stood tense beside Luke, pencil poised over her pad. "I'm sorry. What was it you wanted? A vodka what?"

The college kid who'd manhandled her leaned forward and stared down Luke. "You can back off now, Monroe. Lighten up, for Christ sake. If she didn't want the attention she wouldn't dress like that."

The only reason Luke didn't clock the guy was because Rachel placed her hand on his arm just before he snapped.

"Luke, please. Don't."

"Let's blow this place." The guy and his friends stood. "Uptight asshole."

Luke let the insult slide. He let the guys go without trying to smooth things over. But he did apologize to the nearby patrons who'd focused on the showdown and motioned to Nell, who was working as hostess tonight, regarding a sudden opening for a table of four. Then he focused on Rachel. "You okay?"

Eyes downcast, cheeks flushed, she gave a stiff nod.

Damn. "Come with me." He placed his hand at the small of Rachel's back and guided her through the crowd. He caught Gena's gaze and she nodded in understanding. He'd be back.

For the moment, he ushered Rachel into his office and shut out the chaos. When he turned, she had her back to him, her hands braced on his desk as if trying to catch her breath or needing to bolster shaky legs.

"I'm sorry," she said in a small voice.

"What? Don't apologize, honey. I'm the one who told you tighter clothes might encourage greater tips. I don't get a lot of gropers in here. I didn't anticipate—"

"I don't think I can go back out there."

Luke moved closer, his stomach in knots. "Sure you can. Don't let an isolated incident put you off."

"I don't like it when people stare. I don't like standing out. If I walk out there now—"

"Then don't. Take a break. Hang out here in the office for twenty. Catch your breath." He put his hands on her shoulders and squeezed. He'd meant to reassure, but her muscles bunched. He let go and she turned, tears shimmering in her eyes. His heart stuttered.

"When you championed me like that . . ." Her voice cracked and a tear fell.

Had no man ever stood up for her before? Troubled, Luke cradled Rachel's face and thumbed away tears. He looked into her eyes. Her *expressive* brown eyes. Affection. Adoration. For *him.* Why hadn't he noticed before? Chest tight, he swallowed hard. "Rachel . . ."

She leaned in.

It was all the invitation he needed. Luke gave over to his curiosity and a burning need. He kissed Rachel Lacey with restrained passion. A gentle kiss meant to soothe, yet when she put her arms around him he took the kiss deeper. His heart blossomed and pounded in his ears.

"Aw, hell."

Luke tensed, turned. "Sam."

"I knocked," his cousin said. "You didn't answer." His injured gaze flicked to Rachel. "Now I know why. Sorry." He turned to leave.

"Goddammit, Sam. Wait!" Luke turned to Rachel, who'd slumped back against the desk, face pale. "Wait here. I'll be back." Luke flew out of his office and into a mass of customers. Packed tables, standing room only. Pool balls clacked; music blared. A wash of conversation and laughter battered Luke's whirling senses as he scanned the crush of people in search of Sam. Nell caught Luke's attention and jerked a thumb at the front door. Sam had left. *Shit.*

Luke jammed a hand through his hair, trying to collect his thoughts. *Okay. One crisis at a time.* He moved back toward his office, but Gena whistled and waved him over to the bar. He squeezed in between two patrons and spoke over the noise. "What is it?"

"Rachel blew out the back door."

Damn. "Thanks." He turned and slammed into another one of his waitresses.

"Anna needs you in the kitchen," she said. "An emergency."

He glanced at the back door, then blinked back to business. A packed house and an emergency in his kitchen.

He'd give Sam space to cool off and Rachel time to calm down. Yeah, that was it. It had to be it.

One crisis at a time.

* * *

Jayce felt a flutter of panic when he lost hold of Rocky's hand. He reached out and grasped air. Surrounded by darkness, lost in a maze of creepy antics, he wondered what the hell he'd been thinking when he'd agreed to take Rocky through the Spookytown Haunted Hall. "Dash."

She didn't answer.

A group of giggly, skittish teen girls had rushed past them, squeezing through one of the narrower passages and forcing Jayce and Rocky apart. She had to be near. Just ahead. Or behind.

Jayce turned a corner and spied a body hanging from a noose. The hair on the back of his neck prickled. It was a dummy. A fake body. He knew it. The Haunted Hall was rigged with dozens of props and illusions. Occasionally costumed actors—members of a local amateur theater group—hopped out of secret passages or reached out from behind a curtain or dark corner and grabbed an unsuspecting person. Hence the occasional shriek or scream. The element of surprise delivered the best scares.

To think he used to love this place and the anticipation of being spooked out of his gourd.

Where the hell was she?

He pulled out his cell and texted: *Where r u?*

Someone slammed into him and screamed.

Jayce made out a young girl and boy—twelve maybe.

The girl lapsed into nervous giggles. The boy rolled his eyes. "Jeez, mister. What are you, frozen in fear?" He snorted and they edged around him. The girl shrieked again when she saw the hanging body. "You're such a wiener, Ellie."

"Stuff it, Pete."

Jayce imagined young versions of himself and Rocky and endured a jolting wave of melancholy. The kids disappeared around the next bend. Jayce followed, checked his cell. A text from Rocky.

OUTSIDE. WHERE R U?
ON MY WAY

Jayce booked through the maze, earning curses and grumbles as he shoved his way through the clogged passages. Exiting the maze and gym, he welcomed the brisk night air, scanned the lighted schoolyard . . . and saw Rocky sitting on a bench under a massive maple. Heart hammering, he joined her.

Rocky frowned and raked his hair from his face. "Are you okay? You're sweating."

"It was tight in there. Hot."

"Not that hot."

He sleeved his brow. "What happened to you? Where did you go?"

"When those kids broke us apart, I got shoved through a curtain and ended up in another passage. It was so dark in there. I got turned around. Then one of those actors grabbed me—"

"Are you sure it was an actor?"

"Of course it was an actor." Rocky blinked. "You got scared. Seriously scared. You thought someone nabbed me." She palmed the side of his face. "Or worse. Jesus, Jayce. It's the Haunted Hall. You know what that place is about. You've been through it hundreds of times."

"I know." He caressed her hand, then kissed her palm. "Marry me, Dash."

She gaped and Jayce's stuttering heart stopped.

"Christ." He leaned back against the bench. "I can't seem to get this right. I don't even have a ring."

"I'm thinking this was some sort of freaky knee-jerk re-action to the scare," Rocky said, avoiding his gaze. "Let's just, you know, forget it." She leaned back against the bench, too. "Talk to me, Bello."

Jayce stared at the colorful lights of the carnival rides, breathed in the comforting scents of local foods, and re-laxed a little as Rocky leaned in and interlaced her fingers with his. As he knew she wasn't a fan of PDA, the show of affection meant the world. "I had a friend in Brooklyn, Mrs. Watson. Sofia Watson. She owned the co-op next to mine. My neighbor for nine years.

"She took me under her wing the day I moved in, treated me as an adopted son," he went on. "She saw my girlfriends come and go. Watched me grow cynical and then almost apathetic about my detective work. One day she told me a story about her deceased husband—a long romantic story about a very short-lived courtship and marriage."

"Why short?" Rocky asked.

"Because he was killed in Vietnam. He was going off to war just before they married."

"She knew he might not come back and she married him anyway?"

"She wanted to make the most of their time no matter how long or short. Instead of pitying herself, she pitied people who played it safe. According to her, there was nothing more sad than a missed opportunity."

"She sounds like a pretty cool lady."

"She was."

"Was?"

"She died two months ago. Heart attack."

Rocky squeezed his hand.

"I was with her when it happened. She'd cooked me dinner . . . Christ she was always worried I didn't eat right even though I did." He stroked a thumb over Rocky's knuckles. "She brought up her husband, how they were soul mates, her one-and-only. I thought it was sentimental slop. That's what I wanted to believe anyway. Except you were always on my mind, in my mind. Mrs. Watson knew about you. The memory of you. Her last words were those of undying love, lost opportunities, and vast possibilities. *Tend to your soul,* she said."

Jayce glanced over, locked on to Rocky's beautiful face. "I moved back to Sugar Creek to reclaim the life I wanted. That includes conquering a monster demon, surrounding myself with the only real family I've ever known, and spending my life with you. If anything happened . . . I don't want to lose you, Rocky. To anyone or anything." He felt her shock, her apprehension. He braced for rejection. *You're moving too fast. You're smothering me.*

"Oh, Jayce." She brushed a kiss over his mouth, then smiled into his eyes. "Let's go pick up Brewster and go home."

CHAPTER THIRTY-ONE

Luke woke up in a shitty mood for the second day in a row.

He called Rachel first thing.

She didn't answer.

He called Sam's cell. No answer. He tried the man's landline. Luke's cousin, Mina picked up the phone. "Hello?"

"Hey, sweetie. This is Uncle Luke. Where's your daddy?"

"Upstairs helping Ben pick out his costume for the parade."

"Oh. Can you run up and tell him I want to talk to him?"

"Sure." She hung up.

Damn. Luke waited a minute and called back.

"Hello?"

"Mina, sweetie, it's Uncle Luke. Did you tell your daddy I called?"

"Yup. He says he's busy." She hung up again.

Christ. Luke gave up on a phone discussion. He was pretty sure the costume parade started at 10:00 a.m. Once in town, Sam would spend most of the day there with the kids. Saturday was a big family day at the Spookytown Spectacular. Sam would be there as a single dad. Had he dropped in at the Shack last night to invite Rachel along? Luke's gut clenched with guilt remembering how hurt Sam had looked when he'd walked in on him and Rachel. Chrissakes, Luke had shared a beer with Sam, listening to him gush about Rachel and then encouraging him to continue his pursuit. And then Luke had *kissed* the woman. Talk about a betrayal.

Cursing a blue streak, Luke stabbed his legs into a pair of jeans and pulled on a long-sleeved tee. He jammed his feet into sneakers, nabbed a flannel jacket, and blew out the door. No time to shower or shave. He wanted to catch Sam before he left the house. He needed to apologize, to make things right, or as good as he could anyway. He couldn't remember ever screwing up this badly with a family member. He would've called Dev for advice but was too damned embarrassed.

Fifteen minutes later, Luke pulled into Sam's driveway still unsure as to what he was going to say. Should he admit he had feelings for Rachel himself? Or would that only make it worse? Head throbbing, he walked across the manicured lawn marveling that he could feel so confused and depressed on such a clear, sunny day. As he approached the house, the kids bounded outside: Mina, a five-year-old cutie, dressed as a princess. Ben, a serious-minded eight-year-old, dressed as a race-car driver—including helmet and gloves.

Luke stooped to their eye level. "You guys look amazing."

"Thanks, Uncle Luke," Ben said.

"We're gonna be on a float," Mina said.

"That's cool," Luke said. He couldn't believe how much Mina looked like Paula now. Instead of saying that, he said, "I can't believe how much you guys have grown."

"That's what happens when you don't see them very often," Sam said. "Do me a favor, kids. Wait in the truck, will you? And buckle up!" he called when they ran off and disappeared around the hedges.

Feeling like shit, Luke dragged a hand down his unshaven jaw. "I need to talk to you, Sam."

"Make it quick."

"I'm sorry."

Sam stared, that death glare he'd honed in the military. The silence was excruciating.

Luke shifted, scrambled for an explanation that didn't come.

"That's it? *Sorry?*"

"Really sorry." *Oh, hell.* "Just hit me or something, Sam. Get it out of your system. I deserve it."

"Yeah, you do." Except Sam just continued to glare. Then he averted his gaze and shook his head, which was almost worse because it suggested he was not only angry with Luke but also ashamed of him.

Just when Luke thought Sam was turning to stalk off, the man swung around and clocked him with a haymaker. Luke went down hard. His vision blurred and his ears rang. He worked his jaw, certain it was busted. It wasn't. But as Sam walked away, Luke's heart cracked.

* * *

Chloe was in the kitchen making Spanish omelets when Devlin walked in and kissed her on the back of the neck. She smiled. "Morning, handsome."

"Morning, beautiful." He helped himself to a cup of coffee and snatched up the Saturday paper. "I have to say, I'm glad Gram and Connie offered to open Moose-a-lotta this morning. Lazy mornings with you are rare."

"We're trying to switch things up so we can each put in time at the Creepy Cupcake booth. Since Daisy insists on wearing that moose costume for the Spectacular, I'd rather her work the booth in the evening when it's cooler."

"Always looking out for Gram. Just one of the things I love about you."

"Vince is looking out for her, too."

"I know." Devlin lowered the paper and quirked a brow. "You don't have to keep reminding me."

She loaded up two plates and joined Devlin at the table. "Did you hear from Jayce yet today?"

"Called a few minutes ago." His expression sobered as he set aside the paper. "Nothing new. No more threats. No suspicious incidents."

"That's a good thing. Why don't you look happy?"

"Because whether it's an actual problem or not, Jayce planted that stalker scenario in my head."

Chloe toyed with her food. "I have to admit I tossed and turned with the idea last night."

"I shouldn't have worried you with it."

"I'm glad you told me. I can keep my eyes peeled for anything weird while we're working the booth together."

"If you see or hear anything suspicious, call me or Jayce. Don't get involved."

"Don't worry."

"Good luck with that."

Chloe smiled. "What was I thinking?" Devlin Monroe was the most protective and caring man she'd ever known. God, she loved him. Even when he made her crazy.

"After I drop you at the cupcake booth, I'm going to head over and talk to Luke about Adam."

"I can't imagine Adam writing a vengeful note."

"Neither can I. But like Jayce said, you never know. I'm hoping Luke can put any doubt to rest." Devlin sipped more coffee, motioning Chloe to keep her seat when someone knocked on the door.

Chloe sipped her milk, hoping to calm her stomach. She hoped Jayce was wrong and Devlin was right and that note had been nothing more than a warped prank.

"Someone to see you," Devlin said.

Chloe turned just as Monica walked in with a huge bouquet of flowers. "Oh, my God. Those are *beautiful*."

"They're for you," Monica said with a genuine smile. "And Dev. An official congratulations from Leo and me. We're so happy for you."

Chloe's throat clogged. "Really?"

"I'll wait in the living room," Devlin said.

"No, don't go," Monica said. She set the vase of flowers near the sink, then leaned back against the counter. "You both know where my head's been at, and suffice it to say I had a bit of a meltdown after Chloe shared your news. Which," she said, warding off Chloe with a raised hand, "resulted in Leo and me having a long talk. A really long and intense talk. It was good. Better than good. For some reason this time we each were more inclined to really hear what the other person was saying." She rolled back her shoulders, then smiled. "We decided to take a trip. To go off somewhere for three whole weeks. Just the two of us. To kind of, I don't know, rediscover *us* as a couple."

"Sounds like a great idea," Devlin said.

Chloe smiled. "Where are you going?"

Monica beamed. "Europe. We're starting in Paris. Leo said every woman should see Paris at least once." She laughed. "I think he read that somewhere."

"I can't imagine Leo in Paris," Devlin said.

"Neither can I," Monica said, "but that's part of what makes it so romantic. I can't believe he'd go so far out of his comfort zone for me."

"I can." Teary-eyed and heart full, Chloe moved over and hugged her best friend. "I'm so glad things are looking up."

"I'm already lucky in life," Monica said. "I'd just forgotten." She smacked a kiss to Chloe's forehead. "Leo's waiting outside. I should run. See you guys later at the Spectacular?"

"Absolutely."

Monica scooted past Devlin, who was leaning against the doorjamb looking incredibly smug.

"If you say, *I told you so,*" Chloe said as she admired the gorgeous bouquet, "you can forget about the incredible dessert I planned on making tonight."

"Just glad the day's starting on a bright note," Devlin said, giving her butt a playful swat as he returned to his breakfast.

Chloe smiled while setting the vase in the center of the table. "I'm feeling optimistic about the day as a whole. In the words of Tasha, *No bickering or backstabbing. No drama.*"

* * *

Rocky went to bed and woke up with Jayce's voice ringing in her ears. *Marry me, Dash.*

She hadn't taken him seriously at the time because he'd

been in the midst of an adrenaline rush, but those words, the notion, had spoken to her innermost fantasy. It hadn't been much more romantic than the first time he'd proposed, but it was what he'd said after—that he'd moved home to reclaim his life and to be with *her*. *That* had rocked her world.

She'd been all over him on the ride home, had practically tackled him when they'd walked through the door. The sex had been intense and meaningful, and Rocky had clung to Jayce through the night, silent assurance that she was with him—safe and sound, heart and soul. She wasn't going off to war. No one was going to nab her. He'd followed his heart, which had led him to Sugar Creek. And her. She'd been right all along. They were meant to be.

This morning they'd swigged OJ, then taken a long run with Brewster. After a sexy shower, Jayce had checked his e-mail and handled some business while Rocky whipped up a batch of French toast. She felt almost as comfortable in his kitchen as she did in her own. Then again, she'd arranged all the cabinets. His house as a whole was coming along—a touch of Rocky inspired by Jayce. Most important, over the last couple of days she'd focused on infusing every room with some sort of cheer—whether by way of a decoration or by doing something silly or sexy or kind. Her plan was to create so many wonderful memories that there'd be no room left for the bad. She'd never considered herself a do-gooder, certainly not someone who acted frilly or fruity just to get a smile out of a guy. But getting to know Jayce, learning what made him tick, had affected her own view on life. To think she'd wallowed in her misfortune to the extent of losing perspective. No matter her business or financial woes, she'd always had the love and support of her family. Was there anything more precious?

"I can't ever remember being this happy," Rocky said as they drove toward the Red Clover.

"Then why do you look so miserable?"

"Because I'd rather be watching the costume parade with you and Brewster instead of doing this stupid interview." Amber had pinned her down last night, suggesting they film her segment at the Red Clover. "I didn't mind when the crew filmed us baking cupcakes at Moose-a-lotta or working the Creepy Cupcake booth. I just ignored them and did my thing."

"You'll be doing your thing this morning, too," Jayce said while cracking the back window to give Brewster more air. "Talking to someone about the history of Cupcake Lovers and your upcoming charitable efforts. You do it all the time."

"But not on camera. And not with a professional interviewer who looks like a glammed-up Katie Couric." Rocky flipped down the visor and inspected her hair. "I'm beginning to rethink my braids. Maybe you should fuss with my hair. Do that tousled half-updo thing."

Jayce cut her a glance. "Just be yourself and think about the free exposure for the Red Clover."

She grinned. "There is that. It's a double whammy when you think about it. I'll be talking up the Cupcake Lovers and our cause in the comfort and charm of a Victorian B and B. Maybe viewers will be so intrigued, they'll want to visit."

"Just be sure to mention the name of the inn."

"Chloe suggested the same thing. She said that might inspire people to Google the Red Clover. Did I tell you she's helping me beef up my Web site? She's really good at marketing stuff."

"Oh, right. She did a stint in PR when she lived in New York."

"She dabbled in a lot of creative arts, but you'd know that since you investigated her background. Speaking of . . ." Rocky shifted in her seat and broached an uncomfortable subject. "You never said, but I assume you looked into Adam's history."

"I didn't learn anything that raised any red flags and I didn't say because you have a problem with my snooping into people's lives."

"That was before I understood how truly relevant snooping is to your work. Plus I think I was grasping for any reason to maintain emotional distance." Her ancient grudge exploded in her mind. Shame washed over her soul. "I can't believe how petty I was. If I hadn't shut you out that morning and all the years after . . . When I think of the wasted time."

Jayce reached over and squeezed her hand. "I'd rather think about the years ahead of us."

Such a perfect thing to say and yet a shiver iced down her spine.

As if sensing her tension, Brewster poked his head over the seat and licked her ear.

Jayce frowned. "Something I said?"

"It's just . . ." Rocky stroked her dog's head, grappled for the right words. "Remember when I mentioned not ever being this happy?"

"And once again you look miserable."

"I'm happy now. Right now. I'm so stinking happy, somehow it doesn't feel right."

"Like you don't deserve it?"

"Like it's too good to be true. When I think about the future . . . Every time I want something badly, Jayce, somehow I screw it up."

"Do you want me?"

"You know I do."

"Then you won't screw it up."

"How do you know?"

"I won't let you."

Her heart pounded against her tight chest. Yeah, boy, she had it bad for Jayce Bello. She had always had it bad. *I want, I want, I want* . . . "What scares you most in this world, Jayce?"

"Aside from losing you?"

Rocky's pulse skipped. Although they'd agreed to take their relationship one day at a time, it was definitely on the fast track.

"Other than that," Jayce said, "the only thing that scares me is the inability to forgive myself regarding my parents' deaths. Logically I know . . ." He blinked, then shook his head. "I didn't think I'd ever be able to talk about this and I don't know why I blurted it just now. Damn."

Stunned, Rocky gaped at Jayce's somber profile. "What are you talking about? It was an accident."

"One I could have prevented if I'd stopped my mom from driving off." Jayce flexed his fingers on the steering wheel, worked his jaw. "She was drunk, Rocky. Then again, Angie was always drunk. I walked into the house just as she was getting ready to leave to meet Joe at some party. A swingers' party, I assumed, and made a snide comment. We argued and she lashed out with some razor-mean shit. Nothing I hadn't heard in some form before, but that night I snapped. Among other things, I wished her dead."

His stricken expression sliced Rocky's soul. She struggled for the right thing to say, choosing to stay objective. "You got a community service award that night. So did Dev. I remember being in the gym with my whole family and wondering why your parents weren't there to cheer you on. I assumed work." She swallowed around the miserable lump in her throat. "You were a teen, Jayce, and you were hurt and angry. It's not uncommon at that age to say ugly things to a parent in the heat of the moment." She reached over and placed a comforting palm on his thigh. "It's not like you meant it."

"Regardless, I stood by as she stormed out. It's not like Angie hadn't driven under the influence before. What I didn't take into account was that she'd drink even more at the party. And that my dad would indulge to excess as well."

Rocky's heart pounded up into her throat. "There was no mention of your parents being intoxicated in the newspapers, no gossip."

Jayce cut her a meaningful glance. "That's because your dad spoke with the acting sheriff and, working together, they suppressed that piece of information."

Rocky palmed her forehead, mind reeling. "Is that legal?"

Jayce hiked a brow. "Your dad knew I blamed myself. Knew that if the accident was attributed to alcohol it would cast a shadow over my parents, me. Bottom line, he reasoned, it was late, dark, and Joe was speeding on a winding, rain-slick mountain road. He could have lost control even sober."

Rocky chewed on that. She knew that stretch of road and, oh yes, spinning out while speeding in inclement weather was a definite possibility—even sober. "So all that was suppressed was the toxicology report?"

"It's ancient history," Jayce said, "and I could deal with the stink if the news ever came to light. But I worry about your dad's reputation."

Rocky smiled a little, thinking about how courageous and caring it had been for her dad to go out on a limb like that for Jayce. She wasn't shocked as much as proud. "Dad can take care of himself."

"That's pretty much what Dev said."

Rocky nodded. Of course Dev had been privy to specifics. At eighteen her brother and Jayce had still been close to inseparable. She blew out a breath. "Okay. So the fact that alcohol could have contributed to the accident is sad, but . . . it seems to me, given everything you've told me about your parents, a similar accident could have happened at any time. Stopping your mom from leaving the house that night might have saved her, them, for one more day, maybe. Maybe not." She thought about Jayce's work in law enforcement, his intent regarding his cyber detective agency, his dedication to homeless animals. "You can't save everyone," Rocky said while reaching for Jayce's hand. "Regarding your parents, curse their lifestyle, curse fate, but don't curse yourself."

Jayce squeezed her hand. "I'm sorry I unloaded something so heavy just before your interview."

Her heart ached as she wondered what it would feel like having to live with that kind of guilt, wishing she could wish it away. "I'm all right with it, Jayce. The question is, are you?"

He slowed the car as they neared the Red Clover. "Considering I just spewed my darkest regret to you, I guess I'm getting there. Film crew beat us," Jayce said, switching gears.

"What?" Rocky looked ahead and saw Highlife's rented van in front of the Red Clover. Amber was walking around the house, and the two camera guys were shooting footage of the mountain scenery. "Crap. Turn around. I don't need to do this. Not now. I'll call Amber and reschedule. Let's do something fun. Together." All she could think about was creating some incredible wonderful memory, something to cast sunshine on Jayce's troubled past.

He smiled then. "I'm okay, Dash. Really. Do the interview."

She sensed some sort of relief in his being, a new tentative calm. "If you're sure."

"I'm sure."

"All right," she said, trying to perk up for Jayce's sake. "I just wish they hadn't shown early. I need time to tidy the downstairs."

"Brewster and I will give them a tour of the grounds."

"They're already touring the grounds," Rocky noted with a sigh.

"Don't worry. I'll buy you some time."

Her heart swelled. "I appreciate it. At least the contractors started painting the exterior," she said as he pulled into the gravel drive. "Oh, my God, it looks *fantastic!*" She'd gotten so used to the faded and cracked façade, the fresh coat of sunshine yellow nearly stole away her breath. "Since they don't work on weekends, we'll have to wait until next week to see the finished product, but they're going to paint the shutters and gables crimson spice. Can you imagine it?"

"I can. Your attention to detail, inside and out, is impressive, Rocky."

"Hopefully, tourists will agree." Warmed by his genuine enthusiasm, Rocky unbuckled her seat belt. "I just need to whip some tarps off of the furniture. If you can buy me fifteen minutes—"

"Done."

Rocky hotfooted it for the inn, then doubled back just as Jayce let Brewster out of the car. She threw herself into Jayce's strong arms, oblivious of the video crew looking on. "You don't have to be scared, Jayce," Rocky said, close to his ear. "I've got your back."

He brushed an achingly sweet kiss over her lips, then stared into her eyes.

She didn't wait for him to say it first. She knew his heart and she knew hers. "I love you, Jayce."

CHAPTER THIRTY-TWO

Luke was in his office nursing a swollen jaw and a guilty conscience when his big brother strolled in.

"What happened to you?" Dev asked, noting the ice pack.

"I screwed up."

Dev helped himself to a seat. "Want to talk about it?"

"Not really." After picking himself up from Sam's lawn, Luke had driven over to Rachel's rented apartment. He'd dreaded speaking with her, not knowing what to say but knowing he had to address the attraction between them, and Sam's hurt feelings. When she didn't answer her door or her phone, Luke panicked and tracked down her landlady.

"She moved out."

Luke blinked at the woman. "What? When?"

"Sometime in the middle of the night. Left a note under my door."

"What did it say?"

"Not much. Just an apology for the late notice and that it was time to move home."

"That's it?"

"Yup. Aside from including next month's rent—in cash. Always was a thoughtful girl. Sorry to see her go."

Luke couldn't believe his ears. Rachel couldn't deal with the awkward situation between her and Sam and himself so she skipped town? What the freaking hell? *"Where's home? Where's Rachel from?"*

"I don't know. She didn't talk about herself much. Strike that. She never talked about herself."

"Did she leave a forwarding address? Phone number? Anything?"

The woman shook her head. "Sorry." Then she pointed to Luke's face. "You should ice that jaw. Whoever walloped you walloped you good."

Luke shook off the mystery of Rachel and focused on his brother. "What do you want, Dev?"

"It's about Adam."

* * *

She loved him.

Deep down, in his bones, Jayce had believed Rocky loved him. That she'd always loved him to some degree. But when she'd said the words aloud, he'd been dumbstruck. Literally dumbstruck. He should have returned the sentiment. For Christ sake, he loved Rocky so much his soul ached. But the words hadn't formed. He'd stood there like an idiot thinking, *She loves me,* and then, smiling, she'd zipped into the Red Clover to speed-clean for the interview.

Christ.

He'd spent the next hour puttering around the grounds. First giving the video crew the grand tour of the grounds, then contemplating the best positioning for motion-detector sensors on the inn. He'd purchased decorative lighting for the front of the house and flood fixtures to cover the immense backyard. Actual installation would have to wait until the fresh paint had dried on key surfaces of the exterior. Since there'd been no further threats, Rocky had once again questioned the need for security lighting, but she hadn't nixed the idea. All it had taken was Jayce pointing out that low-level security would benefit not only her but also her guests.

The entire time he'd inspected the Red Clover, Jayce had wrestled with conflicting emotions. Part of him breathed easier for sharing that dark night with Rocky. She hadn't judged him, nor had she smothered him with sympathy. She'd empathized while stating logic. Just like Dev. Just like their dad, Jerome. Except she'd reminded Jayce about the awards ceremony. Somehow he'd lost or buried that memory. He hadn't expected his parents to attend but had been hurt when neither had shown. Just another in a lifetime of disappointments where Angie and Joe Bello were concerned, but it had hit hard and had no doubt influenced Jayce's harsh words and shaky judgment that evening. It didn't excuse him for not wrenching the car keys from his mom and locking her in her bedroom, but somehow it put the night in better perspective.

Although his conscience had lightened in that regard, a feeling of dread dogged his spirit. Renovations would be complete within a week. Which meant Rocky would be moving out of his house and back to the B and B.

He missed her already.

For the past few days they'd lived as a couple. Sleeping and waking together. Bickering over stupid things and debating important issues. Performing mundane chores like washing the dishes and scooping Brewster's poop. Why the hell did that light up Jayce's world?

Jayce struggled with the fact that this perfect arrangement was only temporary. Rocky wasn't the only one having a hard time imagining their future. He'd never ask her to give up her dream of running a successful bed-and-breakfast, and at the same time he couldn't imagine himself living at the Red Clover. It wasn't the inn that put him off. The house and property were amazing. It was the thought of living his life, *their* life, in front of strangers.

Mrs. Watson, bless her soul, lectured in his head, *Stop shooting your happiness in the foot.*

Right.

Jayce shoved the uncertainty aside, choosing to believe he and Rocky would reach a compromise. Better to tackle a day at a time than obsess on the future. Bottom line, they were a couple. And she *loved* him.

"You were right," Rocky said, bounding out the back door. "It wasn't so bad. They asked me about the history of the Cup-cake Lovers and once I got started they couldn't shut me up."

Jayce smiled. "I'm glad it went well."

Spotting Rocky, Brewster abandoned his tree sniffing and barreled across the yard, practically knocking Rocky off her feet. Laughing, she stooped and hugged the dog tight. "You were right," she said to Jayce. "Brewster loves the space to run."

"Lots to explore out here." Jayce dragged a hand through his hair, experiencing another pang of dread. He was going to miss the dog, too.

"Amber and the guys took off and I need to get into town, too. The Spectacular's in full swing and I got a text from Tasha that the booth is short staffed." She dropped her fore-head to Brewster's and sighed. "I called Molly, but she can't watch Brewster today."

Jayce crouched next to the pair. "We'll take him back to my house and crate him. He'll be fine, Rocky."

"He'll be cramped."

"Dogs look at crates as a safe place. He'll sleep and I'll run back and check on him after a couple of hours." Jayce had business in town, and he wanted to stay close to Rocky. She'd relaxed, thinking Billy or whoever had gotten bored with hounding her, but Jayce had the edgy feeling of the calm before the storm.

"Can't he stay here?"

"What if he gets anxious and chews up a leg of your fur-niture or destroys an antique? What if he gets into some-thing harmful? There are paint cans upstairs and—"

"What about the back porch? Renovations are done there. It's spacious and there's nothing but an old wicker set that I want to replace anyway. I'll put out a water bowl and grab his stuffed toy from the backseat of your car. He can sleep on the cushioned settee, watch the birds and squirrels through the screened windows."

Brewster barked as if casting his vote.

"Four hours in the booth and then we'll come back for Brewster and do something fun together," Rocky said. "The three of us."

Jayce liked the sound of that. He also knew when he was beaten. "You win." He cupped the back of Rocky's head, then kissed her forehead. "But if he chews up that wicker set, don't say I didn't warn you."

"I'll take my chances." She sprang to her feet and called for Brewster to follow. "Told you he was a softie," she said to the mutt in a conspiratorial voice.

Jayce rubbed an ache in his chest and smiled.

Rocky's cell phone rang and she paused to take the call. "Yes, this is Rocky. . . . Oh, Miss Day. Yes, thank you for returning my call." She glanced at Jayce and smiled—Harper Day. The woman who'd purchased the old Rothwell farm.

"Say that again?" Rocky furrowed her brow, stepped left, then right. "I'm so sorry, Miss Day. We seem to have a bad connection."

Brewster barked, vying for attention.

Rocky moved away, seeking quiet and a better signal.

Jayce led the dog to the back porch not wanting to eavesdrop, but damn, he was curious. He wanted her to land that decorating gig . . . and he didn't. What if she got so busy between the Red Clover and her proposed sideline that she had no time for Jayce and the future he wanted for them? He told himself to get a grip. He had no right to dictate her business. He'd never felt so damned possessive of a woman in his life. It pricked an ugly thought. Had he inherited a trait from his father? Obsessed with a woman, would Jayce expect her to live the life of his choosing?

That thought unsettled Jayce as much as the possibility that Rocky was being stalked. Gut knotted, Jayce kept a keen eye on her while he got Brewster settled.

A minute later the woman who loved him came bounding onto the porch. "You're not going to believe this. Harper—she asked me to call her by her first name—wants to fly me out for an in-person interview!"

"To Los Angeles?"

"She checked out my Web site. Not that it's great, but it does feature several photos of the interior, giving her a feel for my sense of style—which she liked! I told her how familiar I am with the Rothwell farm and tossed out some thoughts regarding a makeover. She wants to meet with me. See if we hit it off. If we connect, she'd like to speak to me about redecorating another one of her investments. Can you believe this?"

Jayce frowned. "Why can't she fly in here? Interview you while doing a walk-through on the Rothwell property?"

"She has business obligations."

"So do you."

Rocky blinked. "You're not happy about this."

"I'm not thrilled about you flying across country to meet with a stranger."

"Molly met Harper. Said she was kind of prissy and uptight, but pleasant. She's a highly successful businesswoman, Jayce, not a psychotic killer."

Irritated by Rocky's naïveté and snarky tone, Jayce folded his arms over his chest. "How do you know? Did you research her background?"

"Why would I . . ." Rocky narrowed her eyes. "Don't you dare poke into Harper's life."

"If you're going to work closely with someone you've never met, especially on an isolated property like Rothwell's, you should know something about them. Their business practices at the very least. It's common sense."

"It's paranoid." Rocky spun on her heel and paced. "I can't believe this. You're the one who pointed out my talent for decorating. You're the one who got me fired up by giving me your credit card and carte blanche. Do you know what a thrill it's been for me to transform your house? The shopping and the actual decorating? I'm good at it and I love it. With a little luck and devotion, I could be successful at it." She threw her arms wide, gesturing to the inn. "I don't know that all these structural and exterior renovations are going to increase business for the Clover. I'm sick of struggling financially. I'm tired of feeling like a failure. Every other Monroe *ever* has run a successful business."

Jayce stared, stunned at the vehemence of her tone, stymied by the glimpse of insecurity. "There are different levels of success, Rocky. You've turned this old property into a warm and stunning showcase. That's a hell of an accomplishment. You contribute volumes of time and energy to the charitable efforts of the Cupcake Lovers. You've made a positive difference in the lives of countless soldiers and assorted people and causes in need. That's huge." He resisted the urge to reach out. He wanted to pull her into his arms, but experience told him—in her agitated state—he'd only get a sock in the chin. "You don't have to prove anything to the world. You don't have to compete with your brothers. And you damn well don't have to worry about finances. You have me."

She stopped in her tracks, glared. "So, what? You expect me to not work? To give up my passions? To freeload off of you? Are you nuts?"

"Call me old-fashioned, but is it a crime to want to take care of you? Provide for you?"

"Yes!' she snapped, fists clenched. "It's a crime against my independence."

Brewster whined and circled, sensitive to the heated exchange.

Jayce scrambled not to repeat history. This moment smacked of the same vibe thirteen years ago. Him trying to do the right thing, speaking from his heart, and royally pissing Rocky off. Her cheeks flushed. Her eyes sparked. He knew that look. *Damn.*

"I love that you moved back to Sugar Creek to slay demons and to win my heart," she said in a tight voice. "You *have* my heart, Jayce. But it's not fair for you to expect me to fall in with whatever fairy-tale version you have of us now. Just like it wasn't fair for me to expect you to meet my fanciful expectations thirteen years ago."

"What I'm envisioning isn't fanciful, Dash."

"Don't call me that. Not now. Not when I'm so . . . angry.

Dammit, Jayce, I can't be the cure-all for your horrible childhood."

She may as well have whacked him with a baseball bat. He was stunned. Was that what she thought? Was that what he was doing? *No. Yes and no.* "Rocky—"

"I can't . . . I don't want to talk about this anymore. Not now. Not in the heat of the moment." She fussed with Brewster's water dish, fluffed a chaise pillow, then kissed the dog's head. "The Cupcake Lovers need me," she said without making eye contact, and then hotfooted it toward his car.

Reeling, Jayce followed. She was right. They both needed to cool down. And he, for one, needed to reassess. *Had* he put the responsibility for his happiness on her shoulders? The notion shook his recently grounded world.

* * *

Instead of stewing over her fight with Jayce, Rocky devoted her attention to the Creepy Cupcake booth, hoping time and a clear head would provide her with better perspective on their future. The last thing she wanted was to make a hasty decision or say something awful that she couldn't take back. Although she may have done that already. Her crack about being the cure-all for Jayce's crappy childhood had been low. But dammit, he'd cast a shadow on her possible shiny new career and that had hurt. Why did she have to choose between him and her version of success? Why couldn't she have it all?

Not that she was stewing.

Rocky washed down two Tylenol with a swig of apple cider, hoping to ease the pounding in her head. She didn't know what to do for her heart. She'd been on an emotional roller coaster since the crack of dawn, and the freaking mind-and-gut-jerking ride continued.

Working alongside Tasha for the last three hours had been unusually unsettling. Their relationship, for lack of a better term, had always been strained, but Rocky was used to snippy comments or out-and-out rude remarks, not cold silence. Rocky still smarted over their brief confrontation the day before, and she wasn't even sure what she'd done to set Tasha off. Given the "no drama" decree and the fact that the video crew was still popping in and out at the booth, Rocky bit her tongue and focused on business. CL business.

The Monster-Mash Cakes were a hit, although she was certain the kids would have loved just about any free cupcake. The real treat, for Rocky, was the success of the charity cupcake sale. The reason the booth was so short staffed was because they'd run low on cupcakes and several of the members, including Chloe, had retreated home to bake and replenish supplies. At this rate, the Cupcake Lovers would have a pretty hefty sum to donate to Sugar Tots for the new playground. Thinking of Sugar Tots made Rocky think of Rachel. Excusing herself, Rocky retreated to the back of the booth and, for the second time today, tried calling the reclusive CL member. Again, no answer, just an automated voice inviting the caller to leave a message—which Rocky did. Frowning, she pocketed her phone and edged back in next to Tasha, who was taking orange tickets and handing out Monster-Mash Cakes with a brittle smile.

"I just want you to know," Rocky said, "that I've tried Rachel twice today. I'm hoping she'll get back to me before the end of the day," she plowed on when Tasha didn't react. "I'll mention how busy and strapped we are and try to get her to work the booth for a while. That way Amber can at least get a shot of Rachel in action."

"I'm not counting on it."

Rocky dug deep for calm. "Why are you mad at me?" she asked in a low voice while rearranging the dwindling supply of Ethel's Chocolate Pumpkin Spices.

"I'm not mad at you, Rocky," Tasha said in an equally calm tone. "I'm mad at the world." Her phone pinged, and after reading the text she whirled away, "Excuse me," and left the booth.

Ethel sidled over and took a ticket from a young boy. "I have to say I'm impressed," the older woman said to Rocky. "Tasha's put in more hours at this booth than any other CL member. And she's actually been nice to the kids. Well, as nice as Tasha can be. She's sort of awkward with genuine pleasantries."

"She's certainly determined to put on a good show for the camera," Rocky said.

"Normally, I'd agree, but I've been watching and I get the sense that she's actually trying to put her best foot forward for the club and the community. She said something to me about wanting to make Randall proud."

Rocky blinked. "You're kidding."

Ethel shrugged. "A passing remark. I didn't pursue it because she looked like she regretted saying it the moment the words left her mouth."

"Huh." Blessedly distracted from her own personal problems, Rocky watched as Tasha weaved through the crowd, frowning when she saw her point of destination. Decked out in full uniform, Deputy Burke was leaning against the ticket booth next to the kiddie carnival rides and games. Tasha crossed her arms over her chest as she approached, then stood stiffly as Billy leaned in and whispered something in her ear. Tasha nodded, then backed away. She disappeared into the crowd, and damned if Billy's weasel gaze didn't float over to the Creepy Cupcake booth and lock on Rocky.

Watch your ass, Rocky. I am.

"That does it."

"Where are you going?" Ethel asked as Rocky untied her apron.

"To whack a weasel."

* * *

Jayce had spent the afternoon trying not to dwell on his fight with Rocky and watching her back instead. He maintained visual contact from a distance while handling business via his smart phone. E-mails. Calls. A quick Internet search on Harper Day—who was, at least on the surface, a respected and well-connected Hollywood publicist.

Meanwhile his senses buzzed with the sights and sounds

of the popular festival. Sugar Creek was packed with locals and tourists. Several people he knew, including Sam Mc-Cloud and his two kids, had stopped to talk with Jayce when they'd spied him sitting on a bench or leaning against a tree, seemingly taking in the festivities of the Spookytown Spectacular. All the while, Jayce had kept a keen eye on Rocky.

More than once he'd berated himself for being paranoid. She was in public, in a cupcake booth, surrounded by friends and hordes of families enjoying multiple activities. The sun was shining, and temps were mild. A local band cranked out country folk music. There was nothing ominous about this day. So when Jayce got a call from Dev asking him to meet him at J.T.'s, he shelved his paranoia and hoofed it one block over to the bustling department store. Dev had promised to broach the subject of Adam with Luke. Jayce assumed Dev hadn't liked what he'd learned. He hadn't sounded happy on the phone.

Jayce scaled the stairs to Dev's office two at a time. He knocked on the partially opened door, then walked in.

Dev looked up from a mound of paperwork. "You're not going to like this." He held up a specific document for Jayce's inspection.

Curious, Jayce moved forward and took the pristine page. A photocopy of the toxicology report on his parents. *Shit.* Pulse erratic, he glanced back to Dev. "Where'd you get this?"

"Barry Stein, executive editor of the *Sugar Creek Gazette.* Said it was delivered to him, anonymously, along with this typed note."

Jayce took another page from Dev and read out loud. *"Jerome Monroe and Jayce Bello conspired to bury this evidence. Is Bello the kind of man we want policing Sugar Creek?"* Jayce blew out a breath. "Obviously instigated by someone who believes the rumor about me running for sheriff."

"Could be Stone," Dev said. "Hell, it could be Billy. He wouldn't be keen on working under you. At any rate, Barry turned it over to me, saying he didn't feel right about making this public until he'd at least given the family a heads-up. I told him you had no intention of running for sheriff. Tried to reason with him about dredging up dirt for the sake of dirt. Barry's a decent man and I'm pretty sure we can count on his discretion, but that doesn't mean another photocopy won't land at the *Pixley Tribune* or any one of several northern Vermont papers."

Jayce chewed the inside of his cheek, reviewed the report one last time.

"I called Dad. He wants to speak with you first, but his advice is to let Barry run the story. Get it out and over with and he'll do damage control." Dev's lip twitched. "You should have heard the heat in the old man's voice. He's primed for the fight. In a warped way, I think this is a good thing. For him. And you." Dev regarded Jayce with a calm and caring expression. "With this secret out in the open, maybe you can finally let go and move on."

Jayce nodded. It did indeed seem like the final tie that needed severing. "I'll call your dad. Let's do it."

As if on cue, Dev's phone rang. "Devlin Monroe. No problem. What's up, Gerry?" He listened, then shot to his feet. "Who phoned it in? . . . No. . . . Yeah. We're on our way." He hung up, then nailed Dev with another look—this one pained. "The Red Clover's on fire."

* * *

Rocky pushed through the crowd, tears blurring her vision, panic obscuring clear thought. *Must get home. Purse. Keys. No, Jayce drove. Phone. Pocket.* She'd almost made it back to the cupcake booth when someone grabbed her by the shoulders.

"Dash."

"Oh, God. Jayce."

"You heard," he said while finessing her through the masses.

"Was talking to Billy. His walkie-talkie squawked and

someone said, *Ten-seventy* at *One-oh-one Pikeman Lane.* That's my address," she choked out.

"I know, hon." Jayce helped her into the car, buckled her seat belt.

"Asked him what it meant. He looked sort of stunned. Then he mumbled something about dreams going up in smoke, and stalked off."

Jayce squeezed her arm and shut the door.

Rocky's stomach convulsed as he rounded the car and climbed behind the wheel. "It means 'fire,' doesn't it? 'Ten-seventy,'" she said. "I heard sirens."

"Listen, babe, I need you to stay calm. I was with Dev when he got a call from Gerry Rush."

The captain of the fire department. So it was official. Rocky wrapped her arms around her aching middle. "Oh, God."

"Someone phoned it in. Anonymous call. Fire trucks are on their way. Police, too. Dev's en route and he's calling Luke."

"Brewster—"

"Is a smart dog. As soon as he smelled smoke, he probably panicked and busted out."

"H-how?"

"You left the window partially opened for fresh air, remember? The screen."

But she hadn't left it open enough for Brewster to squeeze his body through, had she? She imagined his teddy-bear face and the one ear that flopped over, the way he followed her everywhere, the way he liked to snuggle. "I feel sick."

"Think positive."

If she hadn't been holding herself together with locked arms, she would've punched him. "My freaking house is burning down, Jayce! Everything I own. Everything I love."

"It might not be that bad, Rocky."

But as his car raced faster and closer, she could see the smoke. Ugly black smoke billowing against the blue sky and vibrant mountains. Her eyes burned, and she retched. Her throbbing brain raced. She'd made hot tea for the film crew.

Had she left the burner on? Had something sparked due to the rewiring in the house?

She saw it then. The fire trucks. The raging fire.

But no dog.

"Brewster!"

Jayce was still braking to a stop and she already had the seat belt off. She pushed open the door.

"Goddammit, Rocky!"

Hitting the ground in motion, she tripped and fell to her knees. Stood and ran. People shouted. Flames ravaged. Water gushed from hoses, yet the heat seared and pulsed in suffocating waves.

Jayce tackled her just as an explosion rocked the earth and shattered her heart. She wanted to puke. She wanted to die. Her body shook with fury and sobs as Jayce hauled her off of the grass and into his arms.

She clung and wept, her heart in tatters as she imagined Brewster. She could see his face. She could hear his bark.

"Dash."

The noise was deafening. Crackling, burning. Firemen shouting. *Barking.*

She felt something warm and wet on her cheeks. A tongue. A big sloppy tongue and bacon doggy-treat breath. She opened her eyes. *"Brewster."* Her voice cracked from abuse and emotion. Rocky wrapped her arms around her furry friend and hugged him with all her might. She felt Jayce stroking her back, felt someone else squeeze her shoulder. She looked up just as her big brother stooped down.

"Jayce told me Brewster was here," Dev said in a low voice. "I informed Gerry, and his crew called for Brewster as soon as they arrived. He ran out of the woods just before you got here, Rocky. He's unharmed, but it's not safe here. Let me put him in my car and let Jayce move you further from the house."

What house? she wanted to ask, but the words wouldn't come. Her throat was thick with misery, relief, and acrid smoke. She gave Brewster another hug, then let her brother lead him away.

Jayce framed her face with his hands. "Rocky, look at me."

She blinked at him through a haze of tears. She'd never seen him look so somber.

"It'll be okay, hon. Are you listening?"

She flashed back on the creepy note. *You crushed my life, now I'll crush yours.*

Except the Red Clover wasn't her life. Her family and friends were her life. *Jayce* was her life.

What if the fire hadn't been an accident? What if someone had set it intentionally? And what if that same person crushed Rocky further by going after Jayce?

Panic whispered through her veins. Fresh tears blurred her eyes. If she pushed Jayce away, if he wasn't a part of her life, maybe then he'd be safe. Chaos and sadness ravaged Rocky's heart, mind, and soul. "Nothing will ever be right again."

CHAPTER THIRTY-THREE

"You need to calm down."

Jayce looked at Dev. "Did I say anything?"

"You didn't have to. I've known you a long time and I know when you're upset. Rocky's in shock, Jayce. People say things they don't mean under extreme circumstances. Losing her home and business, *all* of her belongings? That's extreme."

Jayce tried to relax on the sofa in Daisy Monroe's house. A sofa he'd sat on hundreds of times through the years. He tried to slow his racing, battered heart. Tried to reap assurance from Dev's logic. But all he could hear was Rocky's refusal when he'd tried to take her back to his place, the home she'd so lovingly decorated. The home so full of her. Of *them*.

I can't do this. Us.

She may as well have told him to piss off, because she'd proceeded to shut down just as she had thirteen years ago.

"Gram and Chloe are with her now. Just give Rocky a little time."

Jayce imagined her sitting on a canopied bed in one of the many bedrooms of this enormous house. He imagined her looking at all the antiques and collectibles and thinking about everything she'd lost in the fire. He didn't blame her for being devastated. She'd put everything into the Red Clover.

Her creativity, hard work, and all of her finances—plus some of Dev's. That inn had been her dream, yet over the years it had proven little more than a hardship and ultimately a heartbreak.

Jayce hoped Daisy and Chloe were reminding Rocky that she had the moral and financial support of a large and lucrative family. That's what he'd be saying if she hadn't pushed him away. He'd also remind her that she had Brewster. And, whether she liked it or not, she had Jayce. Unlike the first time she'd rejected him, he wasn't going anywhere.

Luke walked in from the kitchen carrying three beers. He handed one to Jayce.

Jayce met the younger brother's eyes and noted a spark of mutual concern for Rocky. There'd be no fighting now, no grudge regarding the past. Time to pull together. No matter their beefs or quirks, the Monroes always pulled together in times of trouble. Jayce reflected on how many times he'd banded with them in the past. How he'd always been included. How he was still included. Throat tight, Jayce accepted Luke's grand gesture and sipped beer.

Luke sank down in an opposing wingback chair. "Just got off of the phone with Adam. He heard the news—everyone's heard by now—and he was calling to make sure Rocky's okay. He was genuinely shook up." Luke held Jayce's gaze. "You can't blame the guy for caring."

"I don't." And he meant it. He was pretty sure he'd allowed jealousy to taint his judgment where Adam was concerned. Still . . . "Can't blame me for being cautious."

Luke raised a brow. "I know Sheriff Stone and Captain Rush said there was no obvious sign of foul play, but after what Dev told me . . . I mean, come on. Practically the whole of Sugar Creek's fire and police department were on-site with the exception of Billy."

Jayce set his bottle on a coaster and leaned forward. "Stone said Billy was on his way over when he got an emergency call from his wife."

"Convenient," Dev said.

"And suspect," Jayce said, "considering they're separated."

"Which was news to all of us," Dev said, "including Sheriff Stone."

"Stone said he'd look into my concerns and there'll also be a formal investigation into the fire." Jayce dragged a hand through his hair, tempering his frustration. "I don't blame Stone for doubting my suspicions about Billy. A lot of things don't add up."

"Timing for one," Dev said. "He was with Rocky, in town, when the fire was reported."

"Could have rigged something with a timer," Luke said. "Or maybe he set it, then drove like a bat out of hell into town. Fifteen-minute drive."

"Ten if you fly," Jayce said.

"But what about motive?" Luke asked. "What are we talking? Revenge? A grudge? Granted Billy's an asswipe, but an arsonist? What would push him to risk his career and prison?"

"I don't know," Jayce said. "But I'll find out. As soon as I'm sure Rocky's okay, I'll be all over this."

"I'd advise cooling off first," Luke said with a raised brow. "Last thing Dev and I want is to have to bail you out of jail for attempted murder."

"What about assault?" Jayce asked.

Dev shot him a look.

"Not to take away from my sister's case," Luke said, picking at the label on his beer, "but I might need to hire you myself, Jayce."

"For what?" Dev asked.

"Never mind," Luke said. "Bad timing."

Jayce noted Luke's tense body language. "We'll talk."

"I called Dad and Mom," Dev said, his own spine stiffening. "They're flying up tomorrow."

"Took a crisis to pull them out of paradise, huh?" Luke shook his head. "I can't believe they stayed down south so long without buckling for even one weekend visit home. Every time I brought it up they mentioned one or another conflict. The one time I considered flying down to visit *them*, Dad made me feel guilty as hell about leaving the Sugar

Shack. If I didn't know better I'd think they didn't want to see me."

"About that." Dev glanced at Jayce, then back to Luke. He sipped beer, then rolled back his shoulders. "There's something you need to know. I'll fill Rocky in when she's stronger. It's about Dad."

* * *

Rocky sat on a yellow-and-red-flowered bedspread surrounded by lots of beautiful things, two caring people, and one needy dog. But for all of the comfort and love, her heart felt empty. Gram said she was in shock, but Rocky was pretty certain she was dead inside.

"If you don't want to live with Jayce," Gram said, "you can live here. For as long as you like, sweet pea. There's plenty of room. And after next week, I won't be here at all. Unless you want me to stay. I can postpone my plans to move in with Vincent. He'll understand."

"Yeah, but *why* don't you want to live with Jayce?" Chloe said. "You love him and he loves you. I don't get why you're pushing him away."

"Every time I want something badly," Rocky said, "somehow I screw it up. Things go wrong. Bad things happen. Do you know how long I dreamed about owning the Red Clover? I've dreamed of being with Jayce twice as long and I want him much, much more."

"So you think if you have Jayce something bad will happen to him?" Chloe asked.

"What, like he'll get shot or have a heart attack or something?" Gram asked.

Chloe elbowed the older woman, and Rocky glanced down at her grass-and-ash-stained jeans. "You think I'm being ridiculous."

"No," Chloe said.

"Yes," Gram said. "Listen, sweet pea. Life is short and a man like Jayce doesn't come along every day. I've known he was special from the first day he rode his bike over here for

Sunday dinner. He was only yay high," she said to Chloe, "and he pedaled clear across town. Stopped along the way and picked me a bag of apples from a nearby orchard. Said he would have bought me flowers, but he didn't have enough change. Later I learned from my neighbor that he didn't even have money for the apples, so he offered to rake her yard in exchange. He could've swiped the apples, but he didn't. He didn't have to give me a gift, but he wanted to." Gram reached over and squeezed Rocky's hand. "Jayce is a good, honest, hardworking soul. Just like you. Don't shy away from a golden opportunity just because you're scared. Scared, schmared."

Chloe grasped her other hand, and Brewster scooted over and rested his head on Rocky's lap.

"I say spit in the eye of fate and grab all the happiness you can for as long as you can," Chloe said.

"Nothing more sad than a missed opportunity," Rocky said, thinking about Jayce's friend Mrs. Watson.

Brewster barked.

Rocky's dead heart rallied just as the door cracked open. It was Dev. "You need to come downstairs," he said to Rocky.

It wasn't a request. Curiosity motivated her as much as her brother's intense expression. Knees wobbly, she slid off the bed and, holding hands with Gram and Chloe, followed her brother. Brewster brought up the rear. With every step, Rocky's heart pounded a little harder. She didn't know what to expect, but it sure wasn't the sight of Tasha and Randall Burke standing in Gram's living room.

Randall had been at odds with Rocky's dad for years, and before that Randall's dad had butted heads with her Grandpa Jessup, Gram's deceased husband. Tasha was the only Burke who'd ever been in this house, and that was purely because she was a Cupcake Lover.

"What's going on?" Rocky asked.

"That's what we'd like to know," Jayce said.

Her eyes went immediately to his. Her pulse raced and her stomach flipped. So much for being dead inside.

Randall spoke first. "My wife has something she wants to tell you."

Gram motioned everyone to sit, including the Burkes.

Randall shook his head. "Thank you, but we won't be staying long."

The only reason Rocky sat was because she worried her legs might give out. This was bad. Jayce, who'd been standing, sat next to her on the sofa and held her hand. Her brothers remained standing.

"I'm not sure where to start," Tasha said. Her voice sounded raspy and choked. She swallowed hard and looked at her husband. "I don't think I can do this."

Randall reached over and interlaced his fingers with his wife's. He gave a little squeeze, and Rocky's own throat tightened at the show of genuine affection and support.

Tasha squared her shoulders and gave a stiff nod. "First," she said, looking directly at Rocky, "I want to say how sorry I am about your house. I never thought . . ."

She cleared her throat and pushed on. "A couple of months ago, Billy started flirting with me. I'm ashamed to say I flirted back. It's what I do. I like attention." She bit her lower lip, nibbling off most of her signature red lipstick. "Randall was so busy and Billy always seemed to be around, feeding my ego. Nothing squicky every happened. I swear," she said with a nervous glance at Randall. "But Billy got it in his head that I was toying with him. He became obsessed with impressing me, thinking he could win my affections. He was always surprising me with gifts or showing up unexpectedly and giving me a ride. He e-mailed and texted. He ignored his own wife to the extent of alienating her. I tried to ignore him. I tried to handle the situation on my own. I didn't want to tell Randall because I didn't want to cause strife between father and son." Tears filled her eyes. "But mostly I didn't want Randall to be disappointed in me. I didn't want to risk . . . risk losing him."

Her last words sort of croaked out, and mascara streamed down her face along with tears. Rocky knew for certain she wasn't the only one in the room who felt like they were witnessing a freak show. Tasha Burke crying? Tasha Burke embarrassed and contrite? But Rocky knew from little things Tasha had said over the past week and a half that her misery was genuine.

"Billy knew that Tasha and Rocky were longtime rivals," Randall continued for his wife.

"Everyone in Sugar Creek knows that," Luke said.

"But he also knew how devastated and humiliated Tasha was when she was forced to give up her role as president of the Cupcake Lovers," Randall said, "and Rocky took her place."

Rocky flushed. Even though Tasha had been asking for it, Rocky *had* humiliated her. In front of the entire club. Publicly at the Shack.

"My son got it in his head that if he rattled you enough," Randall said, "if he scared you, Tasha might be . . . entertained."

"That's sick," Gram said.

"He told me he was spying on you," Tasha blurted. "He wanted to spook you. I told him to stop."

"The letter," Jayce said. "And the underwear."

"He told me about that, too," Tasha said. "He stole the panties from Rocky's house and as for the note . . . he wanted to confuse you, Jayce. Maybe shed suspicion on someone else while terrorizing Rocky at the same time."

Rocky hadn't realized she'd worked her way to the edge of the seat. She couldn't believe her ears. Gripping the sofa's cushions, she braced for more.

"This is like something out of a movie," Chloe said.

"Except it's real," Dev said.

"Unfortunately," Gram mumbled.

"I knew things were bad," Tasha said, "but I didn't realize how bad until today. Billy bragged to me that he crushed you. He promised you'd fall apart. That you'd drop out of the club and the presidency would be mine for the taking. He told me he'd torched your world, your home." Her legs were trembling now, and Randall put his arm around her waist to bolster her.

Rocky felt sick but couldn't tear herself from Tasha's words. As if sensing Rocky's anxiety, Jayce placed a comforting palm at the small of her back. Strength shot up her spine.

"I called it in, Rocky," Tasha choked out. "I tried to save the Red Clover and then I went to Randall and told him everything. I can't believe . . . I don't know what I've done to deserve his support."

Randall whispered something in Tasha's ear and she faltered.

"Where's Billy now?" Jayce asked.

"I don't know," Randall said. "I think he got a dose of reality when he realized Tasha had betrayed him and tipped off the fire department. We're heading over now to speak with Sheriff Stone. We just wanted to tell you first."

Tasha palmed her stomach as though she was going to be sick. "I'm so sorry, Rocky."

"My son has always been a bad seed, but I chose to turn a blind eye. I'm as guilty as my wife in this matter," Randall said. "Whatever happens with the insurance company, Rocky, I'll still make restitution. As far as Billy . . . I'll let the law handle this, although I feel compelled to pick up his legal bills. I hope you understand."

Rocky didn't know what to stay. She stood when Jayce stood, still grappling for words.

"I'll come to the station with you," Jayce said.

"Me, too," Dev said.

Tasha was wringing her hands when they turned to leave.

"Wait," Rocky said. She hurried over to her longtime nemesis, her best furry friend glued to her side. "I know how hard it was to come here and . . ." Rocky anchored her trembling hands on her hips and blew out a breath. Tasha had come here and humiliated herself in order to right a wrong with Rocky and to save her marriage to Randall. Rocky was humbled and impressed. "I was hoping you could do me a favor, Tasha."

The woman blinked. "Anything."

Even though no one in the room moved, Rocky could feel

everyone leaning forward in anticipation. "I'm going to be very busy, what with trying to rebuild my life."

Tasha flushed.

"It will be a while until I'm in the right frame of mind and have the proper time that's needed to carry out the responsibilities of the president of the Cupcake Lovers. You've handled the deal with Highlife Publishing beautifully and I'd be relieved if you'd oversee the ongoing progress as well as the traditional aspects of our charity work . . . just until I'm back on my feet. Kind of an acting president thing. I'm sure Gram and Chloe can clear it with the club."

Gram raised a penciled brow.

Chloe smiled. "We can try."

Tasha shook her head. "I couldn't . . ."

Randall squeezed her hand.

"I'd be honored, Rocky. Just until you're back on your feet."

Dev led the Burkes to the door.

"God, I love you," Jayce whispered in Rocky's ear, then followed the Burkes.

Rocky tingled from head to toe. Knowing Jayce loved her and actually hearing him say the words were two very different but wonderful animals. How could she feel so miserable yet happy at the same time? How could everything that had been so muddled only hours before suddenly be so crystal clear?

"This calls for a cocktail," Gram said.

"I'll join you," Luke said.

Chloe palmed her forehead. "I'll sit here and catch my breath."

Rocky hurried after Jayce. "Wait," she said, catching him at the door. "You're coming back here, right?"

He smoothed his knuckles over her cheek. "To kiss you good night, Dash. Absolutely."

"No. I mean to take me home. With you. Me and Brewster." She caught Jayce's hand and placed it over her heart. "I take it back. I can do this, Jayce. I want to do this. *Us.* But I need you to work with me. Meet me halfway in our goals. I want marriage and a family, but I also want a career. I'm going to fly to Los Angeles, meet with Harper Day. It's not about succeeding; it's about contentment." She knew that now. She didn't need to be rich or famous, but she did need purpose and passion. With the Red Clover gone, her direction was clear.

Jayce swallowed hard. "Don't do this, *us,* just to make me happy, Dash."

Words she'd said in anger. Her mouth curved into a gentle smile. "You should know me better than that."

He nodded, then pulled her into his arms. "You'll have to handle some details before heading to California. The police, insurance company. If you let me, I'll help you with as much of that as I can." He kissed the top of her head. "Then I'll drive you to the airport myself."

He was meeting her halfway. Rocky absorbed the moment, their future. A dueling sense of calm and excitement rioted throughout her being.

"My timing's wrong as usual," Jayce said. "And I still don't have a ring. But I have to ask, Rocky."

Heart full, she pulled back and shushed him. "Please don't. It's my turn," she added, smiling up into his expressive eyes. "Will you marry me, Jayce Bello?" She held her breath then, truly sensitive to what it was like to put that life-altering question out there, ready to rally if he countered with some old-fashioned *the guy's supposed to propose* crap.

Jayce grinned, that sexy, arrogant smile that had been revving her heart and fantasies since she was a girl. "Hell, yes."

HONORARY CUPCAKE LOVERS
Submitted Recipes and Tips from On-Line Members

GERMAN APPLE CUPCAKES
(submitted by Molly Monte of New Jersey)

1 cup sour milk (set aside)
1 tbsp vinegar or lemon juice
2 cups apple chunks (set aside)
2 ¼ cups flour
2 tsp baking soda
2 tsp cinnamon
½ tsp salt
½ cup shortening
½ cup brown sugar
1 cup sugar
2 eggs

- Prepare the sour milk [pour 1 cup of milk into measuring cup less 1 tbsp. Add 1 tbsp of vinegar or lemon juice to sour the milk and set aside]. Peel, core and chop 4 small apples to make 2 cups. Set aside.
- Blend or sift together: flour, baking soda, cinnamon, and salt. Set this aside.

- Cream shortening and add both sugars, mixing until well blended. Add eggs one at a time, mixing thoroughly after each one. Alternate the flour mixture with sour milk until all is mixed and smooth. Stir in apples by hand.
- Pour into papered cupcake pan ⅔ full. Bake at 350° @ 45 minutes or until toothpick comes out clean. Cool cupcakes in pan and add powdered sugar on top of warm cupcakes or frost with buttercream frosting mixed with 2 tsp cinnamon.

I make this in a 9 × 13 pan and dust with powdered sugar. I will use cupcake tins when making these for lunches. The original recipe was one my mother always used and committed to her memory. After many years my sister found a copy in my mother's handwriting, tucked away in a knitting bag.

S'MORES CUPCAKES
(submitted by Sara Strunk of Wisconsin)

For cupcakes:
1 box Devil's Food cake mix (plus water, oil, and eggs called for)

For topping:
12 standard sized marshmallows, cut in half

For frosting:
2 cups shortening
2 tbsp vanilla extract
2 pounds powdered sugar
¼ cup water
½ cup Biscoff spread or "Cookie Butter" from Trader Joe's

- Prepare and bake cupcakes as directed on box.
- Meanwhile, prepare frosting by beating shortening and extract together until well-combined and smooth. Add powdered sugar and water and beat until stiff. Add Biscoff

spread/ cookie butter and beat until well-combined. Set aside.

- When cupcakes have 3 minutes left to bake, carefully place cut marshmallows on top of cupcake. Place under the broiler until just toasted. When removed from the oven, gently press toasted marshmallows down.
- Prepare pastry bag or heavy zipper-top bag with Biscoff-spread frosting. When cupcakes are cooled, frost top of cupcakes with ample amounts of frosting.

Enjoy!

FALLING FOR YOU PINEAPPLE UPSIDE-DOWN CUPCAKES
(submitted by Dawn A. Jones of New Jersey)

Ingredients
1 box Duncan Hines Signature Pineapple Supreme
   Cake Mix
1 jar Maraschino cherries—without stems
2 cans Dole pineapple slices in 100% pineapple juice
1 cup marshmallow fluff
½ cup Domino Light Brown Sugar Premium Pure
   Cane Sugar
½ cup butter

Cake Directions
1. Preheat oven according to cake mix.
2. Follow directions on box of Cake Mix.
3. Heat butter on stove or microwave and spoon a little in your muffin pans.
4. Take a spoon and take a little brown sugar and add a little to your muffin pans.
5. Take pineapples and add them to your muffin pans.
6. Take your cherries and cut them in half and add ½ to the center of your pineapples muffin pans.

7. Add your cake batter and bake according to cake mix. Cake is done when it springs back to the touch or when a cake tester or toothpick inserted in center comes out clean.

Center Directions

- Using a steak knife, cut out a plug (piece of cake) from the center of each cupcake and put it aside, then use a teaspoon and add a small amount of marshmallow fluff, then replace the plug (piece of cake).
- When they are cool, take a knife and loosen the edges and turn the muffin pans over onto your plate.

Makes about 24 cupcakes, depending on cake mix.

GENERAL CUPCAKE RECIPE "CHEAT" TIP
(submitted by Pam Ackerson of Florida)

Take any cupcake recipe you like. Instead of eggs, substitute ½ cup of cream cheese and a tablespoon of whipping cream. Follow directions for your favorite recipe and find yourself a new favorite!

Read on for an excerpt from

anything but love

—the next enchanting romance from
Beth Ciotta and St. Martin's Paperbacks!

CHAPTER ONE

"Forget love—I'd rather fall in chocolate!"
—Sandra J. Dykes

Sugar Creek, Vermont
December 23

Luke Monroe was by no means a Scrooge. He was all about family and giving and good times with friends. He co-owned and ran the Sugar Shack, a local pub and restaurant devoted to camaraderie via top notch food and drinks, and a cozy atmosphere. Like every other year, this year he'd decked the Shack's halls with boughs of holly on December 1st—*fa-la-la-la-la*. He'd helped decorate two other family businesses, too. J.T. Monroe's Department Store—owned and operated by his dad, Jerome Monroe, and Luke's older brother, Devlin Monroe. And Moose-a-lotta—a kitschy café owned and operated by his grandma, Daisy Monroe, and Dev's lady love, Chloe Madison. Lots of red and green and a good dose of silvery white due to the latest snowstorm. Overall the entire town of Sugar Creek looked like Santa's Vermont Village. Normally, Luke felt like a giddy kid for most of the month of December. This holiday season, for reasons that eluded him, Luke was bluer than blue. *Fa-la-freaking-la.*

Considering Luke and his entire family had a lot to celebrate, first and foremost, his dad's ongoing recovery from a scary bout of cancer, this seasonal funk really pissed Luke off. No way was he going to rain on anyone's holiday parade, so he'd been putting up a cheery front for weeks, waiting for the funk to fade and the joy to commence. No moping. Life as always. Hence why he was with family just now instead of home alone, swigging beer and watching sports?

Sunday dinner at Daisy Monroe's was a Monroe family tradition. Only last month Gram had moved out of her long-time spacious home and Luke's sister, Rocky, and her fiancé, Jayce, had moved in. Just before that, Gram, who'd grown eccentric and reckless, had officially agreed to let Chloe (a kick-ass gourmet chef) take over the planning, prepping, and cooking. So now Sunday dinner was at *Rocky's* house and Chloe oversaw the meal.

In essence, nothing had changed. (With the exception of Luke's brother and sister and even his grandmother now being in committed relationships.) As always, not every member of the Monroe family and their extended clan attended the traditional dinner *every* Sunday. As always, you never knew who you'd end up seated by at the table. Since it was the night before Christmas Eve and a *really* big family shindig, only a core few Monroes were in attendance. There'd been more food than people, but Luke had doubled up on a few portions and he'd offered to take home leftovers since Rocky's fridge was crammed with the next day's feast. Amazing that he had room for dessert, but he did. Lately Luke had had a real weakness for sweets and, in addition to other holiday goodies, there was a boatload of cupcakes left over from the holiday party Rocky had hosted last night for the town's number one social and charity club—the Cupcake Lovers.

While Rocky, Dev, Chloe and Gram laughed and fussed over last-minute decorating in the living room, Luke battled the blues and lingered over the nearby dessert buffet. He'd been lingering for a while.

"Seriously? That's your fourth cupcake, Luke."

Grinning, Luke glanced at his sister while licking sweet, tangy icing from his fingers. "Yes, but it's my first—" He glanced at the card tented near this particular batch, focused on the three words and waited until the letters stopped swirling in his brain. "—Chocolate Peppermint Surprise."

"Leave him alone, Rocky. Obviously our poor boy is eating to fill some emotional void."

That observation was a little too keen for Luke's comfort. He shifted his gaze to Gram—hell on wheels at the spry age of seventy-five. "Did you read that psychobabble in *Cosmo*? And don't tell me you're not reading that glam mag, Gram. I saw it sticking out of your 'Make Love, Not War' tote bag along with a copy of *Simple & Delicious*."

"I'm trying to spice up my life," Gram said while repositioning one of three nativity scenes on the fireplace mantle.

Luke opened his mouth as did Rocky, but Dev beat them to the punch. "You recently moved out of this grand old colonial and into a rustic log cabin with your *boyfriend*," Dev said while climbing a step stool to straighten the crooked tree topper. "Your life is spicy enough."

Luke was surprised that his brother left it at that. Dev had always been anal and overprotective. Although he wasn't half as bad as he used to be since hooking up with Chloe, a bit of a free spirit who went with the flow.

"It's not a log cabin," Chloe said, sticking up for Gram who also happened to be her business partner. "It's a saltbox farmhouse."

"And Vincent is my roommate and companion," Gram said, moving in alongside Chloe to rearrange a few ornaments. "'Boyfriend' sounds silly considering his mature status."

"Silly, huh?" Luke smiled and talked around a mouthful of chocolaty goodness. "Gram, you're wearing glitzy reindeer antlers and pointy elf slippers." She'd also dyed her springy curls flaming red, and had swapped cat-eye specs for a pair of blingy green-tinted bifocals. Oh, and she had blinking snowmen dangling from her wrinkled lobes.

"It's called being festive," Gram said as she rearranged the presents under the massive Christmas tree she and Rocky had decorated to death. "It's almost Christmas after all."

Like Luke needed a reminder. Christmas was Rocky's favorite holiday. Before her home and business had burned down, she used to decorate the hell out of her Victorian bed-and-breakfast. Obviously she'd invested some of her insurance money into replenishing her Christmas holiday décor and then some. There wasn't a square foot of Gram's, strike that, *Rocky's* house that hadn't been touched by an angel, snowman, snowflake, holly, garland, ice cycle, St. Nick, reindeer, candy cane, nutcracker, toy soldier, wreath . . . Usually Luke was all for holiday cheer, but . . .

Cripes. He'd almost thought: *Bah, humbug.*

Noting that nagging emptiness in the pit of his stomach, Luke eyed the desserts. Maybe one of these Oggneg . . . He did a double take at the printed tent card and slowed his mind. Aw, hell. *Eggnog.* Maybe an Eggnog Cupcake would inspire some Christmas joy. Just as Luke bit into the moist rich confection, a furry, big-eyed mutt bounded into the room. "Hey, Brewster."

"Don't feed him any people food," Rocky said. "No matter how much he begs. It's not good for him."

"Gotcha," Luke said while letting the dog lick crumbs from his fingers.

"Got the wood." Jayce Bello, Dev's oldest and closest friend, and Rocky's obsession, crossed to the fireplace with a canvas tote of chopped logs. "Sorry it took so long. Brewster was wound up and I figured it was better to tire him out with a few minutes of fetch, rather than risk him going on a tear in here." He motioned to Dev. "Can you get a fire going? I need Luke's help whipping up Daisy's after-dinner cocktail."

Luke frowned. "What are we in for this time?"

"Candy Cane Cocktails," Gram said with a fist pump. "Yes!"

"Disgusting ingredient?" Rocky asked.

"Strawberry vodka," Jayce said while brushing a kiss over Rocky's cheek.

Luke's heart squeezed when his sister smiled and blushed. Must be nice to be so freaking in love and for that person to freaking love you back.

"Remember to make Chloe's a virgin," Dev said.

"Got it." Luke caught a sweet look between his brother and Chloe, who palmed her barely swelling stomach, and his heart squeezed again. Well, damn. His brother had lucked out in the love department too and the woman *he* loved was pregnant with his baby. It's not that Luke hadn't been in love. He'd been in love thousands of times. He had a way with women. In fact, seducing women was his one and true talent. But he'd never experienced the bone-deep forever love Rocky felt for Jayce or Dev felt for Chloe. Although he'd felt a glimmer of something different, something special a couple of months back with Rachel Lacey. He thought about their one ill-fated kiss, the sizzle that had damned near singed his senses, then immediately shoved that mystifying woman from his mind. Rachel had been a mistake and she wasn't even a possibility. The woman had skipped town and had moved on to wherever. Rachel was history.

Jayce rapped Luke on the shoulder as he strode toward the kitchen.

"Right. Candy Cane Cocktails for six—one virgin. Let's do this. I assume I'll need candy canes," he said to Jayce as they sailed through the dining room. "What else?"

"Creme de menthe. Cranberry juice. Here's the recipe Daisy gave me." Jayce slapped a folded page from a magazine into Luke's hand as they breached the state-of-the-art kitchen. "I located Rachel Lacey."

Luke stopped cold. His brain zapped. His heart jerked. "I thought you gave up."

"I only told you that so you'd stop hounding me for an update twice a day."

"I didn't—"

"Yes, you did."

Jayce had years of experience in law enforcement, first as a cop with the NYPD, then as a successful private investigator. Now he ran a cyber detective agency and Luke had hired him to find Rachel Lacey. Two freaking months ago.

"The reason she was so hard to track," Jayce said, "is because when it comes to hiring someone to create a false identity, Rachel can afford the best."

"What are you talking about? Rachel lived on a shoestring." She'd dressed in frumpy clothes and she'd driven a beat-up car. When she'd lost her job at the daycare center, Luke had hired her as a waitress. She was desperate for the work, desperate for money. She'd said so. *"I need the money, Luke."* Her shy, anxious gaze haunted him . . . sort of like that sizzling kiss.

"Maybe you should sit down," Jayce said.

Heart thudding, Luke dragged a hand through his shaggy hair. "Is she dead?"

"No."

"Dying?"

"No."

"Hurt?"

"She's alive and well in Bel Air, California. Her name is Reagan Deveraux. She's a trust fund baby. An heiress. As of tomorrow, her twenty-fifth birthday, she'll be a millionaire."

Luke blinked, then snorted. "You're kidding me, right?"

Jayce shook his head.

Luke gawked. "That's screwy. That's . . . impossible. You've got the wrong girl, Jayce."

The PI plucked his iPhone from the pocket of his leather jacket, thumbed through bells and whistles, and then showed Luke an image of Reagan Deveraux.

Holy . . . It was Rachel, but it wasn't.

Luke leaned back against the kitchen counter, willing starch into his legs and air into his lungs. "What the hell? Why the ruse?"

"I don't know."

"She lived in Sugar Creek for almost a year," Luke said. "She was a member of the Cupcake Lovers. A beloved teaching assistant at Sugar Tots. She was shy and awkward and freaking mousy. That chick in the picture, that's not mousy, that's . . . that's . . ."

"Hot. I know." Jayce raised a brow, then thumbed something else on the screen. "I can't tell you why Deveraux pretended to be someone she wasn't, but I can fill you in on her background. I downloaded the report. Here. You can read—"

"No, you read it." Luke pushed off the counter, nabbed a cocktail shaker from the cabinet. "I'll make Gram's cocktails." Trying to read all that information . . . the letters would dance and swim in front of Luke's eyes and he'd end up staring at the screen looking like an idiot while he tried to get the words right in his head. Jayce didn't know Luke was dyslexic. No one knew. His family thought he'd beaten his reading disability when he was a kid. He'd just learned to hide it, to fake it, really, really well. Only one person—Rachel—had seen through his polished ploy and he had no idea how. It's not something they'd ever discussed. But in his gut he knew she knew.

While Jayce recited *Reagan Deveraux*'s background, Luke nabbed ice cubes, cranberry juice, and the liquor. He mixed up the holiday cocktail without one glance at the recipe. He'd been a crack bartender for years. He could wing it. The more Jayce revealed about the *trust fund baby*, the more Luke felt like a fool. When he thought about the strife Rachel had caused between him and his cousin, Sam . . . When he thought about the way she'd abandoned the Cupcake Lovers in the midst of their big recipe book publishing deal . . . the way his sister and the other Cupcake Lovers had fretted over her disappearance . . . the nights Luke had wrestled with guilt and worry . . .

"God*damn*," Luke exploded just as Rocky poked her head into the kitchen.

"Everything all right in here?" she asked.

"Just mixing up some Christmas cheer," Jayce said.

"Fa-la-freaking-la," Luke said, then passed the chilled shaker to his sister. "Fill martini glasses with this and garnish the rims with candy canes."

"Where are you going?" Rocky asked as he stalked toward the back door.

"I've got a bone to pick with an heiress."

CHAPTER TWO

Reagan Deveraux shifted from the snow-white leather club chair to the snow-white leather sofa in yet another attempt to find comfort in her mother's luxurious Bel Air home. The furnishings were sparse and expensive. The decorative accessories tasteful, bordering on sterile. Not one area of casual clutter. Even the holiday decorations were meticulously arranged.

Classical music played softly in the background, compliments of a new programmed stereo system, hidden away somewhere—otherwise Rae would've dialed up a livelier playlist. Instead, she endured the stuffy music while scrolling through real estate listings on her Android. She'd only been back in California and living under this roof for three days, and it was two days too long. She glanced toward the grand stairway, wishing her mother and stepfather would dress a little faster. Rae had been ready for an hour. The sooner they got this evening's pretentious holiday dinner over, the better.

"Bah humbug."

There, she said it. She'd been thinking it all day. Rea had never been a big fan of Christmas. Mostly because it had never lived up to her expectations. As an only child of a celebrity socialite who preferred the limelight to home life, Rae had spent a good majority of her childhood keeping company with her very own TV. Holiday programming highlighted the importance of family and friends, the spirit of giving, and the magic of believing.

Rae had never lacked for presents, but there'd been no festive activities with family. No gathering around the piano to sing carols. No sleigh rides, no tree trimming, no baking of holiday cookies. Oh, there'd been decorations, but her mother had hired a company to trick out whichever mansion they were living in at the time. And there'd been parties, but they'd been the Hollywood kind or the business-related kind, depending on which man her mother had been married to, and certainly not the kind that welcomed kids.

Christmas Eve had always been Olivia Deveraux's night on the town, bouncing from one glitzy party to another. Never mind that Christmas Eve was also her daughter's birthday. Surely the fact that Rae got presents *that* day in addition to Christmas morning was celebration enough.

This year was no different. This morning Olivia had presented Rae with diamond earrings, a special gift for her twenty-fifth birthday. "*Really, sweetie,*" she had said, "*you're independently wealthy now. A legitimate heiress. Time to start dressing and acting the part.*"

Olivia had been dressing and acting the part for years. She'd never been the real deal. Rae was the real deal. Thanks to Olivia's first husband, the father Rae had lost at age two.

Just now Olivia was upstairs with husband number four, a man Rae despised, taking forever and a day dressing for the first of three parties on their meticulously calculated social calendar. Amazingly, Olivia had invited Rae along. Although maybe not so amazing. Rae was stinking rich now, a magnet for attention, something Olivia breathed like air.

Not wanting to insult her mother, especially since Rae was trying to forge some sort of genuine bond, she'd sucked it up, agreeing to attend the dinner party being hosted at the Beverly Wilshire. Rae had never been a social butterfly, but she could endure a formal dinner, and besides, the proceeds went to a local children's hospital. She'd simply beg off after, leaving the wilder, drinking parties to Olivia and Geoffrey while she took advantage of their state-of-the-art kitchen.

Rae planned to spend her Christmas Eve birthday whipping up a holiday cupcake that would make the Cupcake Lovers proud, then chowing down while watching a marathon of sappy holiday movies on the Hallmark Channel. Movies celebrating friends and family, old-fashioned values, open hearts and love. Movies that celebrated the kind of Christmas Rae had always craved and—double whammy—reminded her of the down-to-earth lives she'd been surrounded by in Sugar Creek, Vermont. Being filthy rich couldn't compare to being happy.

Rae eyed her mother's professionally decorated, artificial tree, weathering a wave of melancholy as her mind exploded with the visions and scents of naked Vermont pine. Over the last two months Rae had done her best to forget her attempt at lying low and living incognito in the Green Mountain State under the guise of Rachel Lacey. All she'd wanted was a few months of anonymity, time to assess a dicey situation with Geoffrey, time to contemplate her future without her shallow mother breathing down her neck.

Losing herself to find herself.

Hiding until she had the funds to fight fire with fire.

Being a nobody had paid off in ways she'd never dreamed. Working with the children at Sugar Tots had been a dream. Joining the Cupcake Lovers and baking cupcakes for charitable causes had been a joy. If only Sam McCloud hadn't fallen for her. (*How could any man fall for drab, shy Rachel*?) If only Rae hadn't fallen for Sam's cousin, Luke Monroe.

Another dicey situation.

Disappearing, *again*, seemed the best course. No one would miss her, right? People came and went all the time—at least in Rae's life.

"Stop moping. *Jeez*." Disgusted with her blue mood, Rae pushed to her feet and smoothed the wrinkles of her cocktail dress. "It's your birthday. You're a millionaire. Whoop-de-flipping-do."

Time to find new happiness. Honest joy and real contentment. As for love . . .

There was always the Hallmark Channel.

"Someone to see you, Miss Deveraux."

Rae blinked, startled by the depth of her daydreaming. She hadn't heard the doorbell. She hadn't even heard Ms. Finch, her mother's latest housekeeper, enter the room. "Who is it?"

"Said he's an old friend."

That heightened Rae's curiosity. True friends were sacred, a rarity in Rae's life, and she was certain she didn't have any in Bel Air.

Ms. Finch, who struck Rae as having a broomstick up her butt, raised her fastidiously penciled, coal-black eyebrows. "He seemed harmless so I allowed him access through the security gate and asked him to wait in the foyer."

"Oh. Right. Thank you." Rae dragged her fingers through her Bordeaux-colored, newly cropped hair. In her desperate need to cut ties with Rachel Lacey, she'd invested in a stylish makeover and a chic wardrobe. Months ago she would have been wearing a mid-shin peasant dress and clunky, flat-heeled sweater boots. This afternoon she'd zipped herself into a knee-length emerald green sheath with an empire waist and donned Jimmy Choo platform pumps. A dash of holiday spirit combined with an air of sophistication—perfect for the dinner at the Wilshire.

Rae bolstered her shoulders as she moved across the pristine living area and then through two other rooms in order to greet her *old friend*—who was more than likely a smooth-talking reporter or an annoying member of the paparazzi. She'd begged Olivia not to brag about her inheritance but that was like asking her mother not to pose for the camera. Nothing would have surprised Rae. Except . . .

"Luke." His name scraped over her constricted throat, sounding choked and raspy and, to her utter embarrassment, besotted. Rae had never considered herself shallow, but she'd fallen for Luke Monroe's boyishly handsome face and incredible body the first time she'd laid eyes on him—much like every other woman in Sugar Creek. His ornery smile and easy charm were irresistible and his devotion to family and friends admirable. The fact that he openly dated several women at the same time should have been a turn-off, except he was honest about his no-strings-attached intentions and that was oddly refreshing.

As always, he was dressed down in faded, baggy jeans and a snug tee that accentuated his muscled torso. He'd rolled up the sleeves of a blue flannel shirt that hung unbuttoned and untucked, and he was wearing heavy boots more conducive to the snowdrifts of Vermont than sand and sun of California. Rumpled and unshaven, he looked incredibly out of place in Olivia and Geoffrey's ostentatious mansion.

Luke Monroe's presence . . . here, now . . . was surreal and though stunned, Rae couldn't suppress a giddy thrill. "What are you doing here? How . . . how did you find me?"

"It wasn't easy."

His clipped tone betrayed his anger as did his grim expression. Luke was one of the most jovial, easy-going men she'd ever known. She'd seen him harried once, frustrated, but never angry. Well, except for the fateful night a randy college kid had grabbed her butt when she'd been taking a drink order. Luke had interceded and he'd been angry, no, *outraged* on her behalf. She'd been smitten with Luke for months, but that night she'd fallen in love.

Rae's cheeks burned while she grappled for words, while Luke dragged his gaze down her body, soaking in the stylish transformation. She struggled not to fuss with her cropped hair or to tug up her scooped neckline. There was absolutely nothing she could do about her bare legs, and kicking off her pumps would be ridiculous and embarrassing. She'd never been one to flaunt her curves and there was nothing promiscuous about this dress, yet Rae felt naked.

Exposed.

"Born and raised in privilege," Luke said in the wake of

her silence. "Exclusive private schools. Extended lavish vacations."

Rae flinched at Luke's caustic tone. He spouted the cards she'd been dealt as though she'd been lucky. As a teen, she'd been shipped off to various locations and pawned off on assorted relatives so as not to cast a shadow in her mother's spotlight.

"College graduate with a master's degree in education. A freaking *master's*," he said in a low, tight tone, "yet you were working as a teacher's assistant at Sugar Tots and then came to work for me as a freaking waitress in a freaking *bar*. You said, and I quote: *I need the money, Luke*." He stuffed his hands into his jeans' pockets, swept a disgusted gaze over the opulent foyer, then back to Rae. "What the—"

"*Hello.* Who do we have here?"

Rae cringed at her mother's sultry tone and knew without turning that the woman was shrink-wrapped in a sexy gown and no doubt slinking down the white carpeted staircase. Rae watched as Luke turned his attention to her mother, saw the moment he recognized her as the tabloid famous Olivia Deveraux, one-time starlet, all-time sex kitten. Rae waited for Luke to get that bewitched, lustful expression most men, ages eighteen to eighty, got when they saw her voluptuous and overtly stunning mother in person. Instead, he just looked annoyed.

"Friend of yours?" Olivia persisted, moving in alongside Rae, and reeking of Chanel #5 and fruity martinis.

"We worked together," Rae blurted, because *friend* didn't really describe their association. Especially not now.

"Luke Monroe," he expanded, while offering Olivia a hand in polite greeting. More than he'd done with Rae. "Pleased to meet you, Ms. Deveraux."

"Are you *really*?" she asked in a coy tone, clasping his palm and pursing her crimson lips in a sexy pout. "You don't *look* pleased."

"Blame it on the long flight and the holiday crush," he said in a gentler tone, which only made Rae feel worse. Instead of celebrating Christmas with his family, he'd flown across the country . . . for what? To give Rae hell?

"You just flew in from China today?" Olivia asked, looking mildly shocked. "Good heavens, Reagan. Invite the man in for a drink. I'll join you." She looped her arm through Luke's and guided him toward Geoffrey's well-stocked bar.

Rae's heart pounded as she hurried after them, wondering how she was going to wiggle her way around another colossal lie. Wondering what Luke was thinking just now and wishing she'd booked herself into a hotel rather than buckling under Olivia's invitation to stay here while seeking a new home suited to her birthday inheritance.

"Maybe Luke will tell me more about your volunteer work abroad," Olivia said over her shoulder to Rae before turning her wide, kohl-lined eyes on Luke. "Every time I ask her about her work with those children, she declares those days the best days of her life, then changes the subject. It must have been *horrid* working in such a remote location," she said to Luke, then pointed out the premium back bar. "I don't suppose you know how to mix up an appletini?"

"I think I can manage," he said with an enigmatic glance at Rae. "Vodka or gin?"

"I'm a vodka girl. And as Bond would say . . ." Olivia winked and purred. "Shaken, not stirred."

Just as Luke reached for Grey Goose and vermouth, Geoffrey swaggered into the reception room in a dapper Armani suit, his salt and pepper hair slicked back from his handsome, aging face. "Olivia, sweetheart, what the hell?" he asked while checking his gold watch. "We're late as is and . . ." He noticed shaggy-haired Luke in his rumpled tee and flannel shirt mixing drinks behind the Italian marble bar and frowned. "Do we know you?"

"This is Luke Monroe, dear," Olivia said with a beaming smile. "A friend of Reagan's."

"Really."

Rae couldn't tell if Geoffrey was frowning because he didn't like the idea of Rae entertaining a virile, young man or because he was peeved about the way Olivia was ogling said virile, young man. Knowing the way her mother's mind worked, Olivia was no doubt mentally comparing Luke to one of Hollywood's young hunks, in this instance Ryan Reynolds, and imagining herself starring alongside him as the mature love interest. Olivia was constantly lamenting how Sandra Bullock was stealing all of her roles.

Instead of acknowledging Luke, Geoffrey eyed Rae. "Dinner starts promptly at five."

"Maybe Luke could join us," Olivia said.

"There's a dress code," Geoffrey said. "Reservations for three." He spared Luke an annoyed glance. "No offense."

"None taken," Luke said, but he didn't take the hint and leave either. Instead he poured sour apple liqueur into the shaker, then reached for the lemon juice.

Clearly he meant to have his say with Rae and it wasn't a discussion she wanted to have in front of Olivia and Geoffrey. In a way, Rae was grateful for Luke's obstinacy. The less she had to endure Geoffrey's company—the man who'd threatened her in this very house *last* Christmas—the better. Also, Olivia was already three-sheets-to-the-wind. She wouldn't miss Rae for long, if at all.

Feigning nonchalance, Rae moved behind the bar and stood beside Luke. Her skin tingled, her pulse tripped. He'd only held her once, kissed her once, yet she recalled every detail of that tender and then searing encounter. A brush with passion that would haunt her for the rest of her life. "Actually," she said, speaking past the lump in her throat, "I've decided to skip the Wilshire in favor of spending time with Luke. He flew all this way and—"

"You're going to waste a five-hundred dollar plate?" Geoffrey asked.

"No waste," Rae said, holding the industry kingpin's intimidating gaze. "All proceeds go to charity. You two go on. Don't give me a second thought," she said, unconsciously leaning into Luke. "I'm in good hands."

"Do tell," Olivia said with raised brows.

Geoffrey worked his clean-shaven jaw. "What is it you do, Monroe?"

"You mean aside from mixing a mean appletini?" Luke asked, shaking and pouring.

While Olivia sampled his creation, Luke snaked an arm about Rae and held Geoffrey's cold gaze.

Rae's heart pounded. Because of Luke. Because of Geoffrey. Because she was trapped in a web of lies.

"Sweet heaven, this drink is *orgasmic!*" Olivia moaned in ecstasy. "You *must* try it, Geoff."

"Pass. Could I have a word with you, Reagan?"

Rae's stomach turned as the walls closed in. This situation had just gone from awkward to intolerable. The last person she wanted to be alone with was her so-called stepfather. "Aren't you running late for dinner?" she asked. "I know we are." She looked up at Luke, her panicked heart in her eyes. "Ready?"

Hand at the small of her back, Luke prompted her from behind the bar. "Nice meeting you, Ms. Deveraux. Mr.—"

"Stein. Geoffrey Stein. Of Stein & Beecham Industries. And you're Luke Monroe."

"Of the Sugar Creek Monroes," Luke said as he escorted Rae toward a temporary reprieve. "We're in the book."